FIRST CUT IS
THE DEEPEST

Martin Edwards

Contents

Dedicated to my Helena

Introduction

Martin Edwards is a solicitor...and so is his creation, Harry Devlin. But there the similarity ends as, fortunately for Martin (who specialises in employment law - a branch of the law hardly noted for its danger and violence), his encounters with murdered corpses are confined to the printed page.

The author of over forty short stories – and the winner of the Crime Writers' Association Short Story Dagger – Martin Edwards is the editor of the CWA's annual anthology. He is also the author of legal books and more than a thousand articles. Recently he has become deservedly well known for his excellent crime series set in the Lake District featuring Daniel Kind and Hannah Scarlett. However, as a native of Liverpool, I find I have a particular affection for his Harry Devlin novels, the seventh of which is The First Cut is the Deepest.

Harry Devlin operates in the insular world of Liverpool's legal profession and the Liverpool of his investigations is certainly the Liverpool I recognise. From city centre offices, to the Dock Road with its dilapidated warehouses awaiting 'redevelopment' and the swish new apartments near the Albert Dock; from the run down, seedy districts to the affluent suburbs, this is the city I was brought up in and rarely has anybody captured its unique atmosphere as well as Martin Edwards. Liverpool's many notable features are used to wonderful effect in his stories – even the more peculiar ones such as the Williamson tunnels, a labyrinth dug through the red sandstone beneath the Edge Hill area of the city in the early 1800s on the instructions of a retired tobacco merchant, possibly to create work for the unemployed of the time. The tunnels make a dramatic appearance in The First Cut is the Deepest but to say any more would be spoiling the surprise.

It's not an easy matter to create a credible amateur detective but somehow Harry Devlin is completely believable. Harry himself is a damaged, all too human character, a man who is far from perfect but who is driven by a love of justice – a humane and likeable lawyer with good intentions. His estranged wife, Liz, died in tragic and suspicious circumstances in All the Lonely People, the first novel in the series - which was shortlisted by the CWA's John Creasey Memorial Dagger - and, although Harry has a great liking for women, he has never had much good fortune with the opposite sex.

In The First Cut is the Deepest Harry embarks on a torrid and ill-advised affair with Juliet May, the wife of one of Liverpool's greatest villains. In a memorable early scene Harry and Juliet discover the decapitated body of a crown prosecutor during one of their steamy trysts. Then another member of the legal profession is murdered so Harry is forced to ask the inevitable question - who is killing the lawyers? And why is Harry being stalked by a sinister Welshman with an equally sinister agenda of his own?

This is one of Martin Edwards' darkest books, well plotted, intelligent, thrilling and totally enjoyable.

Kate Ellis

Strangers in the Night

...he can direct the elements, the storm, the fog, the thunder: he can command all meaner things; the rat, and the wolf; he can grow and become small; and he can at times vanish and come unknown. How then are we to begin our strike against him?

How long have you been afraid of me? Last night I noticed your glance in my direction when you thought I wasn't looking – and I saw the dread deep in your eyes. I kept my secret for so long, but in the end you were sure to learn the truth. Perhaps you guessed sooner than I realised. After all, it's simple when you know: you recognise the clues which were there all the time, make sense at last of so many oddities, things that didn't quite add up. And now that you know, you are being eaten away by fear.

Do you remember telling me once why the law drew you like a moth to the flame? All of us need rules, you said, and we must believe in rules. Rules which draw a line between right and wrong. What is left for us if we don't have faith, if we can't cling to the belief that life is more than chance and accident? Without justice, the world is wild and dangerous. But the law's a lousy mistress, we should have learned that by now. She's fickle and shameless. Each time you put your trust in her, she lets you down.

So let's forget the law; it can't deliver us from evil. The time has come to face reality. Inside your heart, you know I'm killing you.

No more deceit: the choice is simple. One of us has to die. And I'll be honest with you, I'm scared too. Yet there's no escaping our destiny. My flesh tingles as I close my eyes and picture in my mind the darkness that lies ahead of us.

Chapter One

'Forget it, it's too risky.'

'That's half the fun, isn't it?' asked the voice at the other end of the line.

'What if he finds out?'

'No-one need ever know,' Juliet May whispered, 'apart from you and me.'

Outside in the corridor, someone banged on Harry Devlin's door, made him jump. 'The last client who said that to me,' he muttered, 'finished up with five years for money laundering.'

'Then thank God it's your body I'm after, not your legal advice.'

Harry tightened his grip on the receiver. 'Hey, whatever happened to safe sex?'

'Overrated, don't you agree? Listen, there's nothing to worry about.' She was amused, her tone persuasive. She'd have made a good advocate, he thought, could have persuaded a hanging judge to let her off with a neck massage. 'Casper is in London until tomorrow evening. Everything's perfect. The house is in the middle of nowhere. This may be the best chance we ever get.'

The door rocked on its hinges. Jim Crusoe was standing outside, hand on hips, forearm raised to show the face of his wristwatch. Harry saw the time and gave his partner a caught-in-the-act grin. He could feel his cheeks burning. Cupping his hand over the mouthpiece, he said, 'Sorry, I forgot. With you in half a minute.'

Jim grunted and slammed the door. Harry said into the phone, 'I'm late for a meeting at our bank. A date with the Loan Arranger.'

A giggle. 'Don't tell me, he's got a sidekick called Tonto. Does this mean you have to take out an overdraft to buy the champagne for tonight?'

It was a bitter day in November. The morning news had warned of gales and now he could hear them roaring in from the waterfront.

The office heating had broken down at lunch-time and the cold was seeping into his room through cracks in the window frames. Yet his palms were damp and anticipatory lust wasn't entirely to blame.

'I haven't said I can make it tonight.'

'Don't play hard to get,' Juliet said. 'You want what I want.'

Was that true? He was breathing hard, conscious of the pounding of his heart. 'Adultery isn't good for your health.'

'You're not commiting adultery. It's years since your wife died.'

This wasn't the time to quibble about matrimonial law or the proper interpretation of the Book of Leviticus. He didn't want to finish up like a discredited politician, arguing that his deceits were 'legally accurate'. 'If Casper hears about this,' he said, 'we'll both finish up in intensive care. Maybe worse.'

'Forget him. You ought to relax. The trouble is, you're too uptight.'

'He's dangerous. You've said so yourself.'

'I can picture you tensing up,' she said softly. 'Don't worry, we can have a nice soothing bath together.'

He couldn't help imagining her arms as they stretched around him, her long fingers probing the cavities beneath his shoulder blades, the sharp red nails starting to dig into his back. Closing his eyes, he could smell her perfume, taste the champagne on her lips, feel the thick mass of her hair brush against his cheeks, then his chest.

'But...'

'No buts, Harry. Remember the Tarot reading I gave you? You're in for a life-changing experience.'

That's what I'm afraid of. He sucked air into his lungs. It was supposed to be an aid to rational thought.

'Seven thirty,' she said, filling the silence. 'It's less than four hours away. I can hardly wait, can you?'

Another angry knock at the door. Harry let out a breath. So much for rational thought. Well, whoever chose as an epitaph – 'he was always sensible'?

'No,' he said. 'I can't.'

Carl Symons swallowed the last loop of spaghetti and wiped his mouth clean with his sleeve. He turned up the volume on the portable television on his kitchen table. The bellow of the wind outside was drowning out even the determined cheeriness of the weather forecaster.

'Not a night to be out and about, with storms across the region and the likelihood of damage to property. And a word for all drivers from our motoring unit: don't travel unless your journey is absolutely essential.'

Carl belched. The wind and rain didn't bother him: he wasn't going anywhere tonight. He'd left work at five sharp so as to get home before the weather worsened, the first time in months that he hadn't worked late. Even so, it had seemed like a long day. Unsatisfactory, too. He'd emailed Suki Anwar, asking her to come to his office at four, and the bitch had sent an insolent reply, refusing on the pretext that she had an urgent case to prepare. As if that wasn't enough, on his way to the car park, he'd caught sight of Brett Young behind the wheel of his clapped-out Sierra. For a moment he'd thought Brett was putting his foot down, trying to run him down as he was crossing Water Street. He'd had to skip through the traffic to gain the safety of the pavement on the other side. He'd felt himself flushing and he could picture Brett giving a grim smile at his alarm. *Bastard.* A lying bastard, too, one who had got what he deserved. Carl wasn't sorry about what he'd done.

He laughed out loud and sang in a rumpled baritone, '*Je ne regrette rien.*'

It made him feel better. He'd forget about Suki and Brett. Better to spend a couple of hours working on his report for tomorrow's meeting. It would assuage his conscience for that prompt departure from the office. And he did have a conscience about it. His parents were long dead, but they had inculcated in him the puritan work ethic; he prized diligence above all things. Not even his worst enemy – whoever that might be; he suspected that he was spoiled for choice – could accuse him of laziness. Later, he might relax with a film. Channel 4 was showing an old black and white movie called *Nosferatu*.

He wondered whether to have a Mars bar and decided against it. The lager had better stay in the fridge as well. Tomorrow he intended to wear his best suit and he'd noticed that the trousers were getting tight. He'd always nourished a deep contempt for people with pretty faces, people like Suki and Brett. Only fools judged by appearances: good looks were a mask for weakness. Yet he'd always secretly prided himself on his flat belly. He'd lost his hair young and he'd never been a Robert Redford, but at least he wasn't overweight. Truth was, he needed to look the part at the meeting: nowadays presentation mattered in everything, including the prosecution service. So – how best to present the latest conviction rates? The figures were looking good; the trick was to make sure everyone got the message that the credit belonged to him. No-one could deny he'd justified his promotion. A Principal Crown Prosecutor owed a duty to the taxpayer. He'd told the appointment board that it was vital to be selective. No point in pursuing the ones who were sure to get away. The secret was to target cases where the evidence was cast-iron so that not even a Liverpool jury could fail to bring in a verdict of guilty.

A deafening crash outside almost knocked him off his feet. He swore loudly. A roof tile gone, by the sound of it. He'd already spent a fortune renovating this place. Trouble was, it was too exposed. He'd bought it after receiving confirmation of his promotion in the summer, intrigued by its setting on the bank of the Dee, looking across to the Welsh hills. Once upon a time, before the silting of the river had destroyed the old Dee ports forever, there had been a small anchorage here. This house had once belonged to the harbour master. Now its isolation was part of its charm to Carl; he liked his own company best. Over the years, he'd realised that he didn't have much time for his fellow human beings. So often they whined about being used, when in truth they had asked for it. The prospect of evenings alone held no terrors for him: he was no longer his own boss during the working day, but still he preferred to do as he pleased. But if the cost of maintaining the house continued to rise, rising further in the hierarchy would no longer be merely an ambition. It would be a necessity.

He turned on the outside light and opened the door which gave on to a York stone courtyard at the side of the house. The wind stung his cheeks and blew the rain into his eyes as he stood on the threshold. Shivering, he blinked hard and finally made out the fragments of slate scattered across the paving and the grass beyond. On the other side of the low wall, the waves were lashing the shore like flails on the back of a galley slave. He had never seen the Dee so wild. A sudden gust caught the wooden door and almost snapped it off its hinges. He swore, then heaved the handle and shut out the night.

Why did I say yes?

Harry killed the engine of his MG and sat hunched over the steering wheel, staring through the rain-streaked windscreen into blackness. On his way over here, radio reports had told of the gales leaving a trail of destruction from the mountains of Snowdonia all along the north coast of Wales. A woman swept away in a swollen river, a dozen caravans tossed into the sea. Now the storm was ripping through Wirral. He couldn't help shivering, but it had nothing to do with the elements.

He should not be here. Not so much because of guilt, more because he was sure that one day his affair with Juliet would end in tears. Perhaps worse. Casper May had betrayed his wife a hundred times, or so she reckoned. He beat her too: Harry had seen the bruises and his tears of rage had trickled over them. Casper had, it was true, come a long way since his days as loan shark, charging rates of interest that would have made Shylock's eyes water. His security firm was due to go public soon and nowadays he saw more of government ministers than pleading debtors. The politicians were keen to build bridges with business and to wine and dine an entrepreneur famed for his charitable fund-raising: he might be persuaded to volunteer a donation to party funds. But respectability was only skin deep. If he realised he'd been cuckolded by a small-time solicitor, honour would need to be satisfied.

Harry had heard the story of a rival security boss who had undercut Casper for a contract to look after a dockside container terminal. A week after he'd gone missing, he'd been found inside one of the containers with a hood over his head and a gag in his mouth. The body was discovered on the same day that Casper was lunching with a task force from the Regional Development Agency, sharing ideas on how to make the north-west a better place to live in. He'd sent flowers to the widow, a woman he'd slept with in his younger days. The names of the scallies who had kidnapped the man and left him to die were common knowledge in the pubs of Dingle, but no-one had ever been charged. When Casper May was involved, it made sense to look the other way.

It still wasn't too late. He could turn the MG round now and set off for home. Why not settle for beer rather than the bottle of Mouton Cadet he'd stashed in the boot, maybe watch the late vampire film on Channel 4 and admire Max Schreck's uncanny impersonation of an inspector from the Inland Revenue? He could call Juliet tomorrow and make an excuse. Even if he said something about seeing her around, she'd guess that it was over. No great loss for her: she would soon find someone else to amuse herself with.

But as he buttoned his coat up to the neck to keep out the cold, he realised that for him it was too late after all. No longer was it a matter of choice. She was waiting for him in the lonely cottage. He could not help but seize the chance to be with her again.

Carl turned the key in the mortice lock, but there was no escape from the wind in the living-room chimney. A frantic sound, he thought, the sort a beast might make if caught in a trap. He shook his head, surprised at himself. He wasn't given to flights of fancy. Imagination was a nuisance. It played no part in the preparation of a case for court, in the effective prosecution of criminal offenders.

He cursed as the picture on his television began to flicker and the actor's voices in the Fiat commercial became garbled and discordant. Suddenly the programme cut off and the fluorescent overhead light went out.

Blindly, he stumbled towards the hall, cracking his knee against a cabinet as he crossed the uneven floor. He had to remember to duck his head under the low beams as he went through the doorway. Everything seemed unfamiliar in the dark. He tried the light switch next to the stairs. Nothing. A power line must have been brought down in the storm.

Shit, shit, shit.

At least he was prepared for a black-out. He prided himself on his organisational abilities and he always had supplies to enable him to cope with a crisis. Experiences like this, he told himself, proved the wisdom of such foresight. He crept back into the kitchen and found a packet of candles and a box of matches in a drawer. The flame was weak and the room was full of shadows, but anything was better than pitch darkness.

He tried the transistor radio. The Meteorological Office was issuing another warning of severe gales. *Tell me something I don't know.* He retuned to Radio 3 for a bit of background Beethoven whilst he pulled the paperwork for tomorrow's meeting out of his briefcase. Perhaps if the power didn't come back on, he would only work for an hour or so. He'd already done the hard graft. It wouldn't do any harm to turn in early and make sure he was fresh and ready for the meeting. If all went well, he could hope for another promotion marking at his next performance appraisal. His sights were set high. A move to another office wasn't impossible if no vacancy cropped up in Liverpool. He wasn't prepared to waste his life away, waiting to step into dead men's shoes.

A knock at the front door. For an instant he confused the noise with the rage of the storm. After all, no-one in their right mind would be out on a night like this. But it came again, the sound of the heavy brass knocker hammering against oak.

It must be one of the Blackwells. Either the mother who lived at the cottage up the slope, the only person he could possibly describe as a neighbour, or her drink-sodden son if he happened to be around. Perhaps they weren't equipped to deal with a power cut. He toyed for a moment with the idea of driving a ruthless bargain for a candle and a couple of vestas. The mother looked as if she had a decent body, considering her age. She hadn't let herself go, he liked that in a woman. The thought made him smile as, carrying the candle in its holder, he unlocked the door.

It was freezing outside and so dark that it took him a moment to focus. Then he saw the light glinting on the blade of the axe in his visitor's hand.

The cottage belonged to Linda Blackwell, personal assistant to Juliet in her public relations business. Harry couldn't face the prospect of sleeping in Casper's bed and his own flat was out of bounds because one of his neighbours was a client of Juliet's and they couldn't run the risk that she'd be recognised. In the past, their trysts had taken place in anonymous hotels in places like Runcorn and Frodsham, where they could be confident they wouldn't bump into anyone they knew. Tonight was supposed to be different. Special. She had given him directions, detailed and specific, warning him that the place would be difficult to find in the dark.

'It's called the Customs House, but it's only tiny and you could easily miss it. She bought it after her husband died. Once you've branched off the main road, ignore the signs to the country park. Carry on for half a mile past the nursery and the tumbledown cottage until you come to the end of the lane. Tucked away underneath the trees are a couple of lock-up garages. The one on the left is Linda's. She's let me have the key, so I'll park my Alfa inside there. You leave your car in front of the door. For God's sake don't block her neighbour's access. She can't bear him. I don't know why, but I can guess.' A laugh. 'He's a lawyer and you know how difficult they can be.'

Harry wished now that he'd asked the neighbour's name. The last thing he wanted was to bump into someone he knew. What could he say? 'Can't stop, I'm just off for a tryst with the wife of a gangster'? In theory, it might do wonders for his image – as long as Casper May never got to hear of it. He checked again to make sure that even the most pedantic conveyancer could not complain that his right of way had been obstructed and set off down the path which led into the spinney which bordered the lane.

'For God's sake, don't forget to bring a torch,' she'd instructed him. 'There are no lights and the path twists and turns on its way through the wood.'

Good advice, he reflected, as he shone the pencil beam through the darkness. Without the help of a light, he would soon be hopelessly lost amongst the trees. Juliet obviously knew her way here of old. Had she explained this route before, to a previous lover he'd heard nothing about? If so, was it any of his business?

The path was muddy underfoot and he found himself wondering why anyone would want to live here, in the back of beyond. The city he had left behind twenty minutes earlier seemed already to belong to a different world. He could imagine that in the height of summer this wooded walk might be idyllic, but only a fool would trade the warmth of home on the wildest night of winter for the rain drenching his hair and the wind stinging his cheeks.

The gale dropped for a moment and he heard a rustling amongst the trees. He shone his torch and could dimly perceive dark shapes above his head. What sound did bats make? He was a townie; natural history had never been a strongpoint. To think he might have been in his flat this evening, watching a vampire film on the box, rather than experiencing the Grand Guignol of a date with a murderer's wife. If ever there was a night for the un-dead to rise, this was it.

He tripped over a tree stump but somehow managed to keep his grip upon the holdall which contained the champagne and a few overnight things. The torch slipped from his other hand and rolled away. He scrabbled around in the darkness and when he picked it up, found that the bulb was smashed. In a fit of temper, he hurled the thing away into the undergrowth before squatting on his haunches and cradling the bag with the bottle whilst he told himself to calm down. Pity it wasn't full of whisky; he'd have brought a hip flask if he'd realised the scale of this endurance test. Perhaps Juliet had dreamed up the assignation as a challenge, a measure of the scale of his obsession with her. When he arrived at the Customs House, he'd probably find that there was a dual carriageway running straight past the front door. He inched forward and realised that the path was beginning to fall away beneath his feet.

'When you reach the edge of the cliff, the track starts to wind down. There's a hand-rail and you'd better cling on. It will be slippery with all this rain.'

She was a mistress of understatement, he decided. Unable to see where he was going, he clamped his left hand around the wet wooden railing and put one foot gingerly in front of another. He knew that, ahead and below, flowed the river that divided England from Wales, but he could see nothing of it. On either side of him, trees swayed like monstrous exotic dancers mocking his timidity.

'Soon the path forks. Make sure you follow the left branch. Steps lead down to the Customs House. The other way takes you to the lawyer's cottage.'

He missed his footing and almost fell again. These must be the steps. He told himself that he was almost there. Inching down the pathway, he saw the dark outlines of a house loom in front of him: it must be the place. Yet why were there no lights? He felt suddenly sick and wondered if, for some unknowable reason, she had betrayed him. If he walked in, would he find himself greeted by Casper May, rather than his wife?

'I'll leave the door ajar. You won't need to ring the bell.'

He found himself on a cinder path running up to a small porch. As he moved forward, he saw the front door open, framing the slender figure he couldn't stop thinking about.

'Come in, quick,' she urged. 'You'll catch your death out there.'

As consciousness returned, Carl Symons became fuzzily aware that his head was hurting. Hurting as it had never hurt before. The haft of the axe must have struck him on the temple, a blow so sudden that he'd not even had time to raise his hands in an attempt at self-defence. He forced his eyes open, trying to blink away the tears of pain. The skin of his cheeks and hands was grazed and sore. He'd been dragged inside and laid out on the floor of the kitchen. The stone was cold against his flesh. By the flickering light of the candle, he could see a pool of blood. It had leaked from the wound in his temple and on to the ground.

The candle wavered. With a desperate effort, Carl tried to shift his head so that he could follow the pool of light. Even the slight movement made him want to squeal.

A face emerged from the shadows and bent down towards him, as if to judge the extent of his suffering. Carl could see two hands as well. One held the axe, the other a sharpened stave.

The face was familiar to Carl but there was a strange light in the eyes that he had never seen before. The face came closer still but did not answer. Hypnotised, he watched as a tongue appeared and began to lick the pale lips. The axe was held aloft. White teeth bared in a savage smile.

Carl tried to form a single word and heard his own voice, croaky and pleading.

'*Please.*'

But even as he spoke, the axe began to move towards him. Carl knew it was too late to beg for mercy. His bowels loosened.

Chapter Two

'Think of it this way,' Juliet said as she slipped his shirt over her own bare shoulders. 'What could be more romantic?'

Harry gave her an exhausted grin. His body was aching and he was still breathing hard. The flesh of his back stung where she had raked him, but he didn't care. They were lying with their arms wrapped around each other in semi-darkness, listening as the wind roared through the trees.

'You mean just you and I together with a bottle of champagne to finish off by candle-light?'

She snuggled back under the duvet. 'Exactly.'

He gestured at the redundant lamp and the wet towel on the bedside table. 'Forgetting the storm, the power cut and the imminent likelihood of pneumonia?'

'You've nothing to worry about, darling. I've dried every bit of you and you can see everything you need to see.' She moved so that the light from the flame fell on her breasts. Her nipples were glistening from his kisses. 'I've kept the promise the Tarot made. What more could you wish for?'

As they had bathed together before making love, he'd noticed the dark stain of a fresh bruise on her upper arm. So many questions lacked answers. Why did she stay with Casper? Surely it wasn't simply through fear? She'd once told him that the sex she and her husband had when he was ready to make up after giving her a beating was the best she'd ever known. The day she'd said that, he'd been sure his relationship with her would die before it had come fully to life. But she always confounded his expectations. That was one of the reasons why he could never resist her.

He said quietly, 'I wish he'd never hurt you again.'

'Don't worry about me. I can take care of myself.'

'Are you sure? What if he finds out about us?'

'Stop fussing,' she said, punching his stomach. 'Casper will be tucked up in the Waldorf with some leggy teenager even as we speak. No-one's going to spoil our fun. Right now, this is the safest place on earth.'

Not for the first time, the thought slid into Harry's mind that he might be her revenge against Casper for all those leggy teenagers. But he was intoxicated, and not just because he'd downed a few glasses of champagne. If he was being used, he wasn't sure that he really cared.

'And what about Linda Blackwell? Can you trust her to keep her mouth shut?'

'Linda and I go back a long way. She's never let me down.'

'She knows about you and me?'

Juliet put a warm hand on his thigh. 'She knows there's someone. Obviously. But no names, no pack drill. I gave her a call this afternoon, just before I rang you, to see if she could spare this place for the evening.'

'What did you tell her?'

The hand became adventurous. 'If you must know, I said that Casper had gone to a meeting in London, all to do with getting more Lottery money for Liverpool. He's in good citizen mode at the moment, you know. Reckons there's a knighthood in it for him at the end of the day. I told her that while the cat was away, this particular mouse was in the mood to play. She said no problem, she'd sleep over at Peter's.'

'Peter?'

'Her son. You met him once when you came round to the office, remember? He'd popped in to see his mum.'

'Right.' He remembered a big surly man in his early thirties. 'We didn't really talk.'

'Peter may seem a misery guts, but he's been a good son to Linda, he took care of her after her husband died. She said she'd go round to his place tonight. She stays there sometimes, she didn't

15

even need to go home to pack a case. She said he doesn't get out much, he was sure to be around.'

'She sounds like the perfect personal assistant,' he murmured. Her fingers were teasing him and he wasn't finding it easy to concentrate, didn't really want to concentrate.

'She's always been loyal. I was sure she'd help me out. Though when the power was cut, I started wondering whether my idea was quite so clever.' She sat up and grinned at him. 'Luckily, it's all worked out for the best.'

'I'm glad you found the candles,' he said, unable to drag his eyes away from her lean body. The pale flesh was marked here and there with chicken pox scars, but he liked the blemishes that weren't made by her husband. Each little imperfection reminded him that she was a real woman, not a fantasy he'd conjured up in a lonely dream.

'Tell you the truth, I rang Linda to let her know what had happened. I had her son's number in my bag. Only trouble was that not only are the phone lines down, but the battery of my mobile was just about to pack up. Luckily I managed to get through to her on the second ring and we had a quick word before the battery ran out. She told me where one or two things were. The rest I was able to work out for myself.'

'Never stayed here before?' he asked softly.

She bent forward and started to kiss the hairs on his chest, looking up only to say, 'Does it matter?'

He patted her rump. 'No. Besides, it's none of my business.'

'Then everything's fine ... Christ! What on earth was that?'

At first he thought a bomb had gone off outside the front door. The noise was so loud and close at hand that he was sure it must have been an explosion. Instinctively he closed his eyes and tightened his arms around her, fearing that the house was about to erupt in flames. But what followed was silence.

They looked at each other. Her eyes were wide with astonishment. 'A tree's fallen,' she said, gently disentangling herself from him. 'I can't think what else it could be. Hang on a minute, I'd better get up and see what's happened.'

She had left a towelling gown and slippers on the floor. Climbing out of bed, she slipped into them and blew him a kiss before disappearing downstairs. He stared at the timbered ceiling of the bedroom, his thoughts in a jumble. Soon he heard her footsteps hurrying back up the creaking wooden staircase. She was breathless, her hair and shoulders drenched.

'I had a look out at the front,' she gasped. 'Do you remember seeing a huge sycamore as you came up the path? It's toppled over on to the utility room at the side of the house. It's smashed the roof in. God knows how bad the damage is. I haven't dared go into the kitchen yet. If anyone had been in there, they'd have been killed. Poor Linda, it's heartbreaking!'

'Let me see,' Harry grunted.

He struggled into his boxer shorts and picked up the flashlight that Linda evidently kept for emergencies. As soon as he entered the kitchen, he realised the scale of the calamity.

The utility room had, he guessed, been tacked on to the house in recent years. It was a single-storey extension which led from the kitchen and contained a washing machine, tumble drier and freezer. The trunk of the tree had torn through the roof and wall. Through the gaping hole he could see the starless sky. The window sills, the quarry-tiled floor and every work surface were covered in rubble and sheared-off branches. A large lump of masonry filled the sink. All the equipment was filthy and dripping wet.

He went back to the front door and put his head outside. The rain had eased to a steady drizzle. Even the wind was moaning more quietly, as if chastened by the scale of the wreckage it had caused. He walked across a patch of sodden lawn and shone his light on to the tree. It must have been fifty feet tall. Now it was leaning at an acute angle, its root mass ripped from the ground, its crown hidden behind the devastated utility room.

He trudged back to the bedroom. Juliet was sitting on the carpet, with her back to the bed. He saw to his dismay that she'd put her bra and pants back on underneath the gown. Her face was red with temper and she was gripping the mobile phone as if she hated it, punching numbers at random in frustration.

'Useless bloody thing!' She sent the mobile skimming across the floor.

'You were trying to reach Linda?'

She nodded. 'I have to tell her, Harry. I owe her that, at least.'

'Can't it wait until the morning? There's nothing anyone can do tonight.'

'Have you seen the damage?'

'It's bad,' he admitted. 'Like you say, it's a miracle no-one was hurt.'

'Well, then. Harry. We must do *something*. I mean, we can't just climb back under the covers and forget about it.'

Harry wanted to do precisely that, but care was needed if the evening were not to disintegrate into a squabbling anti-climax. 'Okay, I see your point. But what do you have in mind? Let's face it, this place isn't overflowing with telephone boxes.'

'What about your mobile?'

'Left it at home. Pager ditto.' He groaned. 'I didn't want us to be disturbed.'

She shrugged. 'I suppose the only option is to try the neighbour. His house is only about a hundred yards away. We can throw ourselves on his mercy.'

'Not a good idea,' he said quickly. 'Remember, you said that he and Linda don't get on.'

'I hardly think he'd refuse to let us use his phone in view of what's happened.'

The icy note in her voice made her sound like someone he'd never met before. A warning sign. Yet he couldn't help pressing. 'Who's to say he's got a mobile?'

'Come on,' she snapped, 'how many solicitors do you know without one? Besides, I should have thought it would be mandatory to have a portable back-up in an out-of-the-way spot like this. At least there's no harm in asking.'

'Are you sure about that?' Harry's heart was thudding. 'This solicitor, you don't know anything about him, do you? He might turn out to be someone I did battle with in court today. The cat would be well and truly out of the bag then, wouldn't it? How long before word got around? You know what Liverpudlians are like. Their idea of a secret is something you mustn't tell to more than three people. Who's to say that Casper wouldn't get to hear of it, sooner or later?'

'All right, all right,' she said sulkily. 'I'll go on my own. I'll tell him I turned up here because I needed to call on Linda urgently. Something to do with work. Then I saw the tree had come down.'

'What if he offers his help, wants to come over here to take a look-see?'

'Don't worry. It won't be hard to put him off.' She waved a hand. 'I'll make up a story.'

The throwaway remark jolted him. He realised that she enjoyed making up stories, took it in her stride. Her creative imagination ought not to have come as a surprise, he supposed. She did make a living from promoting the image of solicitors, after all. But he felt like a fly caught in a web.

'Okay. If you think it's for the best.'

'Yes, I do.' She stared at him, her eyes narrowing. 'I'm not just some old nympho, Harry. I have some idea about doing the right thing. I'd never let Linda down.'

'I only meant...'

'Oh forget it.' She pulled on her suspender belt and stockings. 'If you like, you can go home now. Let's face it, the evening's been ruined.'

'I'm staying,' he said doggedly.

'Up to you.' She finished dressing in silence. When she spoke again, her tone had softened. 'Harry, I'm as sorry as you are about this. We were doing fine, weren't we? Too good to be true, I suppose. I won't be long, promise. Ten minutes should do it. You'll probably be proved right and there'll be nothing much Linda can do about this until the morning. But I won't be able to take it easy until I've broken the news. I owe her that.'

'Sure,' he said. 'I'll be waiting for you. And whatever happens, we can finish the champagne, can't we?'

Left alone in the candle-light, he padded around, trying to get his bearings in the unfamiliar house. He'd often spoken to Linda Blackwell on the phone and he'd met her at Juliet's office. He recalled a smart woman with metal-rimmed spectacles and blonde hair in a bob. She was a widow, he gathered, in her early fifties but looking ten years younger. Her manner was always crisp and business like. It came as no surprise that her home contained neither chintz nor clutter.

The bed he'd shared with Juliet had a hard mattress and a plain British Home Stores duvet. The furniture was functional pine. There weren't many personal touches apart from a symmetrically arranged group of framed photographs on the dressing table. Linda on her wedding day; she looked about nineteen, slim and pretty. Her late husband had been a tall handsome man with a mane of long fair hair. There were snaps of the couple with a baby in dungarees, who became an awkward gap-toothed schoolboy, a young man standing proudly outside medical school and finally a morning-suited bridegroom kissing a blonde in a low-cut white dress. It took Harry a moment to identify him as the gruff chap he'd met at Juliet's office. Another picture showed Peter, a few years older, standing next to a signboard at the front of a low-level industrial unit bearing the legend *Blackwell Prostheses*. Perhaps Peter would be useful to know, Harry thought, if Casper chopped his legs off. Although he hadn't taken to Peter on brief initial acquaintance, he was uncomfortably aware that the Blackwells had done Juliet and him a favour by allowing them the opportunity to spend the night together. And now it had all gone wrong.

Linda's bed was a double, presumably for comfort rather than company: there was no evidence of any boyfriend and only a single toothbrush in the bathroom. There was a cardboard box marked in neat lettering *Peter's school reports*. Linda Blackwell was a devoted mother and Harry sighed, composing a mental picture blurred by time of his own long-dead parents. Would they have kept souvenirs of his childhood? How different would his life have been if they had survived?

Even from glancing round the cottage, he could guess that Linda was the perfect secretary, someone who took pleasure in filing things in their proper order. Thank God he'd never married someone so obsessively tidy; she'd have filed for divorce on the grounds of messiness within a matter of months. The downstairs rooms were equally neat, except for the sofa cushions which he and Juliet had swept aside during their first embrace of the evening. Women's magazines filled a rack; Delia Smith and Catherine Cookson dominated the bookshelves; the cd tower was stacked with Enya and Phil Collins. The vinyl of the kitchen floor gleamed; the place would have suited a photo-shoot for an article about ideal homes if it were not for the tree trunk making the utility room look like a stage set for theatre of the absurd.

Perhaps Juliet was right. This did not feel like a gossip's home. He could persuade himself that the person who lived here could be trusted with the secret. But even if Linda kept her mouth shut, what future could he and Juliet possibly have together? She was a woman who had fads. Reading the Tarot, more recently Feng Shui. He didn't deceive himself; he was one more short-term craze, a change from the usual run of well-heeled men she fancied. Some day soon she'd find someone else who amused her more.

He sprawled on the sofa and flicked through a magazine he'd pulled from the rack. There was a double page spread about addiction, aimed at mothers with problem children. The snippets of information in the sidebars struck a chord: there was talk about shopaholics and binge eaters, cases where enjoyable activity became compulsive. The causes of addiction, a psychiatrist was quoted as saying, were usually emotional. A period of stress rooted in unhappiness was almost always to blame. It made sense. Time had passed since his wife Liz had been murdered, but the wounds had yet to heal.

He'd met Juliet after Jim had asked her if she could improve the firm's profile and he'd been smitten at once. At first he'd tried to fight his instincts; it was easy to come up with a dozen good reasons why an affair was doomed. But the excitement of finding that she reciprocated his interest had drowned the still small voice of common sense. Their affair had begun one night in the spring and now he found it increasingly impossible to imagine life without her. Whenever he felt lonely, he needed to pick up the phone and talk to her. Once when he'd called her at home, Casper had answered and he'd had to pretend to be a market researcher for a timeshare company. By the time Casper had said, 'I've already got a five-bedroom villa on the Algarve, so why don't you stop wasting my time and just fuck off?' and banged the phone down, his shirt had been wet through. The health warnings didn't need to be spelled out: sleeping with a violent man's wife could seriously damage your health. The trouble was that he couldn't bring himself to give her up.

The magazine article didn't offer much help. A doctor advised that the only way to conquer the problem was to avoid temptation. The best course for addicts was to supplement an avoidance strategy backed-up with regular self-help group meetings. Somehow Harry couldn't see that working. Nicotine skin patches and chewing gum were no more use than hypnotherapy, acupuncture or methadone. Nor could he rely on family support. He didn't have a family, it was as simple as that. He'd been an only child and his mother and father had been killed in a car crash when he was a teenager. With no-one around to reinforce his memories, sometimes he found it hard nowadays to remember much about them. Liz had left him for someone else and been stabbed to death a couple of years later. It seemed natural to him to be alone. Only on odd occasions, when Jim spoke about his own wife and children, did Harry wonder what he might be missing. Jim might not be quite the textbook family man – Harry had once caught him *in flagrante* with a woman police officer – but he did have someone to go home to. Maybe there was something to be said for a conventional way of life, if the alternative was sleeping with the wife of another man who might kill you if he ever discovered the truth.

'Harry!'

He heard her call his name at the same moment that the front door crashed open. Her voice was breathless and frightened. His skin tingled.

'What is it?'

He raced into the hall. Juliet was standing on the threshold, gasping for air. Her face was streaked with tears. As he put his arm around her, she began to weep. It was a dreadful sound, desperate and afraid. Her body heaved and he hugged her urgently, whispering words of comfort.

'It's all right, darling. I'm here. You're safe.'

'It's – it's not all right,' she wept.

'For God's sake, what's happened?'

'He's dead! He's dead! And – his head ... oh Christ!' She gulped in air as greedily as if she were drowning. 'It's ... it's been cut off.'

Chapter Three

Twenty minutes passed and still she sobbed. Her body rocked against him as again he raised the tumbler to her lips.

She winced as the brandy burned her tongue. 'Thanks,' she said in a muffled voice.

'Have some more.'

Straining hard to smile, she said, 'Sorry, I'm not usually hysterical. But it was so vile...'

They clung to each other. He brushed her cheek with his lips. 'You're not being hysterical. It's only natural.'

'His head,' she said thickly. 'The eyes were staring at me. Oh God, Harry, I – I've never seen a corpse before. Let alone ... shit, it was so horrible ... you can't imagine, you just can't imagine.'

He ground his teeth, wishing he could say something to help. There were no words for comforting someone who had just seen a decapitated corpse. When he spoke, it was less gently than he'd intended. 'I've seen a dead body more than once, remember?' He paused. 'Including my wife's.'

She flinched as if he had slapped her face. 'Oh, Harry, I'm sorry. I remember you once told me about going to the mortuary after she was stabbed.' The words were starting to come a little more easily now. 'God, how could you bear it? I know you were head over heels in love with her. This is a man I've never even met, but even so ...' She touched his hand. 'Guess I'm not as brave and devil-may-care as you thought, eh?'

He squeezed her fingers and said quietly, 'So much the better. I suppose it *was* the neighbour?'

'No idea.' She frowned and pulled away from him. He realised how strong she was; already the shock was beginning to give way to the first stirrings of speculation. It would take time for the full enormity of what she had witnessed to sink in. 'I – I assumed it was him. If it's someone else, Linda's *bête-noir* has a lot of explaining to do.'

'That's for sure. Okay, then. You left here...'

'The storm was dying ... oh Christ, what a choice of words!'

'Doesn't matter, doesn't matter. You took the other fork in the path, found the house not far away?'

'Yes, I was afraid I might get lost, but the trees thin out. The place is near shore level, I couldn't miss it. There's a brass knocker on the door, much the same as the one here. When I lifted it, the door opened. Not properly shut. So I stepped over the threshold, flashing the light and calling, "Anyone there?"'

'Did the house seem empty?'

Her eyes widened as a fresh terror swept over her. 'You're not suggesting that – whoever did it was still there when I walked in?'

'Just asking.'

'Oh Jesus.' She hesitated, her eyes glazing for a moment as her imagination worked. 'I heard nothing. That bothered me. I thought someone must be there, if the door wasn't locked – so why weren't they answering? I remember shivering, but I walked into the hallway. I could see a mobile on an occasional table. Perfect. But I could hardly make my call there and then. It would have been too embarrassing if the owner had popped out of the loo or bathroom and found me standing there, chatting away on his portable phone without a by-your-leave. So I shouted out two or three more times.'

'Still no answer?'

'Nothing. Then I noticed that the floor was covered in pieces of broken glass. Bits of mirror. There was an empty hook on the wall. It was as if someone had grabbed it from the hook and smashed it on the ground. I was scared by now. Even if the man had gone to bed early in some kind of temper, he surely couldn't have slept through that storm.'

Through her thin clothes, he could feel her heart beating faster as she relived the scene. 'I'm amazed you didn't turn round and leg it back here.'

She nodded. 'I thought about it, believe me, but I told myself not to be such a coward. I looked round one door. It was the living-room. No-one there. Same with the little dining-room. At the end of the hall was the way into the kitchen. I peered inside. He – he was lying there.'

She shed more tears, burying her face in his chest. He increased the pressure of his grip on her. 'You're safe with me, love.'

She looked up at him. 'How can you be sure?'

Harry moistened his lips. 'Whoever did this will be long gone. Promise. Now – did you see a weapon of any kind?'

'Nothing. But I wasn't looking out for one. The sight of the body hypnotised me. He'd been stabbed, for good measure. At least I think so. His chest was soaked in blood. Saturated. I hated it, I wanted to throw up, but I was paralysed. I couldn't tear my eyes away. It felt as though I'd been staring at it for hours. Really, I suppose it was a minute at most.'

'Sure. You weren't out so very long.'

'Long enough. The moment I was outside, I did puke. I couldn't help myself.'

'Best thing.'

'Maybe. I tell you, I've never moved so fast as I did on the way back here.'

'I suppose the next thing is to call the police.'

'You – you think we have to?'

He stared at her, trying to fathom what was going on behind the tear-streaked face. 'What's the alternative?'

'I was just wondering ... I mean, do we really want to get involved?'

'Better face up to it. We are involved. It's the last thing I'd wish for, but we can't forget what you've seen.'

She shuddered. 'Understatement of the year. Why do we have to say anything to anyone at all?'

'I'm a lawyer,' he said helplessly. 'Believe me, I often wish I wasn't. But we don't have a choice. There's no option but to report the death.'

'This isn't the right moment to go chasing a good citizenship award.' Her face was pinched with tension. 'We have to be careful. You and I shouldn't be here together. Casper has friends in high places. Believe it or not, he plays golf with a superintendent once a fortnight. We could be in big trouble. People talk.'

'Of course they do. That's why we need to use our heads.' He paused, then said gently, 'Think for a moment. Suppose we do steal away into the night. What happens? Linda Blackwell is left well and truly in the shit. All of a sudden, that tree becomes the least of her problems. Sooner or later a body is discovered in the next house along the path. The police come calling on her, wanting to know if she was here tonight, whether she heard or saw anything. You told me she and this neighbour, whoever he is, weren't on good terms. Assuming he's the victim – and the smart money says he is – she'll be treated as a suspect.'

'You can't be serious!'

'You may think it's crazy, but what if the two of them have been locked in some kind of dispute? The police are bound to check her out, if only to eliminate her.'

Juliet pulled away from him. 'You're exaggerating. I can't see a problem. She has an alibi. She can explain that she was staying at her son's house this evening.'

'On a night like this, you might expect a widow who lives in a place as remote as this to stay at home, keeping an eye on her property. They'll dig around, you can depend on it.'

'You're worrying over nothing.'

'It's not nothing,' he said, obstinacy hardening his tone. 'If this man has been murdered, the police aren't going to treat it like a parking offence. Their forensic people will take his house apart. There'll be trace evidence, you'll have left your fingerprints. You weren't wearing gloves when you picked up the mobile.'

'Strange as it may seem for the wife of Casper May,' she snapped, 'they don't actually have my fingerprints on file. Nor my DNA.'

'Won't they wonder who was sick outside the house?' He grasped her by the shoulder. 'Listen, your husband isn't the only one with friends in the Merseyside Police. I have a few, as well. And I promise you, they aren't going to skimp on this one. Let's not take too many chances. If the detectives do find out that we were here and then did a runner after you discovered the body, all hell will let loose. We'd both be pulled in for questioning. Try explaining that to Casper. You're relying too much on your PA's discretion. To say nothing of her son's.'

She eased out of his grip. Her brow was furrowed; he sensed that she was weighing the risks in her mind. 'Peter, yes. Linda's strong, but he's different. He's not an easy guy, he's had a rough time lately. I mean, he's no fool. At one time he was training to be a surgeon. After he gave that up, he built up a good little business. But it's all fallen apart. His wife left him, his company failed. One of the problems is that he likes a drink. I'm not sure I'd stake my life on him keeping his mouth shut.'

'Well, then.'

A low groan. 'All right. You win. But what do we tell the police? How can we explain why we're here? We can't tell the truth, that's for sure.'

'When you're in a hole, the first rule is – stop digging.'

She leaned forward and seized his wrist. 'Harry, swear to me you won't even hint that we're having an affair. We have to come up with some good reason for being here. It's for your sake as much as mine. If Casper gets the faintest hint…'

'Okay, okay. I'll think of something.'

'It had better be good.'

'You're not the only one who can make up a story. Life as a defence lawyer sharpens the imagination.'

She forced a smile. 'Perhaps you should have gone in for public relations. So how do we contact the police? Don't forget, the phones are down. I'm not going back to that charnel house to use the mobile. Not for anyone.'

'I'll do it.'

'Are you sure?'

'No choice.'

'But what about me? What if whoever did this...?'

'Like I said, he'll have long gone. I'm sure of it.' He paused, realising that he was much less confident than he sounded. 'But lock yourself in, all the same. Just as a precaution. Don't open the door to anyone else. I'll bang on the front window when I'm back.'

'I tell you, it's – it's not a pretty sight.'

'Dead bodies never are,' Harry said harshly.

'There's a poker by the fireplace. Take it, will you?'

'Uh-huh.'

'And when you go over there, don't look in the kitchen, whatever you do.'

He shrugged and said nothing. When she'd told him about the body next door, he had first been horrified, then fearful. Now he was becoming conscious of a familiar yearning, mixed in with the terrors. It was like an emptiness in his belly, a hunger. He realised with a shudder of guilty self-awareness that it was a pang of curiosity. Did he know the murdered man? Soon he would find out.

The wind had become little more than a sigh through the pine leaves and the rain had eased to a fine drizzle. The path was steep and narrow and as he walked, his shoes kept sticking in the mud, but he forced himself on, knowing that time was precious.

He gripped the poker so hard that he risked crushing the bones of his hand, yet he knew he could never bring himself to use it as a weapon. He hated violence and did not dare contemplate the possibility that he might need to protect himself, that his life might depend on a willingness to strike the first blow. It would never happen; he had to believe that. The killer must be long gone, surely. There were other things he ought to worry about. Like what he should do when he reached the cottage.

He must be careful not to wipe fingerprints off the mobile. He doubted that the killer had touched it, but all the same, he would use a paper tissue when picking it up. He mustn't do anything that might prevent the police from solving the crime. First he would call Linda and explain what had happened, make sure that she would go along with his plan before he dialled 999. He'd soon find out whether Juliet was right in believing that her PA had steel nerves. He needed to make sure she came over at once. West Kirby wasn't far away. If she put her foot down, she could get back home before the police arrived at the murder scene.

The police would check on calls made from the mobile. They would want to know why he'd rung the number of Linda's son. He'd have to say Linda had asked him to tell Peter what had happened, maybe see if she could stay overnight with him in West Kirby. Christ, this was going to get complicated. Should he change his mind, call the police first? No, he'd have to risk it. If Linda wouldn't help out, he'd need to come up with another story. He'd fob the detectives off, tell them that he wasn't thinking straight. Not far from the truth, actually. It would seem flimsy and they were sure to be sceptical, but he'd have to chance it.

As he picked his way down the path to the dead man's house, he rehearsed in his mind what he would say when the police came to take statements. He, Juliet and Linda would have to sing from the same hymn-sheet. Their version of events would need to be capable of standing up to scrutiny, not merely from the investigating

31

detectives, but also from Casper May if need be. It was crucial to avoid arousing suspicion of any kind.

Like most lawyers, he had over the years learned the basic principles of lying. Keep it short. Keep it simple. And keep it as close to the truth as you can. The first challenge was to find an innocent explanation for his visit to the Customs House on a night when no-one in his senses would venture out of doors.

He would say that he needed advice from Juliet on an advertising campaign. Someone from *Enterprise Spotlight* had rung him that morning, urging him to participate in a feature about legal help for businesses. Trying to fob off the sales rep had been as fruitless as arguing with a doorstep evangelist. In the end he had found himself agreeing to look at the rates for an ad in an issue focusing on the north-west's captains of industry. The rep had pressed for a decision, offering as an incentive a supposedly unrepeatable discount. So it was just about plausible that, before taking the plunge and agreeing to spend money the firm could – according to the Loan Arranger – ill afford, a prudent lawyer might wish to pick expert brains right away. And Juliet had said she would draft the advertising copy for him that very evening.

It didn't take long to map out Juliet's statement. Suppose she said that, with her husband out of town for forty-eight hours, she'd arranged to spend the evening with Linda. They had been together for years; they were friends as much as employer and employee. She might tell them she'd intended to pick up Linda so that they could go out for a drink, but when Harry rang, she suggested that he meet them at Linda's house. Since the weather was so grim, the evening would not be unduly spoiled. When the tree had crashed into the house, Juliet had volunteered to ask the neighbour for the use of his phone to call the emergency services. But then she had discovered the body and come rushing back in deep distress.

Jesus, it was thin. But what else could he say?

Everything depended on Linda. Without her help, he found it impossible to dream up any innocent explanation for his and Juliet's presence in the isolated cottage. She had to return and support them in their story. At least it was safe to assume that, tonight of all nights, she would not have strayed from her son's fireside.

Twigs cracked under his feet as he followed a bend in the path. As the trees cleared, he saw his destination immediately in front of him. The house was a little larger than Linda's. A slate nameplate bore the legend *Harbour Master's Cottage*. The house had been built just above the water's edge. Harry could hear the waves slapping against the shore on the other side of the building. The front door was swinging backwards and forwards, banging against the jamb.

Would he and Juliet get away with it? If he thought long and hard, perhaps he could come up with a better solution to their dilemma. There might be flaws in his plan that he could not foresee. He took a deep breath. Better not think about what might go wrong or to indulge in flights of fancy. In ordinary times, he and Juliet shared a fascination with mysteries. Tonight, though, he'd had more than enough of tales of the unexpected. This wasn't the time to indulge in wild guessing games – *what if the body has disappeared?*

He crunched up the wet gravel and paused on the threshold. Impossible to walk into a house of death without a second thought. But a moment's hesitation was all that he allowed himself before he stepped into the hallway and slammed the door behind him.

The flashlight revealed a stone-floored passage with a low beamed ceiling. He moved forward, his footsteps echoing in the silence. The only article of furniture was the small mahogany table; the mobile was where Juliet had left it. Shards of glass lay on the floor. He stared down into the largest fragment of the shattered mirror and saw a wary, hollow-cheeked face. For an instant he did not recognise it as his own.

There was a musty odour. Rising damp, yes, and food smells, but he also caught the whiff of death. He could feel his bowels churning. Should he make the calls, then run away? It was a far cry from the mortuary, with its sweet sickly smell, where he had been taken to identify the corpse of his wife. He didn't *need* to see this body. But then, he hadn't needed to spend the night with Juliet. He clenched his fists, digging the fingernails into his palms. No time to panic, he told himself. Curiosity wouldn't kill him.

Grinding his teeth together in concentration, he shone the lamp into the kitchen. It lit on a sprawled naked figure scarcely recognisable as human. Tears of horror pricked Harry's eyes, as if to protect him by blurring the horror. He could dimly make out that the arms and legs were stretched out wide, as if trying to escape the torso. A dark mess saturated the chest and throat. The head lay inches away from the shattered neck.

Nothing Juliet might have said could have prepared him for this. Even though he'd seen corpses before, he'd never encountered a scene so unnatural or savage. How could one person have done this to another? Easier to believe that the man on the ground had fallen victim to a wild and pitiless creature. Harry felt vomit rise at the back of his throat as he smelled the dead man's urine. His beam wavered as his hand shook; for a moment it settled upon the face staring up towards the ceiling. The mouth was open as if uttering a soundless plea for mercy. The eyes stared as though they could see through the gates of hell.

For a few seconds, his memory stalled and he could not put a name to the face, for all the familiarity of the bald scalp and black bushy eyebrows. He could not associate it with a living man who harried witnesses, glared at opponents, smirked at jokes cracked by magistrates. But as the horror soaked into his mind, he remembered.

Carl Symons, the prosecutor. Not a man he cared for: a famously ugly loner engaged in a long-term love affair with himself. But not a man who deserved to die like this. No-one deserved to die like this.

Standing outside the kitchen, gazing at the remains of Carl Symons, Harry found himself speaking aloud.

'Who could have hated you so much?'

'So,' Linda Blackwell said half an hour later, 'I've – I've never left the cottage all evening?'

'You've got it,' Juliet told her. 'We all stick to the same story, okay? Then no-one will get the wrong idea.'

'No,' Linda said. She had a dazed expression, as if someone had struck her over the head with a mallet. There was a note of bewilderment in everything she said and her eyes didn't look as though they were focusing properly. When she'd stood up to pour herself a brandy a few moments earlier, she'd seemed unsteady on her feet even without the help of the alcohol. Her hands kept trembling.

Understandable, Harry reflected. Since she'd walked through the door ten minutes earlier, she'd found her house wrecked, her next-door neighbour murdered and her boss imploring her to lie to the police about it all. Talk about a night to remember. Wasn't that the title of an old film about the last voyage of the *Titanic*? This evening had turned into their own personal disaster movie.

'Are you all right?' Juliet put an arm round the older woman. 'I realise it's a lot to ask.'

'Yes, yes, I'll be fine,' Linda said, although Harry was not convinced. 'It's just difficult to take it all in. But of course I know what Casper's like. He mustn't get to hear of this.'

'I do think Harry's explanation is a good one,' Juliet said. Her cheeks were flushed, her voice a little louder than usual. The brandy had revived her, as it had Harry. They were relying on that, plus adrenalin, to get them through. 'It's not so far from the truth.

We won't be misleading the detectives about anything essential, anything connected with the crime. There's no point in causing unnecessary pain.'

Nicely put, Harry thought. Linda knew as well as they did that more than Casper's ego would be dented if the affair became common knowledge. But perhaps everything might work out. So far he had to admit that Linda was living up to her advance billing: a true friend who was willing to massage the truth in order to save their skins.

'Tell me,' Juliet asked. 'Had you realised Harry and I were...?'

Linda looked at him and shook her head. 'I worked out some time ago that you'd found someone. I was glad. You deserve better than Casper, much better. But I had the shock of my life when I heard Harry's voice on the phone. It never once crossed my mind that he might be the man. To be honest, I was really startled.'

Harry didn't find her answer altogether flattering, but that was the least of his worries. 'Thanks for agreeing to come over. And for not firing too many difficult questions all at once. I'm sorry to land you with all this. But we do need to discuss what happens next. Like I said, the police are sure to want to segregate us, test our statements for inconsistencies. The people first on the scene at a murder are always the obvious suspects.'

'My head's still spinning,' Linda said.

'What did you tell Peter?' Juliet asked.

Linda coloured. 'Oh, I don't know – just that there was a problem here. A tree had blown over in the storm.'

'I was afraid he'd insist on coming over with you,' Juliet said. 'I know he's a good son.'

'He is,' she said, her voice softening. 'One in a million. But – no, he's staying at home.'

'Just as well. I mean, I'm normally delighted to see him, but I don't really think this is the ideal time. And – I'm not quite sure how to put this...'

'I won't tell him about you and Harry,' Linda said quickly. 'I can keep my mouth shut when I have to, even with my own boy.'

'I've been mulling it over,' Harry said. 'You may have no alternative but to give him a clue. After all, it's a racing certainty that the police will check Peter out as well. He has to back you up.'

'Then he will,' Linda said. 'I promise you that.'

Juliet patted her hand. 'God, I'm lucky to have you on my side. When we've talked to the police we can set about getting your house put right. At least Casper's contacts may come in useful. His security people work for several building companies. Don't worry, everything will soon be back to normal.'

Linda shivered. 'But not for Carl Symons.'

'How well did you know him?' Harry asked.

A frown. 'He only moved next door in June. I didn't see much of him. It's a dreadful thing to say, but he – he wasn't a pleasant person.'

'Didn't you say you'd had a row with him?' Juliet asked.

'It was nothing,' Linda said quickly. 'We didn't hit it off, that's all. A pity, since he's my only neighbour. An elderly couple used to have that cottage. They were twitchers, fanatical birdwatchers, that is. We used to help each other out if ever there was a little problem. When they left, I hoped someone decent would move in. There are plenty of people around here in the summer months, walking along the shore, but in winter, it's a lonely spot. Quite cut-off.'

'Tell me about it,' Juliet said.

Linda smoothed out an errant strand of blonde hair. Even in these circumstances her instinct was to keep things neat and tidy. 'This man, Symons, he wasn't sociable. Liked to keep himself to himself. But his manner was always superior, he obviously regarded me as a woman of no importance. He complained a couple of times when Peter parked his car in front of his garage. A silly thing to make a song and dance about: Peter was in the wrong, but this past year he's been distracted, he's had a lot on his plate. I'm sure he'd have been only too happy to move the car at once if he was asked. But no, Carl Symons sent me a formal letter, threatening to seek compensation if it ever happened again.'

'Quite a charmer, then,' Juliet said.

'Put it this way. If I ran out of something, there was no question of my popping round to his house to borrow a bag of sugar or whatever. He'd not only have charged, but demanded interest on top.' She hesitated. 'I'd say he was the sort who would make enemies, plenty of them.'

'You said you knew him, Harry?'

'Vaguely. Before he became a prosecutor, he was in partnership with a couple of other lawyers. It broke up a while ago.'

Juliet leaned forward. 'Acrimoniously?'

'Looking for suspects already? You're worse than me. But yes, there was a bitter dispute, or so I heard. Nothing unusual in that. Partnership's like a marriage. Divorce is never easy.'

'So the poacher turned gamekeeper?'

'Good way of describing it. He moved over to prosecuting. I suppose he rather liked that. I should imagine he was good at it, too. I always had the impression that he was efficient, disciplined. You could usually bet that if he prepared a case, the defence would have a hard time persuading the court there was reasonable doubt of guilt. He liked to pick winners, did Carl Symons.'

Juliet turned to Linda. 'Was he married?'

'If he was, I never saw her. After the trouble over Peter's car, I kept out of the chap's way.'

'Was he gay?' Juliet demanded of Harry.

'No idea. He and I were no more than acquaintances. For all I know, he might have been sleeping with half the members of the Liverpool Legal Group. I don't keep in close touch with the grapevine.'

'Liar,' she said. 'You love gossip and scandal as much as I do.'

He forced a grin. 'I plead the right of silence. You won't...'

He was interrupted by a fierce knock at the door. The three of them looked at each other. Harry mouthed the word '*Police*'.

Juliet gritted her teeth. 'Okay, then. The story we agreed, the whole story and nothing but that story. All right? Let's do it.'

Chapter Four

*I had killed a nightmare. Or – shall I say? – I had given
my enemy peace by liberating his soul. Yet I could not rest.
As the first shafts of daylight penetrated my little room,
I paced back and forth over the stone flags. So much
accomplished. So much yet to do.*

Daniel Roberts leaned back in his chair, rubbing eyes made
sore by the glare from the screen. He blinked hard, trying to
cleanse his mind of the bloody image imprinted on it, then saved
the document and closed down the computer.

The cottage was cold; he had little money and didn't waste what
he had on heating. The old clock chimed six. He shivered, knowing
that it was time to start his journey. He had not had a moment's
sleep all night and yet he was tense and alert. His life was entering a
new phase. Since early childhood, he had felt that he was in search
of something, without being clear about the object of his quest. At
last he knew what it was – and what he had to do to get it.

His van bumped down the stony puddled track that led from the
cottage, the tools in the back rattling like a prisoner's chains. The
track wound through woodland that covered the mountainside. The
tops of the fir trees were wreathed in mist. He loved this place,
had chosen it for his home simply because it reminded him of his
favourite book. He knew the words by heart, could quote them in
chunks. '*Soon we were hemmed in with trees which in places arched
right over the roadway till we passed as through a tunnel; and again
great frowning rocks guarded us boldly on either side.*'

He took the left fork, even though it meant he had to drive an
extra mile before he hit the main road. This way he would miss the
truckstop: it was safer. There was always the danger that Rhodri
would spot him as he drove past the kiosk and wave him over for

a chat. Things were quiet at this hour and Rhodri was incurably nosey. He would want to talk about the havoc wreaked by the storm of the previous afternoon and ask where Daniel was heading and why.

He was a cautious driver but in the early morning traffic was light on the A55 and inside two hours he had reached the outskirts of Liverpool. He did not care for cities and kept well clear of them unless there was a special reason to endure their dirt and dust and noise. Nudging through the rush-hour queues, he found a parking space in a multi-storey off Paradise Street. Still he was early. He decided to kill time by striding over to the waterfront. Although the weather had calmed, here and there he saw relics of the gales' ferocity: smashed fencing, skewed road signs and shattered panes in a hot dog stand.

He gazed across the Mersey, peering through the haze to see if he could make out Moel Famau in the distance. He was unfamiliar with the old port but he'd bought a book about it in a second-hand shop in Bangor. He wanted to learn about the city where the man he was seeking lived. Now he had arrived, his whole body was taut with excitement. He'd had a lifetime's practice in suppressing his emotions, though, and he would not let his control slip today. No-one who met him would guess how he felt, deep inside. They would see a tall lean man whose dark hair was splashed with grey around the temples. The leather jacket, sweatshirt, jeans and boots all reflected his taste for black.

A glance at the clock on the Liver Building told him it was almost nine. Time to move. Leaving Mann Island, he crossed the six-lane Strand with care and headed up James Street before turning off into a narrow side street. Half a dozen stone steps led down to the basement of a tall Victorian building, the upper floors of which were decorated with fading *To Let* signs. A stainless steel nameplate outside the door told him that he had arrived at the headquarters of the Liverpool Legal Group.

He stepped inside and found himself in a large room. The far wall was lined with floor-to-ceiling bookshelves and a young woman with her back to him was leafing through a thick looseleaf volume. The decor was aggresively unDickensian: spare and Scandinavian with lots of spiky pot plants and uncomfortable-looking chairs. A table was piled high with leaflets emblazoned with the legend *No Win – No Fee*. A woman in her mid-forties sat behind the front desk, languidly examining her make-up in a pocket mirror. A paperback was turned upside down on her desk, its title *How To Cope With Stress At Work*. A badge on her beige jacket announced that her name was Pamela and that her title was Reception Executive.

When Daniel coughed, she looked up with a start. Something in his expression seemed to unsettle her and she gabbled, 'Good morning, welcome to the offices of Liverpool Legal Group, how may I help you?'

'I believe you keep a register of lawyers here?' As was his habit, he spoke so softly that it was almost a whisper.

'A database of solicitors and barristers, updated monthly, that's right,' Pamela said, getting into her swing with well-rehearsed brightness. 'We receive funding from both the Law Society and the Bar Council, but we remain an independent registered charity committed to the promotion of local legal services for the benefit of clients in Liverpool and the wider community of Merseyside.'

As she paused for breath, Daniel said, 'I'm interested in one solicitor in particular.'

Two spots of colour appeared on her powdered cheeks. His demeanour was evidently bothering her. Perhaps it was the sheer intensity of his gaze. She said, 'I – I can check for you, if you'll just bear with me. They've put in a new computer system and I've not quite got the hang of it yet.'

As if alerted by the tremor in her voice, the woman at the back of the room looked up. She put her book down on a table and met

Daniel's gaze. She was painfully thin with slanting green eyes and high cheekbones. Her scarlet lipstick made a vivid contrast with the pallor of her skin. The black hair which she'd swept back from her forehead reached down to her waist.

She said softly, 'Perhaps I can help, Pamela. Excuse me, I couldn't help overhearing.'

Her eyes met his. He guessed she was accustomed to attracting attention. Yet it wasn't simply her looks that jolted him, made him feel as if he'd had an electric shock. No mistake about it; there was something *about* her that was extraordinary.

She hesitated, as if having second thoughts about interrupting. Perhaps somehow she had sensed the intensity of his reaction to her and been disturbed by it. But it was too late for her to walk away. She cleared her throat. 'I used to work in one of the law firms round here. Can you tell me the name of the person you have in mind?'

'Yes,' Daniel Roberts said. 'He's called Harry Devlin.'

Harry had arrived home at four in the morning. He'd not even attempted to sleep after the police had finished with him. Predictable as the interviewing process had been, he'd found it an ordeal. The best thing that could be said was that it had sobered him up. The morose sergeant who was first on the scene was someone he'd never met, but it was obvious from his manner that he didn't like solicitors. His ideal outcome was plainly that one lawyer would confess to having killed another: two birds with one murder. Harry's head kept thudding as he stumbled through his version of the evening's events. The sergeant listened to the tale with Eeyore-like gloom and it was a relief when an inspector called Mitch Eggar, whom Harry did know, finally turned up. Eggar suggested pleasantly that it would be best if Harry, Juliet and Linda came down to the station as volunteers to help with inquiries while the forensic boys did their stuff. It was futile to say no. *Talk to you tomorrow*, Harry mouthed at Juliet as she was ushered out of the cottage ahead of him.

The three of them were taken in separate cars to different police stations. The police were taking no chances about collusion. Harry finished up at Birkenhead with Eggar. He wrote out the statement himself, blinking at the perjury declaration, but telling himself that he had no choice but to stick to the plan he'd agreed with the women. Lying about the reason for his visit to the cottage was the lesser of two evils.

'Presumably you crossed swords with Carl Symons from time to time?' Eggar said. He was a well-fed man with a red face and thinning sandy hair. In his younger days, he'd been a useful cricketer and now he umpired on summer weekends. Harry could recall an occasion during his own playing days when he'd turned out for the Legal Group against the Police. Mitch had given him out leg before, a dubious decision given with a beam that brooked no argument. As an interrogator, he favoured an amiable, confiding style. Over the years, it had lured a number of Harry's clients into the trap of self-incrimination.

'We were on other sides of the fence. I won't pretend we were bosom buddies. But there are plenty of prosecutors I know better than Carl. He hadn't been around all that long.'

'Ever have any run-ins with him?'

'None worth mentioning. He was good at his job. When Carl took a case to court, you could bet he was going to win it. I never had any complaints.'

'You liked him?' Eggar gave Harry a father-confessor smile.

'Different question. He'd win no prizes in a charm contest. But you don't climb the greasy pole by being Mr Nice Guy all the time.'

Eggar pursed fleshy lips. 'We'll need to talk again later. But that's enough – for now.'

The moment Harry got back to his flat, he stripped off his clothes and climbed into the shower, as though hoping that the water could cleanse him of everything that had happened overnight. Driving back through the old tunnel under the river, he'd felt guilt gnawing at him, like a rat nibbling inside his stomach. It was as if his affair with Juliet was somehow responsible for the death of Carl Symons. But although he stayed in the shower until his body could no longer bear the sting of the hot water jets, he found it impossible to drown the picture that kept bubbling to the surface of his mind: the sight of the decapitated body in the silent cottage.

As he gulped down a mouthful of coffee, fatigue began to hit him, the cumulative weariness of work, frustrated lust and horror. It was nothing new for him to spend the night in a police station: that was the way he earned his living. But usually he was observing, murmuring a few words of advice whenever the questions took a dangerous turn. Having to find the answers himself was a thousand times harder. He lay down on his bed, but his eyes stayed open as his thoughts swirled around in circles. He'd left his CD player on in the living-room and the words of sixties soul songs swirled around in the air. Aretha Franklin's classic cover of 'I Say A Little Prayer' struck a chord. He needed a little help from up above to get through this in one piece.

Eventually he rolled off the bed, shaved, dressed and strode in the direction of the city centre. For once he was glad of the cold morning gusts from the river smacking his cheeks. Anything to help him stay awake: it was going to be another long day. He didn't wish to be alone, wondering what would happen if Casper May ever found out about his liaison with Juliet. It was safer to keep himself occupied. He had work to do, but there was something else, something that mattered more. Carl Symons was dead and he wanted the mystery solved. The sooner people lost interest in what he'd been doing out at Dawpool, the better. Besides, despite the horrors of the past few hours, he felt the familiar hunger for understanding. Why had someone wanted to destroy Carl with such savagery?

He decided to patronise the early morning cafeteria close to the law courts. Queen Victoria scowled disapprovingly at him as he crossed Derby Square. The forces recruitment office had windows full of advertisements for those who might be seduced by the prospect of learning to operate 'the most sophisticated weapons systems in the western world'. Perhaps he should have considered a career in the army. Right now it seemed like a safer kind of existence.

The Condemned Man served cheap and coronary-inducing breakfasts immensely popular amongst people who used the courts. It was owned by a woman formidable in her girth, temper and disdain for the laws of food hygiene. Cynics reckoned that to all intents and purposes Muriel Scawfell enjoyed immunity from prosecution: her customers included half the city's judges, while the portly members of a masonic lodge played darts in her back room every lunchtime.

It was early yet and the place was deserted except for a melancholic court usher and a couple of doe-eyed constables, who were holding hands at a corner table. Muriel's vast bulk loomed behind the counter. Not for the first time Harry couldn't help wondering if her blue and white apron had been made up from a circus top.

'Usual, Harry?' she bellowed.

He approached the counter, but shook his head. The smell of frying bacon which wafted over from the kitchen made him want to heave. He could almost taste the grease of the sausages on his tongue. As for black pudding – well, he'd had enough of blood products at Dawpool to last a lifetime.

'Just a coffee. Mug, not a cup.'

Muriel's double chins wobbled suspiciously. 'You all right, young man?'

Harry wasn't flattered; anyone under forty-five was young to Muriel. 'Yeah, sure. A bit short of shut-eye, that's all.'

'You're not the only one. Have you heard the news?'

He realised at once that she was talking about the death of Carl Symons. Muriel's customers included scores of policemen for whom the high-fibre, low-cholesterol menus now favoured by their own canteens were anathema. What she didn't know about crime in the city wasn't worth knowing. Senior detectives despaired at the money spent on a new computer system when the most formidable intelligence-gathering network since the Stasi's prime could be found down a passageway off Lord Street.

'What news would that be?' he asked cautiously.

'That creep from the CPS has been found dead. You know, the ugly bugger. Carl Symons.'

He opted to feign bewilderment. Acting baffled was something he was good at; often it wasn't much of an act. 'Seriously?'

'I'd say it's pretty serious for him,' Muriel said with a laugh that sounded like a clap of thunder. She prided herself on her macabre sense of humour. 'Used to brag about never eating meat, y'know. Reckoned it shortens your life. Load of bollocks, I say. Fat lot of good all those lentils and beansprouts did him, eh?'

Muriel's hatred of vegetarians was legendary. She regarded the craze for healthy eating as a sinister conspiracy designed to cheat decent working folk of honest employment. Never mind abhorrence of cruelty to animals; if it were left to Muriel, all the trendy nutritionists and their disciples would be dispatched to the abattoir without a second thought.

'What's the word?'

Muriel tapped the side of her nose with a beefy forefinger. 'Ask no questions and you'll get no lies, young man. All I'll say is that I'm told foul play is suspected.'

Harry breathed an inward sigh of relief. So word hadn't yet reached her on the grapevine of his own involvement. Before long she would find out and be furious that he hadn't told her what he knew. But he was prepared to face her wrath on another day. This morning, he could not bear to talk about his visit to Carl Symons' house.

'Hard to believe,' he mumbled.

'You think so? I'm not so sure.' She spooned enough coffee into a vast mug to keep him awake until the evening. 'He rubbed folk up the wrong way, you know. I had an inspector in here only last week playing merry hell because Symons wouldn't prosecute a couple of drugs dealers from Kirkdale. According to Symons, there was only a fifty-fifty chance of getting a conviction. He liked to back winners, did that feller. It's not the way to make friends and influence people.'

Harry stared. 'You're not suggesting a disgruntled copper killed him?'

She disappeared behind a haze of steam as she filled the mug with hot water from a tottering urn that had somehow escaped the notice of the health and safety apparatchiks. 'Course not. But he had enemies. Take it from me, there's more than one person in this city who'll be dancing on his grave.'

'For instance?'

'Now, Harry Devlin. Am I a blabbermouth?'

Does peeling onions make you cry? 'Perish the thought, Muriel. Sorry. I never meant to ask you to tell tales out of school.' He picked up the mug and turned towards the tables.

'Mind, I'm not sworn to secrecy or anything like that,' she said quickly. 'As I said to that young sergeant half an hour ago, I reckon it's only right to pass information on if they think it might be relevant.'

He glanced back over his shoulder. Muriel was leaning over the counter, her bosom casting a shadow over a large tray of crockery. 'Of course it is,' he said. 'Your public duty, really.'

'My very words! Well, I'd say no more, but at least you're another one who can hold your tongue when it suits you.'

'Sure.' He moved towards her and lowered his voice. 'Matter of fact, I seem to remember that he had a row with his partners when he was in private practice. Nerys Horlock and whatsisname.'

'Brett Young,' she said. 'That's right. There was a massive bust-up. Mind, I won't hear a word said against Nerys. Not after the way she stuffed that good-for-nothing ex-husband of mine. I don't suppose that pair will shed many tears for Carl Symons. But I was thinking of someone else.'

'You were?'

She put a finger to her lips. 'This is strictly between you and me, all right?'

'Swear to God and hope to die,' he said, his fingers crossed behind his back.

'That black girl had it in for him.'

Harry frowned. 'Black girl?'

'You know the one. Has all the fellers with their eyes out on stalks. She leaves her blouse unbuttoned when she thinks she can get away with it. Suki Anwar.'

Well, well. Suki worked for the Crown Prosecution Service, part of the Riverside branch like Carl Symons. She was attractive, and she knew it, but that didn't make her a trollop. Muriel would have threatened a writ if anyone had suggested she was a racist, but Harry had never noticed a black face serving behind her counter. Mind you, she wasn't unique amongst Liverpudlian employers in that.

'Suki and Carl didn't get on?'

Muriel stretched her head and upper body so far forward over the counter that he feared she would lose her balance. 'At one time they did. One of my regulars told me he'd seen them together in the court building. Symons had his hand on her bum when he thought no-one was looking and from what I heard, she wasn't exactly kicking and screaming about it. Later on, things changed.'

'Did they have an affair?'

'If they weren't,' Muriel said darkly, 'it strikes me he had a funny idea of teaching her the ropes about prosecuting.'

'Okay, suppose they had something going at one time. Suppose even that he chucked her. She's a good-looking woman. Why should she worry about missing out on Carl Symons? I'd say it was a lucky break. She could do much better for herself with someone else.'

'Men,' Muriel said with a shake of her thinning curls. 'You don't understand women that well, do you?'

'Never pretended to,' he said with a weary sigh.

'Maybe it was just because Suki does fancy herself that she took it so badly when she and Carl Symons broke up. I heard her confiding in Nerys Horlock. Not that I got every word, mind, I'm no eavesdropper. They were sitting at that table over there. Suki had been crying and Nerys was telling her she ought to do something about it.'

'Are you sure they were talking about Symons?'

'I know what I heard, Harry Devlin, even though she did try to change the subject when she spotted me clearing the cups from the next table. There was hatred in her voice when she mentioned his name.' Muriel's bloodshot eyes gleamed with malice; she was almost salivating as she repeated herself: 'And I'll tell you something else. She said she wished he was dead.'

Chapter Five

Deep in thought, Harry trudged across from the Condemned Man to his office in Fenwick Court. He had learned over the years that it was a mistake to underestimate Muriel, but all the same he boggled at the idea that Suki Anwar had crept out to the Harbour Master's Cottage and butchered Carl Symons. He'd come across her several times since she'd moved up from London. She was young with a lot to learn and although he didn't know her well, he could not bring himself to believe that she was capable of such savage violence.

Back in his room, he pulled a matrimonial file out of the cabinet. At ten o'clock he was due to attend an appointment before the district judge with counsel and a client who was seeking a divorce. Her husband was a property speculator who had made a small fortune out of construction projects around the marina. To celebrate their wedding anniversary, he'd bought his wife a sapphire eternity ring. Her pleasure in the gift had been compromised when, on going through his pockets, she had found a receipt from Boodle and Dunthorne for two identical rings and she had kicked him out of the house within half an hour. He was now living with the other recipient of his generosity, a svelte nineteen-year-old called Tammy.

Next stop the law courts. The whole building buzzed with conversation. As well as the usual hum of minor villains making last-minute business deals on their mobile phones, groups of lawyers were huddled together eagerly exchanging gossip. A single name was on their lips. Harry heard it time and again as he took the steps of the main staircase two at a time.

Carl Symons. Carl Symons. Carl Symons.

The men and women who made their living here were accustomed to crime. Murder trials were commonplace. But this was something new. One of their own was dead: a man who had often strode down these corridors, conferring with counsel, shaking his head at any hint of a last-minute plea-bargain. For once a killing had come close to home.

Harry wanted to learn more about Carl Symons. If he could understand the man, he might have a chance to fathom why he had been killed. Only if the case was wrapped up soon would he be able to breathe again. If the inquiry stalled, the police might put him under the microscope – and he didn't want that. He couldn't deny that he'd had the opportunity; they might use their imagination so far as motive was concerned.

Turning right at the top of the stairs, he headed for the rooms reserved for legal representatives. In the consultation rooms there was no sign of Suki Anwar or any of the other prosecutors. Neither his client nor the barrister instructed on her behalf had yet arrived and he wasn't in the mood for exchanging prurient tittle-tattle with his professional brethren. Especially if word had seeped out that he'd been the one to find the body. The law library should be open by now; he might as well skulk in there until it was time for his conference.

After the hubbub downstairs, the silence in the library was as welcome as breeze in a heatwave. Feeling like a barbarian at the gates of Rome, he gazed at the long rows of books. Finally he pulled down a fat and ancient volume from the metal shelving. *Broom's Legal Maxims*. On his rare visits here as a trainee solicitor, he had always indulged himself by stealing a glance at its solemn precepts. Their remoteness from the real world of legal practice never failed to divert him. He opened the page at random and picked out a Latin phrase, freely translated for the benefit of those who lacked a classical education. *Ubi jus, ibi remedium*. Where there is a wrong, there is a remedy. He grunted: who was old Broom trying to kid?

He put the book back and moved into the area by the counter where the librarian was peering at a computer screen. Hunched over a desk on the other side of the room was a woman whose back was turned to him. But the leather jacket draped over the back of her chair was unmistakable. A doorstop of a textbook, *Rayden and Jackson on Divorce*, lay unopened in front of her. She was staring out through the window, but Harry was sure that she was not spellbound by the prospect of the Mersey beyond the office blocks outside. He wondered if in her mind she was picturing the tableau at the Harbour Master's Cottage, with the SOCO team clustered around Carl Symons' body.

He sidled up to her and murmured, 'Finished with *Rayden?*'

Her head jerked. He couldn't remember ever having seen Nerys Horlock look startled before. She always liked to be in control and relished her reputation for ruthlessness. Other lawyers nicknamed her Cruella. Possibly she'd had more in common with her old partner Carl Symons than people thought. She had her own firm these days, a low-overhead operation in a Toxteth waste land. A temp who had once spent a fortnight with Crusoe and Devlin had come straight from a period working there. She'd had the unenviable task of providing holiday cover for Irma, Nerys's famously long-serving and long-suffering secretary, and she'd hated every minute. According to her, Nerys didn't subscribe to the fashionable nostrum that her firm's human resources were her most important asset. For her, employees – other than the eternally loyal Irma – came some way down the list, well below paper clips and staples. Harry thought of her as the archetypal sole practitioner and found it hard to imagine her sharing power with Symons and Brett Young. Perhaps that was the point: their firm had scarcely lasted five minutes before the inevitable break-up.

'Checking a point of law?' she asked. Her accent was unvarnished Scouse. She'd never forgotten her origins – born and bred in Toxteth, daughter of a stevedore and a lollipop lady – and there was no danger of her letting anyone else forget them, either. This morning she was full of cold and more catarrhal than ever. 'Not like you, Harry.'

'There's a first time for everything.'

'Yeah. Yeah, I suppose so.' She shoved the book towards him and with her other hand stifled a yawn. There were bags under her eyes and Harry thought she looked as weary as he felt. 'So – taking your deerstalker out of mothballs, then?'

'I hardly knew Carl Symons,' he said evasively.

'You didn't miss much.'

'So I gather.' He took a breath and said, 'Sorry he's dead?'

Hard blue eyes bored into him. 'No.'

'At least that's honest.'

'We do enough fibbing in the course of duty every day of the week, don't we?'

'Do we?'

'Come on,' she said wearily. 'You're no saint yourself.'

His mind flashed back to the previous evening and he gave an uneasy shrug. 'That's true.'

'And by the way, don't think I didn't notice. You avoided my question. Going to poke your nose into this one? Fancy playing the poor man's Sam Spade again?'

'It's a bad habit,' he said. 'I keep telling myself to break it. Leave everything to the professionals. They know what they're about.'

She made a scoffing noise. 'You sound like an errant husband, promising to keep his dirty little paws off the dolly birds. They never do, y'know.'

He shrugged. 'I can't pretend I'm not intrigued. All the same, this is one case I'd rather sit out.'

'Too many suspects? After all, Carl didn't exactly court popularity.'

'That's one reason. I'd never have time to talk to them all.'

'You're not making a bad start. My name's sure to come up when the police decide to check out whether my late lamented ex-partner had any enemies. Their only problem is, they'll be inundated.'

'I heard the split was bitter.'

'Yeah, the three of us finished up hating the sight of each other. Looking back on it, Symons, Horlock and Young was a marriage made in hell.'

'Most marriages are,' Harry said on impulse.

She gave a harsh laugh. 'At least it's one trap I never fell into.'

He guessed that probably she frightened most men off. And yet, even full of cold, she exuded both sexuality and danger. He knew enough about perfume to recognise 'Poison' and even here, in the sober surroundings of the Queen Elizabeth II Law Courts, he could believe that beneath the crisp dark lawyer's suit lurked a creature of the wild. Her teeth were small but sharp. Easy to imagine her snarling and biting, taking pleasure in savagery. Without thinking, he took half a pace back.

'What's up?'

'Nothing.' He faked a coughing fit. 'Sorry. I had a bad night.'

'You and me both. I didn't get a wink.'

He raised his eyebrows. But teasing Nerys Horlock was about as wise as tickling a tiger.

'You needn't get excited,' she said drily. 'I wasn't locked in the throes of passion. It couldn't have been more mundane, actually. You'll have noticed I've got the dreaded lurgi. I can't even remember what it feels like to breathe normally. In the end, I got out of bed and started snuffling over a set of month-end accounts.'

'Beats counting sheep.' He paused. 'So, you found Carl Symons impossible to work with?'

'Don't get me wrong. He was a smart lawyer and he worked hard. That's why I went in with him. Same goes for Brett Young. But I soon realised it was a big mistake.'

'What went wrong?'

'Well, the government didn't help, sticking the knife into the legal aid budget. That fat cat on the Woolsack slashed our income and all the time he was living it up like a medieval pope.'

'Come on. There must have been more to it than that.'

She coughed. 'Let's just say I prefer the single life.'

'And Carl?

'I suppose he was a loner too.'

'Which just left Brett?'

Nerys bit her lip. 'He wasn't made of the right stuff, if you ask me. He wanted to keep the ship afloat, but it was never going to work. We bitched at each other constantly. Of course, Brett had most to lose.'

'How do you mean?'

She hesitated. 'Well, he'd bought a swish new house in Formby, his borrowings were sky high.'

Harry sensed that she was keeping something back. 'Surely you were in the same boat?'

'At least when I baled out, I managed to pay off what I owed and set up on my own with the minimum of capital outlay. Carl didn't fancy being self-employed any longer, so he became a prosecutor. We cut our losses. For Brett, it was – different.'

'I've not seen him lately. Last I heard, he was temping for a cowboy outfit which handles tribunal cases for a contingency fee. What's he doing now?'

'God knows. We don't keep in touch.'

'How did he react when you broke up the firm?'

She coloured. 'There was nothing he could do. Last time I bumped into him, he said his house was being repossessed. It wasn't a long conversation. He told me he found it impossible to forgive and forget. He said I'd let Carl destroy him. You see, Carl was the one who issued the formal papers dissolving the partnership.'

Harry stared at her. 'You're not suggesting that he killed Carl?'

'I'm not suggesting anything, Harry,' she said fiercely. 'And by the way, aren't you forgetting that you've resolved not to take an interest in this particular can of worms?'

'Sorry. You're right. I made the mistake of having breakfast at the Condemned Man this morning. Carl's death was Muriel's sole topic of conversation. I suppose I shouldn't have listened.'

'Muriel?' Nerys's eyes narrowed. 'What did she have to say?'

'She made it clear she was a member of your fan club.'

Nerys shrugged. 'Her old feller deserved to be taken to the cleaners. Bad case of middle-aged-man syndrome. But never mind that. If anyone has picked up any inside information about the murder already, it will be Muriel. Did she tell you anything?'

Her curiosity intrigued him. 'She didn't put you in the frame, if that's what you're wondering. On the contrary. She reckoned that Symons' worst enemy was neither you nor Brett.'

'Who then?'

'Suki Anwar.'

Nerys started. 'Suki?'

'A woman scorned, that's Muriel's theory. She reckons Suki and Carl had an affair.'

'For Chrissake!' Nerys was hoarse with anger. 'I never heard such bullshit!'

'Stranger things have happened.'

'You don't have any idea what you're talking about!' She shoved the textbook towards him. 'Here you are. I have to get on with my work.'

As she hurried out of the library, Harry put *Rayden* back on the shelf. One thing he'd learned was that the answers to the puzzles that really mattered to him were never to be found in legal textbooks. Or in Latin maxims.

Daniel Roberts ground his teeth as Pamela experimented with the search facility on her computer. The dark-haired woman was standing by his side, shifting from one foot to another. Maybe she shared his impatience, maybe she was simply ill-at-ease. She was nothing like the few double-chinned lawyers he'd come across over the years. He had an impression of suppressed tension as she stared at the screen, sensed that she was trying to shut out the consciousness of his presence beside her. Was she afraid of him? Instinct told him that she was. He could even guess why. He felt exhilarated, yet he knew he mustn't surrender to his obsession. This wasn't the time to let things get out of hand.

'What – what do you want to know about Harry Devlin?' she asked suddenly.

'What can you tell me?'

'He's a partner in a small firm called Crusoe and Devlin. They have an office in Fenwick Court, five minutes from here.'

'You know him?'

'I've met him briefly and I've heard a bit about him.'

'What have you heard?'

The woman turned to face him, her eyes wide. 'His wife was murdered.'

Pamela gave a little gasp. She'd been like a spectator at the ring-side, watching boxers sparring before the main fight. The mention of murder gave her an opportunity to edge her way back into the conversation. But neither of the others paid her any attention. Daniel Roberts' gaze was fixed on the younger woman. He was taken aback, but he contrived not to reveal it, save for a momentary flickering of the eyelids.

'And – when was that?'

'Two or three years back, I think.'

'The person who killed her was caught?'

'No-one ever faced trial. From what I gather, the murderer died or disappeared or something. There was a mystery about what actually happened.' She was talking rapidly, as if glad to have found a safe topic of conversation. 'By all accounts, Harry Devlin's been mixed up himself in one or two murder cases since then. I once heard someone say that he fancies himself as an amateur detective. Criminal law's his main speciality, so perhaps it's not too surprising.'

Pamela resumed her pressing of buttons on the keyboard, apparently at random. Choosing his words with care, Daniel said, 'Sounds like an interesting character.'

'Bit of a loner, I think.'

'There are worse things than being a loner.'

Suddenly Pamela exclaimed in triumph. 'Ah, here are his details! It's just a question of knowing the right directory to check. Now you can read it for yourself.'

Daniel peered at the screen. The text listed the name, address, phone and fax numbers of Harry's firm. It revealed that he had taken his law degree at Liverpool Polytechnic and learned his trade with Maher and Malcolm before setting up with Jim Crusoe. He dealt with crime, family law and civil litigation.

'Is that what you were looking for?' Pamela asked, basking in her new-found command of the technology.

'It's a start.' Daniel frowned. 'But it doesn't tell me much. Where can I find out more?'

'Why don't you give him a call? Our job is to help promote firms like Crusoe and Devlin. If you like, I can print this data up and then you can fix up an appointment.'

'I'd be grateful for the print-out. But – I don't wish to meet him just yet. How could I find out more about him?'

The dark-haired woman studied him as Pamela printed the file. 'Difficult to say. If you could give me some idea of what you're trying to discover...'

'Never mind,' he said, picking up the sheet as it slipped out of the machine on her desk. 'I need to give this a little more thought. You have both been very helpful. Thank you.'

With that he was gone. As the door closed behind him, Pamela turned to her companion and said, 'Creepy, wasn't he, Andrea? What was all that about, do you think?'

The other woman shivered. 'I have no idea. No idea at all. But you're right. I wonder if Harry Devlin knows that someone is asking questions about him.'

Chapter Six

'Mrs May called you,' Suzanne the receptionist said as Harry walked through the door. 'I said you were out on a court appointment, but she asked if you'd ring back as soon as you got in. Said she needed to speak to you urgently.'

His stomach lurched even as he forced himself to give an elaborately casual nod. It wouldn't do for Suzanne to pick up the idea that Juliet was anything more than a tediously persistent marketing consultant. The switchboard girl had a genius for gossip; in comparison, Muriel Scawfell was the soul of discretion.

'I'll give her a buzz when I have a moment.'

'Do you want me to ring her back now?'

'It'll keep,' he said, with an effort of will. 'I expect she simply wants me to proof-read the text for the advertisement we're planning.'

'She sounded unhappy,' Suzanne insisted.

'Maybe she's spotted a couple of printers' errors,' he said through gritted teeth. 'Don't worry, it won't be important. I'll get back to her as soon as I can.'

Suzanne put down a creased paperback edition of *Feng Shui Can Heal Your Life*. Juliet, in evangelical mood, had lent it to her and she'd become an enthusiastic convert. Folding her arms, she scowled and said, 'Well, don't say I didn't pass the message on. And by the way, did you realise that reception's laid out all wrong? No wonder you don't get a better class of client when there's so much bad Chi.'

He escaped to his room. As he slumped into his chair, he realised his hands were trembling. It would take more than a commitment to Feng Shui to put things right. Closing his eyes, he asked himself why he had ever allowed himself to become involved with the wife of Casper May. Their relationship was starting to resemble a suicide pact.

Of course, it hadn't always been like that. At the outset – if he was honest with himself – he had been flattered by her interest in him. After all, there was no doubt that she could have her pick of men. He'd been in the mood for someone new; the woman he had been seeing for over a year, a solicitor called Kim Lawrence, had been made an offer she couldn't refuse of a high-profile job in London. Juliet was sexy and funny and she liked many of the things he liked. Crime, for instance. It fascinated her. She loved mysteries and arguing about such things as whether the murdered cotton broker James Maybrick really was the author of the diaries of Jack the Ripper. For a time after getting to know her, he'd tried to keep his distance. He was scared not only of Casper May, but also of himself. But one evening when Casper was away she'd persuaded him to join her at the Philharmonic Picture Palace for a John Dahl double bill. *Red Rock West* followed by *The Last Seduction*. Inevitably, they'd finished up in bed together afterwards. From that night on, he'd been lost.

The door opened and he heard Jim saying, 'Bit early for a siesta, isn't it?'

He opened his eyes. 'I didn't get any sleep last night.'

His partner winced. 'Too much to hope that you were catching up on your backlog of legal aid claims?'

'It is, really.'

'All right. The suspense is unbearable. I'll regret asking, but who cares? What kept you up?'

Harry let out a breath. 'You'll have to be told sooner or later. Fact is, I stumbled over a body.'

Jim's craggy features froze in bewilderment. 'Go on. Tell me this is your idea of a joke.'

The phone rang and Harry picked up the receiver. 'There's a Detective Inspector Eggar to see you.' Suzanne was breathless with excitement. 'He says – he says it's about a statement.'

'Sorry,' he said to Jim, putting his hand over the mouthpiece. 'The police have turned up already. I suppose they want to check a few details.'

Jim uttered a low groan. 'Why did I ever get mixed up with you?'

'You must admit it,' Harry said ruefully. 'Life's seldom dull.'

'Look, old son, I'm a conveyancing lawyer from choice. Title deeds turn me on. Anything more dramatic than a dispute over rights of way brings me out in a rash.'

'Then sod off before they arrest you for obstructing the course of justice.' He spoke into the phone. 'Send DI Eggar in, will you?'

With a despairing shake of the head, Jim said, 'Aren't you going to tell me who the body belonged to?'

'A brother solicitor.'

Jim's expression lightened a touch. 'Oh well. Every cloud, eh?'

'Seems a bit odd, that's all.'

There was a note of disappointed puzzlement in Mitch Eggar's voice that almost made Harry want to confide in him, to set the record straight. But then he thought about Eggar's senior officer confiding in Casper May over a beer at the nineteenth hole and dug his nails into his palm. The truth about his affair with Juliet mustn't be told.

'I don't see why.'

'Well, Harry, it's like this. With all due respect, your firm isn't famous for its high profile in the media. So why, on the worst night of the year, do you trek out to the far side of the Wirral for a chin-wag with a marketing consultant about some bloody advertisement? It doesn't stack up.'

'You've said it yourself. We need to brush up our image. Jim's been harping on about it for years. Finally, I've been convinced. We brought in this lady to help us, we're spending money we can barely afford. It seemed right to take it seriously. Jim and I are new to this game. We need the best advice.' Warming to his theme, Harry stretched his arms in an open, nothing-to-hide gesture. Hadn't Juliet once told him about the importance of body language in getting a message across to a sceptical audience? 'Frankly, there are plenty of things I'd rather have been doing last night than driving to the back of beyond to talk about a bloody press campaign. Let alone discovering a body and spending half the night in a police station. But given the deadline for approving final copy, it made sense to go to Mrs May for help.'

'Real expert, then, is she?'

Harry gazed sorrowfully at the detective. It was a shamelessly candid look, one he'd copied from his most disingenuous clients. 'Well, between you and me...'

'Yes?'

'I gagged a bit when she insisted that we should use power words in the advertising copy.'

A frown. 'Power words?'

'Yeah, that's the jargon. Proven sellers, she calls them. Words like "new", "fast" and "guarantee". Mind you, I told her I draw the line at "money back".'

As if sensing that the conversation might be drifting out of control, Eggar said sharply, 'How long have you known her?'

'She first came to see Jim earlier this year. He persuaded me we needed to invest in expertise. She has a good track record.'

'You know who she is, don't you?'

Harry rubbed his chin. 'Well. I read her c.v. when we first interviewed her. She's worked in local television and for one of the big agencies.'

'I mean,' Mitch Eggar said with exaggerated patience, 'who she's married to?'

Harry experimented with a baffled stare before saying, 'Oh yes. The chap who does a lot for charity.'

The policeman sighed. 'Come on, Harry. You weren't born yesterday. You know all about Casper May.'

'Never met the bloke.'

They looked at each other for a while in silence. Eggar wasn't soft. He could tell that he was being spun a line. But he was patient, willing to give plenty of rope. He probably thought he could rely on Harry to hang himself sooner or later.

'Fine, if that's your attitude, let's move on. You claimed you had only a passing acquaintance with Carl Symons?'

'Right. I'd encountered him in the courts a few times. We never talked much to each other. He'd probably have regarded it as fraternising with the enemy.'

'Yet not so long ago he was in private practice, same as you.'

'Our paths seldom crossed, but there's one thing that was pretty obvious. With Carl, his career was everything. Once he joined the CPS, his aim was to rise through the ranks as quickly as possible. He'd already been promoted once.'

'So the fact it was you who happened to find his body was a complete coincidence?'

'As I explained last night. At great length, I thought. I wanted to give you every possible help. I don't like the idea of solicitors as murder victims. The profession doesn't want the public getting ideas. So I hoped that if I volunteered a full statement, that would help you to make rapid progress in catching the murderer.'

'It was a full statement, all right. No complaints about that. Or about the level of co-operation from Mrs May or Mrs Blackwell.'

'Well, then.'

'One thing puzzles me. All three of you told exactly the same story.'

Harry put his elbows on the desk and groaned. 'Wouldn't it have been rather more sinister if the statements hadn't tallied?'

'As you lawyers like to say: on the one hand, yes – but then on the other hand, no. Call me hard to please if you like.'

'You're bloody hard to please,' Harry said. He chose a cold tone, thinking that he'd missed his vocation. Perhaps he should have taken up acting.

'Fact is, all your statements were astonishingly similar. I mean, practically word for word. When I looked at them, something made me wonder if they might have been carefully rehearsed. Made me wonder if I could really believe everything I was being told.'

'So we can't win,' Harry said sulkily.

Mitch Eggar nodded. 'That's life, isn't it? A bit like when you used to play cricket. You just can't win.'

He tested his story on Jim once Eggar had departed. Its plausibility didn't improve with retelling. Jim's eyes rolled once or twice as he listened, but at least he seemed willing to suspend disbelief.

'Not your lucky night, then.'

'You could say the same about Carl Symons.'

'There won't be many people mourning him.'

'Don't tell me you knew him?'

'No. I always keep as far away from crime as I can. Being in partnership with you is bad enough. But I'd heard about him from Brett Young. Nasty piece of work, by the sound of things.'

'I didn't realise you knew Brett.'

'He and I were at law college together. We were never bosom buddies. He was always a nervy bugger. Worrying about the exams, fretting that he might not manage to get qualified. He flunked his finals in the end, but he must have passed his resits. Much good it did him, eh? I lost touch with him after college, but over the past two or three years we've bumped into each other now and then.

Last time I saw him, he'd just finished a tribunal case in the Cunard Building. It was obvious he was in a bad way. His suit and shoes were even scruffier than yours.'

'You're so good for my ego.'

Jim bared his teeth in a grin. 'Listening to his tale of woe made me realise that you and I couldn't afford to split up. Mind, if you keep falling over bodies, I may have to reconsider.'

'I promise you, I don't mean to make a habit of it.'

'So what do the police have to say?'

'Mitch Eggar isn't giving anything away. It's early days. First, he needs to eliminate the three of us from his inquiries.'

'That won't take long, will it?'

'Hope not,' Harry said meekly. 'For all I know, there may be a truck load of forensic that leads them to the killer inside the next twenty-four hours. God knows, there was enough blood there. It was as if the poor devil's body had been drained of it. It was a nightmare for Juliet. She told me she'd never seen a corpse before.'

Jim grunted. 'Getting mixed up in a murder inquiry wasn't the sort of profile-raising venture I had in mind when we hired her. Once the Press find out you were involved, they are bound to start asking questions.'

'We'll need Juliet's advice on how to answer them.'

'I'm not so...'

The phone trilled. 'What is it, Suzanne?'

'Mrs May is on again for you. Insists that it's urgent.'

'Put her through ... Juliet? We were just talking about you. I'm with Jim at the moment. Would you like a word with him?' Harry spoke quickly, before she could say anything, then handed the receiver to his partner.

Caught off balance, Jim said, 'How are you, Juliet? Ummm ... yes, Harry's been telling me. Sounds horrific. Sorry you've both had such an experience ... the police, yes ... no, personally I'd be happier if you could keep me out of it. Right, you'll be wanting to discuss things with Harry. Fine. Be in touch.'

His face red, he clambered to his feet and mouthed, 'Talk to you later.'

As the door closed behind him, Harry said quietly into the phone, 'You okay?'

'I've had better days. Christ, what a night! Where did you finish up?'

'Birkenhead. And you?'

'Upton. They took Linda to Bromborough. Both of us were interrogated for ages. You'd almost think they genuinely regarded us as suspects. I tell you, there were times when I cursed you for persuading me that we should call the police.'

'Imagine their attitude if you'd kept mum and then they'd discovered that you'd been present at the scene of the crime.'

'It's Linda I feel sorry for. Dragged into it through no fault of her own.'

'How is she?'

'Shattered, as you might expect. We agreed neither of us would bother with work today. Thank God for answering machines, eh? She and I both had a follow-up visit from a detective inspector this morning. A man called Eggar. He seemed pleasant enough, but...'

'You're right, there's usually a "but" where Mitch Eggar is concerned. Matter of fact, he left here half an hour ago. You need to watch him, he's not convinced.'

'I promise you, I did my best. So did Linda. We both stuck to our story.'

Harry thought it would be imprudent to mention that Eggar regarded even that as grounds for suspicion. Instead he said, 'You've done the hard part now.'

A pause. 'I don't know, Harry. Eggar was asking all sorts of questions about Casper, as well as about you and me. I can't be sure that he believed me.'

'Don't fret. He may be curious, but he can't waste time on trivia. He'll soon start focusing on the real suspects.'

'It's all very well saying that. This is familiar territory as far as you're concerned. Remember, I'm not used to dealing with the police. I know Casper has lived dangerously in the past, but I was never a part of that. He kept me away from it all.'

'Sure,' he said, although he wasn't sure whether he could believe her.

'The same goes for Linda. When we spoke on the phone she was weeping. Last night she was so strong, but now things are taking a toll.'

'Keep your eye on her. Tell her not to panic. This will all blow over quicker than you expect.'

'We need to talk. Sooner rather than later. The three of us could meet tonight.'

'You're including Linda?'

'She's wound up, Harry, she needs to be reassured. I don't want her to crack up. The truth is, she's not as strong as you may think.'

Now you tell me. 'Uh-huh.'

'Then there's her son to consider. She's confided in him, as we agreed. It was just as well, even if he is a bit of a loose cannon. The police have already questioned him. At least he stood up to it, according to Linda. She's staying at his place for the time being. Obviously she can't go back home at present.'

'The more the merrier,' he said gloomily. 'Are you sure this is a good idea?'

'Listen,' she said, an acid note entering her voice. 'Linda and Peter have bailed us out of a mess. They didn't have to do that. We owe them. Let's face it, we're all in this together.'

The address Juliet had given him proved to be a flat at the end of a tree-lined street leading from the West Kirby promenade. It was above a Greek restaurant and as Harry pressed the bell of the adjoining door he was assailed by the pungent aroma of steamed fish and a lusty performance of 'The White Rose of Athens' on the bouzoukis.

Linda answered. She was wearing a sweatshirt and tight denim jeans. Even casually dressed, she was strikingly attractive for a fiftysomething. To his surprise she kissed him hard on each cheek and clasped his hand in hers. 'It's good of you to come,' she said.

Remembering his reluctance to drive out here and thank her again in person for her help, he felt a jolt of shame. 'The least I could do,' he mumbled.

'Juliet's already here,' she said, jerking her thumb upwards. She seemed as calm as ever. Maybe it was an act, but he couldn't help wondering if Juliet had exaggerated her jumpiness. Did she want to keep him on his toes? He followed Linda up a steep and narrow staircase. When he'd joined her on the landing, she opened a glassed door and ushered him through.

The living-room was cramped and airless. Harry could smell stale cooking, as if odours had wafted here from downstairs and become trapped in the furnishings, a worn three-piece suite and curtains in a floral design that might have been popular in the seventies. The wail of the bouzoukis was coming through the floorboards.

A tall fair-haired man in a sleeveless pullover which revealed frayed shirt cuffs stood with his back to them, gazing out of the front window. He was whistling an accompaniment to the music from the restaurant. Curled up on the sofa, Juliet was nibbling at her fingernails. Dark rings curved beneath her eyes and Harry could hear the strain in her voice when she said hello.

Linda said, 'Darling, this is Harry Devlin.'

The man at the window paused in mid-chorus and turned round. He wasn't bad looking, Harry thought. The blue eyes and curled lip were reminiscent of a minor aristocrat from *Brideshead*

Revisited, but the effect was spoiled by his blotchy complexion and the careless way in which he'd shaved. As Peter offered a hand with grubby fingernails, Harry cast his mind back to the photographs of the smart young man in Linda's bedroom. The past few years hadn't done his host any favours.

'Peter Blackwell. We've met before, haven't we?'

'Briefly. When I called round at Juliet's office.'

Peter raised his eyebrows. 'You introduced yourself as one of her clients, as I recall.'

'It was true.' Harry was irked by the defensive note in his own voice.

'Glad to see the relationship has gone from strength to strength.'

'That's enough, Peter,' Linda said sharply.

'Sorry, Mother.' He flushed. 'Don't mind me, Harry. I can be a sour bugger at times, I don't need telling. You've had a traumatic time this last twenty-four hours. Can I offer you a drink?'

Harry spotted a bottle of supermarket sherry on top of the bookcase and caught a whiff of the alcohol on his host's breath. 'Not for me, thanks. I'm just sorry you and your mother have been dragged into this. But I'm grateful for everything you've done.'

'Think nothing of it. Makes a change.' Peter gave a surprisingly high-pitched laugh. 'I've – never been questioned by the police before.'

'You've stood up to it better than any of us,' Linda said, putting an arm round his waist. The instinctive maternal gesture made her son look for a moment like a schoolboy gone to seed. 'It's an experience I don't want to relive in a hurry.'

'Did they give you a hard time?' Harry asked, sitting down next to Juliet.

'In retrospect,' Linda said, 'this morning was worse than last night. That man Eggar came to see us. He didn't seem convinced by what I was saying. It was different the first time they questioned me. After I came back to the cottage, I was so stunned by what had happened that the trip to the police station seemed like part of a dream. I could have said anything and persuaded myself that it was true. It's taken all day for the reality to sink in.'

'I agree. Eggar doesn't believe us,' Juliet said.

'Why should he doubt you?' Peter said brusquely. 'You're respectable people...'

'I'm not sure he would regard the wife of Casper May as respectable,' Juliet interrupted.

'Even though these days the politicians do.'

Linda said, 'You're not responsible for Casper or what he may or may not have done in the past. You've never broken the law. I've said it enough times. The only mistake you made was to marry him.'

Peter strode briskly around the room, swinging his long arms. Harry thought that any moment now he would send either Juliet or his mother flying. 'We all make mistakes about marriage, Mother. What about Tuesday?'

'Don't say I didn't warn you,' Linda said fiercely. 'I wouldn't treat a dog the way she behaved to you.'

He turned to Harry. 'My wife and I divorced recently. She found someone else, it's the old, old story, but God, did she clean me out. You'd never imagine that eighteen months ago I was living in a four-bedroomed house in Hoylake, running a decent little prosthetics business, would you? All kaput now, of course. And all because I was dumped by Tuesday.'

'I know it isn't easy,' Harry said softly. 'A few years back, my wife left me for another man.'

'Really?' Peter leaned forward. 'And tell me this – did you ever forgive the bitch?'

As Harry shifted on the sofa and started to mumble something about time the great healer, Juliet said, 'As a matter of fact, Harry's wife was murdered.'

'Oh.' Peter flushed. 'Sorry. I didn't know.'

'Doesn't matter,' Harry said.

Linda was absent-mindedly folding and refolding a copy of the *Liverpool Echo*. Harry guessed the pair of them had been poring over the story of Symons' death. He'd glanced at it himself, but it told him nothing he didn't already know. She said, 'I'm just praying the police will leave us alone now. We've spoken to them twice. Surely that's enough?'

'Our best hope,' Harry said, 'is that they soon find out who did kill Carl Symons. Until then we won't be out of the spotlight, even though from what I can gather there are plenty of likely suspects.'

'I can believe that. He was horrible to Peter.'

'But he didn't deserve to die like that,' Juliet said. 'I'm glad you didn't see the body, Linda. I'll never forget it.'

She blinked hard. Harry saw tears forming at the corners of her eyes and put his arm around her.

'Hey, what's all this?'

'Oh, don't mind me,' she sniffed. 'Sorry about this, everyone. I suppose it's just reaction setting in. Whilst we were working out what to tell the police, the adrenalin was flowing. It kept the horror at bay. Now I feel as though I could sleep for a year.'

'Come on, Peter,' Linda said. 'Let's make some coffee in the kitchen whilst this pair have a few private minutes together.'

'Forget coffee,' he grunted, picking up the sherry bottle. 'I think I need something a little stronger.'

As the Blackwells left the room, Harry turned to Juliet and said, 'It's going to be all right. Promise.'

She shivered. 'Eggar's no fool. He's guessed he's not been told the whole truth.'

'Sure, and he might not be averse to giving me a hard time because of it. But he'll soon discover I had no axe to grind with Symons. He needs to concentrate on people with a motive. Whoever murdered Symons meant him to suffer. Remember the blood?'

He realised it was the wrong thing to say as soon as the words left his lips and he bit his tongue as she flinched. Tears crawling down her cheeks, she said, 'Jesus, Harry. How could I forget?'

From downstairs came the familiar strains of 'Zorba the Greek'. He squeezed her shoulder. 'Listen. We'll get through this. Linda's done her best for us. Peter too. As long as he stays sober.'

'You can't be too hard on him for liking a drink,' Juliet snapped. 'Linda told me he's not been able to find a job since his company went down the pan. In the space of eighteen months he lost his father, his wife and his livelihood.'

Abashed by her sharpness, he mumbled, 'It's rough, but as long as he keeps his mouth shut...'

'I think he will.'

'Then we'll be fine. Anyway, so far, so good. And when it's all over...'

'Yes?'

He suddenly realised that he did not have a clue what would happen when the murder was solved and they were able to breathe again. It seemed inconceivable that things could carry on as before. Murder, he thought, changes everything. Even when the victim is someone you disliked.

'I don't know,' he admitted lamely. 'But you're the expert on telling the future. What has the Tarot got to say?'

Chapter Seven

'Do something outrageous,' Juliet suggested the next afternoon.

Jim wrinkled his nose and nodded towards Harry. 'I leave that sort of thing to my friend here.'

'You need to be noticed,' she persisted, 'to stand out from the crowd.'

Jim leaned his elbows on the small pile of books about management theory that he kept on his desk. He'd picked them up second-hand from the book fair in the Bluecoat Gallery to show Juliet they meant business about adapting to the challenges of the competitive legal marketplace. Titles like *When Giants Learn To Dance* and *In Search Of Excellence* set Harry's teeth on edge and he was deeply sceptical about *The One-Minute Manager*. Perhaps he might try *Thriving On Chaos*. His partner spotted his jaundiced scanning of the paperback spines and scowled.

'We did have the feller in charge of the murder investigation round here yesterday, but if that's what we need to rebrand our image, perhaps we'd be better keeping a low profile instead.'

'Well, you did ask.'

She gave a shrug and a weary smile. Harry could not remember seeing her in such subdued mood, yet he understood precisely why her face beneath the light make-up was drained of its usual colour. His own limbs felt heavy, as if he were still short of sleep, even though he'd slumbered through the alarm that morning and turned up late at court. Shaking off questions from inquisitive professional colleagues had proved even more taxing than putting together a plea in mitigation for a serial car thief.

He chewed at his lower lip. For both of them the enormity of events at Dawpool were sinking in. Juliet was finding, as he had found more than once, that the most testing murder puzzle of all was not 'whodunit?' but 'how could this cruelty have been inflicted, whatever the provocation?'

And yet – the show must go on. Under their contract with her, she called in every fortnight to hold their hands for a half hour review as they took their first tentative steps along the tightrope of public relations. Today the theme was pitching for new business. Jim had the idea that this was the way of the future for the business-oriented legal practice, responding to invitations to tender with slickly packaged brochures extolling the virtues of the firm's commitment to partner-led delivery of high-calibre professional services, delivered in prompt and practical manner and yet at reasonable cost. He'd mooted the possibility that the two of them might attend a course for training in presentation skills. Harry had demurred on the basis that if he'd wanted to become a salesman, he'd have spent the past ten years on the Costa del Sol flogging timeshares to tourists with more money than sense. But he had the familiar feeling that it was an argument he was bound to lose in the end.

Jim leaned back in his chair and said lazily, 'What about this advertising feature in *Enterprise Spotlight*, then? Worth a shot, do you think?'

Harry jerked up straight in his chair. During the talk about beauty parades, he'd had to fight to keep his eyes open. Why didn't commercial clients simply check out the Yellow Pages rather than forcing their prospective legal advisers to mince down a catwalk, murmuring platitudes about quality standards and added value? But that particular advertising feature was something else. The supposed reason for his visit to Linda's cottage. Oh God, if only he'd come up with something more credible.

'Juliet ruled it out on grounds of cost,' he muttered.

Jim's eyebrows shot up. 'Oh really? I thought their rates were supposed to be highly competitive?'

Harry tensed. Had Jim seen through the subterfuge? The big man was no fool. Because he was a large awkward man who spoke slowly and in a broad Lancashire accent – which broadened further whenever he found himself in the company of people who patronised him – he was often underestimated. That was one mistake that Harry never made. He glanced across at Juliet. She was pursing her lips, giving the question serious thought. He'd better leave it to her to allay suspicion. It was something she was good at.

'Leave it until after Christmas,' she said in a tone so judicious as to make Solomon seem whimsical. 'I'll be able to negotiate a keener discount for you when the market's a bit flat, with everyone spent up.'

'Really?' Jim seemed to be on the point of pressing her further, then thought better of it. He stood up, a signal that he needed to be off to his next appointment. 'Well, you're the expert. As to beauty parades, I'll keep an eye on the business press for invitations to tender. Maybe I'll put in a quote as an experiment, see how we make out.'

'Why not?' She fiddled with her wedding ring. 'Nothing ventured...'

'I'll show you out,' Harry said.

As the door closed behind them, she touched his hand with cool fingers. 'That was a close one. Do you think he's guessed about us?'

Think positive. 'No, he's just curious, that's all. We've been very discreet.'

'Not easy, is it?' She grinned, although he sensed that it was an effort for her. 'Specially when I'm itching to get my hands back on you.'

'Uh-huh.'

He brushed his hand against her backside. She always had the capacity to excite him; even standing next to her in the draughty corridor, he was headily aware of her physical presence, aware too of his temperature rising, of a mounting excitement that was difficult to contain. Yet even when they were together, he could never quite rid himself of lurking doubts, the suspicion that he didn't turn her on as much as she would have him believe. For her, he feared, their affair was a game in much the same way that murder mysteries were entertaining conundrums, not really to do with life and death. Perhaps the amusement lay in the sheer contrast between Casper and himself, perhaps she was like a small child learning the first lessons of independence, testing the boundaries of what one can get away with in the big bad grown-up world.

After leaving Peter's flat the previous night, Juliet had suggested they go for a quick drink before parting. They'd picked a small pub Harry had never even noticed before, but he'd kept glancing over his shoulder, half-expecting to be seen by someone who knew him – or Juliet and her husband.

'What's the matter?' she'd asked.

'I don't think I'm cut out for this,' he said at last. 'Must be my old Catholic roots. Perhaps I'm rediscovering them. I feel as though I'm drowning in guilt.'

'Try going to confession and it'll all be fine. Face it, Harry, we've been lucky. Linda and Peter have been marvellous, the way they've backed us up.'

'Ummm. Linda is fine, everything you said was right. But the son still bothers me. He's difficult to read. Moody.'

'You'd be moody too if you'd been through as much.'

'You keep saying that,' Harry complained.

'Well, it's true. His father wrapped his car round a crash barrier on a motorway because some kids on a bridge were throwing stones at the traffic for a lark. Then his wife walked out. She was a bit of a scrubber, by all accounts, she'd been having it off with her boss, but it hit Peter hard. Like he said, his business folded under the strain. No wonder he's cracked up, taken to drink, that sort of thing. You or I would do the same in his shoes, I bet. But when the police interviewed him, he toed the party line. What more could you ask for?'

'Okay, but what if Mitch Eggar catches him on an off day?'

She slid her warm palm under the table and on to his thigh. 'You don't exactly look on the bright side, do you?'

With a doleful grin, he'd said, 'At present, I'd take some convincing that there is a bright side.'

'You've got me, what more do you want?'

He shook his head. 'Wrong. Casper's got you. He's the man you married.'

'You only live once.' Her hand had begun to explore.

They'd finished up smooching in the doorway of a grocer's shop and he hadn't arrived back until the stroke of midnight. Later he'd lain awake for a while, wondering if she was right, that Peter could be trusted to keep his mouth shut and that Casper was too busy bedding bimbos and cuddling up to Cabinet ministers to be concerned about what his wife was playing at when he left her alone during the long dark nights.

Now she said, 'You're still worried about Peter spilling the beans, aren't you?'

'About that amongst other things.'

'Talk to him again, if you like. One to one. Satisfy yourself he'll button his lip.'

The very suggestion told him that she was more anxious about relying on Peter than she was willing to admit. 'Okay. I'll nip round there this afternoon if I get a chance. Somehow I get the impression he'll be holed up at the flat. He doesn't seem to have much going on in his life.'

'You're good at persuasion. I'm sure he'll understand how important this is to you and me.'

'We'll soon find out.'

'How about a reading from the cards?'

He shook his head. 'No thanks. On second thoughts, I'd rather not know what else fate has in store for us.'

'Blissful ignorance? You don't look too blissful at the moment, Harry.'

'Sorry. I suppose I haven't forgotten Carl Symons, lying on that floor.'

'No,' she murmured, 'nor have I.'

The door at the far end of the corridor swung open and Suzanne bustled through. 'So there you are, Harry!' she exclaimed. 'I've been looking for you everywhere! I had no idea you were still chatting to Mrs May.'

He cringed inwardly. Why didn't she just pick up a megaphone and announce that he was deep in intimate conversation with an attractive woman who wasn't his wife? 'What is it, Suzanne?'

'I have a call for you.'

'Why don't you take a number, say I'll ring back?'

'She's in a callbox, so you can't do that,' Suzanne proclaimed triumphantly. 'She offered to hold whilst I found out what you were up to.'

'I'd better be going,' Juliet said. 'I'll be in touch, Harry. Let me know if Jim has any luck with tendering for new business.'

Harry nodded. His private guess was that the average blue chip company was as likely to appoint Crusoe and Devlin as its lawyers as to distribute all its dividends to the homeless in a gesture of commitment to social equality. Back in his own room, the phone was shrilling.

'Hello?'

'Harry. This is Andrea. That is, Andrea Gibbs.' She spoke softly, sounded tongue-tied. 'You won't remember, but we've met a couple of times. I trained with Symons, Horlock and Young.'

'Of course I remember.' She wasn't easily forgotten: a striking girl he'd bumped into on a couple of occasions, either when she'd been sitting behind counsel in court or at functions organised by the Liverpool Legal Group. He wasn't sure what had happened to her after the firm she'd been working for suddenly imploded. 'What can I do for you?'

'It's – oh, I don't know. It's probably nothing. I thought you should know, but now we're talking it seems so silly, so trivial.'

'What is it?'

'No, I'm wasting your time. It was just about a new client.'

'A new client?' Harry repeated, baffled.

'At least, he implied he was a new client. Or did he? Oh God, I'm being stupid. I'm sorry to have bothered you. Very sorry. Goodbye.'

The line went dead. Harry glared at the telephone, then called Suzanne. 'I was cut off.'

'It wasn't my fault, I didn't do anything!' Suzanne believed that the best form of defence was attack. 'Sure she didn't just hang up on you?'

He banged the receiver down. What had that all been about? An idea occurred to him; he buzzed Carmel Sutcliffe and asked her to come in. Carmel was Jim's assistant, a recruit taken on a few weeks ago in the hope that her presence would help the firm to cope if work flooded in as a result of all their marketing initiatives. So far she'd spent much of her time employed in key tasks such as helping Jim with the preparation of the new office manual, a weighty tome whose existence was a condition of funding under the legal aid franchise scheme. Its turgid contents seemed to Harry to have about as much bearing on the sharp end of legal practice as did *Broom's Legal Maxims*, but at least it kept her out of mischief. Carmel was an exuberant and flirtatious young woman and he'd heard that, during her time on the committee of the Northern Association of Young Lawyers, her raunchy sense of humour – coupled with her enthusiasm for the law of real property, which struck most people as pretty kinky in itself – had earned her the nickname of Carmel Sutra. He liked her enormously but had resolved on the day Jim offered her the job to resist any temptation to misbehave where she was concerned. Life was complicated enough.

'And what can I do for you, Harry?' She had a mass of thick dark hair and lots of teeth which showed when she smiled. As she often did. 'You name it. I can help out with some of your work, if you'd like. Jim asked me to amend his standard client care letter, but I'm struggling for synonyms for "pay up or we'll sue the pants off you".'

Harry grinned. Talking to Carmel always lifted his spirits. She loved life, that was her gift. Perhaps she'd joined their firm simply to test her capacity always to look on the bright side. 'When you were chair of NAYL, did you ever come across Andrea Gibbs?'

'*La Belle Dame Sans Merci*,' she said. Her French accent was about what Harry would have expected from the daughter of a Kerry colleen and a miner from Bold. 'Broke a few hearts, did Andrea. Bone structure to die for. My vice-chair lusted after her, used to pass her romantic notes during seminars about the Public Interest Disclosure Act. Disclosing his interest in public didn't do him any good at all, I can tell you. She liked older men. Personally, I thought she was pretty weird.'

Harry couldn't help protesting. 'Liking older men isn't weird.'

Carmel wrinkled her nose. 'Not in itself, no. But she was seriously strange. Drama queen, liked to be noticed, but you couldn't say she was a mixer. She'd never turn up for the meals out we arranged, said she didn't have much of an appetite. Anorexic, that was my guess. Most of the blokes fancied her like mad, but she had a pretty high turnover in boyfriends. Like, not many of them made it past the first date.'

'Their choice or hers?'

'Bit of both, I guess. Dare I ask why you're interested?'

Harry told her. 'It was an odd conversation. It left me feeling baffled, curious.'

'If it's any consolation, she had that effect on the lads in NAYL. Funny that she called, though, especially just after the man she used to work for has been killed. Makes you wonder if it's a pure coincidence.'

Carmel was no fool, Harry reflected. 'How did she get on with Symons, any idea?'

'None at all. Obviously, it was a firm with problems. We had a helpline for trainees who were given a hard time by their principals, but so far as I know, Andrea never used it. That's par for the course with her. If she had troubles, she's not the sort who'd be likely to share them. Probably she bottled a lot up. It must have been tough, seeing the firm she worked for going down the pan.'

'What happened to her?'

'I heard she transferred her training contract to Windaybanks. She qualified eventually, but then she left private practice. I've not seen much of her lately but then, I never did. To be honest we didn't hit it off. Not a lot in common. I'm not sure where she works now, but I could find out, if you like.'

'Leave it,' he said, 'it's probably something and nothing.'

She clapped a hand to the side of her head. 'One other thing. I nearly forgot. She did get on well with at least one of the partners in Symons' firm. Last I heard, she was having a torrid affair with him. Bloke by the name of Young. Brett Young.'

'And did the affair survive the break-up of the partnership?'

'That's the funny thing. As far as I know, it did.'

In mid-afternoon, he packed a set of files into the boot of his car. It was a way of easing his conscience: he told himself that even though he was taking a couple of hours off, he could put in more time during the evening. All being well. He couldn't settle until he'd had another word with Peter Blackwell, but first he wanted to make a detour via Dawpool.

He left the MG at the country park, a mile away from Linda's cottage. Here the path curved gently down through a little dell to the Dee. Within five minutes he was walking along the wet sand that edged the river. The sky was the colour of slate and the air was damp. But he found the breeze refreshing and as he stretched his legs the tension in his body began to ebb away. Apart from a middle-aged woman in a Barbour throwing sticks for her spaniel to retrieve, there was no-one else around. He could see grey boulders scattered around the shoreline and the reddish sandstone slabs that were the sole surviving remains of the ancient jetty. Behind him, small boats bobbed around the marina at West Kirby, further on the river turned into salt marsh. The impression he had was of loneliness and peace. Hard to credit that less than forty-eight hours earlier his torch had illuminated the butchered corpse of Carl Symons, only a stone's throw from here.

There were buildings ahead, one or more cottages just above the high-water mark. Lifting his eyes above and beyond them, he could glimpse through the trees the half-hidden homes of Linda Blackwell and the late Crown prosecutor. In daylight, when the wind had dropped, everything was very different. In the dark, this place had seemed wild and dangerous. Now it was a picturesque spot, not menacing at all.

Hands in pockets, he ambled on towards the track that led up to the cottages. Dark clouds, he noticed, were gathering over the Welsh hills. It would rain again before the day was through. The breeze wafted faint voices over to him, he thought he even heard the sound of a walkie-talkie. The police were still busy up there.

An oyster catcher screamed. It occurred to him that coming here wasn't the smartest thing he'd ever done. What if Eggar subscribed to the school of thought that holds that a murderer always returns to the scene of his crime? The killing had brought him back, not from guilt, but because of a yearning to understand why Symons had met his fate. He needed to make sense of it for his own peace of mind. That so savage a crime might have been committed for no reason at all was too terrible to contemplate.

But there was nothing he could do. He stopped in his tracks and after a moment's thought retraced his steps back to the car. Time to call on Peter Blackwell and make sure that he was going to keep his lip buttoned.

'Oh, it's you,' Peter said as he opened the door on to the street. His tone was brusque, his eyes icy with suspicion. All in all, he made Harry feel as welcome as a gypsy peg-seller.

'Just passing by,' Harry lied. 'Thought I'd drop by to have a word. Say thanks again for all your help.'

'I was on my way out.' It wasn't an excuse; he was wearing an outdoor jacket and boots and a canvas bag was slung over his shoulders. 'Just popping round to the off-licence down the road.'

'I'll walk with you,' Harry said quickly.

'If you've nothing better to do.'

Peter might be down on his luck, but he could still muster a formidable curl of the lip. Harry cast his mind back again to the photographs in Linda's cottage. Peter was an only child and his behaviour still betrayed traces of the spoilt brat. Not that parents always spoiled only children. Harry's mother and father had brought him up to toe the line, hadn't been afraid to smack him when he broke the rules. Every now and then he wished he'd had the chance to talk to them as an adult, to get to know them better.

As they headed down the street, Harry said, 'I don't know how to put this. You'll forgive me for mentioning it, I hope. But – you do realise how important it is to Juliet and me that no-one gets wind of our relationship?'

'Especially her husband, eh?'

'Since you mention it, yes. Especially her husband.'

'You needn't worry,' Peter said in an off-hand way. 'My mother can't stand Casper May. A few years ago, when she first started working for Juliet, he tried it on with her. She might not be in the first flush of youth, but she's a hell of an attractive woman for her age. I'm sure you'll agree.'

'Well, er, yes, of course.' Harry coughed, unsure what to say. 'Definitely.'

'He obviously thought he could get away with anything. From what I hear, it's not so far from the truth.'

Harry could manage no more than an affirmative grunt. He was struggling to keep up. Peter had set a brisk pace, his long legs taking enormous strides along the pavement. Evidently the booze hadn't sapped all his strength.

'She was happily married to my father, people used to say they were the perfect couple. So there was never any question of her getting involved with a rogue like that. She believed in fidelity. So do I, come to that.'

Harry felt waves of disapproval flowing towards him. No point in protesting that *he'd* been faithful to Liz, until she'd left him for good. 'Sure,' he said cautiously.

'May took it badly. Not used to being rejected, that's for sure. They've ignored each other ever since. Juliet found out what had happened, realised Mother was someone she could rely on. And she's done Mother a good turn or two, I'm the first to admit it, especially after Dad died. Mum's devoted to Juliet, wouldn't do anything to harm her. So – why should I?'

They had reached an off-licence at the corner of the road. As Peter held the door open, the assistant greeted him by name. A good customer, Harry guessed. 'Thanks again. You'll keep in touch if Mitch Eggar contacts you again?' He reached inside his wallet. 'Here's my office phone number if you need to give me a ring.'

Peter frowned at the business card. 'You're a solicitor? I didn't know that.'

'Yes, Juliet advises us on marketing. That's how we met.'

'I knew she liked a challenge,' Peter said. For the first time in their acquaintance Harry saw the trace of a smile on his thin lips, although there was no humour in his eyes. 'Even so, that must be the toughest yet. Improving the image of a firm of lawyers, eh? I'd say it was easier to rebrand Satan as the King of Hearts.'

Chapter Eight

'We ought to talk,' the voice on the phone said.

Harry made a face at the receiver. *We must talk.* Everyone seemed to be saying it. Any moment now, he'd be contacted by counsellors who specialised in caring, sharing heart-to-hearts with people who stumbled over dead bodies. The Liverpool grapevine had worked with its usual efficiency over the past forty-eight hours. Everyone knew now that he'd been the one to find Carl Symons' corpse. People must be wondering what he'd been doing there in the first place. He didn't much care what they thought, as long as they didn't guess the truth. All morning he'd been fending off questions from people hungry for tit-bits of inside information. At court, two lawyers who were no more than nodding acquaintances had invited him for elevenses in the cafeteria; in the office, Suzanne had offered him a chocolate eclair, an act of unparalleled generosity, as she tried to worm her way into his confidence. Now it was the turn of Ken Cafferty, a friend as well as chief crime reporter on one of the local rags, to ferret away in the hope of learning fresh and lurid details about the crime.

'You sound like Liverpool's answer to Oprah Winfrey,' he muttered. 'I've already told you everything I told the police. There's no more to be said.'

'There's *always* something more to be said. Don't you know that's the first rule of journalism?'

'What's the second rule?'

'Isn't one enough to be going on with? Come on, Harry. We go back a long way. This is quite a story. "Police baffled" always sells newsprint. Can't you help me out?' He added in a throwaway manner, 'For instance, why don't you tell me a bit about the murder scene? Anything – unusual there?'

'If there was, it was soaked in the blood.'

A pause. 'The blood, yes. Tell me about the blood.'

Harry was staring at the framed certificates on the wall of his room; he kept them there as a reminder that he really was respectable, that he had actually qualified as a solicitor of the Supreme Court of Judicature. But in his mind he saw only Symons' beheaded corpse lying on the kitchen floor. He didn't want to mention the decapitation, even to Ken. Eggar had asked him to say nothing to anyone about the circumstances of the murder whilst the investigation was at a delicate early stage; it was a reasonable request and he intended to comply with it.

'It was like a slaughterhouse. If that's what you mean by unusual, yeah, it was unusual.'

'There is one other thing.' Ken seemed to be choosing his words with care more befitting a judge than a journalist. 'What about the mirror?'

'What mirror?'

'Way I heard it, there was a broken mirror at the scene.'

'Getting desperate, aren't you? I can't imagine it will fascinate your readers, but I did see fragments of glass on the floor in the hall, if that's what you mean.'

'Well, well, well. Interesting. Anything else that struck you as – odd?'

'You've lost me. Stop trying to be enigmatic, it doesn't suit you. What does a smashed mirror signify, apart from an enormous slab of bad luck for poor old Carl Symons? Maybe he gazed into the looking-glass once too often. Symons was no oil painting. He looked more like a bit part player from *Papillon* – and that's off the record, by the way.'

Ken gave a heavy sigh. 'Come on. Be serious.'

'Believe me, I wasn't laughing when I found his body. I didn't care for him, but no-one deserves a fate like that. All the same, I don't see what you're driving at. So there was a struggle when

Symons was attacked by his killer. So what? Things do get broken when there's a fight. Especially a fight to the death.'

In the silence that followed, Harry could picture Ken pursing his lips as he weighed up whether it was worth probing further. Finally, he heard a long sigh. 'All right. I'll leave it there for now. But promise me one thing, will you? If anything occurs to you, call me first.'

Returning to the magistrates' court in the afternoon, Harry was conscious of surreptitious stares from people he hardly knew. Perhaps this was what celebrity was like: a prickly sensation on the spine as you sensed that your every move was being watched. An uneasy thought occurred to him: had he been in others' shoes, he too would have been prey to ungovernable curiosity.

Ten minutes before his case was listed for hearing, he was hailed by Nerys Horlock. 'I'd been hoping to see you,' she said, putting down her briefcase. 'I think I owe you an apology.'

Harry gaped at her. It was like hearing Margaret Thatcher say that on mature reflection she regretted all those nasty things she used to say about striking miners.

'I didn't mean to chew you out in the law library,' she said, fiddling with the zip of her leather jacket. 'I suppose I'd got out of bed the wrong side and, really, the idea of Carl and Suki having it off with each other was so ridiculous. Besides, I was wound up after hearing the news about Carl. Even though we had our fights, we were partners once.'

'No problem,' he said, still trying to come to terms with the notion of Cruella expressing remorse. 'Think nothing of it.'

'Funny, innit? Partnership's a bond. Like I said, I've decided I'm one of life's sole practitioners. But losing Carl – in a strange sort of way, it's like the death of a distant relative. Someone who made your toes curl last time you met them at a wedding or a funeral. But once they're gone – you regret all the harsh words that passed between you. All the wasted time. Families are strange like that, y'know.'

'If you say so. My parents died a long time ago.'

'Then you missed out,' she said. 'Seems a long time ago now, but my memories of childhood are still the most precious. That's one of the reasons I take divorce cases so personally. It's the kids I feel for. Their ruined lives.'

'Yes,' he said uneasily, unclear where the conversation was heading.

Nerys squared her shoulders. 'You didn't mention that you were the one who found Carl's body.'

So she was getting to the point at last. 'No,' he said.

A catarrhal laugh. 'Don't tell me it slipped your mind.'

'I'd answered questions from the police for hours. I wasn't in the mood for any more.'

'All right, I can understand that. But now you've had a chance to get over it ...' She lowered her voice. 'Did you see anything?'

'I saw Carl Symons' body. That was enough.'

'I mean – anything that might give you an idea about who had killed him?'

Harry stared at her. 'Nothing. Why are you so interested?'

'Well,' she said, forcing a smile as if to suggest that she was making a joke of it. 'I wouldn't like to think that someone out there had a grudge against former partners in Symons, Horlock and Young.'

'Sorry. I can't help.'

'Oh well, I'd best be off. I'm due to see a client in the office in ten minutes and it will take me quarter of an hour to get through the traffic. I'll see you around.'

His day took an unexpected turn for the better when he secured an improbable acquittal for an elderly client, a grizzled and arthritic thief who was living proof of the adage that old burglars never die, they simply steal away. Bustling out of the courtroom in an unaccustomed haze of self-satisfaction, he cannoned into a woman carrying a stack of buff files. She gasped in surprise as a couple of the folders slipped from her hands, the papers they contained fanning out over the floor.

'Oh God, I'm sorry,' he said. 'Here, let me help you pick up...'

As he bent down to gather the documents, his voice faded as he realised who she was. Suki Anwar, the Crown prosecutor who had – according to Muriel – told Nerys that she wished Carl Symons was dead. Well, well, well.

'Here.' He handed her a few sheets and she slipped them back inside the file covers. Straightening, she smiled at him. She was as tall as him, with a lean, athletic build. Her hair was long and dark; she had a habit of constantly flicking stray strands of it out of her eyes. She was wearing dark red lipstick and a lot of eye shadow, more make-up than most of the women solicitors he knew. He wondered if it was a sign that she lacked confidence. Pity to think ill of the dead, but he couldn't imagine any reason why a woman with a strong self-image would have a fling with anyone as unprepossessing as Carl Symons.

'Hello, Harry.' Her voice was husky and warm. 'Don't worry about it. How are you? Or is that a silly question in the circumstances?'

He took a breath and waved a hand at their surroundings. 'Don't apologise. If people couldn't ask silly questions in the magistrates, we'd all be out of a job.'

Almond eyes gazed into his. Her expression resembled that of a nurse at a gallant soldier's bedside. 'It must have been awful for you.'

'As long as they don't lock me up.'

'Ah, Suki, my dear! Splendid! I've found you at last!' The voice hailing her from down the corridor belonged to a middle-aged barrister who in girth and gait bore a startling resemblance to a penguin. His face was split by a smug beam as he waddled towards them and Harry sensed that he thought she fancied him.

'Uh-oh,' she said under her breath. 'I'm late for a con with counsel. Nice to see you, Harry. We ought to talk some time, okay? Will you be at the Legal Group seminar tonight?'

Harry frowned, vaguely trying to recall the junk mail he'd binned the other day. 'All about professional negligence, right?'

'That's it!'

'Well...'

'Not that you'd ever be negligent, I'm sure. But it does us no harm to be kept up to the mark, does it? And you can count it towards your tally of continuing education points. See you there, I hope.'

She moved away to greet the barrister, her face a mask of charm. As he turned to leave, Harry realised that she had not said a word about Carl himself, the victim of the crime. If Suki was heartbroken about Carl's death, she was hiding it well. He remembered Muriel's account of her conversation with Nerys Horlock.

Walking back down Dale Street, he wondered why she seemed keen for him to attend the seminar in the evening. Perhaps she was simply trying to drum up numbers; he had a vague idea that she had been elected to the committee of the Legal Group in the summer. Even if she was burning to know more about Carl Symons' death, it might simply be a prurient interest in the death of a former lover from whom she had parted on bad terms.

In normal circumstances he would find a Legal Group seminar on professional negligence as enticing as a couple of hours of self-flagellation. If he turned up this evening he might also face the hassle of having to fend off questions about Symons. But perhaps that was a price to be paid if he wanted to understand the prosecutor's fate. And he did want to understand it. Badly.

After rifling through his desk drawers, he came up with the pocket diary the Group issued to its members. It was crammed with useful information about how to create a website and conduct investment business, but Harry used it to note the price of vinyl LPs he fancied from the second-hand shop downstairs. He'd never before consulted the seemingly endless list of professional development courses. Tonight's subject was sure to touch a nerve. Everyone made mistakes from time to time: it was common knowledge that each time the *QEII* set sail, half the luxury cabins were occupied by beneficiaries of estates overpaid in error by dozy probate lawyers. A further check revealed that the venue for the seminar was to be the Titanic Rooms. Perhaps the Group's committee had an unexpectedly sly sense of humour.

Jim bustled in, clutching a sheaf of bills and red reminder notices. 'We'll soon be touching the new overdraft limit. Maybe the Loan Arranger was right and we ought to cut back. We should think about pulling the advertising campaign.' He saw Harry's feet on the desk and scowled. 'Knocked off for the day?'

'Good morning in court. I even got old man Goater off.'

'Jesus, that's a crime against society in itself.'

'Miracles do happen.'

'Like us making some decent money?'

Harry considered his partner. It was never easy to read Jim's mind. 'You're really worried?'

'Things are tight. I put in a tender for new business yesterday, but the legal aid cuts don't help. It's the old story. The courts are open to everyone. Same as the Ritz.'

'My sentiments exactly. I've realised I've been burying my head in the sand about the threats to our livelihood. So I'll be going to the Legal Group talk on avoiding negligence tonight. A chance to keep ahead of the game, pick up a few tips on best practice.'

Jim frowned. 'What are you up to? Is the speaker some gorgeous blonde?'

Harry was all injured innocence. 'Why do you always suspect me of having an ulterior motive?'

'Because you're Harry Devlin, that's why.'

The phone rang. Suzanne chanted Juliet's name in an irritatingly suggestive manner. Harry wondered whether the girl was getting the wrong idea. Or rather, the right idea. He shook his head at his mounting sense of insecurity. *Just because you're paranoid, it doesn't mean they're not out to get you.* Putting his hand over the mouthpiece, he said, 'Would you like to speak to Juliet May? Tell her you want to cancel the marketing plan?'

Jim pulled a face. 'Better leave it till I've done a bit of number-crunching. Can you speak to her, put her off for a bit?'

She's not easily put off – believe me, I know. 'Leave it to me.'

As the door swung behind his partner, Harry asked Juliet how were things.

'It's going to be all right, I'm sure. Nothing more from the police. I bet they must have a few leads now. With any luck, they'll arrest someone soon and we won't be troubled again.'

'Don't bank on it. I was talking to a journalist half an hour ago and as far as he can tell, they haven't got a clue.'

'So many suspects they can't figure out where to begin, that's their only problem. If this man Symons could antagonise the Blackwells, he could upset anyone. I can't believe he's much of a loss to the legal profession.'

'Being a nasty piece of work isn't a barrier to entry. In some firms I know, it's part of the job description. Why else do you think we keep crying out for an image makeover and help from people like you? Though I ought to warn you, Jim's fretting about money. He may change his mind about the media strategy.'

'No problem. I have contacts, I can negotiate hefty discounts. He needs to trust me the way you do.'

Do I? Harry changed tack. 'When does Casper arrive home?'

'Half seven. He rang me on his mobile from Euston a few minutes ago. He was talking about taking me out for a slap-up meal, sounded really pleased with himself. His bimbo must have been in good form last night. I'm almost tempted to make him jealous.' She giggled. 'Only joking.'

Harry laughed too. But nervously.

Daniel Roberts walked down Old Hall Street and bought a newspaper from a vendor with a pitch opposite the main entrance to the Titanic Rooms. There were a couple of paragraphs on the front page about the continuing investigation into the death of Carl Symons. A superintendent was quoted as saying that his team was following up a considerable number of leads. Daniel took that to mean that they didn't know where to start in their investigation. He'd read somewhere that the more time that passed after the discovery of the body, the less likely it was that a culprit would ever be charged. A thought occurred which caused him wry amusement. Perhaps they could do worse than call on Harry Devlin for help.

He'd driven over from his cottage in the mountains and spent a productive afternoon in the basement archive of a local newspaper. He was thirsty to know more about Harry. The more information he had, the better. It had occurred to him to check on press cuttings. He'd needed to tell a few lies to the plump woman responsible for archive material, but he didn't mind that. All his energies were directed on one goal; he could not allow himself to be deflected. He had himself become a hunter. The thought pleased him, prompted a grim smile. The experience would be grist to the mill when he next worked on an entry in the Journal.

Harry Devlin's name cropped up several times in connection with sudden, violent death. It was almost as if he were *drawn* to it. Daniel skimmed through reports of criminal cases in which Harry defended killers. In one case, he'd been a witness, giving evidence in the trial of someone who had done away with three people in a converted church. Above all, there was the stabbing of his wife Liz. From the guarded wording of early reports about her murder,

Daniel guessed that Harry himself had been a prime suspect at first. Odd how the story had fizzled out; the police had intimated that the case was closed, but it seemed as though no-one had ever been brought to justice.

The file contained clippings with smudged photographs. Liz had been caught in a holiday snap, an attractive wide-eyed woman laughing at the camera. And then there was Harry. Daniel gazed at the strangely familiar face. Harry's jaw had a determined set, but his features were creased in bafflement, as if he were puzzling over a secret that someone was keeping from him.

Daniel glanced to his right and his left. The woman in charge was discussing her diet with a colleague at the far end on the cellar. He slipped a pair of nail scissors from his pocket and snipped out the photograph of Harry, tucking it inside his wallet.

He'd walked over to the woman and thanked her for her help. On his way out of the building, he had exulted silently, clenching his fists in a fierce passion as he told himself that he now possessed a picture of the man he was seeking.

Before he returned to his cottage for another night without sleep, he wanted to see Harry. It was important now that he could put a face to the name. He was wary of keeping watch outside Crusoe and Devlin's office. A preliminary reconnaissance the previous day had convinced him that he must rule out Fenwick Court. It was too overlooked. Far better to bide his time.

The information sheets he'd picked up at the Legal Group's offices had mentioned a seminar on professional negligence at the Titanic Rooms tonight. All members were urged to attend. He could not be certain that Harry would show up for it. But he'd decided to come and look out for him, just on the off chance. With the newspaper folded out in front of his face, he stationed himself on the steps leading up to the doorway of a bank that had been converted into a wine bar. From his vantage point, he could keep an eye on everyone who entered the building.

A fine rain was falling as people began to drift towards the Titanic Rooms. A couple were carrying huge umbrellas emblazoned with their firm's name which threatened to poke out the eyes of anyone walking in the opposite direction. Suddenly he noticed a man in an overcoat which had seen better days approaching from the direction of Exchange Flags. His collar was turned up against the cold but even though the photograph filched from the newspaper was poor in quality, Daniel had no doubt. *This* was Harry Devlin.

Excitement ran through his body like an electric current. At last he was closing in on the man he had been seeking for so long. As Harry pushed through the revolving doors, Daniel had to make an effort of will to resist the urge to advance from the shadows and follow his quarry inside. He breathed deeply, trying to master his emotions, unaware of the raven-haired woman he'd met the previous morning at the Legal Group's offices. She was crossing the street when she caught sight of him gazing after Harry. She paused in mid-stride as she recognised him. Then she hurried into the building, as if frightened that she might catch his eye.

Harry hadn't been inside the Titanic Rooms before. The building had once housed the offices of one of the city's smaller shipping lines and after the company had collapsed it had stood empty for more than a decade. An enterprising developer had bought it for a song, given it a new name and turned it into a conference centre. The doomed ship had sailed from Liverpool and the chance to cash in on an Oscar-winning movie was too good to miss. The foyer was full of White Star Line memorabilia supposedly carried away by survivors of the tragedy. Harry suspected that most of it had been manufactured during the past eighteen months in a factory out in Bootle or West Derby. Probably by the same people who turned out Beatles artefacts by the lorryload for sale to credulous souvenir hunters.

He claimed a vacant seat at the far end of the front row, nodding to a couple of solicitors he knew. Turning up at the last minute had spared him the need to dodge their questions. He was conscious of people staring at him and shifted uncomfortably: what must it be like to be an animal in a zoo, constantly goggled at by the masses? All he'd done was stumble across a murder scene, for God's sake.

Suki Anwar was sitting immediately below the dais for the chairman and speaker; she'd donned a conspicuously short skirt in honour of the occasion. The seminar was to be given by a doyen of the Yorkshire Law Society, introduced by Rick Spendlove, the recently elected chairman of the Group. The guest was sipping from a tankard of Boddingtons and muttering that he earned less in a year than the Lord Chancellor spent on wallpaper for his toilet. Rick nodded absent-minded agreement whilst engaging in a minute survey of Suki's long legs.

Glancing round, Harry saw Andrea Gibbs following him in. Their eyes met, then she coloured and looked away. Why had she made that abortive call to him? Perhaps he would have the chance to ask her before the evening was over. Turning his head, he caught Suki intercepting Rick's gaze. She raised her eyebrows and Rick treated her to a full-wattage smile.

Rick was a tall, powerfully built man who had played rugby for Cambridge University and made sure that everyone knew it. The game had flattened his nose and scarred his jaw, giving him the appearance of a nightclub bouncer, albeit one whose c.v. included not only a Blue and a first in law but also a rating as one of *Enterprise Spotlight*'s Lawyers for the Millennium. He'd have figured prominently, also, in any listing of Sex Addicts for the Millennium. Since his second wife had left him some time back, he'd been playing the field as if his life depended on it. When he wasn't checking into hotel bedrooms, he strode the corridors of

Boycott Duff, where he was one of the senior partners. The firm was the biggest and most prosperous in the north of England. It was also famously ruthless, but had recently been embarking on a marketing offensive to show that the partners' hearts were in the right place. Only last week Rick had, amidst a fanfare of publicity, launched a fund to build a hospice for AIDS sufferers in memory of Diana, Princess of Wales. Any day now, he'd be making an impassioned speech in support of the victims of landmines.

Dragging his eyes away from Suki with evident reluctance, Rick got to his feet. 'Ladies and gentlemen, thank you for turning up in such splendid numbers. We have a first class speaker tonight. I think many of you know Willis Arkwright from Batley. He never pulls punches, doesn't Willis, and I expect he'll be landing a few tonight on those of our fellow professionals who let us all down by being guilty of sloppy legal practice.'

Rick coughed and switched on his caring expression. 'But first, it's my painful duty to express on behalf of the Liverpool Legal Group our sense of loss and grief following the death the night before last of a well-known local practitioner. I refer, naturally, to Carl Symons. Carl was known to many of you first during his time in private practice and latterly as a prosecutor. He was an able solicitor and we extend our sympathy to the Crown Prosecution Service in its loss.'

It wasn't much of an epitaph, but perhaps there wasn't much more to be said. No-one in the room seemed woebegone as Willis Arkwright began his talk. Cautionary tales of couples who married bigamously because harassed lawyers had forgotten to sort out the decrees ending their previous marriages and brain-dead conveyancers who thought that buying holiday homes in Spain raised the same legal issues as purchasing a bungalow in Southport.

Ah well, Harry thought, there but for the grace of God. His mind began to wander. Perhaps Carl had had a secret life which might explain his barbaric killing. The best way to find out would be to talk to the people who had known him best. Since he was such a loner, that seemed to point towards the people he'd worked with. Like Nerys, Brett, Suki and Andrea.

Once Willis Arkwright had finally run out of breath, the formal part of the evening was over. Andrea disappeared immediately in the direction of the ladies' and while Rick was doing his good-host bit, Harry walked up to Suki and asked if she'd like a drink. Ten minutes later she was on her second vodka and lime and he judged the moment right to ask if she knew whether Symons had any family.

'Not that I know of. He was an only child. I think his father died when he was at school and he lost his mother years ago.' A sharp, bitten-off laugh. 'He wasn't the kind you associate with the phrase "nearest and dearest".'

Harry wondered if people said the same about him. Banishing the thought, he said, 'A workaholic?'

'Something like that.' Suki looked him in the eye. It was a trick she had, flattering yet doubtless effective as a means of eliciting confidences. 'So did the police give you a hard time?'

'I've had happier experiences.'

'Did Eggar give you any clue as to what they were thinking?'

'Such as?'

'Well ... I mean, it's weird, isn't it? Who could have done such a terrible thing? And it *was* terrible, wasn't it?' She bent forward and whispered in his ear. 'I've heard the inside story from a young constable I'm friendly with. He told me Carl's head was cut off. Why would anyone want to do such a thing?'

'If the police do have any ideas about motive, they haven't taken me into their confidence.'

She brushed a hair out of her eyes. 'People tell me you like to play the detective. Haven't you picked up any clues?'

'Sorry. Perhaps I don't deserve my reputation. What about you? Don't you have any ideas why anyone would have wanted to kill Carl?'

She spread her arms. 'It's a complete mystery.'

'Presumably the police have talked to you?'

'Oh yes, along with everyone else in the office. Not that I could help them much.'

'You didn't know him well?'

She gave him the smile that was, he suspected, her customary first line of defence. He told himself not to be disarmed. There was no denying that she was attractive; the real question was whether, as Muriel believed, she had something to hide.

'He wasn't the sort of man who told you his life story over a drink in a bar.'

A careful answer, he realised. Even with a couple of drinks inside her, Suki wasn't going to give much away, either. He saw her stealing a glance at her watch and guessed that she'd wanted to pump him, to see if he knew anything she didn't. Not exactly flattering. Now that she was satisfied that he couldn't shed any light on the killing, she wanted to be away.

'You'll miss him, then?'

She shrugged. 'Carl was a good lawyer. Rick was right. He'll be a real loss to the CPS.'

'Taking my name in vain?' Rick had shoved through the crowd to join them, leaving Willis Arkwright to hold court before a group of keen young litigators. He still moved with the muscular swagger which had helped him to score a couple of tries in the Varsity Match of twenty years ago. 'Evening, Harry. Glad you could make it. Especially in the circumstances.'

Harry said, 'Yeah, well. I like to keep up to date with best practice.'

Rick almost spilled his gin and tonic but managed to bite back a cutting rejoinder. 'So tell me. One or two of us have been wondering. I mean, how did you happen to call at Symons' place? The Dee coast isn't exactly your regular beat, is it?'

It may only have been an idle enquiry, but Harry was aware of Suki leaning forward, her upper body almost touching his as she waited for his answer. He could see Andrea Gibbs, too, standing behind Rick; she seemed to be listening intently. 'It's a long story. Let's just say I finished up in the wrong place at the wrong time. After listening to Willis, I'm starting to wonder if finding a brother solicitor dead isn't a breach of some Law Society rule. I'm half expecting my insurance premium to go up next year as a result.'

Rick snorted with amusement for Suki's benefit. He liked playing to the gallery; perhaps in his mind he still imagined himself acknowledging the roar of the crowd at Twickenham. 'Didn't they once make a film about you? *The Trouble With Harry*? Oh well, good to see you. Now, if you'll excuse me, I have one or two boring bits of committee business to discuss with Ms Anwar here.'

Suki gave him her habitual teasing smile. 'Sorry, Rick. I'd love to, but I was up early this morning and I'm in court first thing tomorrow. I think what I need is an early night. Another time, perhaps.'

'I'll look forward to it.' Cutting his losses with the ease of the accomplished womaniser, Rick turned and exclaimed, 'Andrea, good to see you! My God, you're looking more gorgeous than ever tonight.'

Harry had wondered if Andrea might have been hanging around in the hope of catching his eye, rather than Rick's, perhaps to follow up her enigmatic phone call. But when she smiled at Rick, he dismissed the idea. Better not fall into the trap of believing that all these women craved his company. Leave those delusions to the Ricks of this world.

A mournful man who was in-house solicitor for a firm of undertakers tugged at his sleeve and asked if he knew who was handling the arrangements for Carl Symons' funeral. It took Harry ten minutes to escape. By now the room was clearing; Rick and Andrea were nowhere to be seen. Vaguely dissatisfied, he made his way towards the exit. He hadn't learned anything from Suki and he still didn't know why Andrea had bothered to phone him. Perhaps he might be better giving the whole detective thing a wide berth.

As he left the building, he saw Rick on the opposite pavement, talking to Andrea Gibbs. As if to emphasise a point, he slipped his arm around her shoulder. For a moment she seemed to freeze, then she looked up into his eyes and they moved closer together.

Suddenly a Sierra that had been parked a hundred yards away revved up and drove towards the pair. Rick glanced round and, as Andrea said something, took a step away from her. The car screeched to a halt beside the pair of them. Rick ducked down and took a look through the passenger's window. Something he saw there must have alarmed him, for he muttered a few words to Andrea and then scuttled off down the alleyway which led to the multi-storey behind Rumford Place.

The window was wound down and Andrea bent down to speak to the driver. Harry watched as she put her hand on the door, then removed it as if scalded. He guessed that the driver had made a remark she hadn't liked.

'You're crazy! You're absolutely crazy!' Her voice rang out, high and clear in the still evening air.

As Harry watched, she moved away from the car and broke into a run, her long hair flapping as she disappeared round the corner into Tithebarn Street and out of sight.

The Sierra did not move. Harry hesitated for a moment before walking slowly towards it. His route home to Empire Dock should take him in the other direction, but his curiosity had been aroused. Drawing nearer, he could see a private hire plate above the vehicle registration number. As he passed the cab, he stole a glance through the window. The profile of the man in the driver's seat, drumming his fingers on the steering wheel, was at once familiar. It belonged to the man who had once been in partnership with Carl Symons and Nerys Horlock. He was also Andrea Gibbs' boyfriend, although right now that relationship looked to be equally ill-starred. He was Brett Young, solicitor turned cab driver.

Chapter Nine

Brett stopped drumming on the wheel and said, 'Hello, Harry. Long time no see.'

'That's right.' Frantically trying to gather his thoughts, Harry glanced at the car. A patch of rust spread from the door handle. Inside, an empty packet of cigarettes lay in the well under the instrument panel. A dog-eared *Liverpool A-Z* was face down on the passenger seat. The beige upholstery was tatty and reeked of smoke. 'How are things?'

As soon as he asked the question, he wanted to bite his tongue. Diplomacy had never been his strong suit. Then again, why should anyone who'd once billed by the hour be embarrassed about a job where he charged by the mile?

'So-so.' Brett spoke almost in a whisper. 'I'm okay. More to the point, how with you?'

'Well. You know.'

'Quite – quite an adventure you had the night before last, by all accounts. Carl Symons murdered, eh?' Brett grunted. 'Couldn't have happened to a nicer bloke.'

'I scarcely knew him.'

'You didn't miss anything.'

'So you haven't shed too many tears?'

'If I covered myself in sackcloth and ashes, nobody would believe me. Why pretend? I'm glad the bastard's dead.' Brett hesitated. 'You live on the waterfront, don't you? Why don't you hop in? I'll give you a lift.'

Harry rested his shoulders on the edge of the window. 'Aren't private hire cars forbidden to pick up in the street?'

'That's the difference between us,' Brett said with a grimace. 'You're still working in the legal profession. These days, I don't have to worry about playing by the rules. Get in.'

'All right.' Harry opened the door. So what if Brett wanted, like everyone else, to try to pump him for information? Two could play at that game.

As he fiddled with the belt, Brett fished a pack of Benson and Hedges out of the pocket of his jacket. Suede Italian tailoring, probably cost a small fortune at one time. Now the elbows were patched and a button was missing. He paused in the act of offering a cigarette. 'You don't, do you?'

'Gave them up a few years back.'

'Wish I could. I seem to need them to get through the day. And night.'

Brett lit up, shifting around in his seat as he did so. He wasn't a big man, but his build was wiry. Early thirties, at a guess, fresh-faced but with an emerging bald patch. His manner was restless; the car seemed too small for him, as though he hated being strapped in and was itching to escape.

'I suppose you saw what happened a moment ago? Andrea and I, we had a few words.'

That's one way of putting it. Harry wasn't a lawyer for nothing: he stonewalled. 'So how long have the two of you been together?'

'You could say it's been an on-off thing.' Brett was breathing hard. 'As much off as on, lately. It's not easy – you could say we're both a bit highly strung.'

'You met at Symons, Horlock and Young?'

'Yes, she was our one and only trainee solicitor and I did a bit of cradle-snatching. I couldn't resist, frankly. When she sets her mind to something ... anyway, at least when the firm collapsed and she lost her job, she didn't blame me. She saw I'd done everything in my power to keep the business afloat. When I had problems, Andrea was the only person who stuck around.'

'I've not seen her working in the courts lately. Who does she work for now?'

'She qualified in the end. People rallied round. Windaybanks let her join them and the Law Society took pity.' There was an odd, sour note in Brett's voice, as if a thought had struck him which had caused him pain. 'By then, she was sick of private practice. Understandable in the circumstances. So she's finished up working on a telephone hot-line. Twenty-four-hour legal advice for consumers. You know the sort of stuff, it's offered as an add-on with your house insurance. She works nights.'

'Can't be much fun.'

'Andrea doesn't mind. The money's not bad and we can see each other during the day. Though maybe not after tonight, I suppose. She never found it easy, dealing with clients face to face. The anonymity of the phone lines suits her.'

Harry made a face. 'All those legal questions.'

'She's always been academic, she's pretty good on tricky points of law. Not like me. I used to dread exams.'

'But you made it in the end.'

A wary look came into Brett's eyes. 'Let's say I knew what I wanted. When I was a kid, I simply got hooked on the idea of becoming a lawyer. I came from a working class family, so maybe it was a status thing. I always intended to be a solicitor of the Supreme Court, I'd never have hacked it at the Bar. I truly believed that once I put up my own brass nameplate, I'd have it made. More fool me.'

He wasn't disguising his bitterness. Harry said quietly, 'So you both work lates?'

'Yeah. I'm usually on six to six. Andrea thought she'd better attend tonight's seminar. The mob she works for aren't lawyers, they don't have any infrastructure. No proper law library, no training, but they'd be quick enough to kick her out if she made a mess of advising over the phone. I offered to pick her up afterwards. I thought we might have time to call back at my flat for an hour before she was due in work. Seemed like a good idea, but it all went wrong.'

'Don't read anything into what happened. Rick must have chatted up half the women in Liverpool since he split from his wife. I expect Andrea was desperate to get away.'

Brett exhaled. The smoke made Harry's eyes water. 'Didn't look much like that to me. Or maybe she was simply hoping to make me jealous.'

Time to change the subject. 'So how's life on the cabs?'

'Different,' Brett said, switching on the ignition. 'When I slogged through law college, I didn't imagine I'd end up driving round darkest Liverpool on the graveyard shift ferrying drunks and whores back home.'

'This is your car?'

'No. When the partnership crashed, I lost pretty much everything except the shirt on my back. I pay the owner a settle – like a rent – in return for the vehicle and use of the radio. He had a problem with his previous driver.'

'Yeah?'

'The lad used to specialise in airport runs, taking people to Manchester to catch night flights. A couple of his customers missed their plane and found someone else to bring them back home. They walked in through the front door and fell over their taxi driver, helping himself to their video recorder and television. Turned out he had a profitable sideline, robbing holidaymakers whilst they were jetting off to warmer climes.'

'Not Billy Rosler?' Harry laughed. 'Small world. I acted for him.'

Brett raised his eyebrows. 'Got five years, didn't he?'

'Can't win 'em all.' Harry coughed. 'So, you enjoy the driving?'

'It's something to do. You meet a few people, get to spend time on your own. I like the solitude. There are worse ways of earning a living. But I miss the law. It still fascinates me, the way it's woven into all our lives. I used to love reading about old murder trials in the days before they abolished the death penalty. Marshall Hall cross-examining defence witnesses to save the life of a client on a capital charge. Those cases had everything.' Brett added in a whisper, 'And a life was always at stake.'

Harry pondered. 'But it's not actually like that, is it? I spend half my time hanging around in courtroom corridors and filling in forms to keep the Legal Aid Board quiet.'

'Yes, yes, you're right. The business of law doesn't have much to do with justice any more. Perhaps it never did. At least as a cabbie, I can please myself. I'm not beholden to anyone. There's nobody from Chancery Lane breathing down my neck.' Brett's face creased, as if at a painful memory. 'So where are we heading? The Colonnades?'

'I'm not in the right income bracket. Try Empire Dock.'

'Could be worse.' Brett gave a harsh laugh as he executed an illicit three-point-turn. 'Beats my place. I've rented a bedsit in Toxteth. The woman next door is on the game. She specialises in S and M, does a roaring trade. The crack of her whip and the punters' groans keep me awake when I'm trying to grab a bit of sleep in the middle of the afternoon. At least if Andrea and I are finished, I'll have time to catch up on my shut-eye.'

'Seriously, I don't think you need worry about Andrea.'

'I worry a lot about Andrea,' Brett said. There was a bleak faraway look in his eyes. 'She's – temperamental. Sometimes we seem to spend more time quarrelling than in bed together.' He let out a breath. 'You know what women are like.'

Do I? He made a non-committal noise which Brett evidently took as assent.

'Anyway, that's my problem. You've got enough on your mind, I guess, after finding Carl. I heard – that it was gruesome. Some bloke I picked up last night said he'd been talking to a friend of a

110

friend, a civilian who works for Merseyside Police. Story goes, they think it was some kind of ritual killing.'

Harry jerked round in his seat. 'What sort of ritual?'

'Search me,' Brett said quickly. 'People are saying all kinds of things. Half a dozen passengers must have mentioned it over the last couple of days. Everyone I speak to seems to have heard a different rumour. I thought you'd be the horse's mouth.'

'I didn't hang around to do an autopsy. All I can say for sure is that Carl met a messy end.'

The car radio crackled and a bored woman's voice asked if anyone was near to Everton Valley. A fare wanted to catch a flight from Speke and had been let down by another cab company. Brett turned the off-switch. 'No long-bonneting tonight.'

'What?'

'Airport runs pay well, even if you don't burgle the customers' house once you've dropped them. If you're nowhere near the pick-up point, the temptation is to tell a fib to control and say you are. So you get the job by cracking on that your car's got a bonnet that stretches all the way to your destination.' Keeping his eyes on the road, he said, 'You don't know whether it's true, then, that there was something – odd about the killing?'

'I'm not sure what you mean.'

Brett pouted. He had an actor's smooth profile; easy to understand why Andrea Gibbs had been smitten by him. But every now and then his mouth curved like that of a child deprived of a favourite toy.

'Listen, Harry. You were there, though God knows why.'

'It's a long story. Believe me, when I went into that cottage I had no idea it belonged to Carl Symons.'

'All right. But if anyone knows whether there's any truth in all the stories flying around, it's you. Must be.'

'Put it like this. I didn't see any pentangles chalked on the floor. There was no smell of incense, either. The only thing out of the ordinary was a smashed mirror. If you call that extraordinary. Bad luck for Carl. And one of the local journalists seems to think it's interesting, but I've no idea why.'

'Someone had destroyed the mirror?' Brett's voice cracked. If it had not been absurd, Harry would have said that he was afraid. 'Are you sure?'

'Yes – but so what?'

Brett flushed. 'Empire Dock, did you say? It's coming up on the right.'

'Why don't you drive on?' Harry suggested on impulse. It must be worth trying to find out more. Filling his lungs with high tar for a few minutes was a price he'd have to pay. 'I'll see you right on the fare. It's been ages since we talked.'

'We never had much in common when I was in practice,' Brett said. 'What is there to talk about?'

'The police gave me a hard enough time yesterday, even though I hardly knew Carl Symons. It's made me interested in him. You must have known him better than most.'

Brett sucked in his cheeks. Harry hadn't quite wound his window up and he could hear the plaintive hooting of a vessel in the Mersey. To their right gleamed the lights of Albert Dock. In the distance loomed the buildings of the waterfront. He travelled along this road every day and yet in the dark it always seemed to belong to a foreign landscape. The block of flats where he lived, the massive Lubianka that was the Customs and Excise headquarters. The development around the marina seemed like a ghost town. *The city's different at night.* Like the lyric to a catchy song, the phrase hummed in his mind. It came from a film; he could hear Jack Nicholson's lazy, nasal voice uttering the words. *The Two Jakes,* that was it.

'I can't believe anyone really knew Carl Symons,' Brett said at last. 'They say no man is an island. He was the exception that proves the rule.'

'You had a row with him. Parting company cost you a huge wad of money. The police must have put you through the wringer even more than they did me.'

'Nothing I couldn't cope with. Only problem was, I didn't have the foresight to arrange myself an alibi.'

'You weren't working on the evening he was killed?'

'I was, as it happens. Only one slight problem. On the night of the storms, fares were thin on the ground. To the point of non-existence. People heard the gale warnings in good time and decided to stay put.'

'Pity.'

'You're telling me. I spent a couple of hours driving round in the hope that there would be someone who was stranded by the weather, but there was nothing doing, so I pulled up off Sefton Park, turned off the radio and had a kip. One of those things. You don't earn easy money in this job.'

'And the police were happy with that?'

'Obviously not. But what could they do? Arrest me?' Brett's voice was becoming shrill. 'Even our local constabulary usually requires some shred of evidence before slapping on the cuffs. And if they don't, the prosecutors certainly will. Fact is, if I'd killed him, I'd have been too proud of myself not to admit it.'

'And Nerys Horlock, what about her?'

'She stood back and let it happen.' Brett swallowed hard. 'You see, I thought I could trust them. One for all, all for one. *Uberrimae fidei*, the relationship of utmost good faith. You know, I was daft enough to believe all that crap about partnership they teach you at law school. I tell you, Harry, I've made some mistakes in my time, but that was the worst.'

They were cruising along Upper Parliament Street; the Anglican Cathedral, floodlit yet strangely menacing, loomed to their left. A bare-legged woman in a leather mini-skirt twenty years too young for her was leaning against a phone box. As they passed, she caught

Harry's eye and gave him a gap-toothed smile. Harry recognised her and smiled back. Not that he wanted to become one of her clients: she was one of his.

'What brought you together – you, Carl and Nerys?'

'I'd been working for Ogley and Mulhearn out at Huyton and I wanted to make a break. I was fed up with working long hours, slaving away in the hope that one day they'd offer me a slice of the equity. I thought it was time to get my own snout in the trough. I'd met both Carl and Nerys in the courts. They were both seasoned litigators, seemed to have the right stuff.'

Brett was talking quickly again. The car, too, was moving faster. Harry glanced at the speedometer and saw that they were well over the limit. 'One day Nerys told me she and Carl fancied setting up on their own and wondered if I'd like to join them. I'd need to put in some capital, help get the show on the road, but they thought the business had a bright future. I jumped at the chance.'

'So what went wrong?' Harry asked, silently bracing himself. Any minute now, they would hit something coming the other way.

'You name it. I suppose we all skipped too many practice management seminars. Cashflow was never more than a trickle. We had plenty of work-in-progress, we just never seemed to get paid fast enough. I persuaded the others we needed more finance. They wouldn't budge, so I traded with them. I'd take the lion's share of the profits and in return I'd take out another loan, give the firm another capital injection.'

'Ah.'

'Call it a calculated risk, if you like. Like jumping this traffic light – *now*.'

Brett suddenly shoved his foot down hard. The car crashed through the red light and slewed into a side road. Harry found himself curling into a ball for fear of impact. He shut his eyes, but nothing happened. When he looked again, Brett had taken one hand off the wheel and and was clenching his fist in a kind of savage jubilation.

'See? Sorry, but you'll take my point. Ninety-nine times out of a hundred, you get away with it. Hundredth time around, you get flattened by a juggernaut.'

'Do you play the percentages with all your passengers?' Harry gasped. It felt as though all the breath had been knocked out of him.

'Believe me, the law of averages is on my side. I've already run into one juggernaut. I was still hoping that we'd turn things round when Carl and Nerys decided that they'd had enough and dissolved the partnership. So much for good faith.' He nodded to the right and said, 'Nerys's new office is half a mile up that road, you know. She's fallen on her feet.'

'I suppose from their point of view...'

'I don't want to hear about their point of view, all right?' Brett shouted. 'They did the dirty on me, don't you understand? They ruined my bloody life!'

After a minute of silence, Harry said, 'Look, Brett, wouldn't it be an idea to ease off on the pedals? I promise, I'm in no hurry.'

'You're not? Good!'

Suddenly the car skidded to a halt. Harry's stomach lurched. 'What are you doing?'

'This is where I live,' Brett said, waving at an old house with a battered green door and steel shutters on the ground floor windows. 'If you're not pushed for time, come in for a drink. I'm up to here with driving for one night. I could use a beer and maybe you feel the same.'

Right now, there was nothing Harry wanted less. Still, better be tactful. He'd watched *Taxi Driver* too many times to have any desire to antagonise a cabbie whose nerve ends were showing. Brett Young looked nothing like Robert De Niro, it was true. But you could never be sure.

'I'd better be going,' he said later, putting his tankard down on the threadbare strip of carpet.

'Have another drink.'

Brett was sprawled across a bed-settee that had leaked a spring. Under the suede jacket, Harry had discovered, he was wearing a T-shirt emblazoned with the legend *My client went to prison and all I got was this lousy T-shirt*. His scuffed trainers were resting on an unopened six-pack of Tetley's. The smoke from his cigarette hung in a haze in the little room, competing with the odour of damp from a patch above the floorboards. His mood had mellowed and for the past half hour he'd been recounting tales of life on the road. The propositions from legless women he brought home from clubs, the need to avoid thugs who would pull a knife rather than pay their fare. The stories palled with inebriated repetition. Every time Harry tried to steer the conversation back round to Carl or Nerys, Brett changed the subject. In the end, he'd abandoned the effort and savoured the taste of the beer on his tongue, waiting for a break in the conversational flow so that he could make his excuses and leave.

Brett hadn't bothered much with home furnishings. A few books: a dog-eared copy of *Learning the Law*, a paperback about pot-holing and a slim volume called *Merseyside's Underworld*. Harry raised his eyebrows at the latter. Some kind of guide to Liverpudlian gangsters? He wondered grimly if Casper May rated a chapter all to himself. On a small cassette player, an Elvis Costello track was playing. One of his best: 'God Give Me Strength'. You could say that again. Harry reached out and turned the music down a shade. Was it his imagination or could he hear the gentle swish of a cane from next door and the low snorts of pleasure from a satisfied customer?

'Thanks, but I need to be up early. I'm in court first thing tomorrow morning.'

'Yeah?' Brett belched. 'Anything out of the ordinary?'

'This couple Jim bought a house for. They've had a run of bad luck and they're blaming a poltergeist. So they decided to sue the sellers because they should have given vacant possession.'

Brett's eyes began to gleam. 'Didn't Andrea once tell me there was a case like that in New York? As I recall, the court decided that as a matter of law, the house was haunted. But I don't think the precedent has ever been followed in this country.'

'That's why the clients were keen to bring the case in Liverpool,' Harry said. 'Anywhere else and they wouldn't have had a ghost of a chance.'

Brett guffawed. 'Come on, have one for the road. I'll drop you off later.'

'For God's sake, you can't drive again tonight.' Harry was out of his chair, standing over Brett with his arms folded. 'You're way over the limit. Don't even think about it. I'm walking. The air will do me good.'

Brett sprang to his feet. 'You don't have to go!'

'It's late,' Harry said. 'Look, I hope you patch it up with Andrea.'

'We're finished,' Brett muttered. 'Finished.'

'Hey, don't get things out of proportion. You know what that bastard Spendlove's like.'

Brett seized his wrist. 'I know what *she's* like. Yes, I do now. I know what she's really like.'

'That hurts,' Harry said, trying to disentangle himself.

Brett's eyes were wide. They didn't seem quite focused. 'She's dangerous, you know, Harry. She's wearing me down, I can feel it. One day she'll kill me.'

'What are you talking about?'

'I'm afraid of her. God's own truth.'

Harry managed to pull free and took a couple of steps towards the door. 'You've had too much to drink. You're not making sense. Go to bed and sober up, eh?'

Brett advanced towards him. 'You don't know what it's like,' he mumbled. 'You don't understand what I've been going through.'

'I do, actually. You're pissed. Simple as that.'

Brett flung a punch at him. Harry dodged to one side and saw the fist miss his cheek by inches. Brett lost his footing and finished up on his knees. Tears were trickling down his cheeks.

'You don't understand,' he repeated. 'She's killing me.'

'I suppose it's fair to say that infidelity made me what I am today.'

Jack Nicholson's voice oozed over the titles to *The Two Jakes*. The belated sequel to *Chinatown* was a film Harry loved; he was protective about it, felt irked when people said it didn't hold a candle to Polanski's masterpiece. Thinking about the movie in the old Sierra had made him want to watch it again when he ought to be in bed, gathering strength for courtroom battle the following day. Perhaps he had a kinship with Jake Gittes, a detective haunted by memories.

'You can't forget what has happened in your life, any more than you can change it.'

Of course it was true. On the long walk back from Toxteth, he'd decided he oughtn't to spend any more time trying to unravel what had happened to Carl Symons, let alone attempting to make sense of Brett's boozy ramblings. But he knew he could never scrub from his mind the picture of the blood-soaked body he'd seen in the gloom of the cottage by the riverside. The image would stay with him for ever.

As he'd made his way down Myrtle Street, he'd spotted Peanuts Benjamin, a pimp and old client for whom he'd been acting at the time of Liz's death. Peanuts was arguing with one of his girls' customers and Harry hurried on, easily resisting any temptation to mediate. But the near-encounter had set him thinking about Liz again – and now he was afraid of sleep. He knew that when he dreamed, he would dream of the woman who had betrayed him, the woman whom he could never let go. Even in death, he realised, she meant more to him than Juliet. Jake was right: the footprints and the signs from the past are everywhere.

'Everybody makes mistakes,' Jake muttered as Harry began to doze. 'But when you marry one, you pay for it for the rest of your life.'

Fire and Rain

...but it was butcher work; had I not been nerved by thoughts of other dead, and of the living over whom hung such a pall of fear, I could not have gone on. I tremble and tremble even yet, though till it was all over, God be thanked, my nerve did stand. Had I not seen the repose in the first face, and the gladness that stole over it just ere the final dissolution came, as realisation that the soul had been won, I could not have gone further with my butchery. I could not have endured the horrid screeching as the stake drove home; the plunging of writhing form, and lips of bloody foam. I should have fled in terror and left my work undone.

Yesterday I cut my wrist. A flesh wound only, little more than a scratch. I scarcely felt pain as the dark red fluid streaked across the pale skin. I bent my head so that my lips brushed against the wrist. The taste was spicy on my tongue. I couldn't help but shudder as I sensed the life force flowing through me, greedily absorbed all the nourishment.

I don't deny that I'm drawn to blood – how could I? I think about it day and night and when I take it in, it makes me high. Yet it isn't a disease: I'm not sick, whatever you might think. Consider it rather as a craving, like the fat man's lust for chocolate cake.

The trouble is that I want more and more. I lack restraint, I've lost all sense of shame. Never mind the rules, forget those old taboos. How many times have I dreamed that one day our blood would mingle – that we might explore eternity together?

Chapter Ten

'You were out late last night,' Rhodri Nash said.

Daniel Roberts glared across the formica-topped table. 'Keeping watch, were you?'

'Hey, no need to lose your rag. I was only commenting.'

'When I need your comments, I'll ask for them, all right?'

'Okay, okay.'

Rhodri sounded hurt. He was a pudgy little man in his forties who had worked at the truck stop for as long as Daniel could remember. They spent a good deal of time together, especially at break times and when they had a coffee together at the end of a shift. Business wasn't brisk outside the summer months, especially since the new road had taken away a good deal of the traffic and when the manager wasn't around, they had little to do but chat. But they didn't have much in common except their jobs. Daniel preferred to lose himself in his imaginings, Rhodri liked to talk even when he had nothing to say. That was the trouble. If his curiosity was aroused, he might mention it to other people. Daniel was a private person; he didn't want to become a topic of conversation. Better try to put things right.

'Sorry I bit your head off,' he said. 'But I had a bad night. I was out yesterday and the van broke down.'

Rhodri grinned. He didn't bear grudges, was always happy to accept an apology. Anything to keep the conversation trundling along. It was his break-time and they were in the café, but the place was deserted except for the buck-toothed girl in the check overall and she didn't count. Serving a cup of tea was about Bronwen's limit.

'Hard luck. Battery on the blink again?' In response to Daniel's nod he added. 'Told you so, boy.'

'Should have listened to you, shouldn't I? I'll know better next time than to argue with the expert.' On the rare occasions when Daniel made the effort, he could be gracious.

Encouraged, Rhodri said, 'Not much I don't know about vans. So where did you get to, then? Haven't seen you around so much lately. Time was when you never stirred beyond this place for one week after another.'

Daniel's jaw tightened. 'Felt like a drive, didn't I?'

'You were out for hours. I called at the cottage when I knocked off mid-afternoon, see. I wondered if you fancied coming round for a pint in the evening, maybe watch the big match. There was no sign. Then, when I was closing the curtains before bed, I saw your lights coming up the track.'

'You had a late night yourself. That must have been around one.'

'Good game. Close thing, though. Went to extra time, then penalties.' Rhodri shook his head. 'Me, I can't think of anything crueller than penalties.'

'Shame I missed it.' Daniel finished his coffee and stood up. 'I'd best be going. Work to do.'

Rhodri squinted at him. 'That's the second time this month you've said something about working. Not got a second job, have you? Or is it just a spot of DIY? What exactly do you get up to in that lonely little cottage of yours? I've often wondered.'

Daniel ground his teeth. 'Ask no questions and I'll tell you no lies.'

Rhodri smirked. 'Secret, is it? Now you've got me wondering, you have.'

'Nothing to wonder about.'

'Maybe I'll pop round one day, take a look-see.'

Daniel gripped the top of the chair, squeezing it so hard his hand hurt. He had to force himself to keep his tongue civil; it was important not to make things worse. 'When I want company, you can be sure you'll be the first I ask round.'

He waved to Bronwen as he left the café. His shoulders were stiff with suppressed tension, but he knew it would be a mistake to let it show. Blame it on the van breaking down. It had been yet another long sleepless night. He was tired, but he'd done what he set out to do. Everything was going according to his plan. He mustn't lose his nerve. Soon the moment he'd been waiting for would arrive at last and he would come face to face with Harry Devlin.

'We've got a problem,' Juliet said as soon as Suzanne put her through.

Harry bit his lip, tasted a trace of blood. He had a sick feeling in his stomach that she wasn't just worrying about the possible postponement of Crusoe and Devlin's onslaught on the media. She sounded as though she were throwing down a gauntlet, expecting him to say *What do you mean, "we"?*

Striving for calm, he said, 'Tell me.'

'Not on the phone.'

'Okay. Where and when?'

'Are you free now? I don't want to wait. But I can't come to your office. We might be overheard. And we need to be careful about being seen together anywhere else.'

He'd only just returned from Widnes County Court and he had plenty to do. In particular, he wanted to talk to Nerys Horlock again. Before leaving home, he'd checked his answering machine; he'd been too tired to do so the previous evening. Nerys had left a message whilst he was out at the Titanic Rooms. She'd never called him at home before.

'There's something I wanted to tell you about,' her disembodied voice had said. 'I almost mentioned it when we met at the magistrates', but it didn't seem right somehow. On second thoughts, I'd like to have a word in your ear. Why don't you ring me? Later this evening if you like. I'll be on the office number until ten. Plenty of paperwork to catch up with.'

He threw a guilty glance at the letters spilling out of his in-tray and remembered Willis Arkwright's strictures on the need to prioritise. Well – first things first.

'I'm starving,' he said. 'Why don't we have a sandwich together?'

'I don't think I could manage anything to eat right now. I just want to talk. In private. Not in your office. Jim will start getting suspicious.'

If he isn't already. 'How about the old Botanic Gardens?'

'At Wavertree? God, I've not been there since I was a kid.'

'It's not exactly Kew, but at least it's quiet. Not much danger of bumping into anyone we know. We'll be able to talk.'

'I'll be there by half twelve. Meet you outside.'

She banged the phone down. He shut his eyes. Had she let something slip? Was it possible that Casper had cottoned on?

'Asleep on the job?' Jim demanded.

Harry opened his eyes and gave his partner a sheepish grin. 'Just collecting my thoughts.'

Jim grunted. 'How did you get on?'

'I'm afraid Mr and Mrs Margetson came face to face with the spectre of failure.'

'The judge threw out their claim?'

'He certainly wasn't moved by the spirit of equity.'

Jim grinned. 'I've been getting a will executed at a rest home in Edge Hill. An old lady's dying and she wanted to leave her goods and chattels to a deserving cause. Everton Football Club, actually. She's expressed the testamentary wish that they use the proceeds to buy a decent penalty taker after last night's fiasco. Tell you something. There's a lot of police activity up in that neck of the woods this morning. Flashing blue lights, screaming sirens, the works. That whole area is swarming with panda cars.'

'So what's new?' Perhaps Brett Young had crashed through one red light too many this morning. For the moment, Harry had other things on his mind. 'By the way, I'll be going out for lunch soon.'

'Once you've collected your thoughts, eh?' Jim gave a sorrowful look at the mound of paperwork and departed with a shake of the head.

It might not be too bad, Harry told himself on his way out of the office. Even if Casper had somehow learned about the affair, it needn't be the end of the world. It wasn't as if the man had been a model of fidelity. Nowadays he was a prominent businessman, a pillar of the community. With any luck, he'd realise that vengeance never achieved anything. Despite his wounded pride, he might be willing to let his wife's lover fade into the background. Perhaps he'd learn the right lesson and start to work at his marriage with Juliet. There might yet be a happy ending.

Then again, wasn't that a formation of pigs flying over the Liver Building?

Juliet's Alfa was already waiting in Botanic Road when he arrived. It was a sleek silver car, not the sort commonly found round here. He gritted his teeth: she paid lip service to the need for discretion, but he was beginning to understand that she was by nature a risk-taker. And, truth to tell, that was part of her appeal. She opened the passenger door and he climbed in beside her. She was tense and breathing hard.

'What's the matter? Is it Casper?'

'No,' she said. 'At least, not yet.'

He breathed out. That was all right, then. 'So why are you worried?'

'It's that bastard Peter Blackwell.'

Oh shit. 'What's he done?'

'Nothing much so far. But he's trouble, I'm sure of it.'

'You've changed your tune. Twenty-four hours ago he was one of the good guys.'

'I know, I know, don't rub it in. But that was before he and I talked alone. He called me yesterday evening, not long before Casper was due home. He'd obviously been drinking, his voice was slurred. I've known him for ages, I thought we were friends, but what he said shocked me. It was as if I was connecting with the real person for the very first time.'

'We all say things when we're pissed that we don't really mean.'

'You don't understand. This was horrible. He said some filthy things about you and me. Said I was a cheap whore. Asked what my husband would say if he found out I was screwing a two-bit solicitor.'

Harry's stomach lurched. 'He threatened to blow the gaff?'

'Not in so many words,' she said slowly. 'It was more as though he enjoyed making me squirm.'

'It was the booze,' Harry said, more confidently than he felt. 'As soon as he dries out, he'll come crawling back to you, full of apologies and promises that he'll never do it again. Look, why don't we have a walk round? You look as though you could do with a bit of fresh air.'

When they were out of the car, she said, 'I wish I could be so sure. Some things – once they are said, they can't be unsaid.'

He turned up his coat collar. 'Have you discussed this with Linda?'

'Not yet. I wanted to talk to you first.'

They turned on to the main road, keeping their counsel as the cars roared by on the dual carriageway. The old stone gatehouse was boarded-up, its drainpipes rusted, its single door padlocked. Pinned to a signboard by the main entrance was a single piece of paper, a notice of election of a municipal councillor for the Smithdown Ward. The polling date was the previous May.

They walked towards the walled garden. He'd once heard that this place had originally been intended as the site for the city's gaol. Instead it had been turned into a botanical garden, but after the Luftwaffe had bombed the borders and wrecked the glasshouses, the plants had been moved to another part of Liverpool and this place had been left to moulder.

He put his hand on hers. 'It'll be all right. You said it yourself, Peter has had a rough time. Probably best to cut him some slack. What's he going to do, anyway? Buttonhole Casper on his way into work? Apart from anything else, I doubt if he'd have the guts. He needs the booze to get through the day. The odds are, he just couldn't hack it.'

'It's too easy for someone to cause mayhem,' she muttered. 'An anonymous phone call. A note. There are all kinds of ways he could shaft us with the minimum of personal inconvenience. I can picture him, sitting in that crummy flat of his and laughing till he wept at the thought of the pain he'd caused.'

'Have a word with Linda. She's on your side. She'll give him a good talking-to.'

'Oh, she's loyal, no question about that. But even with her, I need to watch my step, believe me. Peter is her only child, the only family she has left since she lost her husband. And she's still very much the doting mummy. Her boy can do no wrong. You must have picked that up when you came to West Kirby. It's strange, it's something that sets us apart. I've never had a son, never wanted kids.' A shadow passed across her face. 'That's not quite true, actually. I never got the chance. I had a hysterectomy when I was a student. I was only twenty-one.'

'I'm sorry.' In all their moments of intimacy, she'd never mentioned that before.

'Oh, it doesn't matter. Who wanted a screaming brat anyway?' She halted for a moment under the shadow of a cherry tree. 'That's what I told myself and Casper didn't seem to mind. He never seemed bothered about founding a dynasty. Maybe he's begun to change his mind lately, God knows.'

He brushed against the glossy leaves of a huge old rhododendron bush and cleared his throat. The conversation wasn't getting any easier.

'Sorry,' she said, 'I'm rambling. Back to Linda. I was saying that she idolises Peter, her whole life revolves around him to this day. If anything, she's been even more intense lately. It's her main topic of conversation some days, how badly life's treated him. She was desperate for grandchildren, but her daughter-in-law wasn't the maternal kind. Now Peter's divorced, it's just the two of them together. I daren't say anything that seems critical of him – she might fly off the handle.'

'Listen, she won't want Peter to sour things between you and her. Besides, if she despises Casper as much as you said, the last thing she will want is for her darling son to snitch on you to him.'

Juliet paused by a metal bench. It was smothered in graffiti about the sexual tastes of Noel and Kylie and gleeful quips about the contrasting fortunes of the Liverpool and Everton football clubs. Swallowing hard, she said, 'You're right, of course. It frightens me, though, Harry. I've always been so sure that Casper would never find out about the two of us. Now, even if Peter does manage to keep his mouth shut – I'll never feel safe.'

'This is just a squall. Promise.' He put his arm around her shoulder. There was something oddly comforting in clichés. Perhaps he should have spent more time trawling through soap operas to expand his repertoire.

'Wish I was so sure.' She aimed a kick at the gravel of the pathway, bringing up a flurry of dust. 'Truth is, though, I can't help thinking things will never be the same again. When Casper arrived home last night, I was shaking. Even he noticed, and he's not exactly famous for his sensitivity.'

A pram-pushing mother approached them, a gooey-mouthed infant staggering in her wake. The child leered at Harry.

'Say hello, sweet pea.'

Harry ventured a wary smile. The child responded by allowing her lunch to ooze out of the corners of her mouth. He waved jerkily and hurried on, Juliet following close behind.

'So what did you tell him?'

'Oh, I just said I had a raging headache.' She gave a sour laugh. 'Told him I might be sickening for something, just for good measure. At least he managed to keep his paws off me in bed. He told me he was being considerate, though I wouldn't mind betting his dolly bird in London had worn him out.'

They were strolling past straggly herbaceous borders. There wasn't much colour at this time of year. Cotoneasters poked their branches over the walkways. A few pansies had survived the autumn chills, but so had a scattering of spiky weeds. Over to the right in the inner walled area were a couple of skips full of garden rubbish and a pile of rubble. The bricks in the wall were crumbling; several coping stones had disappeared. Appearances might be deceptive; perhaps the gardeners hadn't abandoned the unequal struggle and an impoverished council hadn't let a lovely place go to rack and ruin. The artistic director from the Tate might have been hired to create an avant-garde ambience of decay and desolation. Very *fin de siècle*.

'So far, he doesn't suspect anything?'

'No, he was in good humour. I wasn't at risk of a smacking, even though I didn't rush into his arms the moment he stepped through the door. At least I've got something to thank his girlfriend for. Plus the government. I gather he's up for a place on a task force, would you believe? He said he'd agreed to let his name go forward. Those were his very words, for God's sake.'

They had reached the perimeter. A curved archway, roofed by a climber's million tiny green leaves, enticed Harry. Slipping his hand in hers, he led her into the tunnel, but after fifty metres they reached a chained gateway dividing the garden from the main road and had to retrace their steps.

'He's offered to put his hand in his pocket over some training initiative. He's buying a chain of residential care homes for the elderly and he's offered to bring a load of young Scousers off the dole to care for them. Aren't the elderly lucky?'

'What's the idea, a maximum security wing for troublesome geriatrics?'

'Oh, it's some kind of scam, of course. I'm never told the details, but I suppose there's some way of washing dirty money by putting it through the books of the homes.' A magpie dropped a piece of bread at their feet. Juliet bent down, picked it up and threw it to a pigeon strutting past the broom hedge. 'His philanthropy is only skin deep. But what do the authorities care? The unemployment figures look good, so does he. Everyone wins.'

'Except for the old people?'

'They're confused, they'll probably bless his name.' She sighed. 'As long as Casper stays in a good mood, I suppose that's something for us to be thankful for.'

They had reached the heart of the garden now. Two battered and empty urns, two headless seated figures in stone. *Decapitated.* He shivered, tried to banish the memory of Carl Symons' corpse.

'And you'll speak to Linda?'

'Maybe.' Her expression was thoughtful.

His thoughts roamed as they walked along the top pathway, glancing back through the gate that led to Wavertree Park. Truanting boys were playing soccer, small children in the distance shrieked as they fooled about in the playground. He felt a touch of drizzle on his cheeks.

'I think you should. She will tell Peter to apologise, everything will be wrapped up nicely.'

'Until the next time he goes on a bender.'

The path curved and he motioned her to join him on a bench. He brushed away the bits of stone and dirt before she sat down, trying to ignore the sickly smell wafting towards them from the litter bins.

'I'm sure there won't be a next time.'

'There's always a next time,' she said.

He didn't drive straight back to the office, knowing he would find it difficult to concentrate on work. Despite what he'd said to Juliet, it was impossible not to dread the prospect of Peter Blackwell, in a drunken fit of bravado, ratting on them to Casper May. And even at the best of times, he often found it difficult to concentrate on work.

A short detour would take him to Nerys Horlock's office. He could turn up on her doorstep, perhaps suggest that they nip out to a café for half an hour. He hadn't had any lunch and his stomach was rumbling. If she wasn't still at court or busy with a client, he could take the opportunity to find out why she had rung him at home the previous evening. The more he thought about it, the stranger it seemed that she had called. They had never socialised together and although they sometimes did battle on behalf of their clients, at present they didn't have any cases on with each other. He could only assume that it was something to do with the death of Carl Symons.

He realised something was wrong as soon as he approached the road where she had her office. A policeman on a motorcycle was parked next to a sign which said *Diversion – Road Closed*. A tape and a row of cones stretched across the road. He followed the arrows pointing him down a street which led in the opposite direction and parked fifty yards down. Even as he climbed out of the car, he was conscious of the churning of his stomach. No longer hunger, he realised, but apprehension.

Avoiding the policeman's eye, he hurried along the pavement. Rain was falling and he almost slipped on the wet slabs. He'd forgotten his umbrella, but it didn't seem to matter. Turning the corner into the adjoining road, he paused to take his bearings. He'd been here once before, to discuss a divorce settlement. Nerys Horlock's office was the last of a small parade of shops. He remembered it as a poky place, susceptible to the smells from a fishmonger next door. Nerys got by with a teenage switchboard girl and Irma, the loyal secretary who had followed her from Symons, Horlock and Young. She ran a tight ship; experience had taught her the need to keep down costs.

He hoped, though, that she hadn't economised on insurance. As his gaze travelled down the row of shops, he saw that fire had blackened the frontages of the last two or three. It wasn't an entirely unfamiliar sight. Inner city Liverpool had its share of arsonists. Nerys's office, he noticed, seemed to be by far the worst affected. The ground floor windows were protected by security grilles but those above had been stoved in and were now covered by temporary sheeting. There was still a smell of burning in the air; the rain hadn't yet washed it away.

He swore. All lawyers dread fire. For all that they have the occasional urge to burn problem files, they know their livelihood is locked inside their filing cabinets. Then again, if it was only Nerys's business that had been destroyed, she might yet have something to be thankful for.

A policeman in a fluorescent wet weather jacket loped towards him as he stood and stared. 'Come on, sir. On your way, if you don't mind. Nothing here for you to see.'

'What's happened?'

'I'd have thought it's pretty obvious, sir. There's been a fire.'

'But Nerys Horlock – is she all right?'

The man's eyes narrowed. 'You know Ms Horlock?'

'I was coming to see her.'

'You're a client? I'm afraid all meetings have been cancelled indefinitely.'

'No, I'm a solicitor. Nerys Horlock rang me yesterday evening. She wanted to talk about something.'

'Yesterday evening?' The man leaned towards him. 'Are you sure about that?'

'Perfectly.'

'And what time would that be?'

'I think she said it was seven o'clock. She was still in the office, planning to work late.'

'Perhaps you'd better have a word with my sergeant, if you don't mind, sir.'

'Has something happened to her?' Harry blinked the raindrops out of his eyes and stared at the policeman. 'Tell me. She's dead, isn't she?'

'Now,' the policeman said, all cordiality wiped from his voice, 'how would you know that?'

Chapter Eleven

'So why do you think she wanted to talk to you?' Eggar asked.

Harry put his elbows on the table and let out a sigh. The bitter taste of police station coffee lingered on his tongue. So far, he wasn't having the best of days. But perhaps to be suspected of a murder he hadn't committed was a lesser evil than coming face to face with Casper May after Peter Blackwell had blown the gaff.

'If I didn't know you better, I'd be thinking you don't believe me, Mitch.'

'You'll be telling me you want to call a solicitor in a minute.'

'Don't bet against it,' Harry said. 'Frankly, this hasn't been the most reassuring conversation I've ever had.'

'Can you wonder?' the detective asked comfortably. 'It really is pretty unfortunate from your point of view. One minute you're chumming up with the wife of a major league villain, the next you're finding the body of an old adversary from the CPS. You give me an explanation so lame it can barely hobble and before I can draw breath, you turn up at the scene when one of your toughest competitors has come to an unpleasant end. I have to ask myself if it's a coincidence – or something else. See how it is, Harry?'

'I take it Nerys *was* murdered?'

'I haven't said that, have I?' Eggar showed his teeth in a mirthless smile. 'You're a lawyer, you ought to be sensitive to the precise use of words. You've been told what's in the statement to the press. Nothing more, nothing less. "The body of a thirty-two-year-old woman has been found following a fire at the office of Liverpool solicitor Nerys Horlock. The police are treating the death as suspicious".'

'Murder it is, then.'

Mitch Eggar folded his arms, said nothing. Time to regain the initiative.

'Was she burned to death – or killed in some other way?'

'Such as?'

Harry swallowed. 'Carl was stabbed in the chest – and decapitated for good measure. With Nerys, was it the same...?'

Eggar was watching him closely. 'What makes you imagine that it might have been?'

'Come on. This isn't your usual patch. Why would you be involved in both inquiries if there wasn't a link between the deaths?'

'Carl Symons and Nerys Horlock were once in partnership together. They're killed within a matter of days of each other. Isn't that enough of a link?'

'Maybe. But you haven't given me an answer. Was her head cut off?'

'All I'll say is this.' The smile had vanished. Harry had never known Eggar's tone so bleak. 'In life, she wasn't such a bad looking woman. In death – not a pretty sight.'

For a few moments both men were silent. They were sitting in a mobile incident room parked across the road from the burned-out building. It was turning into a long afternoon. Outside it was pouring down. Harry could hear the rain slamming down on the roof above them.

'For the record, I didn't kill her. Or Carl. I had no reason to, no reason at all.'

'They were fellow lawyers, both with a reputation for being hard-nosed. The sort who upset other people. Did a legal dispute get out of hand? Maybe they'd given you a rough time in court.'

'If I went around murdering everyone who gave me a rough time in court, the legal profession in Liverpool would be down to single figures by now. And I can think of a few members of the judiciary and tribunal chairmen who'd be keeping the undertaker busy as well. To say nothing of learned counsel.'

Eggar weighed him up, as if called upon to make a tight umpiring decision. 'Let's move on. What do you think Nerys

Horlock wanted to talk to you about? What was so urgent that couldn't wait for the morning?'

'Can't help you. I wish I could. Obviously she wanted to get something off her chest.'

Eggar looked at him curiously. 'You hadn't been screwing her, by any chance?'

'Are you kidding?' Harry didn't know whether to be flattered or appalled. 'She wasn't exactly my type.'

'And what is your type?'

A sexy redhead married to a violent ex-loan shark. He tried out a lazy smile. 'You know, Mitch, I've always had a bit of a soft spot for winsome charm. Hayley Mills, perhaps. Jenny Agutter. Nerys Horlock didn't qualify. She had balls of steel. Not someone to mess around with. And I can promise you, she never showed the slightest interest in me. You may wonder that she was able to resist falling into my arms, but believe it or not, she didn't seem to find it much of a challenge.'

'Yet she rang you,' Eggar persisted. 'Went to the trouble of tracking down your home number. Can't have been business, according to what you told me. So it must have been personal.'

'We'd spoken a couple of times since Carl's death. On the morning after he was killed, I bumped into her in the law courts. Yesterday we had a five-minute conversation at Dale Street. We talked about Carl's death, naturally. It did cross my mind that she was keeping something back.'

'She gave you that impression?'

'Yes. When I found she'd called, I wondered if she'd decided to take me into her confidence after all.'

Eggar cast his eyes to the heavens. 'Doing your detective number again?'

'I found Symons' body, don't forget. It's not entirely bizarre that I wondered who might have killed him – and why.

'Any idea what she wanted to tell you?'

'Been racking my brains. I can only assume it was something to do with Carl. Some secret he'd been trying to hide, maybe.' He spread his arms. 'Not sure. Perhaps she was simply suffering from delayed shock after his death and wanted a shoulder to cry on.'

'Bit odd, though. If the two of you weren't close, why should she choose you?'

'Perhaps she couldn't think of anyone else,' Harry said helplessly. 'She wasn't the kind of woman who had many friends. There had been a couple of affairs that I'd heard gossip about, but nothing that lasted.'

'Tell me more. Did she ever sleep with Symons?'

'Hard to believe she was that desperate. She wasn't blind. As far as I can tell, she always found him physically repulsive. She said as much when I said I'd heard a rumour that Carl and Suki Anwar had been an item. Nerys would have none of it.'

'Suki the prosecutor? That's interesting.' Eggar stroked his chin. 'I suppose Nerys might have been jealous if Suki had supplanted her.'

Harry shrugged. 'The idea never occurred to me. And I still don't think it's likely. Nerys was choosy. She'd much rather live alone than in a relationship that didn't suit her. Above all, I reckon she liked good looks. A few years back, before she set up in partnership, I remember she was seeing a lecturer from the College of Law, a real smoothie. That finished when he emigrated to Canada. A while ago, there was gossip that she'd had a fling with Rick Spendlove. I'm not sure I believed it.'

'Why not?'

'I got the impression it was Rick who put the story about. I wondered if she'd rebuffed him and so he'd decided to get his own back.'

'Do I gather you and he aren't soul mates?'

'He's not my favourite person, I must admit.'

'But he does well with the ladies?'

'Scores more often than Michael Owen.'

'I've heard Spendlove's name. Picked up odd bits from the papers. Doesn't he work for that big firm over at Albert Dock? I keep seeing his photo next to stuff about all the work he does for charity. A lawyer with a heart, it seems.'

Harry scanned the detective's bland expression for irony. 'Let's just say that Rick doesn't believe in doing good by stealth. He lives in a different world from Nerys and me.'

'Business lawyer?'

'Insolvency. Or corporate recovery, as he likes to call it. The legal profession's equivalent of the undertaker, really. Each night he goes to bed, he prays the roof will fall in on the economy.'

'Any day now, he might get lucky. Suppose Nerys did sleep with Spendlove, though. If she dumped him, he might have taken it badly.'

Harry wrinkled his nose. 'I might not be a fan of Rick's, but I can't see him as a killer. Besides, he's had two wives, countless girlfriends. If she did give him the elbow, it would be water off a duck's back.'

'You reckon?'

'Sure. He likes to brag about his favourite chat-up line. Asks a girl if she knows the difference between pizza and oral sex. If she says no, he says, "Fine. Let's do lunch." Believe me, he'd soon have another girl in tow.'

The policeman sniggered. 'Tell me this, then. Was there ever anything between Nerys Horlock and Brett Young?'

'The way he was talking last night, there was no love lost between them. But I don't think that had anything to do with an affair gone wrong. He's a good-looking bloke, but I can't see Nerys mixing work with pleasure.'

'But Young was bitter about the partnership break-up?'

'He used to be a partner in a firm of solicitors. Now he's driving a rusty Sierra round Liverpool in the small hours. Wouldn't you be bitter?'

'I might think I'd begun to move up in the world at last.'

Harry grinned. He was relaxing a little, but in the back of his mind he couldn't forget that this was when Mitch Eggar was at his most dangerous. You could never be completely off guard. Same as in the cricket match; just when you thought the ball that had rapped your pads was swinging away down the legside, he'd give you out and you'd be trudging back to the pavilion.

'Blessing in disguise? I could just go along with that. At least Carl and Nerys gave him a reason to escape the drudgery.'

'You left his place about when? Nine, did you say?'

'More like half past.'

'Where did you go afterwards?'

'I walked straight home, like I said.'

'A fair stretch.'

'I needed the exercise. And to clear my head. By the way, before you ask, I don't have anyone to vouch for me. I did see one of my ex-clients near the Cathedral, but he was fully occupied with a business transaction and I'm pretty sure he didn't see me. Besides, he's a black pimp with convictions for dealing in drugs, so I guess you might not regard him as an entirely reliable witness.'

'I hope you're not implying prejudice,' Mitch Eggar said with pleasant menace.

'Perish the thought. I'm sure you'd listen to him with an open mind and then decide impartially that he was a lying toe-rag. So what it comes down to is this. I have no alibi for either of the killings.'

'Looks bad.' Eggar gave a thoughtful nod. 'Lots of detectives in my shoes would lock you up, you realise? Just on the off chance you were guilty.'

'Sure. And if I'm innocent, it's one more brief out of the way, so who cares?'

'You get my drift.'

'Yeah, but trouble is, you don't believe I murdered anyone, do you? Plus, you don't have any evidence. Not a shred. And the last thing you want is to let me have the satisfaction of sueing for wrongful arrest.'

Eggar did his impersonation of an Easter Island statue. 'Face it, you're a suspect.'

'And Brett Young? He hasn't an alibi, either.'

'Careless. Maybe you and your mate were in it together.'

'One thing you need to face is this, Mitch. Plenty of people might have wanted to kill Carl. Nerys too. They never exactly courted popularity. Have you checked out disgruntled ex-clients of Symons, Horlock and Young? Surely that's where you should be concentrating your inquiries.'

'Don't worry, we haven't overlooked them.' Mitch Eggar bared his teeth. 'No stone unturned, eh?'

'Another thing. I wouldn't call Brett a mate. We're acquaintances rather than friends.'

Eggar narrowed his eyes. 'Putting clear blue water between the two of you, eh? You sound like the Prime Minister when he finds a member of the cabinet has been a bit naughty. Think Young might be guilty, then?'

'Just making sure you don't get the wrong impression.'

'You'd be surprised how often the wrong impression turns out to be dead right. We'll see. Okay, that's it for now.'

'So I'm not under arrest?'

'Not yet.' As Harry got up to go, Eggar said, 'Just one last question.'

'Oh for Christ's sake. Not the Columbo technique.'

'Always admired that show. Taught me a lot.'

'Your shabby raincoat is one of your proudest possessions?'

'Don't push it, Harry. What I wanted to ask is this. I came across Nerys Horlock in court perhaps two or three times over the last few years, that's all. I didn't know her. You did. What sort of woman was she?'

'I told you before, we were never close.'

'Sure, but what was she like?'

Harry considered. 'Tough lawyer. Ruthless. I can see that she and Spendlove did have a couple of things in common. She liked being a crusader. Muriel Scawfell raves about the way Nerys stitched up her old man. Not much private life to speak of, I shouldn't think. If Rick's a sex addict, she's a workaholic. She came from a family with lots of kids and not much money. I think she was proud of her achievements, but somehow they'd distanced her from her background. She'd never found anything to replace it, so she threw herself into her work. I suppose that's what she had in common with Carl. Lawyering had become a substitute for living.'

'Fate worse than death, eh?'

'I can think of worse.'

And in his mind Harry could not help conjuring up a stomach-churning picture of Nerys Horlock's severed head, wearing her trademark sardonic grin

Brett Young was waiting for him when he arrived back at Fenwick Court. He was in reception, reading an out of date copy of *Making a Will Won't Kill You* and sipping a cup of tea, apparently sobered up and oblivious to the admiring glances of Suzanne. Harry could not recall the last time she had made a client of his a drink of any kind. She'd even abandoned her book on Feng Shui. Definitely smitten.

'You're late,' she said as he nodded at Brett and went to pick up his phone messages. 'Mr Crusoe wanted to know where you were.'

'Tell him I've been helping the police with their inquiries.'

She gave him a thrilled look before adding, 'And Mr Young has been here for the past twenty minutes. He doesn't have an appointment, but I assured him that if he was willing to wait, you'd be happy to see him.'

'Sure. Thanks for looking after him.'

'My pleasure,' she said, her cheeks reddening. Harry gaped: a blush from Suzanne was on a par with a visit from Halley's Comet. The phone buzzed and she glared at it for an instant before answering. 'Crusoe and Devlin ... yes, he's just walked in ... no, no, at least I don't think so.'

She pressed 'hold' and said in a gleeful shock-horror tone, 'It's a Ms Anwar. Seems to think you may have been arrested.'

He snatched up the handset. 'Suki. This is Harry Devlin. Why do you...'

She sounded rattled. 'Sorry. But there are all kinds of rumours flying around here. Nerys Horlock has been found dead and someone just said they'd been told Mitchell Eggar had picked you up.'

'Wrong end of the stick. I turned up at Nerys's office and Mitch took the opportunity to ask me a few questions about Nerys, that's all.'

'What sort of questions?'

Harry glanced at Suzanne. She was hanging on his every word. Brett too had abandoned any pretence of reading about the rules of testamentary disposition. 'Look, it's a bit difficult to talk now.'

'I understand ... I don't suppose we could get together later? It's Friday night, I often finish up at the Maritime Bar.'

A trendy place on the Strand, much frequented by the city's yuppy professionals. 'It's on my way home. I can drop in there once I've cleared my desk.' The latter phrase appealed to him so much that he couldn't help repeating it. 'Once I've cleared my desk.' Well, a man could dream.

'Marvellous. I'll see you there.'

He put down the receiver and gave Brett a sheepish grin. 'Sorry to keep you. But I'm glad to see you've been looked after.'

'Perfectly,' he said, handing his cup back to Suzanne with an artless smile that reduced her to something like a special effect from *The Blob*. 'Thanks very much.'

'Any time. Really, any time at all. See you again, I hope.'

'Hope so.'

Brett's gift, Harry thought, lay in his lack of self-consciousness where women were concerned. Whereas Rick's charm was constantly rehearsed, Brett's was entirely natural. No wonder he'd been able to hook Andrea Gibbs.

Once they were in his office with the door closed, Harry sat down in a chair facing Brett on the client's side of the desk and said, 'I take it you've heard the news?'

Brett nodded. 'On the radio. I guess Nerys is the dead woman, but they didn't name her. Do you know anything more?'

'I've just come back from a session with Detective Inspector Eggar. And yes, she's dead. The case is being linked with the Carl Symons murder, but I don't know much more. Eggar plays his cards close to his chest, as you would expect. He wouldn't tell me how she died.'

'When did it happen?'

'The fire took hold some time after ten o'clock, as far as I can gather.'

'I heard sirens,' Brett said. 'Of course, I had no idea Nerys's office was on fire.'

'You heard them from your flat? Surely the fire engines didn't pass right by? It's not on the main route.'

'No, no. After you left, I decided to go for a walk, clear my head. I was overwrought, as well as pissed. Speaking of which, I'm sorry I gave you a hard time.'

'Forget it.'

'Listen, the things I said about Andrea – can you forget them, too?'

'Sure.'

'I was upset. Seeing her with Spendlove hurt. I wasn't thinking straight.'

'Uh-huh. So – you went for a walk?'

'Yeah, I wasn't far away from Nerys's place when I heard the fire engines.'

'I see.'

'Don't say it like that. I was walking round aimlessly, getting the booze out of my system. Trying not to get even more uptight about Andrea. I thought about ringing her at work and trying to patch things up. But in the end I was afraid to call. As for Nerys, I didn't give her a second thought, let alone kill her.'

Harry fiddled with the papers on his desk, not looking at Brett. 'Why were you afraid?'

Brett breathed out. 'It's just that – oh, doesn't matter.'

'Have you been in touch with her today?'

'No.'

'I told you last night, it's crazy to be jealous of Rick. You know what he's like. My guess is, Andrea wouldn't give him the time of day. Why don't you give her a call now?'

'No! Not now.'

'What's wrong?'

'It's just that ... oh, let's just say I don't want to have to crawl to her, beg her forgiveness for what I said last night.'

Harry frowned. Brett's excuse didn't ring true, but he let it pass. 'Think about it. You have enough problems without making them worse. For a start, you're like me. A bit lacking as far as alibis are concerned.'

'I was wondering,' Brett said slowly. 'Maybe we could do ourselves both a bit of good. If we said that you were with me until eleven, say, it would put us in the clear. Save the police from wasting time on us when they could be tracking down the real culprit.'

Harry gave him a sorrowful look. 'Not a good idea. Even if it was, you're too late. I told the police I left you at half nine. Time enough to put us both in the frame.'

'Oh fucking hell! Thanks very much!'

Brett jumped out of his chair and began to pace around the room. 'I wouldn't mind betting that they're battering their way into my place even as we speak. I can't go back there now. I'll have to keep driving.'

'You're overreacting. Of course they want to talk to you. Mitch Eggar isn't stupid. You're a possible suspect. Me too, come to that. But they're not going to bang up a solicitor without plenty of hard evidence. A claim for damages for wrongful imprisonment would bring tears to the eyes of the police authority treasurer. I reckon we're safe as long as we don't do anything stupid. Like doing a moonlight flit.'

'That's what you reckon, is it?' Brett came up close to him, standing there with his hands on hips. 'You're satisfied that I'm innocent?'

'Aren't you?'

Brett's face turned crimson. He waved an arm angrily, knocking over a pile of files. 'For Christ's sake! Whose side are you on!' he shouted.

Harry stood up. 'I take it that means "yes"? Then why don't you stop acting as if you have something to hide?'

The door was flung open. 'Everything all right in here?' Jim demanded from the corridor.

'Fine, fine,' Harry said hastily.

As Jim stepped into the room, he saw Brett and raised bushy eyebrows. 'Hello, old son. I wondered what was happening when I heard the raised voices. You're not consulting my partner for legal advice, by any chance?'

'He's not that desperate,' Harry said. 'Things are a bit fraught this afternoon, that's all.'

'So I gather. What's this Suzanne tells me about you and the police?'

'I decided to pay Nerys Horlock a visit. Only one drawback. She was dead.'

Jim swore. 'You pick your moments, don't you? What's the story?'

Harry ran through what he had gleaned from Mitch Eggar. 'He's playing his cards close to his chest. Can't blame him for that. She may have died during an arson attack. My bet is, she was killed first and the fire started to cover up the crime.'

'Then why were you given a grilling?'

'Brett and I were together last night. But I left his place before Nerys was killed.'

'Wonderful,' Jim said heavily.

'No-one could seriously suspect Harry,' Brett snapped.

'I'd better take that as a compliment,' Harry said.

'You see, it's different for me. Why beat about the bush? It's too late for that. I hated them both. They ruined my life.' Brett expelled a breath. 'Fact is, I'm glad they're dead.'

'Can't fault you for honesty,' Jim said, 'but if I were you, old son, I'd be a tad more discreet when the police interview you.'

'I'm not sure about talking to the police,' Brett said, running his hand wildly through his hair. 'I don't want to find myself fitted up.'

'Come on now,' Harry said. 'That isn't going to happen.'

'You can be so fucking naïve at times! Of course it could happen. You're a lawyer, you've seen what goes on, just as much as I have.' Brett wagged a finger at Harry. 'I'll tell you something. It isn't going to happen to me. I've been screwed around already more than enough for one lifetime.'

146

With that, he strode quickly out of the room. Harry made as if to follow him, but his partner laid a restraining hand on his arm. 'Let him go. He'll calm down soon enough.'

'You think so?'

'He always had a temper. The slightest thing could set him off. So what on earth were you and he up to together last night?'

'He took me for a ride in his taxi.' Harry grinned at his partner's expression of bafflement. 'Didn't you know? He's decided to turn an honest penny, so he's jacked in the law and become a cabbie.'

'After our last meeting at the bank, I can see the temptation.'

'Me too. I bumped into him after he'd just had a row with his girlfriend. Who happens to be Andrea Gibbs, by the way. Ever come across her? Slinky, dark-haired girl. Used to work for Symons, Horlock and Young. Now she's chained to a telephone hot-line over at Queen's Dock. He offered me a lift, we got talking and finished up at his place. You're right, of course, he is a twitchy bugger. He almost throttled me when I teased him about her.'

'You think he could have killed Carl and Nerys, then?'

Harry rubbed the bristles on his chin. 'I suppose the answer has to be yes. And he's bound to be the prime suspect so far as the police are concerned.'

'You don't sound altogether convinced.'

'Correct. There's another way of looking at all this, isn't there?'

'Which is?'

'Two of Brett's former partners have been killed in the space of forty-eight hours. If he isn't the culprit, he might just be the next victim.'

Chapter Twelve

'I can't believe she's dead,' Suki Anwar said.

In the hubbub of the Maritime Bar, Harry had to lean close to hear her low voice. His bar stool wobbled dangerously and she put a hand on it to steady him. He was conscious of her proximity, of her perfume.

The place was packed with people in suits. This was where the city's young professionals came after a hard week's fee-earning to spend a slice of their profit shares on over-priced Harvey Wallbangers. In one corner, a group of stockbrokers were chortling about an insider trading scam, in another half a dozen partners from Boycott Duff were toasting the liquidation of one of the city's oldest ship repair companies. Three hundred people out of work; a dozen smaller suppliers out of pocket and on their uppers; another slice of the city's history gone for ever. But the legal fees would pay a year's alimony for the partners' ex-wives. Harry could hear Rick Spendlove braying with laughter, telling old jokes about the sure signs of an insolvent company: personalised number plates on the directors' Mercs, an aquarium in the reception area, a flagpole in the car park.

'Did you know her well?'

She withdrew her hand, gave him a wary look. 'I suppose you could say that we were good friends. At least, once upon a time.'

'You had a disagreement?'

'It was silly. Something and nothing.' She said it so quickly that he guessed she was underplaying the extent of the rift. 'I suppose we were both to blame. And now we can never make it up. I'll always regret that.'

'No point in regretting the things we left unsaid,' Harry said, more brusquely than he had intended.

She put her glass down on the counter and gave him an enquiring look. 'Are you thinking about your wife? She was murdered, wasn't she? Someone told me. I'm sorry. It must have been dreadful for you.'

'I survived.'

Her gaze became intense. He felt as if she were trying to hypnotise him. 'Yes,' she said softly, 'but you've never found anyone else, have you? Not long-term. The way I heard it, your wife left you a couple of years before she died. A long time ago, but you've never lived with anyone since then.'

He looked away for a moment. Even in the overheated bar, he felt a chill on his spine. 'You've been checking up on me.'

'Don't be cross,' she said. 'We'd bumped into each other in court on the odd occasion, but I knew very little about you. When I heard you were the one who discovered Carl's body, naturally I was curious. So I asked around and learned a few things, okay?'

'Such as?'

'Seems like you're a dangerous person to know. I gather you have a habit of getting involved with murders.'

'Everyone tells me I'm too inquisitive for my own good. This afternoon, I realised they were right.'

'What happened?'

'I popped over to Nerys's office hoping to have a word with her. Before I knew what was happening, I found myself under interrogation.'

'The office grapevine has been working overtime today. We were still struggling to take in the news of Carl's death when someone got word that Nerys had been murdered.'

'I suppose there's no doubt it was murder?'

'The police seem pretty sure, by all accounts. But they're playing their cards very close to their chest. They don't trust us, you know. We're supposed to be on the same side, but you'd never guess it.'

'They think you're too soft, eh?'

'Of course. We insist on evidence before we launch into a prosecution. Gut feel isn't enough. You might think Carl was pretty hard-nosed, but even he didn't take enough cases to court so far as the police were concerned. I don't think they shed too many tears when he was killed.'

'Did anyone?'

'If they did, they composed themselves soon enough,' she said grimly. 'Tell you something. They don't trust us on this one. I don't think they're giving us the full story about Carl's murder.'

'Which was why you wanted to pump me last night?'

She laughed nervously. 'Oh dear. Was I so obvious?'

'Tell you the truth, I did wonder why you called me this afternoon, if not to quiz me about Nerys's death. Do you want to check whether I can tell you something the police are keeping quiet?'

She hung her head. 'I'm sorry.'

'No problem. I'm sure you've already been told, I'm a nosey parker myself. It'd be hypocritical for me to complain that you're asking questions about things that don't concern you. I do it constantly.'

'I wouldn't say Carl's death doesn't concern me.' She was striving for a tone of lawyerly detachment, but not quite achieving it. 'We worked together, don't forget. I reported to him. As for Nerys, like I said, she'd been a friend.'

'How did you meet?'

'Oh, in court one day, I suppose.' She made a vague gesture with her hands. No rings on her fingers, he noticed. 'Does it matter?'

'Maybe not. I can't help you much, though. Mitch Eggar told me as little as possible and, frankly, my main concern was to persuade him that I had nothing to do with either death. I don't have an alibi in either case, you see.'

'Careless of you.' She smiled, then asked with an elaborate lack of concern that he found unconvincing, 'How was she killed?'

'Mitch wouldn't say. There's obviously something he's keen to keep back.'

She nodded. 'Just like the Symons murder.'

He wondered whether to mention the decapitation, but decided to hold his tongue. No need for her to risk nightmares about what had happened to her erstwhile friend Nerys Horlock. And, it occurred to him, it was possible that she knew already, or had at least heard rumours. Perhaps the purpose of her questions was simply to test the extent of his own knowledge. But why would she want to do that?

'You'd better watch out,' she said, teasing him with mock solemnity. 'The killer might think you know more than you admit. Has it crossed your mind that you might be next?'

He said slowly, 'You think there will be another victim?'

She gave an artless smile. 'You're the murder expert, you tell me. But one thing seems clear. Two solicitors dead in the space of a couple of days. Looks as though someone out there doesn't like us.'

'Remember, those two people used to be partners in the same firm.'

She blinked at him. 'You think that's significant?'

'No idea. But if I were Brett Young, I'd be looking over my shoulder.'

'He had some sort of breakdown, didn't he? Nerys used to say he brought all his problems on himself. She wasn't sympathetic.'

'Sympathy wasn't something Nerys was famous for.'

Suki frowned. 'She wore a lot of armour, but she could be kind. Trouble is, she always knew best, had to do things her way. To her, Brett Young was a weakling. I even wonder if...'

'Yes?'

'Oh, it's nothing.'

'Go on. Tell me.' He was sure she wanted to.

'I was only going to say that I'd thought of Brett as a likely victim. Then it crossed my mind that it's just as logical to regard him as a possible culprit.'

'I'm sure that has already occurred to the police. I was with Brett in my office when you called this afternoon.'

She stared. 'You and he are friends?'

'I wouldn't say that. But I bumped into him last night after the Legal Group meeting. He was intending to pick up Andrea Gibbs. You know her?'

Suki nodded. 'She trained with Nerys and Brett, didn't she? A strange girl. Nerys said there was something spooky about her, nicknamed her Lady Macbeth.'

'They didn't hit it off, then?'

'Nerys was so focused on her own career, she never had much time for anyone who wasn't. Andrea was very bright, according to Nerys. If you wanted to know the chapter and verse of legislation, she was fine. But wasn't it John Mortimer who said that what you need to succeed in the law is common sense and clean fingernails? Nerys said she was a dreamer, spent too much of her time with her head in books. I didn't know she was still seeing Brett.'

'For all I know, it may be finished after last night. They had a row.'

'What's Brett doing now?'

'Driving a private hire car.'

'Jesus.'

'Quite a career change, yes? But I'm interested in why you think Brett might have hated Nerys so much that he would want to murder her.'

'She once told me that she didn't have a conscience,' Suki whispered. Her eyes were downcast. With so much noise all around, he had to move closer to her to be able to hear the words. 'She used to boast about it, but it wasn't true. We all – know when we've done wrong, don't we?'

He wondered what was on her mind. 'I think so, yes.'

'I'm sure she felt guilty about Brett. When their partnership broke up, she sided with Carl Symons. Much as she despised him, she thought he had a better business brain than Brett. Which wouldn't have been difficult, from what she told me.'

'She and Carl stitched Brett up, didn't they? He took on the major liabilities of the firm. They walked away and lived to appear in court another day.'

Suki frowned. 'I don't know the details. If you've been talking to Brett, remember he's not exactly impartial.'

'Sure, but what he told me isn't far off the mark, is it?'

'Maybe not. Nerys and Carl hadn't earned much, but they weren't ruined and they were able to put it down to experience.'

'Leaving Brett bankrupt.'

'Nerys realised Brett had a raw deal. Of course, you could say it was his own fault. Everything that happened was perfectly legal.'

'And your theory is that he resented her – and Carl – so much that he killed them in revenge?'

Suki shrugged. 'Nerys used to say he was always a bit strange. He was obsessed with the idea of being a solicitor. The status meant so much to him. God knows why. All I do know is that I can't think of a better explanation for the killings. Can you?'

'Talking murder, are we?' Rick Spendlove demanded. 'All right, then, Harry, you're the amateur sleuth. Whodunit?'

Harry had noticed Rick elbowing his way over to them. He nudged people aside with the same disdain he'd shown when shrugging off the tackles in his rugger days. And he hadn't spilled a drop of his gin and tonic. Now he was studying the curve of Suki's bosom with an interest apparently undiminished by her rebuff of the previous evening.

'You've heard about Nerys?' Harry asked.

'Too right. Amazing, eh?' Rick hiccupped. It was barely seven o'clock, but already he was talking loudly and Harry saw Suki wince as he breathed alcohol all over her. 'I mean, who would have dared to murder Cruella herself? Plenty of people thought about doing her in over the years, I'm sure of that. But who would have the courage to go through with it? Extraordinary.'

'She's dead,' Suki hissed. 'Why don't you shut your big mouth?'

'Oh, excuse me,' Rick said loudly. 'Put my foot in it, have I? *Mea culpa*, as presumably they say in Bootle magistrates'. I certainly didn't mean to offend the lovely Ms Anwar.'

She stood up. 'Thanks for talking to me, Harry. But I'd better be going before I say something I regret.'

Rick put a hand on her wrist and treated her to a broad smile. 'Hey, no need to be like that. Don't run off. Let me make it up to you. What would you like to drink?'

She jerked his hand away. 'Get your grubby paw off me, you shit.'

'Now, now.' Rick swayed slightly. 'No need to get personal, darling. After all, you know what they say about people who live in glass houses.'

'What do you mean?' she demanded.

'Leave it, Suki,' Harry said. 'He's had a skinful, he doesn't know what he's saying.'

'You don't think so?' Rick asked. He put his glass down on the table and wagged his finger in Harry's face. 'Listen, matey, I could tell you a thing or two about your lady friend.'

'Look, Rick. In the nicest possible way, why don't you piss off home and dry out?'

'The knight in shining armour, are we? What's the idea, fancy getting into her knickers, do you? Well, take a tip from me. Keep an eye out for the tattoo on her bum.' Rick grinned broadly. A crowd was beginning to gather round them and, as ever, he was relishing the chance to be centre stage. 'A single rose, very charming, I believe, though I haven't had the pleasure of checking it out myself. Mind you, hope springs eternal.'

Suki picked up the glass of gin and tonic and threw the contents into Rick's face. 'You fucking bastard! I wish it was acid!'

Rick staggered backwards and lost his balance. As Harry watched, paralysed by dismay, Suki stood over Rick and spat on his face. As the gin and saliva trickled down his cheek, she uttered a choking sob and pushed her way with blind fury through the forest of suits in the direction of the door to the street.

Harry was torn between chasing after her and kicking a man whilst he was down. Since he'd had much less to drink than Rick, he discarded both options and, bending down, began to haul the other man to his feet.

'Oh, Jesus,' Rick moaned, wiping his face with his sleeve. 'The fucking cow.'

Harry seized him by the shoulder. 'Don't you think you asked for it? You could do worse than take my advice and call it a night.'

'He's right,' one of Rick's partners muttered. 'You've made yourself look a right bloody arsehole. Here we are, spending a king's ransom on publicity and you go round picking fights with black women. Talk about a sodding own goal!'

'Better find him a taxi,' someone said as Rick began to mumble an incoherent plea in mitigation. 'The sooner we get him home the better. We don't want the legal press getting hold of this. They'd have a field day.'

'Before you go,' Harry said, not releasing his grip. 'What was that about a tattoo?'

Rick scowled at him. 'It's perfectly true, you know. Check out the left cheek of her backside, if you don't believe me.'

'You have it on good authority, then?'

'I do. Although the poor devil's dead.' Tottering slightly, he leaned over to whisper in Harry's ear. 'Between you and me, I wouldn't be surprised if she turned out to be the person who killed him.'

'Who are you talking about?'

155

'Carl Symons, of course.' Rick looked Harry in the eye, then placed a finger to his lips. 'But he passed it on to me in strict confidence. Don't tell anyone I told you.'

Two of his colleagues put their arms under his shoulders and began to help him away. Harry shook his head in disgust and followed at a safe distance. As he edged towards the door, he caught sight of a familiar face in the group of people peering at the scene with fascination.

'A paragraph for tomorrow's paper?' Harry asked. 'High flying lawyer disgraces himself in wine bar?'

'Stories like that are two-a-penny,' Ken Cafferty confided. 'You could write 'em every Friday night.'

'What are you up to here, then?'

'Picking up a bit of background colour on the late Nerys Horlock. A little bird tells me that you turned up at her office this very afternoon. Right?'

Harry nodded. 'Bad timing. The story of my life. So what do you make of it all?'

'Tell you one thing I've discovered. Ms Horlock didn't have many admirers amongst her fellow solicitors. Or are you going to start singing her praises?'

'She never courted popularity. If you wanted someone to fight for you in court, Nerys would have been a good choice. She took no prisoners.'

'Folk tell me her nickname was Cruella.'

'Bestowed on her by a defeated opponent, I dare say.'

'Or someone she sent a hefty bill.'

They moved out into the cold night air. A few yards away, Rick Spendlove was vomiting into the gutter while one of his colleagues waved frantically at an approaching black cab.

Ken shook his head and murmured, 'By the way, you might have told me that Carl Symons' head was cut off.'

Harry stared at him. 'Who said it was?'

'Don't act soft. I told Mitch Eggar, the truth's like a tail-end batsman. It always gets out sooner or later.'

'Eggar told me to say nothing about the crime scene. I've been in enough hot water not to want to upset him without good reason.'

'You don't seriously think they suspect you of killing Symons and Horlock?'

'No, but...'

'How long have we known each other? You can't fool me. I'd bet a month's salary that you're as keen to figure out what's going on as I am. Headless chickens are one thing, headless lawyers quite another. So why not put your cards on the table? I might even do the same.'

'So someone in the police has been talking out of turn?'

Ken smiled amiably. 'I always look after my sources.'

'Who tell you – what?'

'That Symons was decapitated. Horlock too.'

Harry closed his eyes. 'Shit.'

'Can't have been a pretty sight you saw in that cottage,' Ken said softly.

'I didn't like Symons,' Harry muttered. 'Nerys and I weren't exactly friends, either. But I wouldn't have wished that death upon anyone.'

'It's not just the beheading, either,' Ken said. 'I'm told that Nerys was – stabbed.'

'Like Symons,' Harry said slowly. 'He was stabbed in the chest.'

'That's right. Any idea about the weapon which killed him?'

Harry leaned against a lamp-post for support as he cast his mind back to the horrors of the scene in the cottage by the river. 'None. Does it matter?'

Ken beamed. 'Might do. You see, I'm led to believe that both the killings were pretty much identical. In each case the victim was beheaded – but there's something else. The weapon's not been found, but the word is that little slivers of wood have been found in the chest wounds. Perhaps chippings from a wooden stave, the sort you'd have to drive into a body with a hammer or a mallet. You see what it means?'

'The police are hunting for a homicidal handyman?'

'Be serious.'

'Listen, pal, if you'd seen what I've seen, you'd have had enough of being serious.'

'All right. Anyway, about what's happened?'

'Tell me.'

'Both victims had a stake driven through the heart. It's just the same way you might kill a vampire.'

Chapter Thirteen

Sprawled across his sofa a couple of hours later, Harry pointed his remote control at the television set like an absent-minded gunman. He zapped from channel to channel, trying to banish his mental image of Nerys Horlock's headless corpse. His stomach was empty and hurting. He hadn't eaten since breakfast, but he was sure that if he tried even a biscuit he would throw up.

He wondered if she had known her killer, what her final thoughts had been. Had there been bewilderment, terror, a stunned sense of betrayal? He hadn't known her well, but he prayed that she hadn't suffered for long, that death had at least come quickly for her.

Ken was testing out whether there was any mileage in his vampire theory. It amused him and it was just possible – although Harry, a journosceptic, doubted it – that he even thought there was something in it. According to Ken, the shattered mirror in the Harbour Master's Cottage offered corroboration. Vampires don't like looking-glasses; they have no reflections. Symons and Horlock might have been victims of a deranged vampire-fixated sadist who prowled Merseyside by night and murdered innocent people in brutally ritualistic fashion.

'You know what? We could be talking about a signature killer here.'

No question, his cheeks had been *glowing*. It was the sort of story that might sell papers, lots of them. Yet for all his glee, he wasn't confident that the time had come to run it. The police were holding information back, that was certain, and Ken owed them too many favours to want to antagonise them without good reason. Better to gamble on holding off for the time being, whilst he ferreted around for hard evidence about what had actually happened to Nerys. Ken had no intention of getting egg on his face if he could help it. It didn't matter that he couldn't prove the truth of his theory, but if it was obviously ridiculous, he didn't want to face mockery from the crime team who worked for the city's other major newspaper. He'd heard a whisper that they had their sights set on Brett Young as the prime suspect, but the libel lawyers had so far vetoed publishing even the slightest hint that Brett was in the frame. Ken was pinning his hopes on Brett's innocence, but he wasn't ready to gamble his reputation on it.

At first Harry had scoffed at Ken's guesswork, making lazy jokes about bats in the belfry. For him, vampires belonged in lurid B-movies, ludicrous but enjoyable. The mountains of Transylvania were a long way from Toxteth. But now it was late and he was alone in his flat, Ken's fantasy did not seem quite so childish. He recalled, too, that when he had walked into Symons' home, he'd been aware of cooking smells. Thinking back, he'd probably detected a few whiffs of garlic. Just as well he hadn't mentioned it to Ken. He'd probably have wanted to hold the front page.

Harry swallowed a mouthful of black coffee. He hated murder, but it fascinated him to the point of obsession. Murder had robbed him of the only woman, at least since his long dead mother, to whom he had ever said, 'I love you.' Yet he had not been able to rest until he'd learned the truth as to why Liz had died. He wasn't a masochist, he wasn't simply playing games. The need to understand what drove a man or woman to kill their fellow human beings was an urge he couldn't resist, even though he knew that the answers to his questions were never good enough, that the motives he uncovered could not suffice to justify the snuffing out of a life before its time.

He glanced at the screen. In ten minutes, BBC 2 would be screening a film about American law students, *The Paper Chase*. When he'd first seen it, he'd decided that even though he still bore the emotional scars of struggling through his exams at Chester Law College, it could all have been much worse if he'd made it to Harvard Law School. While he waited, he segued from a chat show about child abuse to an erotic melodrama set in Leytonstone. Finally he took refuge in the regional news bulletin.

Of course it was a mistake. The newscaster was already talking about the fire and Nerys Horlock's death. There followed a shot of the scene outside the incident room. A fresh-faced reporter in an over-large anorak was standing on the pavement, doing justice to the gravity of the item by adopting a tense facial expression and staccato delivery style. He said that the cause of death had not yet been revealed. Nor were police commenting on a possible link between the case and the murder earlier in the week of one of Ms Horlock's former partners. Mitch Eggar's face suddenly appeared, wearing a solemn rehearsed-for-TV expression.

'It's early days yet. We are pursuing a number of lines of inquiry as a matter of urgency. Of course we ask any member of the public who might have information pertaining to the fire and the death of Ms Horlock to come forward without delay.'

Then on to the next piece: something about the challenges posed by an ageing population. Harry let out a sigh. It was time to escape from reminders of the killings and of the possibility that if Mitch Eggar and company didn't move swiftly, there might be more deaths. Whoever was responsible was not in rational mood. Neither Carl nor Nerys were easy people, but what could justify the savagery they had suffered?

'...to a company owned by local businessman and philanthropist Casper May.'

The jolt was as sharp as if he had touched an electric cable. The newscaster had been saying something about the old people's homes that Juliet had mentioned.

A new face filled the screen. Strong jaw, dark penetrating eyes. The nose had once been broken and imperfectly reset and the make-up people hadn't quite managed to camouflage the scars that acne had left on his cheeks. Thick hair, turning grey, curled on to the shoulders of his slickly tailored jacket. The smile on his face was like a cheery logo chalked on to a granite tombstone. A caption read: *Casper May, chairman of Third Age Care.*

'We offer a new concept in compassionate elder care,' he said. His voice was a rich bass and he spoke with the confidence of one unaccustomed to contradiction. Harry was almost persuaded that Casper believed what he was saying. 'In partnership with the public sector agencies, we can make sure that all those senior citizens who come to stay with us enjoy the comfort and attention they deserve.'

Then it was time for news that a football manager had been sacked. If that counted as news. Harry switched off the sound. His skin was covered in gooseflesh. It had been scary to see Casper May in close up, as chilling as if his lover's husband had broken into his living-room.

For the thousandth time he asked himself why Juliet stayed with the man and for the thousandth time he realised that if he ever learned the answer, he would not like it. Suppose Peter Blackwell didn't hold his tongue. Casper was unlikely to extend his solicitude to Juliet and the man with whom she had betrayed him.

Harry shifted uncomfortably on the sofa. He'd never seen Juliet as worried as she had been at Wavertree. He didn't believe she was the type to panic, but he'd never seen her under pressure before. People did strange things when they were trapped in a corner. As the credits for *The Paper Chase* finally slid on to the screen, his thoughts were far from Harvard, far even from the burned-out office of Nerys Horlock. He couldn't stop thinking about Casper and the need to make sure that he never learned the truth.

The doorbell woke him the next morning. At first he buried himself under his duvet, hoping that the noise would simply go away. It must be a mistake. No-one in their right mind ever called at this time. He'd stumbled to bed at one o'clock, exhausted as much from lack of food as from the lateness of the hour.

The bell kept shrilling. A memory crawled into his groggy mind of an occasion when he had received an equally insistent summons – that morning he would never forget, when a pair of detectives had come to tell him that Liz was dead. Perhaps Mitch Eggar was at the door. He might have dreamed up a reason to ask more questions. He groaned and glanced at the clock. Half six on Saturday. So much for his customary lie-in. Policemen never went away. Better get it over with. Whatever it was.

He shrugged on a dressing-gown and headed for the door. As he bent towards the spyhole, it crossed his mind that his visitor might be someone else altogether. Within the past few days a killer had called at Carl Symons' cottage, had paid a visit to Nerys Horlock's office. Might that same person now be here at Empire Dock?

The face he saw through the spyhole was pallid and framed by long black hair. As he stared into her green eyes, he relaxed. Impossible to believe that Carl and Nerys had been stabbed and decapitated by this small, skinny woman.

'Hello, Andrea,' he said as he opened the door. 'What brings you here?'

Andrea Gibbs was wearing a long dark coat, but that didn't disguise the fact that her whole body was shaking. Her voice faltered when she asked if she could come in. He moved aside and she stumbled into the hallway. He thought she was about to lose her footing and he put a hand on her shoulder to check her fall.

'I'm sorry ...' she began. She eased free of him, as if in an effort to regain her dignity, but then her face crumpled and he saw tears well up.

'The lounge is through there,' he said quickly. 'Sit yourself down and let me make you a coffee. It'll do us both good.'

He padded into the kitchen and plugged in the filter machine. Glancing back into the living-room, he saw her pacing around, as if she were unable to keep still. From the frown on her face he guessed she was trying to make up her mind about something. The search for clean mugs diverted him for a few moments and then he heard the door in the next room closing softly. He looked again. She had vanished.

He raced out and saw her at the other end of the corridor, waiting by the lifts. He hurried towards her, trying not to imagine what the neighbours would say if they saw him bare-legged and obviously semi-naked under the gown, haring after a distressed young woman. He could sense her fear. Catching up with her, he reached out and touched her wrist. Her skin was so cold that he jerked his hand away in surprise.

'Where are you going?'

The faintest touch of colour appeared in her cheeks. 'I'm sorry. I should never have come here, disturbing you so early in the morning. It was a mistake. Unforgivable.'

'Listen, it's too late to run out now. You've already dragged me out of bed. Come back and tell me what's bothering you. My coffee's not so terrible.'

The lift doors opened. She hesitated, then said, 'You're right. I owe you that.'

He led her back, careful not to brush against her. The chill of her flesh had startled him. Having hung up her coat, guided her into a chair and ascertained that she took neither milk nor sugar, he brought in two steaming mugs and settled himself on the sofa, biding his time until she began to feel more comfortable.

She sipped at the drink, concentrating on it, not lifting her eyes. He remembered the call she had made to his office. At last he had the chance to discover what had prompted it and why, abruptly, she had hung up on him.

'You've been working?' he asked eventually. She was casually dressed, in jersey and jeans, but that signified nothing. In her job, she wasn't on display to the clients; she was no more than a voice at the other end of a telephone.

'At Brunswick Dock, that's right. I work on a legal advice hot-line.'

'Not so hot in the middle of the night, I don't suppose.'

'You'd be surprised how many people have nothing better to do at three in the morning.'

'Is that right?' Over the years, he'd learned the art of putting nervous witnesses at their ease. Talk about trivial things, let their confidence build.

'God, yes.' She even gave a tentative smile, as if relieved to find a safe topic to talk about. 'They can always find something to agonise over. Whether they can sue their neighbours for growing a conifer hedge that blocks the light from their living-room, that sort of thing. It's not exactly high pressure stuff. And even though there's a lot of repetition, it's different from private practice. No filling in time sheets, no running round to court. I don't miss all that, to be honest.'

'You trained with Symons, Horlock and Young, you reminded me.'

'And I hated every minute,' she blurted out. As if she had said too much too soon, she added quickly, 'Believe me, I put my heart and soul into the work, but it was such a let-down. It was so much worse because I hadn't expected that. When I took my degree, I'd fallen in love with the law. It fascinated me. In a way, it still does.'

'Takes all sorts,' he said easily.

'Laws are – oh, I don't know – our *lifeblood*.' For a moment her green eyes shone. 'I mean – how could we survive without them? But when I started off as a trainee, I found that all that mattered was how to work the photocopier and collect the partners' dry cleaning because they were too important to do the menial jobs.'

'You got on all right with one of the partners.'

165

'Oh, Brett was the exception. Not just because he was sweet, but because he treated me like a real person. Someone who mattered. Mind you, by the time the firm collapsed, the other two were treating him with as much contempt as they treated me.'

'So you didn't hit it off with Nerys Horlock?'

'She didn't have any time for academic lawyers. I think she had a chip on her shoulder because she came from the back streets of Liverpool and struggled to pass her degree. Maybe that's why she became a workaholic. She was constantly sneering at me, trying to take me down a peg. When she found out about Brett and me, she hit the roof. She even accused me of wanting to sleep my way to the top. As if. She simply didn't understand me. I'm not ambitious, I just made the mistake of deciding to become a lawyer.'

'And it was a mistake?'

'At least it pays the rent. But I can't see myself staying on the end of a phone line for much longer.'

'What, then?'

'God knows,' she said softly. 'I certainly don't.'

'And you say that Carl Symons was just as bad as Nerys?'

She flinched. 'Worse. He was – horrible.'

There was no mistaking her physical revulsion. She wasn't, he felt sure, simply referring to Symons' ugliness. He wanted to probe more deeply, but instinct told him that he needed to take care. Carmel and Brett had already warned him that she was highly strung as well as bright.

'Must have been difficult for you when the whole business went belly-up.'

'Brett was the one who really suffered. It broke my heart to see what he went through. He tried so hard to make a go of it. I felt so helpless. There was a lot he didn't tell me, I'm sure of that. He took it all on himself. I simply couldn't get through to him. For a long time I thought we would be sure to drift apart.'

'But you didn't?'

'He'd lost his house, he'd been working in the tribunal on a commission basis, but in the end he had to give up even that. He was depressed, he was taking happy pills – much good that they did him. I did my best to care for him. I won't say we haven't had a few stormy exchanges since then. I suppose we're both emotional people. We have highs, but there are plenty of lows as well.'

Harry recalled Brett's hoarse voice, his claim that Andrea was killing him. 'And you're both out of private practice.'

'My training stint made me realise I simply couldn't bear it. As soon as I was qualified, I found myself a proper job.'

'Answering phone calls about consumer disputes in the small hours?'

She shrugged. 'At least I'm working at night. It suits me best. I'm an owl, not a lark. I can make enough to get by, then spend the rest of my time as I please. No office politics, no clients to see. Just the voices of people I'll never meet.'

He smiled, trying to put her at her ease. 'On second thoughts, I see the attraction. Perhaps I should apply. But you didn't come here to talk about life on the helpline.'

'No.' She cast her eyes down. 'I caught sight of you in the car with Brett last night. I was hiding in a shop doorway, feeling like a criminal.'

'He offered me a lift home from the Titanic Rooms. I'd followed you out and couldn't help seeing the little contretemps with Rick Spendlove.'

She said tightly, 'Brett got the wrong idea.'

'I tried to tell him that.'

'He didn't believe you, though, did he? He's jealous. If I so much as look at another man, he imagines I'm about to embark on an affair.'

'At least he cares.'

'He and I have the same fault. We care too much.' She swallowed. 'Did you have much of a conversation?'

167

'We finished up at his place, had a few drinks. Pity I didn't stay longer.'

'Why do you say that?'

'You know Nerys is dead?'

Her pallor was like a mask, he thought. She inclined her head and said, 'On the radio, they are suggesting her death was suspicious. Murder and arson, by the sound of it.'

'Uh-huh. And that's the problem. Two of Brett's partners have been killed and he doesn't have an alibi. As for me, I discovered Carl's body and chose the wrong moment to pay a visit to Nerys's office this afternoon. The police have half an idea I was revisiting the scene of my crime.'

'At least you haven't a motive for killing either of them. With Brett, it's different.' She had started to tremble again, he noticed. 'And now he's disappeared.'

'What do you mean?' Harry glanced at the clock. Brett's shift should have finished an hour ago. 'Is he still out in the Sierra?'

'It's not that. I checked with the owner. Brett should have taken the car back yesterday morning. He didn't – and he didn't get in touch all day. He's switched off the radio, he's out of contact.'

'Don't you have any idea where he is?'

'I turned up at his place yesterday evening, on my way into work. All I wanted to do was to say sorry for the night before – to explain that things weren't the way they looked. There wasn't a sign of him. I've called all through the night, but his number just keeps ringing out.' She leaned forward in her chair. 'I'm worried, Mr Devlin. That's why I looked up your address. You were the last person I'd seen with him. I thought you might know where he is.'

'I met him again yesterday afternoon. He came round to my office, wanting to talk about Nerys Horlock.'

'How was he?' she asked urgently.

Harry grimaced. 'Of course he was uptight. Carl and Nerys have died in mysterious circumstances within the space of a few days. Frankly, Brett is either a prime suspect or a prospective victim.'

She flinched as if he'd slapped her face. 'Did he – did he say where he would be going after he left you?'

'No, but listen. My guess is, he's decided to get away from it all for a while and he's made use of the car to do it. It's too early to send out the search parties. Depend on it, he'll soon be back.'

She closed her eyes. 'I hope you're right.'

He looked at her curiously. 'You hated Carl and Nerys. So did Brett. Why in God's name did he go in with them in the first place?'

'He told me it seemed too good a chance to miss, would you believe? He'd set his heart on making a success out of his career and he thought he'd hit on the right formula. Carl always worked hard, there was no problem there. Nerys wanted to win every case she fought. I can't pretend they were bad lawyers. I could have learned a lot from them myself, if I'd wanted to sell my soul. The one thing they did teach me was that I didn't want to be like them. Perhaps I should be grateful.'

She stared at her long sharp fingernails. He couldn't guess what was passing through her mind, but now was the moment to solve the conundrum that had been teasing him.

'You called me the other day,' he said gently.

'Yes. I'm sorry I rang off. I lost my nerve.'

'That's okay. Can you tell me why you phoned?'

She nodded. 'Of course. I almost mentioned it when I saw you at the Titanic Rooms. Someone is checking up on you.'

'The police?' Harry asked with a frown.

'No. At least, he doesn't look like a policeman. I can't believe he has any official status. I did wonder if he was an inquiry agent, but that didn't add up either. His investigative technique is pretty amateurish, to say the least.'

Harry was nonplussed. He wasn't accustomed to being inquired about. 'What's he checking on?'

'He was asking about you the other day at the Legal Group offices. I'd called in there first thing, to look up the small print of the Consumer Credit Act. I'd answered a call about the legislation the previous night and on second thoughts I wasn't happy with the advice I'd given. I overheard him trying to pump Pamela, the receptionist.'

'What can you tell me about this character?'

She described her first encounter with Daniel Roberts. 'He's tall, early forties, has a Welsh accent. He – he bothered me. I can't explain, but Pamela felt the same. I couldn't believe that he was simply intending to consult you for legal advice. It was *you* he was interested in.'

'Perhaps I should be flattered.'

'Ten minutes after he left, he phoned Pamela from a call box. Apparently he was trying to find out where you lived. It was rather clumsy. He tried to pretend that he knew you had a house near Sefton Park when it was obvious he hadn't a clue and was simply fishing for information. He made Pamela feel uneasy. She didn't tell him anything, but she rang me to let me know. I said one of us ought to mention it to you and she asked me if I'd give you a ring. But as soon as I got through, I realised how absurd you'd find it. I didn't have anything definite to tell you. You'd probably write me off as hopelessly neurotic.'

Neurotic? Well, yes, Harry didn't have much doubt about that. But not hopeless. She struck him as perceptive. If she thought there was something strange about the Welshman, she was probably right.

'Another thing. I caught sight of him again outside the Titanic Rooms before the seminar. The night Nerys Horlock was murdered. He was on the other side of the street. It was as if he'd stationed himself there, so that he could watch out for you. I was just behind as you were going in and he had his eyes fixed on you so firmly he didn't even see that I'd spotted him.'

Harry was baffled. 'Are you sure about this?'

She flushed. 'I promise, I'm not making it up. When I heard about Nerys Horlock, I realised my first reaction was right. I had to warn you.'

'I don't understand.'

'Someone is killing solicitors. This man seems to be interested in – God I don't know – stalking you? You need to be aware.'

'If only I'd realised,' Harry said, trying to make light of it. 'I might have offered him my autograph.'

'I don't think it's a laughing matter,' she said, banging her mug down so hard on the table that the coffee splashed over the carpet. 'I owed it to you to tell you what I saw. Of course, your mind may already be made up. Perhaps you do think Brett is guilty after all. And I suppose you've decided I'm just another hysterical bitch.'

'No, it's just that...'

She stood up and waved a hand to silence him. 'Don't bother to deny it. I can see it on your face. You think I'm unbalanced. Worrying about Brett's disappearance one minute. Imagining you have a secret pursuer the next. I see it now, it was a mistake to come here. Let's forget I've said anything, shall we?'

She turned and walked rapidly out of the room. Harry swore under his breath, then hurried after her.

'Wait a minute. I didn't mean...'

The outside door slammed in his face. He hesitated, wondering whether to follow her outside again. But this time, he guessed, she would not be persuaded back.

Chapter Fourteen

How best to destroy those who exist as the un-dead? This I have made the study of a lifetime. I have pored over ancient manuscripts until the small hours and travelled far to speak in unfamiliar tongues with those who have encountered the enemy and survived to tell the tale, striving all the while to disentangle fact from folklore, myth and legend.

Fire is, I have learned, amongst the most potent of the hunter's weapons. Fire is for ever hungry. In its greed it will devour everything that stands in its way. There is no reasoning with the flames. I dread their fury. Yet as I watched from a safe distance as the red tongue of the blaze licked and gorged on its prize, I could not suppress a thrill of exultation. I had become a conqueror again. I had vanquished another enemy.

Daniel Roberts rubbed his itching eyes as he mulled over the Journal. He'd been straining to read by the inadequate light of the old lamp. Even though sleep had remained elusive as always, he was weary and the words kept jumbling together in his mind, so that nothing he wrote in his small cramped hand seemed to make sense any more. Yet he could not give up now. He must have faith, he must keep going.

The cottage was built out of stone and roofed with slate from the quarry at Blaneau. It offered rudimentary cover from the elements, little more. He'd been told that a shepherd had lived here once. Shepherds were hardy souls, but he was no less resilient. In the height of summer the cottage was cool, a refreshing spot in which to take refuge from the sun, but as soon as the leaves began to fall, he could feel the draughts coursing through the dimly lit rooms. Yet they did not trouble him and when winter came he would take no notice of either the bitter chill or the damp. Comfort meant nothing to him.

He yawned and stretched his arms as the old clock on the mantelpiece chimed the hour. He glanced round the room, taking in the uneven floor with its rush matting cover and the whitewashed walls. The furniture was ancient, the decoration minimal. His tastes were ascetic; in another life, he might have been a monk. There were no cushions here, no soft fabrics. The only personal touches were to be found on the single shelf above the clock, in the row of old books. The titles were as familiar to him as the names of the authors: Le Fanu, Summers and Stoker. He had inherited the clock, the lamp and the books and he would never be parted from them, but otherwise he had little interest in material possessions. He needed the bare essentials of existence; anything else was an encumbrance.

His mind strayed to the path he had embarked upon. There was no question of turning back. Once he finished working at the truck stop, he was answerable to no-one and could come and go as he pleased. Few people were even aware of this tiny place, tucked away on an isolated mountain slope, and the remoteness of the spot suited him well. He prized his privacy and he had always taken care to safeguard it. His home might be small, but it was his castle and he allowed no visitors to step inside. No tradesmen called; mail was delivered to the box at the bottom of the hill and he bought his milk from the garage shop. Several times Rhodri had suggested they have a night in together, just the two of them plus a few beers. But Daniel had always said no.

Once Daniel had overheard Rhodri suggesting to Bronwen that there was something odd in the way he kept himself to himself. Not natural, like. Her reply had been in keeping with her robust character.

'Just 'cause he's not the same as you, Rhodri Nash, that doesn't mean there's anything wrong with him.'

'Oh aye. Fancy him, do you?'

'No,' she'd said tersely. 'But I do feel sorry for him. He seems so alone.'

Standing on the other side of the partition that divided the garage from the kiosk, Daniel had frowned. She was right, of course. He had always felt different. Somehow *apart* from other men, isolated and insecure. Yet it seemed right to stay that way. He had no urge to mix with others.

He recalled eavesdropping on that conversation now, as he climbed off his wooden chair and leaned on the window sill. The room looked out up the hillside. Feeble rays of November sun were crawling in through the gaps in the blinds. He opened the window and breathed in the moist morning air. He'd always loved the peace and quiet amidst the mountains, would never have dreamed of disturbing it with a crackling radio or television with a fuzzy screen. There was no-one to threaten his reveries here. Even on bright days the chirping of the birds seemed subdued and when the squirrels jumped from tree to tree they scarcely made a sound.

Closing his eyes, he pictured Harry Devlin shambling into the Titanic Rooms. Harry wasn't how he'd imagined: tall, lithe and brisk. There was a dogged set to the jaw but the corrugated brow belonged to a man accustomed to being taken aback by the way things kept turning out. Although he did not know it, Daniel reflected grimly, a fresh shock was in store for him.

He'd discovered Harry's address through the simple expedient of checking the phone book. It listed *H. Devlin, Solr* at an address in the Empire Dock – presumably a block of flats by the riverside. There had been no need to make that crass call to the Legal Group offices. A childish spur-of-the-moment error. Daniel hoped that he hadn't alarmed the woman to whom he'd spoken. The last thing he wanted was for her to alert Harry, provoke his curiosity about the identity of the middle-aged stranger who was trying to track him down. Harry would be wasting time if he started to wonder what it was all about. He would never guess.

Daniel picked up the Journal and put it carefully away in the battered sideboard. The time was drawing near when at last he would meet Harry face to face. He could not postpone the encounter indefinitely. Their fates were intertwined. Blood bound them together.

After Andrea's departure, Harry's morning passed in a haze. He spent a couple of hours loafing around in his flat, determined not to let what she had said start bothering him. At least her visit had taken his mind off Peter Blackwell and the prospect that he might blow the gaff to Casper May. He ploughed through the newspapers, trying not too worry too much about whether there was going to be another economic recession. He'd scarcely noticed that the country had recovered from the last one. There were a couple of columns about Nerys Horlock's death – a London-based editor could discount the killing of a single Liverpool solicitor as just one of those things, but a second murder in quick succession had the makings of a circulation-booster – but the report was as excitable as it was uninformative.

When he started turning his mind to the prospect of lunch, he discovered he was out of food, so he drove to a supermarket and pushed a squeaking trolley round and round the maze of aisles. From time to time he glanced at the faces of his fellow shoppers, their concentration intense as they checked discounts and calculated the points they might earn on their loyalty cards. He let them dodge past and thought about murder as he plucked tins and packets from the shelves at random. Perhaps he should be on his guard all the time. Any moment now, Andrea Gibbs's Welshman might emerge from behind a pyramid of cans of peaches.

'Fancy a cheddar surprise, sir?'

Startled, he took a pace back. A plump assistant in the smart green overall was thrusting a biscuit barrel under his nose. Her voice resonated with evangelical zeal. The biscuits had an irresistibly tangy new taste, she assured him.

'It's a special promotion. Try one and see. You'll want another, take my word.'

He took a bite from the biscuit she handed him, conscious of her expectant gaze. 'What do you think?' she asked.

'Let me savour it,' he said, reluctant to tell her that it seemed indistinguishable from the average cream cracker. The woman caught the eye of a passing housewife and launched into her sales patter. Harry seized the chance to slink away. His trolley was almost full and he pushed it towards the racks of wine and beer. A twelve-pack of Tetley's completed his shop; now he was equipped if his nerve began to crack.

As he unloaded his purchases at the checkout, he told himself that Andrea Gibbs must be mistaken. There was bound to be a simple explanation. The Welshman had been looking for legal advice from a small firm who wouldn't charge the earth, but then found someone else to consult. She'd spotted him before the Legal Group meeting and jumped to the wild conclusion that he was some kind of stalker. If so, he wasn't conspicuously patient; there had been no sign of him when Harry had come out of the Titanic Rooms.

The cashier, a fierce young woman evidently fresh from a training course in cross-selling techniques, unleashed a volley of questions as she swiped the bar code on each product. Did he need his car-park ticket validated? *Swipe.* Would he like any extra cash? *Swipe.* Was he interested in twenty-four hour banking? *Swipe.* The bargain offers in kitchen hardware were available for one day only. *Swipe.* How about redeeming the loyalty vouchers he had earned? He could exchange them for a citrus press or opt for the long haul and put them towards a family picnic hamper. Groggily, Harry crammed things into unco-operative carrier bags. Never mind the Welshman, the challenges of everyday living were enough to cope with. Life was too short to worry about the wilder speculations of a woman with nerves as ragged as Andrea's.

The car park was full by the time he wheeled his purchases outside. Drivers were circling like carrion crows, scanning the lanes for an empty space, heedless of the people weaving back through the traffic to their vehicles. As Harry tried to cross to his MG, brakes squealed and he scuttled back to the safety of the pavement, losing control of his trolley in the process. It careered into another coming in the opposite direction and piled high with carrier bags. The accident sent both trolleys crashing into the wall of the supermarket.

'What the fucking hell do you think you're playing at?' a thick voice demanded. 'For two pins...'

Harry's first instinct was to tense as he prepared to defend himself against an acute manifestation of trolley rage. His second impulse was to glance again at the man in the sheepskin coat who was waving his arms in such a menacing fashion. Thought so. It was Rick Spendlove. His face was grey, his eyes bloodshot, but after his performance at the Maritime Bar, it was a miracle that he'd managed to crawl out of bed.

'Sorry, Rick,' he said breezily. 'I just didn't see you there. We'd better not come to blows, eh? The ranks of the Liverpool lawyers are thinning out as it is.'

'Oh.' Spendlove choked back whatever expletives had been on his lips. Perhaps he'd been on the point of threatening to issue a writ. 'It's you.'

Harry retrieved the trolleys and tossed a couple of the bags which had fallen from Rick's heap of goodies back inside. He was pleased to discover that even hard-bitten business lawyers consumed Sugar Puffs and Wagon Wheels as well as plentiful supplies of Alka-Seltzer. Spendlove spotted the smile that played on his lips and turned the colour of beetroot.

'I have the girls over every other Sunday,' he said hurriedly. 'Unless my first wife decides to punish me for some misdemeanour, real or imagined. You know how it is.'

'Not really. I never had children.' Never divorced, either. He'd always hoped that one day Liz would change her mind and give their marriage a second try. One night his dreams had come true and she'd returned, although only out of fear. Within twenty-four hours she'd been knifed to death.

'Unlucky.' For a moment the hard features seemed to have a softer edge. 'Kids almost make marriage worthwhile. That, and being able to leave it to the wife to do the bloody shopping. Oh well, price of freedom, eh? Work hard, play hard, that's my credo.'

'Feeling better after last night?' Harry asked. He wondered if he'd caught a glimpse of the real man beneath the business lawyer's braggadocio, but after seeing Rick's behaviour towards Suki, he wasn't inclined to give him the benefit of the doubt. So he contented himself with the chilly smile he usually reserved for interviewing child-molesters.

'You were there?' Spendlove groaned. Harry could smell the stale whiff of alcohol. 'Christ, I can't remember much about it, tell you the truth.'

'Probably for the best.'

'Made myself look a right prat, didn't I?' Spendlove's flat Yorkshire vowels were more in evidence than usual today. He pushed a hand through his curly black hair and scanned Harry's expression for reassurance. Finding none, he added, 'These young girls, you know what it is. Bloody feminism. They come into the profession – they're outnumbering us now, it's a statistical fact! – and think they're God's gift. Trouble is, the likes of Anwar, they don't have much of a sense of humour. Give me an older woman any day. They don't yell and they don't tell.'

'All the same in the dark, eh?'

Spendlove clapped him on the shoulder. 'You're right, Harry. You know a thing or two.'

Harry sighed. 'One thing you mentioned last night that I didn't know. Something about Suki having a tattoo?'

'Oh, that. Well, maybe the less said the better, eh?'

'I was intrigued, that's all.'

'I bet. You fancy giving her one, then?'

Harry's immediate urge was to bury his boot into Spendlove's private parts, but he simply said, 'It's not that. You said that Carl Symons told you about the tattoo. I didn't even realise you and he were pals.'

'Wouldn't say we were. Business acquaintance, that's all. He consulted me when his practice was on its uppers. He was worried about being made bankrupt. As it turned out, he got off lightly. He and Horlock did a deal which left Young carrying the can. Why the stupid bastard fell for it, I don't know.'

'You were involved in the negotiations?'

'Bit of background advice. Nothing meaty. There's not a lot of money in winding up a small legal practice. A Chancellor of the Exchequer who wants to make a name for himself by restructuring the economy, that's what you need if you want to make a few bob in my line of business.'

'Didn't you have something going with Nerys at one time?'

Rick frowned. 'It was all exaggerated. Tell you the truth – this is just between us, all right? – she gave me the cold shoulder.'

'You kept in touch with Symons, though?'

Spendlove shook his head. 'Our paths hardly ever crossed. It was like you and me. I mean, no disrespect, but you're not a member of my golf club, your firm doesn't sponsor concerts at the Liverpool Philharmonic. We may both be lawyers, but what else do we have in common?'

Certainly not our taste in breakfast cereals and chocolate biscuits. 'When did he tell you about the tattoo?'

'Must have been a couple of months back. I bumped into him at the Maritime. He didn't drink there often, but he was celebrating some case or other and we got talking. The way you do. He said something about Anwar and I said I wouldn't mind a piece. He gave me a sly look and told me about the tattoo.'

'He'd had an affair with her?'

'Let's put it this way,' Spendlove said in a judicial tone, 'he was certainly keen to give me the impression that he had.'

'Showing off?'

'Sure. Obviously whatever had been going on between them was over. Maybe she dumped him, I don't know. He was trying to act like a man of the world. Only trouble was, the poor bastard was so fucking ugly, a woman would have to be desperate before she'd let him inside her knickers. I suppose Anwar must have been after promotion. It happens, Harry. It happens.'

Harry said, almost to himself, 'Suki was involved with Carl Symons and friendly with Nerys Horlock. Now both of them are dead.'

'What are you suggesting? That Anwar killed them?'

'I'm not suggesting anything. I'm just wondering why two lawyers who'd once been partners came to be murdered.'

Spendlove sniggered. 'You disappoint me, Harry. To think you once had a name for being a kind of Scouse Sherlock Holmes. I'd have thought it was obvious to anyone who's ever had to cope with the shit that gets shovelled at a meeting of partners in a law firm. Elementary. Who had cause to hate that pair the most? The partner they stitched up, surely?'

Harry didn't drive straight home from the supermarket. He wanted to see for himself whether Andrea was right and Brett had disappeared without a trace. A short detour took him to Toxteth and five minutes later he was parking outside the disused butcher's shop. The street was quiet except for a couple of bespectacled students carrying bags full of books. He could hear them arguing as he walked down the side passage and rang Brett's doorbell.

'Call it a masterpiece of jurisprudential analysis? I read it from cover to cover and there wasn't a single reference to the moral imperative.'

'But you have to face it. Law is simply a system of rules.'

Harry grinned. A couple of years filling in legal aid forms would knock all that out of them. There was no answer from Brett. He banged hard on the door with his fist, but to no avail and was on the point of giving up when a middle-aged woman came under the archway, her high heels clomping on the paving stones. She had cropped red hair and a crooked nose. He had to look twice as she fished in a huge handbag for a Yale key. Her name, according to the card by the door, was Madame Brigitte.

'Who are you after, chuck?' she asked.

'Have you seen Brett Young lately?'

She pouted, a mannerism that probably wouldn't have been attractive even when she was twenty years younger. 'He's getting more bloody visitors than me all of a sudden. I keep hearing people ringing his bell. The busies have been round. Journalists, too. Has he done something, then? What's it all about?'

Her voice, he thought, was eerily reminiscent of the young Cilla Black's. It wouldn't have come entirely as a surprise if she'd repeated her question by declaiming the first line of 'Alfie'.

'I'm a friend of his. He's gone missing.'

'Come on. There must be more to it than that.'

'His girlfriend's raised the alarm. A couple of old friends of his have died recently and she's worried he might have done something silly.'

'Oh, is that it? I think I know the girl you mean. Looks as though she could do with a good square meal inside her?' Madame Brigitte giggled. 'I shouldn't worry. He does seem a bit moody, but it's true, y'know. The quiet ones are always the worst. Well, I saw him the night before last. Getting on for ten, it must have been. We passed on the stairs. I'd been saying goodbye to a friend, your mate was on his way out. What's the betting he's playing away from home? He's probably had a lady passenger who invited him in for a cup of cocoa. Twenty to one, he'll still be there. That's cabbies for you.'

Harry stepped aside to let her put the key in the lock. The passageway gave on to a small yard ringed by a wall topped with spikes for security. The sharp tips were rusting but they were still more than a match for even the most determined burglar. There was a scattering of broken bricks, odd lengths of pipe and bits of wooden pallet. Convolvulus sprouted through cracks in the uneven concrete and strands of ivy clung to the back wall of the building. Set into the wall was a steel door.

'How long since the butcher's shop closed down?' he asked.

'Search me. Twelve months, maybe more. Before my time.'

'Was the place left empty?'

She nodded. 'Went out of business because of mad cow disease. Quite right, too. Me, I never eat meat. You've got to look after yourself, haven't you?'

With that, she gave him a brilliant smile marred only by the gaps in her front teeth and waved goodbye. As the door swung shut behind her, he heard the clatter of the high heels as she began the climb upstairs to her torture chamber.

He walked round to the front of the building and tried to peer in through the minute gaps between the boards in the window. The security people had done a good job; in this neck of the woods, they had plenty of practice. He could see nothing but darkness.

Suddenly he heard a car approaching and stepped back. When he looked round, he saw that it bore the insignia of Merseyside Police. He put his hands in his pocket and ambled over to his MG. Two young constables sprang out of the police car and cast him a glance before marching under the archway.

No sense in hanging around here. He drove home, unloaded the food and set off on a walk along the riverside in the hope of clearing his head. It was a dull damp day and wisps of mist were still hanging over the Mersey. Every now and then dogs being taken for walks snapped at his ankles, but he paid them no heed.

It was nonsense, he decided, to suspect Brett of murder and decapitation simply because he happened to live above a derelict butcher's shop. There was no reason to suspect that he had even rudimentary skills in sawing off the head of a corpse. It certainly didn't form part of the curriculum at the College of Law; not even the probate course. But it wouldn't help if Madame Brigitte, who'd not be keen to antagonise the forces of law and order, told the constables that she had seen Brett leave his flat on the night of Nerys's death. When they heard that, he would be installed as their prime suspect – if he wasn't already. And perhaps, Harry thought, they were right and Brett was guilty. It had to be more likely than Ken's farrago about the vampire-killer.

His mind flashed back to the scene at the Harbour Master's Cottage. The bloodied head with its ghastly smile. The thought that he might have spent the evening before last swigging beer with a man who could commit such savagery turned his stomach.

It was drizzling as he ambled towards the entrance to the flats at Empire Dock. As he approached, a figure emerged from the shadows by the side of the huge old building and moved as if to intercept him before he reached the door. Peering through the gloom, he saw a woman in a closely fitted dark coat. She was wearing a headscarf and glasses; he could not make out her face. He drew nearer and, raising her arm, she hissed his name.

He stopped in his tracks. Impossible to mistake that voice, even though she was disguising it with a huskiness that made Lauren Bacall's throaty tones sound like falsetto. Yet Juliet and he had agreed she would never call on him at home. If she were recognised, a visit might prove impossible to explain away.

'What's the matter?'

As she reached his side, she gripped his wrist so tightly that he winced. She was wearing no make-up and her cheeks were ashen.

'Something's happened,' she panted.

Casper has found out. He couldn't help shuddering.

'Have you told him about us?'

She stared at him, horrified. 'For Christ's sake! What are you talking about?'

'Your husband knows, doesn't he?'

'No, no. You couldn't be more wrong. In fact – I think we're safe. For ever, with any luck.'

'What are you saying?'

'It's terrible. I don't mean to dance on his grave or anything like that. God, no. It's terrible. But at least our problem's solved.'

'You've lost me.'

She took a deep breath. 'Peter Blackwell died last night.'

Chapter Fifteen

At first the words didn't make any sense to him. For a few moments he lost the power of speech. It was as if this latest shock had caused his vocal cords to seize up. Then he managed to clear his throat and find a few words. 'You – you'd better come into the flat.'

She took off the spectacles to look at her Rolex. He could see dark rings around her eyes. 'I'll have to leave in ten minutes. I've been hanging around here for half an hour and I'm due back home soon. I mustn't be late.'

'We don't want to attract attention. I'll go in first and you follow.'

'No point. I've already spoken to your caretaker.' When he winced, she said, 'I had to. How was I to know which was your flat? I suppose I should have rung first, but I didn't think. I assumed you'd be here.'

The casual phrase struck Harry like a slap on the cheek. As far as Juliet was concerned, he had no life outside the office and their relationship. Then again, was she far wrong?

'Listen, I was desperate to see you, to tell you the news. The caretaker said he'd seen you going out for a walk. He expected you back any time, so I thought it was worth hanging on. I told him I was a client. He offered to let me wait in his cubby-hole, but I said I'd rather keep a look-out for you in the car park.'

'All right. Come inside and tell me about it.'

He waited until she'd put the glasses back on and then led the way inside and nodded to Griff on the desk. 'Found him, then?' the caretaker asked, giving Juliet's figure an appreciative appraisal.

'Yes, thanks,' she said with a forced smile.

Harry grunted, said nothing. Once they were inside the flat, she shrugged off her coat, rubbing her hands as he hung it up. She was wearing a white sweater and leather trousers and the thought struck him that, whatever the crisis, she contrived never to look less than gorgeous. But she was restless, like a cat wanting to sniff out unfamiliar territory. He waved her to the sofa but she wandered around the flat, picking up books, glancing at the covers, putting them back in the wrong place.

'Wouldn't mind a spot of whisky. It'll warm me up. God, it was freezing in that bloody car park.' She looked around and shivered. 'So this is where you live. I've always wondered about it. Pictured you on your own at night, watching the late movie, then pulling the curtains back and staring out over the river. I've wanted to be here with you, dreamed of spending the night in your bed.'

'Peter,' Harry said, his tone harsher than he had intended. 'What happened to him?'

'It was an accident,' she said quickly.

'Car crash?'

'No, not that.'

'What, then?' He felt a surge of impatience. Was it his imagination, or did she sound defensive, afraid of his reaction?

'He must have had too much to drink last night. You remember that steep flight of stairs leading up to his flat? He fell all the way down to the bottom. Broke his neck.'

He stared. 'You're kidding.'

'I've never been more serious, darling. Now, how about that whisky?'

He found a bottle of Bell's and poured for both of them. 'Linda was still staying with him, presumably?'

'Yes, that's the terrible thing. She found his body. Poor woman, it's a wonder she hasn't lost her mind. First her husband dies, then her only child.'

He wrinkled his brow, trying to get things straight in his mind. 'You mean – she was there when he fell down the stairs?'

186

'No, no.' She seemed to hesitate. 'I don't mean that. She'd been so worried about him lately. Drinking heavily, not bothering to eat. These last few weeks, she said it herself, he'd been like a different person. The old Peter, you know, he would never have threatened me in the way he did on the telephone. Linda couldn't get through to him. She was still badly shaken herself. Her house wrecked, all the stuff about her neighbour being killed. She wanted a break from it. So she went for a walk along the sea front, leaving him alone with his bottles while she tried to clear her head. When she got back, she opened the front door – and found him lying there. Of course she dialled 999. But it was no good, he died on his way to hospital.'

Harry swore. His mind was in a whirl. Part of him thought: *he'll never threaten us again.* But he couldn't help feeling guilty at his selfishness. Besides, in his heart, he was not sure that they were yet safe.

'She rang me from Arrowe Park Hospital that night. Of course, she was in a dreadful state. The medics wanted to keep an eye on her, but she hates hospitals. She just wanted to get away, have some time to herself. To start grieving. Trouble was, she had nowhere to go. Her own house is still a wreck. She couldn't face going back to the place where she'd found Peter. So I drove over there and brought her back to Parkgate. We have plenty of room. There's a sort of granny annexe. I'm putting her up there for the time being.'

'How is she?'

'How do you imagine? Of course, she's devastated, not thinking straight. It's only to be expected.' She sipped the whisky. 'Jesus, that's better. One way or another, it's been quite a few days.'

'You're telling me.'

'Even though I've never had a kid,' she said sombrely, 'I can imagine it's the worst nightmare any parent can experience. To have your only son die before you.'

'I suppose there's never been any suggestion that Peter ...' he began tentatively.

'Threw himself down the stairs? It did cross my mind. He was a mixed-up guy, but poor Linda says this was a genuine accident, not suicide.'

'Mothers aren't always the best judges. She wouldn't want to face up to the possibility that the son she loved so much had killed himself.'

'Maybe, but all the same she convinced me. She reckons he was so fuddled, he opened the main door and stepped out into thin air, believing he was walking into the kitchen or bedroom or something. From what she says, the police see it that way too.'

After a few moments' silence, he said, 'I suppose there's no question of – anyone else being involved?'

'What do you mean?' she snapped.

'I mean – is it possible he had a helpful push?'

'Don't be ridiculous!' She scowled and said through gritted teeth, 'I never heard such a crazy idea! Honestly, you have murder on the brain.'

'Is it so surprising? Two lawyers I know have been killed within the past week. You know about the woman who died, Nerys Horlock? She used to be Carl Symons' partner.'

'Sure, I read about it in the newspaper. But take it from me, Peter's death is something else. An accident, pure and simple. Understand?'

There was a menace in her voice that he'd never expected to hear. Flinching, he remembered that this was Casper May's wife. Her husband might beat her up every now and then, but she wasn't soft. He bit his lip. He was familiar with every inch of her body, had kissed her all over, from head to toe. But it was beginning to dawn on him that, despite all that had happened between them, he still didn't know her very well.

Struggling to lighten the mood, he put his hands up in a gesture of appeasement. 'Okay, okay. I give in. It was an accident.'

She swallowed the whisky. 'Sorry if I bit your head off. Is it any wonder my nerves are frayed after the last few days?'

'Same here.'

'I don't know.' She eyed him over her tumbler. 'You may be a worrier, but you don't actually lose it. You don't panic. I've noticed that.'

'There's no need to panic, is there?' he asked carefully.

'No, there isn't. You know, I hate to say this. Linda's a good friend of mine and I would never have wished unhappiness on her. But I'd be lying if I said I was heartbroken. Shocked, yes. I can't believe he's dead. We both know what it means, though. No-one will ever find out about us.'

'You think so?'

She frowned. 'Of course. He was the one person – apart from Linda – who knew what really happened on the night of the storm. Now he's dead, there's no danger any more. No risk that Casper will ever find out. We've been lucky – we've got away with it.'

He shuffled his feet. 'Let's not count our chickens. You're forgetting Linda.'

'I told you before,' she said sharply. 'I trust her.'

He didn't feel reassured. He was painfully aware of his own occasional gullibility. But he couldn't pretend to himself that her judgment was wholly to be relied upon. After all, she'd chosen Casper May for a husband. Himself for a lover.

'You trusted Peter at first.'

'I've known Linda a lot longer than I've known you.' She was snapping again. He suddenly realised she was on the verge of tears. 'She'd never betray me.'

He moved to her side and put his arm around her, but she pulled away with a grunt of distaste and blew her nose fiercely.

'I'd better go,' she said in a muffled voice. 'Casper will be wondering where I am. So will Linda. I made up a story to get away. I wanted to tell you what had happened.'

'Thanks. I'm glad you did.'

'Can you fetch my coat, please?'

He smelled her perfume as he helped her to guide her arms into the coat sleeves. For a moment he was seized by the urge to nuzzle her neck, but he thought better of it.

'When you see Linda, will you tell her how sorry I was to hear the news?'

'You needn't worry,' she said. Her tone was bleak. 'With all Peter's faults, she worshipped him, you know that. His death may destroy her. I hope not, but I'm afraid for her. One thing's for sure. She'll have other things on her mind than gossiping about our affair.'

'Sure. Look, I didn't mean to...'

'Just don't say any more, all right?' she snapped. 'Don't make things worse than they already are.'

He wasn't in the mood to eat any of the stuff he'd bought that morning. After Juliet had gone he poured himself another whisky and lay on the sofa, his feet hanging over the side, turning over and over in his mind the news she had brought.

He had taken a dislike to Peter Blackwell and the threat which Juliet had recounted in the park at Wavertree had frightened him. She was probably right. Peter's death would solve everything; he had no reason to doubt that Linda could indeed be relied upon to keep her mouth shut. Yet he had not wished the man harm and he felt sickened at the picture conjured up by his eternally active imagination. He could visualise the crumpled heap lying at the foot of the staircase in the shabby seaside building.

At least he'd found something that took his mind off Andrea's mystery Welshman, something else to worry about. Suppose that he hadn't been so far off the mark when he'd wondered aloud if Peter might have been murdered? Juliet had done her best to scotch the idea. He couldn't deny that she was right; at present, he did have murder on the brain. But that didn't mean that Peter's death was bound to have an innocent explanation. The police might not be as easily satisfied as Juliet suggested; after all, Peter had recently been interviewed in connection with a murder inquiry. It occurred to Harry that he might himself be in the frame. Never mind the lack of the vampiric hallmarks which had excited Ken Cafferty. Mitch Eggar might still try to link the case with the deaths of Carl and Nerys. But there was a yet more chilling possibility. The only person, apart from himself, who appeared to have a motive for silencing Peter Blackwell was Juliet.

Harry replayed the conversation with her. She was no fool. He suspected that she'd been angry and defensive because she'd guessed he might wonder if she had killed Peter. Understandable. Then again, it might simply be that she was feeling guilty and unable to hide her emotions.

Wearied by the torments of the last few days, he began to doze. When he awoke, it was after seven. As he rubbed his eyes, he decided he wasn't in the mood for any more fretting this evening. Too many people had died. There were too many unsolved mysteries and only one solution. Peter Blackwell and Rick Spendlove weren't perfect role models, but nonetheless the time had come to take a leaf out of their book. He would go out and get pissed.

He didn't want to visit one of his usual haunts and he didn't want to have too far to stagger back home. The Jesse Hartley, a trendy pub on the waterfront named after the stern Yorkshireman who had built the Albert Dock, fitted the bill. At least half the clientele worked in television and local radio and each of the bars was dominated by a huge screen showing baseball or American football on satellite television.

After buying himself a pint, he wandered over to the jukebox. Mostly seventies stuff. It wasn't a sacrifice to pass on Gary Glitter, Showaddywaddy and T Rex. He deliberated for a while, then chose Rod Stewart's cover of 'First Cut is the Deepest'. It wasn't as achingly wonderful as P. P. Arnold's original, but the words still had resonance for him; he'd given his heart to Liz and even after all this time, he still hadn't got over her betrayal. As for Juliet – well, she was many things, but she wasn't Liz.

'Harry Devlin! Just the man I wanted to see!'

The voice interrupting his reverie sounded familiar. He turned to discover that it belonged to a slender young man in impossibly tight fawn trousers. He wore a medallion with his open-neck lumberjack shirt and a precisely trimmed toothbrush moustache. At one time he'd worked as a clerk in the employment tribunal office a short distance away at Cunard Building. Harry had always found him amiable but tediously loquacious. His real name was Eric but everyone called him Errol.

'How are you doing?'

'Lovely, thanks. I'm a personal assistant to Gavin Lacey now, you know.'

'So I heard.'

Gavin Lacey was a weatherman with a broad Lancastrian accent who was celebrated for apologising with an ostentatious wink whenever his predictions proved inaccurate. What he lacked in meteorological savvy he more than made up for in camp charm and his regular forecast of wet patches in Wallasey had become a much-parrotted catchphrase and earned him a cult following.

'You probably read in the papers, he's actually been offered the chance to host that new game show, *Pink Prizes*.'

Somehow Harry had missed that little titbit of tabloid showbiz gossip. As they moved away from the jukebox, he smiled vaguely and squinted round to check the possibilities of escape. They were few and far between. He suddenly realised that he had missed the sign on the door proclaiming that this was Proud Gays Night at the Jesse. He became conscious that, on the other side of the room, a small man who looked like Rowan Atkinson's younger brother was moving in time to the music and giving him a toothy smile.

'You know, it really is a stroke of luck bumping into you like this. You may be able to help.'

'Sure,' Harry said, who was wishing that he'd stayed in his flat. Perhaps he should have bided his time until the Jesse dedicated a theme evening to Guilty Heterosexuals.

Errol leaned forward and said *sotto voce*, 'I heard the gossip, I know you found Carl Symons' body. So you're bound to have an interest in what happened to Nerys Horlock.'

'Uh-huh.' So even here there wasn't any escape from murder.

'You see, it's like this. I have some information – and I simply don't know what to do with it. It's been keeping me awake at nights. Whether to tell the police or forget all about it.'

'Go on.'

'Then again, it may not mean anything at all. That's what Gavin thinks.'

Never mind bloody Gavin, get to the point. 'Try me,' he hissed.

'Well. On my last morning at the tribunal, my very last morning, I picked up a fax from Nerys Horlock. I knew Nerys, she'd acted for me once when she was with Symons, Horlock and Young. I had a car accident, suffered whiplash. It wasn't too bad, I even hesitated before I took any legal advice. She sorted out the other driver's insurance company. I picked up enough compensation to pay for a holiday for two in the West Indies. So I owed her one. But she wasn't an employment lawyer. I'd hardly ever seen her in the tribunal.'

'So what was the fax about?'

'I was coming to that. There was a covering letter and a form claiming sex discrimination. Sexual harassment, to be precise. But you'll never guess who the respondent was.'

Harry said instinctively, 'Rick Spendlove.'

Errol's thin eyebrows shot up. 'The chap from Boycott Duff? No, no, you're miles out. Between you, me and the gatepost, that wouldn't be anything out of the ordinary. I think he's been on the receiving end of three separate claims during the past couple of years. They all settled out of court. He's quite a naughty boy, that Mr Spendlove, he really is.'

'So who was the culprit?'

'Carl Symons.' Errol breathed rather than spoke the name.

Harry was startled. 'Nerys was complaining that Carl had harassed her?'

'No, no, my word, you've got it all wrong. The claim was about an incident at the Crown Prosecution Service, after the partnership broke up. The claim named Carl and his employers. They would have to pay up if a tribunal found him guilty. But there was a snag. The incident had happened three months earlier and the time limit for bringing a claim is three months, too. She was sending the claim in by fax at the last minute, to make sure it was in time. Once the three months are up, that's usually the end of the road. You know how it is. Rules are rules.'

'Yeah, I know.' Errol had always had a streak of the jobsworth in him.

'But in the covering letter, you see, she was asking us not to serve the papers on Carl or the CPS.'

'Why?'

'She said she was still awaiting formal instructions from her client about whether to proceed. She wanted a few days' grace until she found out whether she could get the go-ahead.'

'Any problem with that?'

'Oh my goodness me, yes. Yes, there was. The law says you can't do it. It's quite plain, it's down there in black and white. Once the tribunal receives the claim, it's duty bound to send it on to the respondents. In this case, both the CPS and Carl Symons. I decided to give her a call to tip her off. I owed her that.'

'What did she say?'

'She said she'd speak to her client and ring me back. An hour later, she called again. It was extraordinary. I'd always thought she was a strong woman, but it sounded to me as though she was choking back tears at the other end of the line. Oh yes, she was! I could tell it was a claim she felt passionately about. Nerys was like that, you know. For her, every case was a crusade.'

'What had her client said?' Harry leaned forward, making sure that he could hear the reply above the cheery exuberance of the Village People singing 'In the Navy'. One thing was for certain: Errol had caught his attention now.

'She didn't want to go ahead. Nerys had obviously pleaded with her, but the answer was no. Nerys asked me to tear the claim up. I suppose I shouldn't have done it, but what the hell? I was on my way out of the tribunal and she'd been good to me. So I did as she asked and that dreadful person Carl Symons never even knew what a lucky escape he had. It wasn't justice.'

'Who was Nerys acting for?' Harry asked, although he'd already guessed.

'The woman's name was Anwar. She was a junior prosecutor.'

'And what was Carl Symons supposed to have done to her?'

Errol lowered his voice to a whisper. 'According to her, they'd been working together in the office late one night. He'd made a pass at her and she'd said no. Then he raped her.'

Chapter Sixteen

My work is almost complete. The time has come for me to make the final journey and undertake my last and most terrible task. I cannot deny that I dread to think what the next few hours may have in store, but my nerve will not fail me, not now. I have already endured so much. Heard the scream of horror as the stake drives in. Watched the writhing body, the lips that foam.

Soon it will be over. I shall be able to pity that wretched soul as at last it experiences the wholesome sleep of death. Death, that should have come so long ago. And, reminding myself of the mission entrusted to me, passed on from one generation to another, I shall myself find peace, even at the moment when my knife severs the head from the neck.

Daniel Roberts tapped away at his keyboard. The words were flowing. He'd never realised that it could be like this. The Journal was nearly finished. He could feel his skin tingle as the blank screen filled. The draught in the cottage meant nothing to him. He hadn't even bothered to bring the coal in or light a fire.

There was another reason, of course. The long wait was almost over. This was to be the day when he finally introduced himself to Harry Devlin. He tried to picture the look on the other man's face, but had to give up. He did not lack imagination, but he found it impossible to guess the reaction he would evoke. Would Harry recoil, stammer, run?

Rhodri had offered to tinker with the van, check it over to make sure that despite its age it could handle another long trip. Daniel had accepted readily, muttering something about someone he needed to see a few miles away. He could not match Rhodri's mechanical expertise and he dared not risk another breakdown.

That was important, today of all days. And if Rhodri was motivated by curiosity, if he thought he might find something in the van which revealed more about the mysteries of Daniel's private life, he would finish up sorely disappointed. There wasn't a single thing. Naturally, Rhodri had never seen anything suggesting the existence of the Journal.

He glanced at the clock on the mantelpiece. Not long to go, now. He planned to set out early in the afternoon. He did not know what Harry's movements would be, but that did not matter. Even if he was away from his flat when Daniel arrived, it was fair to assume that he would turn up during the evening. Daniel did not mind biding his time. His search had taken years. At times he had despaired that it would ever reach a successful conclusion. A few more hours would not hurt him. Rather, they would add to the anticipation.

By the time Harry's hangover began to ease, it was mid-day on Sunday. After Errol had finally left him to rejoin Gavin Lacey, he'd sat on a stool at the end of the bar and drunk the evening away. No-one else had bothered him; even the man who looked like Rowan Atkinson's younger brother had become engrossed in conversation with one of the staff. From time to time his eyes drifted to the match on the screen, but he could not remember who was playing, far less who scored. Eventually he'd staggered from the Jesse to his flat and slumped on the bed fully clothed before falling into deep yet unsatisfying sleep.

He dreamed that the Welshman Andrea had described was following him along the dark city streets. In the end he found himself trapped in an alley-way closed off by a brick wall. He had turned to face the stranger and asked, 'What do you want?'

The other man's voice was soft and lilting. 'I was sent by Casper May. He's never liked lawyers, you see. But Symons and Horlock were lucky. They were dead before I started to cut.'

As he swallowed the first coffee of the day, he cast his mind back to his conversation with Errol. If what he said was right, Suki must be in the frame. Yet whilst she had a motive for killing Carl, it was impossible to understand why Nerys should have met a similar fate. All right, Suki may have fallen out with Nerys over the tribunal claim – but a disagreement about tactics with one's legal adviser is scarcely a reason to commit murder. At least, Harry hoped not.

He had to talk to her. It wasn't enough simply to wait and hope that he might bump into her in the Law Courts on Monday morning. He checked the phone book for Anwars and rang the likeliest number. First time lucky.

'Hello?'

'This is Harry Devlin.'

'Oh ... hi.' Very cautious.

'Sorry to bother you on a Sunday, but there was something I meant to ask.'

'Well – go ahead, then.'

'The tribunal case. Nerys Horlock was representing you. A claim of sexual harassment.'

Dead silence. He didn't break it for a full half minute.

'Are you still there? I was asking about the claim Nerys put in for you. Against Carl Symons and the CPS.'

'I heard you.' A different note had entered her voice. For the first time in their acquaintance, she sounded frightened. 'But – I never made any claim. End of story.'

'That's not what I've been told,' he said gently. 'Last night I was talking to one of the clerks from the tribunal. He saw the form, the originating application. Nerys signed it on your behalf.'

'You're barking up the wrong tree,' she snapped. 'Sorry, but I have to go out now. Goodbye.'

The moment she banged the receiver down, Harry started putting on his trainers. She was lying and he needed to know why. He could imagine few experiences more horrific than being raped by a colleague. There were many reasons why Suki might have wanted to keep quiet about it. One thing was clear. The man accused of raping Suki and the woman who had made the accusation on Suki's behalf had both been murdered. He itched to know whether it was a mere coincidence.

The address in the phone book was Vauxhall Hey. He couldn't find a road of that name in his A-Z and guessed from the postcode that it was a new development off the Leeds-Liverpool canal. The area had been ruined by pollution and derelict for years, but lately a ton of Eurocash had been spent on cleaning it up and grassing over the waste land. Rows of new houses had sprung up along the water's edge. It was only ten minutes away. He grabbed his car keys from the hook in the kitchen. Even if Suki slammed the door in his face, at least he would have tried to solve the puzzle.

He drove slowly along Vauxhall Road, squinting at the names of the streets on the left that crossed over the canal to a yellow brick housing estate. After turning off the main road, he soon became lost in a maze of cul-de-sacs. Children were playing football, men fiddling with car engines. He wound down his window to ask the way and was directed to a road that ended in a row of bollards outside a community centre. Suki's house was a neat semi; a red Citroen was parked outside.

He rang the bell long and hard. No sign of life. He rapped on the door until his knuckles hurt. Nothing. Perhaps she was hiding from him. But if she wasn't at home, she couldn't be far. He strolled past the community centre on to a bridge painted sky blue which carried a footpath to the main road. Halfway across, he paused and leaned on the parapet, checking out his surroundings. As he looked down over the dark ribbon of water, he saw a familiar figure in a tracksuit, loping along the towpath away from him.

'Suki!'

She stopped in her tracks and turned round slowly to gaze up at him. 'Leave me alone,' she called.

'I'll only take five minutes of your time.'

'Forget it.'

She flipped her hand, as if dismissing him from her life. As she jogged away, he gripped the edge of the parapet, unsure what to do. Of course she was entitled to her privacy. He was well aware of the lasting pain that rape caused its victims; more than once, he'd seen their distress at first hand. He was supposed to be compassionate, or so people sometimes said. If they were right, he should drive straight back home and forget all about reopening old wounds.

But he couldn't do it. He'd come this far. There was no choice but to go on.

A gate adjoining the main road gave on to the canalside. By the time he'd reached it, Suki was out of sight. He hurried down the long slope and, breaking into a run, followed the curve in the towpath under the next bridge until he caught a glimpse of her lime green tracksuit far in the distance. She moved smoothly, rhythmically, not seeming to exert herself. He increased his pace, but soon she vanished round another bend. It was a while since he'd taken any serious exercise – his footballing days were long over – and presently he felt his heart begin to thud against the walls of his chest. Not for the first time over the past couple of years, he made a mental note that he needed to cut down on the chip suppers in front of the television and make an effort to recover some sort of semblance of fitness. His breath was coming in shallow gasps as he crunched along the pathway. Much more of this and he'd finish up in an oxygen tent. He caught his heel on a brick that some delinquent had left lying in the way and felt the pull of a muscle in his calf. It hurt but he kept on going. He couldn't lose her now.

When she came into view again, he had cut the gap between them to less than a hundred metres, but he realised she was bound to hear his trainers pounding on the gravel. Sure enough, she glanced over her shoulder and slowed to a halt.

'Go away!'

'I just want to talk.'

'That's what they all say,' she scoffed.

'Why don't you want to discuss the tribunal claim?'

'I told you. I never made a claim.' She jabbed a finger at him. 'Are you calling me a liar?'

He'd caught up with her at last. His injured leg was throbbing, his feet were sore, he was huffing and puffing like an old steam train, while she had scarcely broken sweat. But at least he had found her and it didn't look as though she was going to run away again.

'I realise Nerys went too far,' he panted. 'She was shocked by what you'd told her. You said that Symons had raped you.'

Suki flinched. 'It's got nothing to do with you, okay?'

'I saw Symons' body,' Harry said, more harshly than he had intended. 'Have you ever seen a decapitated corpse? Not a pretty sight.'

'He was never a pretty sight,' she said, matching the roughness of his tone.

'He was butchered, Suki. I'd like to know why.'

'You ought to leave it to the police.'

'And the police know he raped you, do they?'

'Nerys broke a confidence. She shouldn't have done what she did. I never asked her to.'

'I suppose she thought she was acting for the best.'

'Yeah, isn't that what most of the trouble-makers through history have said?'

'She believed in justice,' Harry said. 'She was desperate to see it done. And yet – you stopped her in her tracks. What I'm wondering is – why.'

'None of your business.'

'You were keen enough to talk to me before. When you wanted to find out whether I knew how Carl Symons died. When you wondered what the police had told me about the murder of Nerys.'

'That was different.'

'Are you so sure?'

'Yes, I bloody am!' She was trembling with anger. 'This – what you're asking me – is personal. Private stuff. You're crossing the line, Harry, and you don't have the right. You're harassing me.'

He wiped his forehead with his shirtsleeve. 'I don't mean to. I could have scuttled off to the police and told them what I've heard, leave it to Mitch Eggar to have a word with you.'

'And I'm expected to be grateful? You're not a knight in shining armour, you know. You're just a bloody nosey-parker. Always sticking your oar in where it doesn't belong!'

'Sure. I admitted that at the Maritime Bar, remember? But listen, if Symons was a rapist, isn't that something the police ought to know about? You're a prosecutor. You know better than me that it might give them a fresh lead.'

'What makes you think I haven't told them?'

She leaned against the brick wall that divided the path from the flat roofs of a row of garages. The tracksuit emphasised her muscles. The thought flashed through his mind that perhaps she might, just might, have possessed the physical power to cut a man's head from its body.

'Because you seem so desperate to keep your secret.'

'Is that surprising?' She could shift ground as fast as a flyweight in the ring. One day she'd be a great court advocate. 'You're telling me you're not able to understand how I felt? How many rape victims have you known?'

A girl Harry knew had once been raped. Her life had been left in ruins. 'A few,' he said tersely.

'Then are you saying I've made it up? That Symons never touched me?'

He shook his head. 'Somehow I don't have too much difficulty believing he was a rapist. Or that you were his victim. That's not the point. It would have taken plenty of courage to bring the claim. Lots of people wouldn't do it. But you're not short of guts. You'd already told Nerys about the rape...'

'Just between the two of us,' she interrupted.

'Okay. She was up in arms on your behalf. My guess is, she kept on until the last minute for making a claim, trying to persuade you to bring it out into the open. To buy herself a bit of time, she sent the form to the tribunal, so you wouldn't lose your right to compensation. I expect she was still thinking that when push came to shove, you'd allow her to represent you, to expose Symons for the man he really was. Maybe she knew enough about him from their days as partners to be confident that you were telling the truth. But even then, you wouldn't go through with it.'

'Nerys didn't just want me to sue Symons for sexual harassment, she said I should claim against the CPS as well. They employed him. He had the desk next to mine, he was my reporting officer. I said no. I didn't want to screw up my career.'

'If you'd come out in the open, there's every chance Symons' bosses would have taken your part. The odds are that he'd have been sacked and you'd have been free of him for ever.'

She shook her head. 'You just don't understand. I'd never have been free of him. He'd have made sure he destroyed me.'

'There are safeguards. The Press couldn't print your name during the hearing. The law wouldn't allow you to be victimised for bringing the claim, even if you lost.'

'Get real,' she scoffed. 'We both know how the justice game is played, don't we? I've seen plenty of women put through the wringer under cross-examination. Questions about their love life. Whether they wear saucy knickers, watch dirty films. No, thanks. I'd rather be on the right side of the witness box.'

'You're holding back on me.'

'And you're treating this like a bloody cross-examination,' she said through gritted teeth. 'I don't have to answer your questions, okay?'

'And I don't have to resist the temptation to tell Mitch Eggar what I've found out. But my impression is, you don't want me to do that.'

'Can't stop you, can I?'

'I'm not promising to keep my mouth shut if the police ask me straight questions, whatever you tell me now. All the same, I won't go mouthing off to all and sundry. It's up to you.'

She hooked her thumbs in the waistband of her tracksuit trousers. 'You're wondering if I killed Carl, aren't you?'

'I never said that. I'm curious, that's all.'

'What is it to you? The world's a better place without him. Isn't that all you need to know?'

'What about Nerys? Is it all for the best that she's dead, too?'

She ground her heel into the path. 'You know, I've decided Nerys had things in common with Carl. In different ways, they were both selfish. Couldn't see anyone else's point of view.'

He moved closer towards her, felt her warm breath on his cheeks. 'Selfishness isn't a capital offence.'

A couple of kids approached them, a boy and girl aged fourteen or fifteen. He had his hand inside her T-shirt; she was pretending to wriggle away from him. As they passed, the girl glanced at Suki. Harry guessed she was seeing a woman with her back to the wall, confronted by a man with only one thing on his mind, and drawing her own conclusions. She gave Suki a sidelong smile, as if to say: *they're all the same, aren't they?*

'Okay,' Suki said when the teenagers were out of earshot. 'Is that it?'

'Not quite. How did Nerys react when you told her to withdraw the claim?'

She shrugged. 'It was her fault. She should never have done it. I'd told her I didn't wish to make an issue about what Carl had done to me. She and I were close, I trusted her to respect my feelings. I'd never asked her to act as my lawyer.'

'So when she let you down, that was the end of a beautiful friendship?'

'She was furious.' Suki closed her eyes. He could tell she was reliving the past. 'You knew her. She was a fighter, always. For her, it was impossible to understand that I might not be able to cope with the flak in a tribunal hearing.'

Harry agreed with the dead woman. Suki still wasn't telling him the whole truth; his advocate's instinct told him that. There was no point in pressing her further, though. Not yet.

'She went ballistic, accused me of making the whole thing up. Lying to win her sympathy because I knew she detested Symons.'

'Did you manage to persuade her that it wasn't a lie?'

'In the end, I didn't even try to make her see sense.' She opened her eyes and looked straight at him. 'If she chose to believe that I'd been fantasising, that was up to her. No-one who really understood me could imagine that I was capable of inventing something like that.'

'Nerys rang me just before she died.'

Suki stared at him. 'To say what?'

'I wasn't there to take her call, so I'll never know for certain. She left a message, but I never had the chance to ring back before she was killed. My guess is, she wanted to share her knowledge about Symons being a rapist. Not to point the finger at you, simply to test my reaction. Perhaps she hoped I'd tell the police without involving you or her. There might have been other victims. It would have opened up a fresh line of inquiry.'

Suki said slowly, 'I wasn't the only woman he chanced his arm with. There was Andrea Gibbs, too.'

'Is that so?'

'So Nerys told me. When she found out her partner was trying it on with their trainee, Nerys put a stop to it. There was never a formal complaint. But Symons was an animal. He thought of nothing and no-one but himself. His own pleasure.'

'Muriel Scawfell reckons the pair of you had a thing going on at one time.'

'She's got a vivid imagination,' Suki said shortly.

'So you were never his girlfriend?'

'For Chrissake. He made my flesh creep. Always.'

'But he took liberties with you in public. Touched you up, fondled your bum.'

She shrugged. 'He disgusted me, okay? But we worked together. I was afraid of making a scene. Women in the law have to put up with a lot. Nerys knew that. She should have trusted me. She let me down. I deserved better, after all...'

'After what?' Harry demanded when her voice trailed away. 'After all you'd been through together?'

She clenched her fists. 'What are you suggesting?'

'Like you said earlier, it's none of my business.'

'Spit it out!'

'Well ...' Harry hesitated. 'I mean, you say the two of you were close friends. I was just wondering – how close?'

She bowed her head. When she spoke again her voice was muffled by tears. 'It's still none of your business, but you've guessed anyway. That stuff about Carl Symons – it ruined everything Nerys and I had together.'

Harry exhaled. He wandered over to the edge of the canal, picked up a pebble and threw it into the water. It made a loud splash; he stood with his hands in his pockets and watched the ripples spreading out.

Eventually she broke the silence. 'What's up with you?'

He turned to face her, gave a grim smile. 'Simply this. The more I learn, the more I realise there's so much I don't understand.'

They retraced their steps along the towpath. Harry was limping and Suki had to slow her pace to accommodate his. At the gate nearest to Vauxhall Hey, they parted with a muttered goodbye and he climbed back into the MG. He sat at the wheel for a long time before he switched the engine on, mulling over what she had told him. For sure, the waters of the canal were less murky than the events surrounding the murders of Carl Symons and Nerys Horlock.

He wasn't ready to go back home and so he spent a couple of hours driving round aimlessly, trying to straighten his thoughts. He took the road north to Southport, passing the windswept sand-dunes and the pier that stretched over the apparently endless beach to the distant sea. As the grey of afternoon gave way to twilight, he threaded along the lanes of Lancashire back towards Liverpool, but when the Empire Dock complex loomed ahead of him he still felt as weary and confused as ever. After his race along the canalside, his thighs and feet were hurting and there was still an ache in his guts from all the booze he'd knocked back the previous evening. Perhaps he'd better write the day off to experience, settle down in front of an old black and white movie and hope that things made more sense tomorrow.

The parking places nearest to the entrance to the building were all occupied, so he left his car three or four rows away. As he locked it, he heard a low voice calling to him.

'Harry Devlin!'

He peered through the gloom. Someone was standing in the shadows, perhaps a dozen paces ahead of him. A tall man wearing dark clothes, barely distinguishable from the gathering night.

'Who is it?'

'We've never met.'

The man began to walk towards him. His voice had a Welsh lilt, no doubt about it. Harry didn't recognise his face. His guts began to churn. This was the stranger Andrea Gibbs had warned him of. At last he had decided to make himself known.

'What do you want?' Harry demanded hoarsely.

The man paused. Harry glanced round. There were no other pedestrians in sight, although he could hear the engine of a car as it shuttled round in search of a free space. The man was in a direct line between him and the entrance to the building. He dare not risk making a dash for the sanctuary of the old warehouse building. He was stiff after all the driving. Even if he turned on his heel and headed for the Strand, the man might easily outpace him.

'I've been waiting for this moment for longer than you could ever imagine,' the man said. He sounded croaky, as though he were tense with expectation and his throat had dried. As he spoke, he began to thread his way between the parked cars. He was wearing a leather jacket, Harry saw. Was a gun or a knife concealed in one of the pockets?

Harry decided he did not want to find out. He would risk making a break for it. He spun round, lowered his head and charged in the direction of the car park exit.

There was never a chance that the driver of the Sierra could have missed him. He ran straight into its path as it turned into the lane where he had parked. At the last moment before impact, he glanced up and into the windscreen, to see the horrified face of the man behind the wheel. As the wing of the car tossed him off the ground, his last conscious thought was of the irony that, rather than coming to his rescue, Brett Young rather than the Welsh stranger would be the one to kill him.

Let It Bleed

The blood is the life! The blood is the life!

I always longed for immortality. To live forever was to achieve perfection. Now I'd say it was closer to perdition.

There's something you don't know. When I was fifteen years old. I came home from school one afternoon and went upstairs as usual to get changed. I found my mother in the bathroom, drenched in blood. She'd slashed her wrists; a problem with some man or other, I believe. She didn't leave a note to explain or to apologise. For a long time I hated her, called her a heartless bitch for what she'd done, but as I grew older I began to understand. I forgave her years ago for ending it all; that was her right. What still torments me is her failure to explain to me what was in her mind, even if only in a few lines, random jottings scrawled on a page torn out of an exercise book. A page like this, in fact.

Since that day, things for me have never been the same. I've thought about it ceaselessly, trying to make sense of the absurd. Lately I have come to realise that it isn't only death that we fear. We fear the dead themselves. My mother has haunted me since she killed herself. I've come to wish that she had taken me with her, on that journey into the dark unknown. For I have begun to recognise that eternal life would be a curse. Nothing to ache for, nothing but endless time and space for suffering.

So much better to die young – wouldn't you agree?

Chapter Seventeen

'Did you hear what I said? There's someone to see you.'

The woman's voice was muffled. It was as though she had a bandage over her mouth. The words did not make immediate sense as Harry stirred in his bed. Even the slight movement made him want to weep. His face and ribs were sore, his left leg numb. Was he paralysed, dying? He tried to scream, but no sound came. Slowly, very slowly, he forced his eyes to open.

A pinched face was hovering above his. The woman's eyes were narrow, her lips pursed. The severity of her expression suggested that she expected to be dissatisfied with his reaction. She resembled a schoolteacher marking the work of the class dunce. He blinked, trying to adjust to the brightness of the strip light in the ceiling.

'Uhhh ...' The sound rattled in his throat.

'Take your time,' she commanded. 'There's no rush. You're not going anywhere at present.'

He shifted his gaze – even his eyeballs were aching – and saw she was wearing a white uniform, polo shirt and trousers. He'd finished up in hospital, rather than the morgue. A wave of relief washed over him and he offered a silent prayer to the God in whom he was never quite sure whether he believed. He was in a small room for one, rather than a ward. Yellow flowers in a vase on the bedside table, umbrella plant silhouetted against the window. He tried to lever himself up, but was barely able to raise himself off the mattress. All the strength had drained from his body and he slumped back with a groan. Into his mind came the picture of Brett Young's frightened, helpless stare as the car lifted his body into the air.

'What ... happened?' He felt saliva dribbling from the corner of his mouth, but wasn't sure whether there was anything he could do about it.

'You were in an accident.'

Well, yes, I've gathered that. Irritation smothered the discomfort for a moment. The thought crawled into his mind that it was a good sign, it showed that in some small way he was on the mend.

'Bad?'

He held his breath as he waited for the answer. There was no sensation in his left leg. He had a sick feeling in his stomach and guessed he'd been doped up with painkillers.

'Could have been a lot worse,' she sniffed. 'You were lucky.'

'Ah.' The tension hissed out of him like air from a burst balloon.

'You'll need to take it easy, that's all.'

He made an attempt at a smile. She wrinkled her nose, but he couldn't blame her for that. The way his cheeks were stinging, he probably looked like something out of *The X Files*. He began to cough, a hacking, old man's noise. The aching of his ribs told him that coughing wasn't a good idea. Perhaps the painkillers were wearing off. 'It will be a while before I run a marathon.'

'You'll be right as rain if you show a smidgeon of common sense. Now, you have a visitor.'

'Who?'

'Your partner, Mr Crusoe. Are you fit enough to have a few words?'

'Send him in.'

The face bobbed away. He tried to stretch his limbs. They didn't like it and the sharp stab of reproof brought tears to his eyes. He swore hoarsely. Never mind. Think positive. He'd survived. The Welshman hadn't managed to kill him after all. Neither had Brett Young.

The door swung open and Jim said, 'Another fine mess, eh? How are you feeling?'

Harry made as if to reach for his partner's hand, but his ribs were still hurting. So much for the discipline of positive thinking. 'Shitty.'

'You're lucky to be alive.'

'Don't start telling me I should count my blessings. It's true, I realise. Just don't remind me.'

'You had a narrow escape, old son.'

'Yeah. Jaywalking can seriously damage your health. What time is it?'

'Five o'clock. Some of us have done a day's work. I was in the office before seven this morning. And before you ask, it's Tuesday.'

'Tuesday? Jesus. I've lost two whole days.'

'Yeah, all that chargeable time. You've been drifting in and out of consciousness ever since you stepped under the wheels of that car. This is the third time I've turned up here at the General, wondering if I'd catch you in a lucid interval. The triumph of hope over experience, you know...'

Harry grunted and rubbed his scalp gingerly. 'I feel like someone's been using my skull as a punchbag.'

'You hit the ground head first, apparently. The nurse told me you were knocked senseless. I explained there must be some mistake. You never had any sense to start with. Just as well you didn't talk me out of setting up those insurance premiums, eh?' He rubbed his shovel-like hands together. 'We're probably going to make more money whilst you're in here than if you were out doing the duty solicitor rota.'

'Don't say you had me run over as a way to make money.'

'If I'd thought of it first, I might have been tempted.' Jim straddled the visitor's chair. 'Can you remember the accident?'

'Everything's blurred. It wasn't Brett's fault, though. I was trying to get away from the Welshman.'

Jim scratched his stubble. 'I don't know what you're talking about. Sure you're *compos mentis*?'

'A splitting headache doesn't mean I'm doolally,' Harry said. 'Let me spell it out for you. I'm not blaming Brett Young for the accident. I walked straight under the wheels of his Sierra. No matter what he tried, he couldn't have helped hitting me.'

'So it *was* Brett.'

'Meaning what?' For once, he wasn't in the mood for riddles.

The big man pulled his chair closer to the bedside and said softly, 'The police are looking for him. In connection with the murders of Carl and Nerys. He's disappeared, no-one can find him. Last time anyone other than you saw him was when he came to our office the day after Nerys was killed. He's not been back home. The story goes that his girlfriend is beside herself with worry over what he might be up to on the run. His Sierra's turned up, though. Things are falling into place – he must have dumped it in a panic after he hit you. He left it near the Catholic Cathedral. I've heard Mitch Eggar giving a statement on the regional news. He says he believes Brett can assist with their inquiries, and we all know what that means.'

'Did Brett bring me in here?'

'No fear. An ambulance was called. Not by Brett, I'm pretty sure of that. Some passer-by at the other end of the car park saw a vehicle hit you and rushed over. He found you sprawled across the ground and dialled 999. Just as well he did. In the dark, a car could have run over you at any moment and finished the job off.'

The room was stuffy, but suddenly Harry felt cold. It had not occurred to him that Brett might have left him to die. 'And the Welshman?'

'What Welshman?'

He closed his eyes, felt his head lolling back on the pillow. Talking had exhausted him. There were still plenty of questions, but finding out the truth about what had happened to him would have to wait. 'Have they said how long I need to stay in here?'

'Itching to get back to your desk, eh? No, I had a word with the sister before I came in. They've been worried about the concussion.

A couple of ribs are cracked and you've made a mess of your leg, tore a lot of skin off, but not badly enough for you to need a graft.'

'Marvellous,' Harry mumbled.

'No problem,' Jim said with the brisk assurance of a man who'd never suffered a day's illness since childhood. 'It'll heal soon enough. Mind, even by your standards, you're not a pretty sight at present. You took a hell of a whack when you hit the deck. That's why they wanted to keep a close eye on you. I gather they did a brain scan. Reckon to have found something there, by all accounts.'

'You're all heart,' Harry said wearily. He was fighting to keep his side of the conversation going, but it was a losing battle.

'That's me,' Jim said. 'A true lawyer.'

He fell into a shallow sleep, dreams coming in fragments. The sight of Carl Symons' staring eyes, the thick blood necklace beneath his head. Suki Anwar running away into the distance, his body aching with defeat as he lost ground, realised that he could never catch her up. The dark shape of a stranger, pacing forwards in slow motion. *I've been waiting for this moment for a long time. I've been waiting for this moment for a long time.* As the phrase was repeated, the lilt disappeared so that the catarrhal Scouse growl was disguised no longer. A shaft of moonlight fell upon the man's face. It belonged to Casper May. In his hand was an axe with a gleaming blade. *I beat the truth out of my wife months ago. Yes, I've been waiting for this moment for a long time.*

He jerked back to consciousness, sweat running down his cheeks. Oblivious to the warning twinge from his rib cage, he shifted his position in the bed, raised his arms. He needed to touch his neck, make sure that it had not been cut. The skin beneath where he shaved was smooth, his Adam's apple bobbing nervously. He opened his eyes and looked into the face of Juliet May.

'Just as well I didn't bring any grapes,' she said. 'I'd have finished them off all by myself, waiting for you to surface.'

'I was – dreaming.'

'Nightmare, by the look of things.' Her tone was light, she was trying not to smile. He hadn't seen her so relaxed since they had made love in Linda Blackwell's cottage. 'See, you've thrown your bedclothes off. Bad boy. The nurse will put you across her knee. And don't think you'll enjoy that. She's a real Gorgon.'

'Whatever happened to the angels you see in films and telly programmes, all sexy in their starched uniforms and black tights?'

'Disappeared in the health service reforms, I guess. That lady looks like she wears knickers made out of emery paper. So what were you dreaming about? Being cosseted back to health by Hot Lips Houlihan while "Suicide is Painless" plays in the background?'

'As it happens, I was thinking about Casper.'

'So it *was* a nightmare. What are you worrying about him for? There's no problem, none at all. He has enough on his plate at the moment, wondering how to cash in on the geriatrics he's taken under his wing. I've been left to my own devices this evening, so I thought I'd pop in and see the invalid.'

'Thanks.'

She sat down and crossed her legs. 'Remember this skirt?'

It was a leather mini. She had wonderful legs, she could dress like a nineteen-year-old and get away with it. She'd been wearing the same skirt the first night they had made love.

'Brings back memories.'

'Some life left in the old dog yet, then. God, it's hot in here. Why are all hospitals over-heated? I'm sure it's not healthy.' She gestured to her purple jersey. 'Mind if I take this off?'

'Be my guest.'

She pulled the jersey off over her head. Underneath she was wearing a white top that revealed a flat midriff and her lack of a

216

bra. Harry felt the first stirrings of desire. Perhaps lust was the best medicine.

'I brought you something to while away the time,' she said with a grin, handing him a green Penguin edition of *The Daughter of Time*. 'It's the one about the hospitalised detective. Couldn't resist it somehow. Do you like the flowers I sent, by the way? Don't worry, I didn't give the florist my name. No-one here knows who they came from. I've done my best to be discreet. I told the nurse I was one of your clients.'

Terrific. Really credible. How many clients visit their brief in hospital? 'Uh-huh,' he said with a grumpy cough.

'So how are you, darling? Getting better, so I hear.'

'Allegedly.'

'Feeling sorry for yourself, eh? All men are the same. They like to be coddled. Low pain thresholds. You'd never survive giving birth.'

'Maybe not.' He had cramp in his leg and let out a groan. 'Christ, I'm dying of thirst. Can you pour me some water?'

There was a jug next to the bedside bouquet. She filled a tumbler and handed it to him. 'So tell me, did you jump in front of the wheels of this car or were you pushed?'

'It's a long story.'

'Visiting time is up in twenty minutes. Let me prop you up on a couple of pillows and you can give me the gist.'

He gave a short account of the events he could remember from Sunday. Even to order his thoughts in a semi-coherent fashion was tiring. She sat next to him, holding his hand almost in an absent-minded way as he talked. When he'd finished, she lifted his fingers to her lips and kissed them one by one.

'You poor thing. So Brett Young has done a runner?'

'He'll be afraid the police have him in the frame for killing his two ex-partners. Rational thought isn't his strong point.'

'Makes you wonder how he ever qualified as a solicitor. I thought that was what you were all supposed to be good at. Detached, objective judgment.'

'You obviously don't know that many solicitors.'

'One I know very well indeed, thank you,' she said, squeezing his hand. 'And that's quite enough. Mind you, I'm very glad he's not been too badly injured. Though I have to say, darling, I have seen you on days when you've looked more gorgeous. Swollen lips, yellowing bruises, they're not my favourite turn-on.'

Yet you sleep with a man who hurts you. Harry felt a sudden flame of jealousy spurt up in his heart. He moistened his lips and said, 'Let's just say I'm in no hurry to look in a mirror.'

'Sensible,' she said with mock gravity. 'Okay, so where are we? Brett's the prime suspect so far as the police are concerned, but no-one apart from you and this Gibbs girl have any idea about this chap with the Welsh accent who's keeping you under surveillance. Are you absolutely certain you don't have any idea who he might be?'

'Cross my heart and hope not to die. I've been racking my brains ever since Andrea first mentioned him to me, but I've drawn a total blank.'

'A client whose case you messed up? Sort of Phantom of the Law Courts?'

'You may not believe this, but I don't make a habit of treating my clients so badly that years later they set about stalking me with a view to murder.'

'We all make mistakes.'

'Maybe I make more than my fair share. Even so, none of this stacks up. I've known plenty of Welsh people. You can't spend a lifetime in Liverpool and not. The bloody country's only just round the corner. Yet I can't imagine who this feller could be. Even when I heard him speak, his voice didn't ring any bells.'

She furrowed her brow. 'Then there's only one conclusion, isn't there?'

'That it's the same man who killed Carl Symons and Nerys Horlock?'

'Got it in one. Someone with a grudge against lawyers. Maybe he's not an embittered ex-client, just someone who dislikes solicitors in general.'

'The Lord Chancellor's bad enough.'

She waved away his feeble attempt at humour. 'Perhaps he's simply picked names from a list at random.'

'And he chose me.'

'Remember what the Tarot said that time? That something special and unexpected was going to happen. You were going to be sought out.'

'I thought it meant my numbers coming up on the Lottery.'

'You always were a sucker for wishful thinking.' She fired a quick smile, as if she'd wondered if he might misunderstand and think she was referring to their relationship. 'Cheer up. He can't get you in here. The place is bristling with security cameras, chaps in uniforms on the look-out for baby-snatchers and nurse-bashers. You're quite safe.'

'For how long? I can't live off the National Health Service for the rest of my life.'

'You won't be moving for a day or two, I guess. Even though the suits will be telling the medics they need your bed, I doubt they'll turf you out just yet. The sister said they'd be moving you on to a ward tomorrow morning. You can have a few words with the police. If you can remember enough to come up with some sort of description, they may be able to pick this fellow up before you're discharged. Perhaps he's already known to them, someone who used to be a patient in a psychiatric unit, something like that.'

'Terrific. And if they don't have a clue where he might be, presumably I borrow a neckbrace from orthopaedics to give me a bit of protection for the next time he decides to try his luck.'

'The police may be willing to offer you a guard. Or you could keep your head down for a while. Take a holiday.'

'What, go into hiding until the *fatwa*'s lifted? I'm not the legal profession's answer to Salman Rushdie, you know.'

'Fed up with the Satanic nurses, are you? Well, you've had a rough time, you could use a break.'

'Yeah, and if I mess Jim about any more, he'll probably break my neck himself.'

'Don't be silly. You can't help it. There's this lunatic out on the streets and until he's caught, it makes sense to take precautions. If you're careful, there simply won't be a problem. He may even have been scared off on Sunday afternoon. Perhaps Brett spotted him and he panicked. That's why he didn't try to finish you off.'

'Presumably he thought Brett had done his dirty work for him,' Harry said gloomily. 'It was bad enough when I thought I only had Casper's wrath to fear. Now that seems like the good old days.'

Juliet stretched her limbs. 'I hate to sound unsympathetic...'

'That's what people say when they're about to be *very* unsympathetic,' Harry interrupted.

'Okay, okay. I'm truly sorry about what you've been through. But I was talking to Linda this afternoon. If you think your life's in a mess, what about her? She worshipped Peter. His death has ruined her life.'

After a pause, Harry said, 'You're right, of course. I'd forgotten all about her. Selfish of me. How is she?'

'She's still staying in our annexe for the time being. She's been keeping busy, she says it's her way of staying sane after everything that's happened to her lately. The last couple of mornings, she's even insisted on coming into the office, helping me to keep up to date with work. And she's been over at Peter's flat, going through his things.'

'Has she any other family?'

'No-one close. She doesn't even have much in the way of friends apart from me. She's always lived for her son. Apart from Peter, she's devoted herself to her work. The best assistant I could have. I wish I could do something to help her. There's money, sure, I can put my hand in my pocket. But it comes down to this: nothing can bring her boy back.'

Harry thought about Liz. Same thing: you could fix a damaged roof, but people were irreplaceable. 'You need to keep an eye on her. Make sure she doesn't do anything silly.'

Juliet nodded. 'I'm worried. Whenever we talk, she goes to great lengths to convince me she's calm and in control, but I'm sure it's all an act. Deep down, she's in turmoil. Trouble is, she's a proud woman. Strong, independent. We've known each other a long time, but she's very self-contained. Keeps her feelings to herself, so you can never be sure what's raging under the surface. Someone like that is hard to look after.'

'Tell her I'm thinking of her, will you? She saved us the night Carl Symons was killed.'

'You're dead right. We owe Peter too, despite what he said to me when he was drunk.' Juliet paused. Her hesitancy was uncharacteristic. The thought struck him that he couldn't recall having seen her blush. Embarrassment was foreign to her. But something was on her mind. 'Look, I don't know how to say this, but there's one thing I'd better get off my chest. When I told you Peter was dead, this weird look came into your eyes. It was as if you were looking at a stranger. Someone you were scared of.'

The conversation was moving into dangerous waters. He sensed a need to plot his course with care. 'It came as a shock, what you told me. That must have been it.'

221

She took a breath. 'I wondered – if you suspected that I might have had something to do with his accident.'

He wasn't mobile enough to squirm, but he felt as uncomfortable as he had when he'd first woken up in the hospital bed. 'I don't know why...'

'You're not good at evasion, Harry,' she said, softly insistent. 'I'm right, aren't I?'

He couldn't bring himself to admit the truth. It seemed to him that if he did, their relationship was finished. At the back of his mind, there also lurked a fear that that might not be the worst that could happen. 'You're making something out of nothing. I know you wouldn't harm him. Your friend's boy.'

'I did say that I wished him dead, remember?'

How could I forget? 'It was the heat of the moment,' Harry said. 'He was a sad mixed-up drunk who deliberately set out to hurt you.'

'I'll be honest,' she said, and it was as if she were talking to herself. 'It's a good thing I didn't have a gun at the moment when he threatened me. I might have pulled the trigger. You know me. I'm a bit crazy at times.'

You know me. Not even warm: she remained a mystery to him. He was even beginning to think that the more he got to know her, the less he understood what made her tick. 'Most of us are a little crazy, every now and then,' he said. 'The police are satisfied Peter's death was an accident, aren't they?'

'Yes.' She swallowed. 'Yes, they are.'

'There you are, then.'

'You wondered, though, didn't you? Wondered whether I had it in me – to kill in cold blood, then make it look like an accident.'

'I wonder about lots of things. That's one of my problems. Life's a lot easier if you don't have any imagination. But of course you didn't kill Peter.'

She took his hand. 'Okay, let's say no more about it. He's gone and we're still here together. That is, unless you've decided you've had enough of me.'

The pressure on his palm warmed him. She'd guessed that at times she frightened him; perhaps the thought even turned her on. But he was afraid of losing her. 'Or you of me.'

She dropped his hand, slipped hers under the bedclothes, raising her eyebrows at what she found. 'Well, well. Seems to me like you're a long way down the road to recovery.'

He gave her a crooked smile. 'When I get out of here, you'll have to be gentle with me.'

She leaned over the bed, let her tongue touch his dry lips. 'So you do want to see me again?'

He could smell her subtle perfume and it made him want to put his arms round her, pull her down beside him. Hoarsely, he said, 'Yes. But what do you want?'

She closed her eyes and breathed out, breasts moving beneath her skimpy top. 'I wish I knew, Harry. I wish I knew.'

Next morning he was transferred to a small open ward. His head and body still ached, but even the hypochondriac in him could accept that he would soon be fit again. A doctor came to have a look at him and said that he didn't expect the concussion to have any lasting effects. There was every chance that he would be discharged within the next twenty-four hours. Encouraged, he chatted idly about soccer with a man in the next bed and after his companion fell asleep he glanced at the paperback that Juliet, tongue firmly in cheek, had brought for him. But somehow he couldn't work up much enthusiasm for re-investigating the mystery of the Princes in the Tower. More pressing things were on his mind. Like whether he should tell Mitch Eggar that Brett had run him over and whether his desire for Juliet still outweighed his fear of the consequences if Casper May found out.

He'd put the book down and was on the point of dozing off himself when he heard the door of the ward being pushed open. His eyelids were drooping and he didn't bother to look up. People kept coming and going; hospitals were always full of passing strangers. Footsteps rapped against the floortiles. He was vaguely aware of someone reaching his bedside. A polite cough roused his attention.

He found himself staring at someone he had seen only once before. The tall Welshman who had pursued him into the path of Brett Young's taxi. The man who had been pursuing him, the man responsible for his present invalid state. He was staring down with undisguised fascination, as if scarcely able to credit that Harry was still alive.

Harry's heart felt as though it were crashing against the walls of his chest. He scarcely dared to breathe. Helplessness swamped him. It was as if he'd been afflicted by paraplegia. A quick glance confirmed that the football fan in the next bed was still slumbering. An old chap in the bed opposite was snoring peacefully. There was a screen round someone at the far end of the little ward. The beds in between were empty. In the heart of a busy hospital, in the midst of a large city, Harry had never been so alone.

'Harry Devlin.' A soft voice, deep but not unmusical.

Harry could barely muster a groan. 'What do you want?'

He'd asked the same question of Juliet the previous evening, but now he dreaded the answer. The Welshman's brow furrowed. His skin was pale, as though he'd spent most of his life indoors, yet he had a spare athletic build. He shifted from one foot to another in an awkward manner, like an overgrown schoolboy expecting a reprimand.

'I've been waiting for this moment for a long time. I can't tell you how long. All my life, it seems.'

He was talking half to himself, in a tone of amazement. His dress was casual, navy blue sweater and dark denim jeans that were worn at the knees. The way his hands were clasping and unclasping reminded Harry of himself on that never-to-be-forgotten day that he'd asked Liz to become his wife. The man was nervous. Not a shadow of a doubt. He might have murder on his mind, but he was as tense as a Victorian virgin on her wedding night.

Under the bedsheets, Harry clenched his fists. All might not yet be lost. Perhaps he could talk himself out of trouble. It might be a vain hope, but anything was worth a try. He loved life, for all that he had experienced some of its agonies, and he would not let it go without a fight.

'I'm flattered,' he said slowly, forcing out each syllable with care, desperate not to reveal his fear. 'But I must be honest. I don't understand.'

'It's a long story, Mr Devlin.'

Good. Let's keep him talking.

'You see, it's about my mother.'

That bastard Freud, he has a lot to answer for. 'Right. You want to tell me about it?'

'I'm sorry. I'm not making much sense, am I? Especially to someone who's recovering from a bad accident. How are you feeling? I should have asked that before anything.'

'Fine. Thanks. Could have been much worse.'

The man nodded slowly. 'Yes. I should have introduced myself, incidentally. My name's Daniel Roberts.'

'Pleased to meet you.'

'The name means nothing to you. Why should it? But perhaps if I give you another name, that will help to explain why I'm here.'

'All right, then. Let's hear it.' Every muscle in Harry's battered body was tense. He was sure that the man was about to tell him something shocking, something to make him cringe with shame. But he could not begin to guess what it might be.

225

'Maria Ellen Brady.'

The name hit Harry like a punch in the stomach from a trusted friend. It was so unexpected. He could not speak, simply gaped at the man in bewilderment.

'Yes, it's true,' Daniel Roberts said. 'She was my mother, but she gave me away. Years later, she married a man called John Garett Devlin. And they had one son. A boy called Harry.'

Chapter Eighteen

'Is that better?' Daniel asked a couple of minutes later.

Harry gulped down another mouthful of water from the tumbler the Welshman had filled. Once again, he'd been knocked flying. He was dazed, unable to make sense of what he was being told, far less capable of deciding whether or not to believe it. His visitor didn't mean to kill him, that seemed certain. Relief washed over him like a tide. But what he said could not be true – could it? Wires must somewhere have become crossed. Daniel Roberts was deceiving himself. It was a case of mistaken identity. Had to be.

Had to be.

'I'm sorry,' Daniel said. 'Stands to reason that I've shocked you. Believe me, I've rehearsed this scene a thousand times and the truth is, I've never got it right yet.'

'Well,' Harry mumbled after a pause, 'that's a feeling I'm familiar with myself.'

'The last thing I'd intended was to introduce myself in this way, at your bedside in a hospital, but it didn't seem right to wait any longer. I screwed my courage up to visit you at your flat and then I messed everything up. It was a mistake approaching you in the car park. I see that now. You jumped out of your skin. Before I realised what was happening, you'd run under the wheels of that taxi.'

'You were the one who called an ambulance,' Harry said slowly, working it out for himself. He had to make sense of things in manageable bits, solve the multitude of mysteries one at a time. 'I'd assumed it was Brett – that is, the driver who hit me.'

'You know him? My God. One thing I can say for sure is, the fellow didn't stop. I glimpsed him through the window and panic was written all over his face.'

'I saw that too.'

'Understandable, perhaps. Even so, he shouldn't have put his foot down like that. He drove straight off. I should have taken his number, but I was in a state of shock myself.' Daniel was talking quickly. Harry sensed he was nervous, perhaps unused to saying much. But now the words were pouring out. 'You were crumpled up on the ground. I was petrified, instinctively thought you'd been killed. Imagine it. I come face to face with my half-brother after all these years and he ends up dead before I've even told him my name.'

Half-brother. The words, the whole idea, were so alien that Harry blotted them out of his mind. He wasn't ready to learn a foreign language. Better to concentrate on the things he could take in. He cleared his throat and said, 'So you were the passer-by, the one who dialled 999?'

'I dragged you out of the way of the traffic, that was the first thing I did. The car hit you a glancing blow...'

'It felt worse than that,' Harry said, rubbing his damaged cheek. It still smarted to the touch.

'Those cuts and bruises don't look too clever, either,' Daniel said, disconcertingly blunt. 'Just as well it didn't hit you head on. The crack when you hit the deck was bad enough. Anyhow, I left you propped up between a clapped-out Mini and a BMW. The sublime and the ridiculous, you might say.'

Harry grunted and swallowed the rest of the water. He felt his headache beginning to ease. Time to take stock. The first question was whether Daniel Roberts was all right in the head. Even if he lacked a darker purpose, he might yet prove to be a wandering eccentric obsessed by a ludicrous fantasy. At first glance he seemed sane enough, but if experience had taught Harry one thing, it was that appearances were deceptive. The very notion that his own mother had given birth to this stranger was bizarre. For the moment, though, there was no choice but to humour him.

'I ran over to the lodge in the dock building where you live.' Daniel chewed his lip as he cast his mind back. 'The chap on duty at the desk didn't waste time. He called the ambulance and said he'd take care of things. I had an attack of cold feet, decided I ought to take my chance to melt away. I'd come so near and yet so far, you see. Needed a bit of time to sort myself out. Besides, there was nothing I could do. You were a hospital case. I told myself the best I could do was to drive back home and then ring up to check on your progress.'

'You live in Liverpool?'

Daniel shook his head. 'Cities aren't my cup of tea. I've heard people say Liverpool's simply an overgrown village, but...'

'It's true, you know.'

'Not my idea of a village, let's say. I have a tumbledown cottage up on a hillside in Snowdonia. My nearest neighbours are a mile away. You won't have heard of the place. Even if you did, you'd never be able to pronounce it.'

Harry sucked air into his lungs. 'I suppose you'd better tell me the story.'

'About how I came to track you down?'

'About everything.'

Daniel swallowed. 'I was brought up in Penmaenmawr. Perhaps you've been there.'

'Uh-huh.' A little resort on the coast between Llandudno and Bangor. Harry had played on the beach as a kid one holiday when the family had been staying in Conwy. He'd built a sandcastle with the help of his mother. Maria Ellen Devlin, the woman he had thought he knew so much about.

'My parents ran a cafeteria on the main road. The Druid's House, it was called.' Daniel half-closed his eyes, remembering. 'They were decent people, well respected. Regular chapel-goers, you know the sort of thing. So they were honest with me right from the start. For as long as I can remember, I've known that I

229

was adopted. But they made me feel good about it, they explained how they had picked me out. I felt a cut above most of my mates at school. Their parents hadn't had the luxury of choice, see. As for me, I was special.'

Harry earned his living listening to people who told lies. He'd spent years conducting cross-examinations, but he'd never imagined interrogating someone who claimed to be his half-brother. Better take it gently; no point in treating the man as a hostile witness. No need to hurry. Let him tell his story in his own way, then pore over it for inconsistencies, the bits that didn't quite ring true.

'What did they say about – your own background?'

'Not much. They weren't trying to protect me, they simply hadn't been told. I was illegitimate, obviously. Born to a young girl who couldn't cope with a child in the days before the permissive society got into its stride. That's really all I knew.'

'But you wanted to find out something more?'

'Not for a long time, I didn't. I was quite content. I went to a local school and that was okay. Then university at Aberystwyth. I read English there. Books always fascinated me, that's why. My father, Dai Roberts that is, he was a great talker. Marvellous yarn-spinner, the customers loved him and so did I. I wanted to follow in his footsteps and tell stories for a living. But things didn't work out the way I'd planned.'

'They usually don't,' Harry said.

'During my second year at uni, he had a heart attack whilst he was cooking breakfasts at the café. Mum struggled on with the café for a while, but it became too much for her. Looking back, I don't suppose I was much help. She sold the place for a song and married one of the blokes who'd worked in the kitchen. He was a younger man with an eye on the main chance. She was pretty, even in her fifties, but she was soft, too. Gullible, really. He cleaned her out and then he dumped her. Six months later, the week after I did my finals, she had a stroke. I came back and took a job in the town while I nursed her. She recovered, but her powers of speech were limited and she wasn't able to walk without a frame. All the same, she was a tough old bird. It took eighteen years for her to die. Eighteen years. I won't pretend it was an easy time.'

'No.' Harry had little first-hand experience of serious illness. Perhaps it helped to explain his hypochondria. He was afraid of the unknown.

'I had thought about training as a teacher, without making any definite plans. I'd enjoyed being a student, wasn't ready to put down roots or turn an honest penny. I wanted to travel, perhaps do a bit of writing. I'd always had this dream of becoming a novelist. Anyway, Mum's stroke put paid to that. I worked in a little bookshop for six or seven years until the proprietor went bust. The theory was that it would keep me in touch with literature. Of course you'll probably tell me it had as much to do with writing a masterpiece as manning the turnstile at Anfield has to do with playing in the Premiership.'

'Uh-huh.' Harry had never given much thought to writing a masterpiece although over the years, one or two magistrates had suggested that his speeches in mitigation qualified as classics of creative fiction.

'After that I had to take whatever came along. I've waited on in hotels, served behind bars, sold clothes and hardware in shops on the high street. I wasn't mobile, you see. I couldn't move away. Carers can't. Your life isn't your own.'

'So it was around this time that you started to get curious about – where you came from?'

'That's right. It began to sneak up on me, this feeling that I didn't understand the truth about myself. I realised that unless I could put the missing pieces of my personal jigsaw together, I'd always be incomplete as a man. It became a craving, the need to learn about my mother and father. It's – it's impossible to explain.'

'I suppose I can guess.' An odd idea struck Harry. Perhaps the need to know that had obsessed Daniel was simply another species of the inquisitiveness that he so often succumbed to himself. It might be a family characteristic, for God's sake. He made a conscious effort to banish the thought. The Welshman hadn't begun to prove his case yet.

'You can? Well, maybe. I hope so, at any rate. But I was scared, Harry. What if it turned out that I was the child of a couple of criminals? All sorts of wild fancies cross your mind when you don't have a clue about your origins. And I was worried about my mum. Mrs Roberts, that is. She'd been good to me, now she was frail and dependent. I felt as though I was dishonouring her, behaving as though what she'd given me for a start in life simply wasn't enough. So I kept my thoughts to myself. I decided I'd do nothing about it as long as she was alive. Otherwise, it would feel like a breach of trust. A betrayal.'

'And when she died?'

'It hit me hard.' Daniel closed his eyes again. 'I'd waited for her to go for so long, and when I was finally released, I couldn't cope. It's a bit like a long-term prisoner who reaches the end of his sentence and then finds that he can't come to terms with the outside world.'

'Bad luck,' Harry muttered. 'Takes a while to recover from something like that.'

'If you ever do.' Daniel shook his head. 'I'd always written, all those years tucked away in my little Welsh backwater, I'd scribbled down bits of prose. Weird tales. Sort of cross between Tolkien and Lovecraft, if you can imagine any such thing.'

'Not my cup of tea. I never picked up *The Hobbit*.'

Daniel gave him a bleak smile. 'I suffer from insomnia. I don't know why, doctors can't explain it. But I don't sleep at night. At least it gives me plenty of time for writing. Once or twice I sent pieces to magazines. They always came winging back through the post. Quite right, too. With hindsight, I see it. I didn't realise at the time, but the stuff was pretty feeble. Plagiaristic, too. It didn't deserve to be printed. But I kept trying. Eventually, I wrote something better. Derivative still, but better. I picked up one or two acceptances. It gave me something to cling to.'

Harry shifted his position on the propped-up pillows. He couldn't see where all this was leading. 'You started looking in earnest for your real mother,' he prompted.

'Eventually. I sold the house, bought my cottage in the back of beyond and decided to concentrate on writing a novel. I took a job at a truckstop a few miles from where I'd grown up, to keep the wolf from the door while I worked on the manuscript. Whenever I got a spare minute, I began to burrow away for information about my past.'

'Difficult?'

'Time-consuming. You don't need me to tell you that the law entitles adopted kids to their birth records. It's mainly a question of trawling through masses of information, hoping for a stroke of luck. I made contact with a tracing agency. They help people like me, offer counselling and practical advice. I discovered that Maria Ellen Brady had been seventeen years old. That name was my starting point. I tried to conjure up a picture of her, the young girl who had given birth to me. I guessed she came from a Catholic family, that in those days getting pregnant was a terrible disgrace.'

'I suppose it was.'

In his mind, Harry was seeing the round, pretty face of his mother. Through the haze of memory, it seemed that she had always been laughing, teasing the old man about his shyness, his self-consciousness in company. She'd died before he'd ever had the chance to know her as a person. He couldn't picture her as a teenager, lonely and scared of the consequences for her life of the human being that had begun to grow inside her.

'Next step was to find her marriage certificate. Sure enough, I turned it up. She hadn't married my natural father, but six years after I was born she became Mrs Devlin. I was excited. At last I was on the track. A bit more detective work gave me an address in Liverpool where that particular family of Devlins had lived. I summoned up the nerve to make a phone call. And then the person I spoke to, someone who remembered the family, broke the news, the terrible news. The couple had died together in a road accident years ago. It couldn't have been worse. A disaster. I wept for hours on end. All those years, I'd dreamed of meeting my real mother. And now it would never happen.'

'What about your natural father?'

'I talked to the social worker who had been given my file from the local authority where I'd been adopted. She gave me his name. He was called Harvey, he was a lecturer. I wondered if Maria was one of his students, though I never checked that out. It all seemed immaterial, because I found that Harvey was dead as well. Cancer. He'd never married, perhaps he wasn't into commitment. Maybe he enjoyed making free with the girls he taught too much. Whatever. He was only thirty-six when they buried him.'

Harry said quietly, 'And where do I come into all this?'

'For a long time, I was too devastated to do anything more. All my efforts seemed to have been in vain. I'd left it too late. I can't explain how much it hurt, Harry. We all need to know where we come from, get to grips with our own personal history.'

'Sure.' *And you're re-writing mine.*

'You see, the simple truth was that I'd never had the chance to speak to anyone who was related to me by blood. Can you imagine how that feels – the isolation, the sense of being abandoned?'

Daniel was leaning over the bed, spreading his long bony arms as if in supplication. Harry wanted to shrink back from him. He was afraid that the man was investing hope in him, as if he believed that Harry possessed a key that would enable him to unlock the secrets of his life.

'So you decided to seek me out.'

'Eventually I started to wonder if the Devlins' marriage had produced any children. After all the searching I'd carried out, the last exercise was the simplest of all. It was easy to establish that a son had been born. It took some time to sink in, that did. I had a half-brother. I made enquiries, eventually discovered that he was a solicitor, practising in Liverpool. Still alive.'

'If only just,' Harry murmured.

Daniel laughed. The man in the next bed stirred at the sound; his eyelids flickered, but then he turned over and went back to sleep. 'I heaved a sigh of relief, I can tell you. I was afraid you might have emigrated to Australia, something like that. Instead, you were practically on my doorstep. I'd come so far, I couldn't possibly let it go. I had to find you.'

He pulled out his wallet and showed Harry the photograph he'd taken from the old newspaper in the archive. 'See, I found your picture. Once I knew who I was looking for, the rest was easy. By the way, here's a copy of my birth certificate. See her name there?'

Harry shifted his position to study the certificate more closely. The movement made his ribs hurt, but he didn't notice the pain. Daniel's story had left him numb.

'I – I don't know what to say.'

'You'd be entitled to tell me to get lost. I've broken the rules, I guess. It's quite wrong to do things the way I have. Turning up out of the blue like this.'

'Not quite out of the blue.'

'What do you mean?'

'The woman you spoke to at the Legal Group office told me about you. I thought I'd got myself a stalker.'

'Oh, God, I'm sorry. I should have contacted you through the proper channels. God, what an idiot I am. There's a protocol for doing these things. Social workers ought to be involved.'

Harry shrugged. 'At least you spared me that.'

The door opened and the nurse appeared. Daniel moistened his lips. 'I'd better leave. Here, I've scribbled my number down, in case you want to get in touch. It's up to you, I don't expect you to say yes or no right now. I've given you more than enough to think about. It must all be a hell of a shock.'

Harry took the crumpled piece of paper, put it on the bedside table without glancing at it. The patient at the far end of the ward had woken and the nurse was talking to him. 'So you're a writer,' he said at last.

'Pre-published, as the Americans say. But that's how I think of myself, as a writer. Always have done. Sounds better than a truckstop attendant, eh? Mind you, I'm still working on the final draft of my manuscript.'

'What exactly is it about?'

Daniel coloured. 'Oh, I don't have too many literary pretensions these days. I've not shown the Journal to anyone yet. It's meant to be a spine-chiller, actually. All about a man in pursuit of a legend. He's the grandson of Jonathan Harker and he idolises his grandfather's mentor, an old professor by the name of Abraham Van Helsing.'

Harry frowned. 'The name rings a bell.'

'So it should. Van Helsing hunted vampires. He's a character who has always fascinated me. You must remember, he was the man who killed Count Dracula.'

'At least he can't be after your money, old son,' Jim said through a mouthful of crisps when he looked in at lunch-time.

236

'I suppose he's harmless,' Harry admitted, shaking his head as his partner offered him the packet. Worcester Sauce flavour had never appealed to him. 'And yet there was something scary about him. The way he'd been devoured by this *obsession...*'

'Runs in the family, obviously,' the big man said with a crooked grin. 'I reckon that proves he's not having you on.'

'Everything he said had the ring of truth,' Harry admitted. 'But there was so much to take in. I was just glad I wasn't going to be murdered in my bed. As for this idea that my mum had another kid – well, it's going to take some getting used to.'

'She never dropped a hint?'

'To me, no. Remember, I was – what? – just fourteen when she was killed. Whether my father had any inkling, I can't even guess. She always seemed so open. A nothing-to-hide kind of woman.'

'We all have skeletons tucked away,' Jim said and Harry guessed his partner was recalling his brief fling with the policewoman. 'Usually it's better for all concerned if they stay out of sight.'

'Sure,' he agreed, thinking about Juliet and Casper May. 'But I can't imagine why he'd want to make up something like this. Let alone forge a birth certificate. If it's all a load of hogwash, I'll be able to prove he's lying easily enough. No, the more I mull it over, the more convinced I am that he must be right. I have a half-brother I never knew existed.'

'Another Christmas present to buy, eh?'

'I always thought I was alone,' Harry said. He was trying to be matter-of-fact about it, but he couldn't keep the note of wonderment out of his voice. 'Then this spooky stranger turns out to be the only flesh and blood I have in the world.'

'You say he's a writer?'

Harry sighed. 'Yeah. And that's what's been bothering me.'

Jim frowned. 'I'm not with you.'

'Look at it this way. The guy's obsessed by a vampire hunter. He told me *Dracula* is his all-time favourite book...'

'Mine's *The Day of the Jackal*,' Jim interrupted, 'but that doesn't mean I'm into assassinating French politicians.'

'Hang on a moment.' He was recalling his conversation with Juliet. 'Ken Cafferty insists there's a vampire connection between the killings of Symons and Horlock. Suppose Daniel Roberts has some kind of grudge against members of the legal profession...'

'Forget it.' Jim stood up. 'If you start looking for people who fit that particular bill, you'll be spoiled for choice.'

'You're letting your imagination run riot,' Juliet said that afternoon.

'Blame it on your dress,' Harry said, stroking her thigh. 'Talk about a pick-me-up. When you leaned over to pour the water...'

She wriggled away from him. 'Behave. I meant – this idea that your half-brother...'

'If he is who he says he is.'

'Come on. You don't seriously believe he'd go to the trouble of pretending to be related to you? Imagine the damage it will do to his credit rating.'

'Thanks a lot.'

'Any time. Look, it's a wonderful thing that has happened to you, can't you see that? It's amazing. Why must you keep looking for the downside? You can't jump to the conclusion, simply because he's writing a book about someone who slaughters vampires, that he has anything to do with the murders. What about the presumption of innocence?'

'Jim said much the same,' Harry confessed. He guessed she was thinking that he'd jumped to conclusions about her possible guilt, as soon as he'd heard that Peter Blackwell was dead. 'I suppose you're both right. I'm still in a daze. Nothing seems to add up any more. So – what do you think I should do?'

'Get to know the man, of course.' Juliet's own hand slipped under the covers, reached inside his pyjama shirt, began to stroke. 'It's the chance of a lifetime. At last you have someone.'

'And I don't have you, you mean?'

The hand stopped moving and she fixed her gaze on him. 'We always said we were having fun together. Nothing too heavy. Are you saying you've changed your mind?'

He chewed at his lower lip. 'I don't know my own mind at all right now.'

'Listen, you and Daniel Roberts belong to each other. You're family. It's pretty special, if you ask me.'

'I can't get over the thought that my mum kept her secret all those years...'

She withdrew her hand altogether and wagged a finger at him. 'That's what hurts, is it? I understand what you mean, but you shouldn't torment yourself. How well can we know another person? You mustn't be angry with her. At least she found happiness with your father.'

He put up his arms in mock surrender; the sudden movement made his ribs protest. 'All right. I give up. So what's the latest from the outside world? Has Brett Young turned up yet?'

'I was wondering when you were going to ask about him.'

The smug note in her voice teased Harry. 'Something's happened, hasn't it? Don't tell me Mitch has arrested him.'

She grinned. 'Could it be that you've changed your mind? If Daniel's in the clear, the poor old plods might be right after all.'

'There's a first time for everything.'

'I don't see why you're so reluctant to accept that Brett is guilty. Let's face it, he ran you down and didn't stop. Hardly the behaviour of a pillar of the community.'

'He panicked. I've been thinking it over. He must have come to see me. I was one person he could trust, so he showed up at Empire Dock. It was my misfortune to run straight under his wheels.

When that happened, his nerve snapped. He thought the police were bound to pull him in.'

'You're too forbearing. My money's on Brett. He has no alibi for either murder. Plus he had the motive.'

'A partnership split isn't a reason for committing murder. If it was, the mortuaries would be full of lawyers and accountants.'

'Sounds tempting. But there is something you don't know.'

At that moment the ward door opened and Linda Blackwell walked in. As she reached his bedside, Harry found himself groping in vain for words of condolence. She was, as usual, well-dressed and carefully made up. Even from his sick-bed, he couldn't help admiring her legs; they might have belonged to a woman half her age. But there was a defeated slope to her shoulders that no smart suit or face powder could disguise.

'How are you, Harry?'

'On the mend, thanks. More important, what about you?'

'Oh, you know. Trying to come to terms with things. I've had some practice at that lately. More than I would have wished.'

'You're doing fine,' Juliet said. 'You just need to take it easy, that's all, not keep gallivanting all over the place.'

'I'm not an invalid,' Linda told her. 'I can't expect you to look after me all the time. Besides, it's better if I keep myself busy. I need to stand on my own two feet.'

'Yes, but...'

'No buts,' Linda said. Turning back to Harry, she gave a wan smile. 'Juliet passed on your good wishes. Thanks. I wanted to repay the compliment, see for myself how you were getting on. One way or another we've all been in the wars lately, haven't we?'

'It's kind of you.'

Juliet said, 'We were talking about the murders. Harry knows this man Brett Young. He has this theory that Young is innocent.'

Linda raised her eyebrows. 'Have you seen the latest, though, Harry?'

'I was just about to break the news,' Juliet said. She bent down and rooted around in her bag, pulling out a copy of the evening newspaper. A crimson fingernail pointed at a headline on the front page. *Missing Man Was Bogus Lawyer.*

'What's this?' Harry demanded.

'Read it.'

He scanned the piece quickly. Even if it hadn't carried Ken Cafferty's by-line, he would have recognised the breathless prose style, quoting 'sources close to the investigation'. An officially inspired tip-off, presumably designed to intensify pressure on Brett Young while keeping media interest in the case alive. Apparently the police had made a check with the Law Society. Brett had never been admitted to the Roll of Solicitors. He'd studied at the College of Law, but flunked his exams and never retaken them. Detectives were anxious to interview him, but he couldn't be found. The only clue was the Sierra he'd abandoned in Hope Street; at first they'd assumed he hadn't gone far. Now they were having second thoughts.

'Jesus.' It was difficult to take in. Harry had never heard anyone express any doubt about Brett's competence as a lawyer. But it seemed he lacked the pieces of paper which would have entitled him to practise, let alone set up in partnership.

'The sad bastard,' Juliet said. 'I mean, of all the fantasies to choose. I don't wish to be unkind, darling, but living a lie by pursuing a phoney career in the legal profession does suggest a certain poverty of imagination. Pretending to be a heart surgeon or an angel of mercy, that I could understand. But who in their right mind would want to bluff their way into the Liverpool County Court?'

'You're so good for my ego,' Harry said.

'Listen, of all the things I like about you, the fact that you're a lawyer has to be bottom of the list.'

He decided not to push his luck by asking what came top of the list. He was conscious that Linda was staring at him earnestly, as if trying to read his thoughts.

'This man Young. You know him, I take it?'

'Not as well as I thought I did, obviously.'

'Does he strike you as someone who might have done – that terrible thing to my next-door neighbour?'

'I was with him the night Nerys Horlock was murdered. He was pretty hyped up, no question of that. And he'd had a few drinks. All the same, when I left his flat, I never...'

'Nobody's blaming you,' Linda said quickly.

'Not yet,' Harry grunted.

'Ever the pessimist, darling?' Juliet asked. 'Anyway, what do you make of this latest development?'

'Obviously it changes things.'

Fragments of conversation were coming back to him, even as he spoke. Brett explaining the fascination the law held for him, the edge to his tone when he described how Andrea had been helped to earn admission as a solicitor after the firm she'd been working for fell apart.

She folded her arms. 'Too right it does.'

He frowned at the newspaper. 'You don't have to read too far between the lines of this report to grasp the sub-text. Carl Symons presumably found out the truth, maybe let Nerys in on the secret. Perhaps Brett was blackmailed. That would explain why he came out of the bust-up so badly in comparison to the other two.'

'Plus the fact it would also give him a pressing motive for murder.'

'Okay, okay. I hate to say it, but you're right.'

Linda said, 'It's a criminal offence to pretend to be a solicitor, isn't it?'

'I sometimes feel nervous about having my own collar felt on that account.'

Juliet grinned. 'There you are, then. Linda and I were working it out on the way over here. Even on what little the two of us know, the pieces fit so easily. Carl was a nasty piece of work. He soaked Brett for every last penny and then found a good job for himself as a prosecutor. Nerys may have been in on it, for all we know. At any rate, she made sure she was sitting pretty with her new firm. Leaving Brett Young bled dry, with only a rented taxi and a mountain of debts to his name. Together with a burning urge to take revenge.'

Bled dry. The phrase chilled Harry. He was picturing Brett in the loneliness of his flat, telling himself that there is only one sure way to kill a vampire. Drive a stake through the heart and cut off the head so that never again can the creature rise from the dead.

Chapter Nineteen

'What else do you remember?' Daniel asked eagerly. 'Did she always live round here? I suppose the Bradys were a Liverpool family?'

Harry rubbed his stubble. He hadn't shaved since leaving hospital. One bonus about not going in to work this week was that he could experiment with a beard. Juliet had once told him that she fancied Sean Connery like mad. All right, so it would take more than a bit of facial hair for women to swoon at his approach. He could dream.

'She grew up in Penny Lane, a stone's throw from the bus-shelter on the roundabout. Her father – our grandfather, he died when she was ten – had a window cleaning round. John Lennon's Aunt Mimi was one of his customers, back in the mists of time. Mum went to the Cavern Club a couple of times, but she reckoned more to Rory Storm than the Beatles. One thing she lacked was a crystal ball.'

'She was keen on pop music?'

'Sure. She once told me she'd had a crush on Elvis in his "Love Me Tender" days. To say nothing of the young Cliff Richard. You weren't her only dark secret, you see.'

They were walking round Sefton Park, their pace slow because Harry's strapped ribs were still aching. It was his first attempt at exercise since leaving the General. Daniel had arranged to call on him at Empire Dock as soon as he was back on his feet. Harry hadn't been able to say no; nor had he wanted to. Yet he dreaded raking over the past. He found it difficult to picture the happy, capable woman he'd worshipped giving up her illegitimate child for adoption. He would have preferred his memories of her to fade untouched, but Daniel's arrival in his life had made that impossible. The past had seemed certain, unchanging, a reassuring contrast to the nervous present and the unguessable future. Now he was faced with the need to relearn his own history. He felt bitter that his mother had kept her secret from him. She'd given up her first-born. Surely she had never stopped mourning her loss. Jealousy gnawed at him. Daniel's story made him feel insecure, unable to place his trust in anything that he had once taken for granted.

Of one thing he was sure. Daniel was telling the truth: they were blood relatives. No need for a DNA test or anything like that. Neither of them was physically demonstrative – that didn't run in the family – and there hadn't been any hugs, nor any tears. Yet there was a strange kind of intimacy between them, something unspoken and impossible to define. It wasn't just a matter of a birth certificate or that Daniel's story hung together. Harry had only to look at his brown eyes, or hear the inflection in his voice when he asked a question, to be reminded of their dead mother and of the fact that she had taken her secret to the grave. Would she have told him the truth when he grew older? He wanted to believe that she would have confided in him, that she wouldn't have kept him in the dark for ever.

Daniel had turned up earlier than arranged, at a time when Harry was still half-asleep. Perhaps that was the price of a morning meeting with an insomniac. Within a couple of minutes of crossing the threshold, he'd begun talking about their mother. Firing questions about what she was like. To gain a breathing space, Harry had suggested that, as the rain was holding off, they might as well go for a stroll in the park. They had driven out here in Daniel's van, but the inquisition had continued with barely a pause.

As they neared the Palm House, Daniel stopped and leaned against a thick oak trunk. 'I haven't inherited a taste for music from her, I'm afraid. Tone deaf, that's me.'

'I'm not saying she was musical. Her singing voice was almost as bad as mine. My first childhood memory is of Mum crooning "The

Story of My Life" to me, hopelessly out of tune. She'd met Michael Holliday once in a pub, she told me. It was a brush with fame.'

'Never heard of him.'

'Liverpudlian, gay. Tricky combination in the fifties. He committed suicide, but Mum had this weird theory that he was murdered.'

'So she's the one who inspired you with a love of mystery?'

'She liked a puzzle. I used to raid her bookcase when I was ten or eleven,' Harry admitted. 'She had a stock of Agatha Christie paperbacks.'

'Which was her favourite?' Daniel asked, leaning forward, unable to contain his thirst for knowledge, any fragment of information about the woman he would never meet. It was as if he were pasting every anecdote, every hazily recalled incident, into a vast mental scrapbook.

Harry buttoned up his jacket. The temperature was in the low single figures and after so long in the warmth of the hospital and his flat, the cold November air was gnawing at his bones. 'It's a long time ago, I'm not sure I can...'

'Sorry,' Daniel said quickly, 'I'm being selfish. I've done nothing but bombard you with demands for chapter and verse since I arrived this morning. You'll be punch drunk soon.'

Harry gave him a weary grin. 'It's good for my soul. Next time I'm in court, I'll remember what it's like to face an intensive cross-examination. I'm beginning to think the wrong son became the lawyer.'

'It's just that – well, there's a lot of catching up to do. I want to know so much about her. You too.' Daniel bowed his head. 'Do you know, when I showed up in the hospital, it was the first time in my entire life that I'd ever had a conversation with someone who was really related to me?'

Harry swallowed, allowing the thought sink in. 'You never wanted to marry, have kids?'

'I never told anyone this before,' Daniel said, his voice dropping to a whisper. 'When I was a student, I fell in love with a girl on the same course. A blue-eyed blonde from Manchester. I'd had no real experience with the fair sex before that. I could hardly believe my luck. We had a fling during our second term. When she broke the news after the Easter holiday that I'd got her pregnant, I had mixed emotions. Scared, yes, but excited too. She was startled by my reaction. She said, "Don't you understand? I've already had the abortion, of course."'

'Shit.'

'When I lost my temper, she told me it was her body, her decision. She was right, no question, but I've never got over it. Never. It froze me, the thought that I might have had a child of my own – and the chance had been snatched from my grasp.'

Harry said slowly, 'After a time it might have been possible...'

'Don't tell me there are always plenty of fish in the sea. Please.' Daniel folded his arms and stared straight into Harry's eyes, as if challenging him to disagree. 'I'm not a fool. I realise it's not logical to allow that pathetic little episode to stifle my life, to use my mother's dependence on me as an excuse for avoiding any other sort of commitment. The problem is, sometimes we can't behave logically. Simple as that. Maybe that's why discovering the truth about my own origins has come to mean so much for me.'

Harry aimed a desultory kick at a stone. 'I can't live up to your expectations, you realise that? I've shown you the photographs, the bits and pieces I've hung on to because they remind me of her – and my old man. But it was all such a long time ago.'

'You knew her,' Daniel said. 'You *knew* her.'

'Did I? Looking back, I wonder. I never got to know either Mum or Dad properly, not in an adult way. I was an only child, if I ever gave the purpose of their lives a second thought, I'd have assumed it was simply to take care of me. I didn't spend much time wondering if they had any private lives, things they might be hiding from me.'

Daniel seized him by the wrist. The pressure of his bony fingers made Harry wince. 'It's only natural. You assumed you had all the time in the world. Perhaps what happened to you was the cruellest. Your parents were snatched from you. I never had the chance to get to know mine. Perhaps what you never have, you never miss.'

'If that were true, you wouldn't be giving me the third degree right now.'

'I suppose so,' Daniel said, releasing his grip. 'All the same, I'll lay off for a while. For Heaven's sake, I don't want to bore my only living relative into a stupor.'

They started walking again, back towards where they had parked the car. 'Tell me more about yourself,' Harry said. 'It's mostly been one-way traffic today. You've heard all about Mum's taste in television and where she liked to go for her holidays. Let's take a break for a while. How's your writing? Are we going to see your name up in lights when the novel's published?'

'*If* it's published,' Daniel grunted. 'I suppose you could say *The Journal of Quincy Harker* is a homage to Bram Stoker. I've adored *Dracula* ever since I first came across it. You've read it, of course?'

'Flicked through the pages when I was a kid. But mostly I know the story through the films.'

'The book's a thousand times better.' Daniel's voice trembled with proselytising zeal. 'Take it from me, Harry, its reputation is no accident. The writing's so atmospheric. People had written vampire stories before Stoker and God knows they've written plenty since. But *Dracula* is unique. He never matched it.'

'I'll have to give it another try. Maybe it will even cast a little light on the murders.'

Daniel gave a sudden dazzling smile. 'Stoker was a lawyer, too, you know. The title of his first book was *The Duties of Clerks of Petty Sessions in Ireland*.'

'Don't tell me. A cult classic of gore and law?'

'No fangs.' Daniel bared his teeth in a grin that Harry found vaguely alarming. 'Mind you, there are plenty of clues to Stoker's legal training in *Dracula*. Do you recall that Jonathan Harker, the narrator, is a recently admitted solicitor? He's been sent out to Transylvania to advise the Count on the purchase of an estate in London.'

'Those were the days. Have quill pen, will travel. That's the trouble, all the romance has gone out of the profession. The furthest I was ever allowed to roam was the Small Claims Court at Macclesfield.'

'Jonathan's an innocent abroad, a young man turning up at this remote castle in the midst of the Carpathians.' Daniel sighed. 'I feel a bit like that about my trips to Liverpool. A yokel in the city. Anyway, Jonathan seeks out familiar things. It gladdens his heart when he examines Dracula's library and his eyes fall on the Law List.'

'Sounds like desperation to me.'

'Oh, believe me,' Daniel said with fervour, 'there's more. Jonathan explains at length to his host how solicitors act as local agents. After the Count has quizzed him about the conduct of various business transactions, he decides that Dracula "would have made a wonderful solicitor".'

Harry couldn't help laughing. 'That's all we need. To be identified with the king of the blood-suckers.'

'Jonathan means it as a compliment. He visualises the Count as a lawyer because "there was nothing that he did not think of or foresee."'

'That proves it. I'm in the wrong job.'

They had reached the van. Daniel paused in the act of unlocking the door. 'You thought I was going to kill you, didn't you?'

Taken by surprise, Harry gave a non-committal cough while he pondered a reply. It had to be convincing; whatever else he might be, Daniel was no fool.

Daniel leaned against the van, resting his chin on his palm as he looked across at Harry. 'My fault. I'd concentrated so much on tracking you down, I never gave a second thought to how you might react when you found someone was on your trail. I'd invested so much – I suppose you might call it emotional capital – that perhaps I was afraid of what you'd say. It was bound to be a shock when I told you that we were family.'

Harry shifted from one foot to another. He wasn't accustomed to talking intimately with another man. Daniel's arrival in his life had opened doors that he had believed to be closed for ever. An agony columnist, he guessed, would urge him to accentuate the positive. He'd been given a chance, a unique chance, to share his life in a wholly unexpected way. He ought to be exhilarated. The only trouble was that he would be sharing his life with a stranger whose conversation sometimes made him shiver.

'You frightened me, I'll confess that.'

Daniel gave his back a gentle slap. 'I promise I don't have any immediate plans to decapitate you. The trouble is, whenever we talk, it seems we're sailing in uncharted waters.'

'I'm afraid you're hoping for more than I can give.'

'Hoping that you can help me get a life? The life I mislaid a long time ago?' Daniel shook his head. 'No, Harry. I'm not naïve. It's enough for me that I've found you. I don't intend to make myself a nuisance.'

'I'm glad you got in touch,' Harry said softly. 'Obviously it was a bolt from the blue. I won't pretend I wasn't shocked. Truth is, what you've told me still hasn't sunk in yet. I guess it will take time. One thing's for sure: you did well to track me down. I've decided you're a better detective than me.'

'We both want the same thing, don't you agree?' Daniel's tone suggested he thought he regarded the idea as reassuring. Harry remembered Juliet on the phone, a few hours before she'd stumbled over Symons' body. She was someone else who was convinced she knew what he wanted. 'To find things out. Even when finding out might be more painful than remaining in ignorance.'

Harry cast his mind back to tragedies that his investigations had in the past revealed. The passion that had caused the death of his wife. The fear that explained the murder of Finbar Rogan. The secret kept by the mother of a strangled teenager. 'I can't deny it,' he admitted. 'Even though it can be dangerous. A drug.'

'I read the press cuttings about you. It seems you simply can't stop getting involved with murder.'

Harry winced. He didn't regard himself as a ghoul, didn't want Daniel to see him that way. 'I didn't have much choice as far as Carl Symons was concerned. And Nerys Horlock was an acquaintance as well. When people you know are butchered, people in the same line of business, it's all coming pretty close to home.'

'I've read up about the killings in the newspaper. You dropped a hint this morning about a vampire connection.'

'Me and my big mouth.' As he'd made coffee in the flat, he had gabbled about the murders for the sake of having something to say.

'Where do vampires come in? I've seen nothing in the Press.'

'No, the police are keeping that aspect of the case – for what it's worth – under wraps. They'll be lucky if someone doesn't blow the gaff any time now in the hope of making a fast buck from the tabloids. I didn't mean to let the cat out of the bag, though. My fault. I should have kept quiet.'

'I don't want to embarrass you,' Daniel said. 'Saying that, I must confess I'm intrigued. Especially given – my own interests. Can you tell me any more?'

Harry shrugged. The damage was done now. Besides, Ken hadn't sworn him to secrecy and the odds were that he might not run the vampire story until Brett was found and he could discover whether there was anything in it. Daniel knew plenty about vampires. Perhaps he could help. 'It's a long story and I don't know a lot of the details. But let's get in and I'll give you a flavour of it.'

As they drove towards the city centre, he described briefly what he knew. 'So there you are. It's not much to go on. A shattered mirror, a whiff of garlic. Stakes through the victims' hearts.'

'Significant that both Carl Symons and Nerys Horlock had their heads cut off,' Daniel said, keeping his eyes fixed on the road. He was a maddening driver, careful to the point of irrational timidity in negotiating Liverpool's one-way system. 'That's part of the myth.'

'Tell me more.'

'After Lucy Westenra became a vampire, Abraham Van Helsing insisted that it wasn't enough to drive a stake through her heart. She had to be decapitated as well. Her coffin was opened and they mutilated her.'

'But why?'

'Because, Van Helsing said, it was the only way to make sure that she would no longer be one of "the Devil's Un-Dead". Only when her head was cut off could she be "true dead". Only then could God have possession of her soul.'

Daniel spoke in the same matter-of-fact tone that a broadcaster might use for reading out the racing results. Harry felt his gorge rising. He wasn't sure which he found the more disturbing: the murderer's modus operandi or Daniel's calm appraisal of it.

'When I think about vampires,' he said, 'and it isn't too often, I picture Christopher Lee in a long black cloak. Apart from that, I'm pretty hazy.'

'Don't be deceived by cheap Hammer Horror films,' Daniel said. 'Vampires represent our deepest fears. Of disease, of sex, of death. They are powerful and dangerous. Human dignity means nothing to them.'

'A bit like game show hosts, then?'

The car halted at a red light. Daniel turned his head and gave the thinnest of smiles. He did not altogether lack a sense of humour, Harry thought, but there was no doubt that it came a poor second to his obsession with the Un-Dead.

'They have died, yet they have conquered the darkness. By feeding on the blood of others, they retain their potency. They are repulsive, yet at the same time strangely glamorous. They drain the life from their victims, sucking all the vitality out of them. And all too often, the victims may be those closest to us.' The lights had changed, but Daniel made no move. When a car's horn sounded behind them, he took no notice. It was as if he were talking to himself, intoning the words like a preacher giving a sermon at a non-conformist chapel somewhere in the wilds of Wales. 'Lucy Westenra was beloved by Arthur Holmwood, yet he had no choice but to drive the stake through her heart. That's part of the reason for our fear of them. Our terror that our loved ones have become lost souls.'

'How do you get on with him?' Jim asked that evening. He'd come round to the flat to check on how Harry's recuperation was progressing whilst they put away a couple of beers. In the background Marvin Gaye was crooning about what he'd heard on the grapevine.

'He's different.' The ringpull of the can opened with a hiss. 'That's one thing I can say for sure. All those years living on his own in the Welsh mountains haven't done much for his social skills. You don't get small talk with Daniel Roberts. Just non-stop cross-examination.'

'Quizzing you about your mum?'

'It's only natural. I want to help as much as I can. I was the lucky one. Even though I lost her, I did have her for the early years.

I keep wondering if I was a disappointment, if she asked herself how Daniel would have compared to me, had she kept him. But whether or not she did, she never gave a hint of it to me. Perhaps that's all that matters.'

'Seeing him again?'

'Tomorrow. I suggested he stay overnight, but he said no, he had things to do back at home. He works at a truckstop, to make enough money so that he can eat whilst he's penning his novel. So he's driving back here again and bringing his manuscript with him.'

'Make a change from all that mystery stuff you read by the yard.'

'I'm intrigued, I admit it. Mind, I've warned him that I'm not too keen on stories of horror and the supernatural. I like my puzzles to have a rational explanation.'

'Then you're in the wrong job, aren't you?'

'At least I did manage to qualify as a solicitor. Not like Brett Young.'

'Yeah, you could have knocked me over with a quill pen when I heard about that. And there's still no sign of him, I gather.'

'He could be anywhere by now. For all we know, he could be putting his experience as a cabbie to good use somewhere else, pretending to be an expert in road traffic law.' Harry yawned. 'By the way, before you ask, I should be in the office on Monday morning and I guess that once I'm back I'll have plenty to do, catching up with the backlog.'

'You're not wrong. The lovely Carmel has done a good job covering in your absence, but somehow the clients miss your inimitable style.'

'You mean because her letters are crammed with advice based on legal precedent, whereas mine usually run to two paragraphs?'

'That's one way of looking at it.'

'You do realise mine are short whenever I'm hazy about what the law actually is?'

Jim wiped the foam from his mouth. 'You know that, I know that. The clients think that you're distilling the wisdom of years of study in concise and practical fashion without running up unnecessary fees. It's like the lawyer in that film you like so much. *Body Heat*. It was on the box the other night. Remember when his mate accuses him of using his incompetence as a weapon?'

'Thanks a lot.'

'Any road, it'll be good to see you behind the desk again. You'll notice one or two changes.'

Harry scowled. 'You've got rid of my spider plants, haven't you?'

'They were dying, old son. It was a kindness. Think mercy killing. Besides, Suzanne raised serious questions about whether they were up to the mark in terms of Feng Shui. Incidentally, it may not be mumbo-jumbo after all. Since I let her persuade me to have reception repainted, business has been brisker than ever. We may even have a slug of decent new work in the offing. All the signs are good, so keep your fingers crossed. Tell you more on Monday.'

'By then I guess I'll be glad of the break. I've spent so long walking down Memory Lane with my new brother. Did I tell you his book is about vampires?' Harry grinned. 'He's batty about *Dracula*.'

Jim's bushy eyebrows shot up. 'That's – topical. Lot of talk in the city at the moment about vampires.'

'Because of the way the murders were committed? I thought the police were trying to keep things under wraps. Ken Cafferty was planning to break the story, but he seems to have got cold feet since Brett did a runner.'

'Word's got round. As it usually does. Mitch Eggar is under a lot of pressure to deliver a result. If he can't track Brett down, then anyone hanging round the law courts wearing a cape and baring his canines is likely to find himself locked up.'

'One or two judges must be worried, then.'

'Yeah.' Jim put his can down on the carpet. 'Have you talked to Daniel about the murders?'

Harry nodded. 'He reckons that there's something in the vampire connection. It's not just the product of a journalist's over-heated imagination. The decapitation is symbolic, it's what the prudent vampire hunter does to make sure that the coffin lid doesn't get pushed open again. To make extra sure, it may be worth destroying the vampire's body. For example by burning it.'

Jim's eyes narrowed. 'Hence the fire at Nerys's office? Well, well. Maybe the police ought to consult Daniel's expertise.'

'Maybe.'

'What's up? You don't look happy.'

Harry sighed. 'It's stupid, of course. But he worries me, does Daniel.'

'You don't seriously think he has anything to do with these killings?'

'I said it was stupid,' Harry said mulishly.

'Come on. Brett had the motive, plus the opportunity. He knocked you down with his car but didn't stop. He's on the run. You're a defence lawyer, I don't expect you to agree, but most people would say those are the actions of a guilty man.'

'I suppose you're right,' Harry said. But for some reason, he couldn't bring himself to believe it.

The insistent shrill of the telephone woke Harry the next morning. His head was throbbing and his mouth was dry. He opened one eye to look at the bedside alarm. Ten to eleven. He swore under his breath. Hadn't Daniel said he'd turn up at ten thirty? He had a vague recollection that he'd carried on drinking alone after Jim's departure. He'd put on a tape of a favourite old Edward G. Robinson film, *Nightmare*, but he'd fallen asleep before the end. It didn't matter; he'd watched the movie half a dozen times before.

When he'd woken up, some bloke in a kipper tie and flares had occupied the screen, sharing with Open University students and other night owls the secrets of higher mathematics. He'd struggled off to bed and although he'd slept deeply, for once he couldn't remember any of his dreams.

The telephone kept ringing. He shambled over and picked up the receiver. His body was stiff and his ribs still hurt: the sudden unwelcome shafts of pain reminded him that he was still weak after the accident.

'Harry?'

At first he couldn't place the woman's voice. She sounded breathless, frightened. 'Who's that?'

'It's Andrea. Andrea Gibbs. When – when I rang your office the other day, I heard you'd been hit by a car.'

Driven by your boyfriend, actually. 'I'll live. So you've been trying to contact me?'

'I called after the news broke about Brett. This stuff about his not being a qualified lawyer. It knocked the stuffing out of me. I don't know, I suppose I wanted someone to talk to. Someone I could trust.'

You hardly know me. You must be desperate. 'Has he been in touch?'

'No, no – but have you heard the news?'

'What news?'

She sounded as though she were gulping for air. 'Don't you know there was another murder last night?'

For all the silence of the flat, Harry thought he might be deafened by the pounding inside his head. He clutched the table for support. For a moment he feared his legs would buckle beneath him. Why did he waste his time watching old movies about nightmares, when every day seemed to bring horrors closer to home?

'What are you talking about?' he said, his voice thick with catarrh.

'It's been on the radio. Television news as well.'

'I've been in bed.'

'Sorry. I – I didn't mean to disturb you. But there wasn't anyone else I could...'

'Doesn't matter. Look, do you know who's been killed?'

Her voice was shaking so much that she could hardly talk. He heard her gulp before her voice steadied enough to make herself understood.

'Another lawyer.'

Chapter Twenty

He felt himself tensing, dreading what she would say next. For God's sake – what if it were Jim? Fighting to keep a tremor out of his own voice, he asked, 'A friend?'

'No. God, no. But...'

She had started crying. Helpless at the other end of the line, Harry tried to soothe her. As the sobbing eased, he said, 'Have they given a name?'

'A few minutes ago. It's Rick Spendlove.'

His first instinctive reaction was one of relief. *Thank God it's no-one I care about, then.* But then shame flooded through him. He hated his own selfishness. He hadn't liked Spendlove, but the death penalty had been abolished years ago. You couldn't be, shouldn't be, slaughtered just because you were a creep. Or just because you were a solicitor, come to that.

'Do you know what's happened?'

She had begun to weep again. 'His car was found in a dock at Birkenhead. The police say they are linking it to the other two murders.'

'Shit.' His thoughts flew to Daniel. Surely it wasn't possible that he was the killer? If only he'd agreed to stay overnight in the flat. And why hadn't he arrived here this morning?

'I'm afraid, Harry. Afraid for Brett.'

'Where is he? Do you have any idea?'

'None, I promise you. He's vanished off the face of the earth.' She was speaking quickly, as if frantic with the need to spit it all out before hysteria overwhelmed her. 'The police are keeping an eye on my flat, I wouldn't be surprised if they're tapping my phone. Listening to this call. But I've had no contact from him. Not a word.'

He bit his lip. A hitherto unsuspected possibility had occurred to him.

It was as if she had read his mind. 'I'm scared. I keep wondering – if he might be dead.'

'You think he may have had an accident? Or been murdered?' He didn't voice the third possibility: that Brett might have committed suicide.

'Either.'

'There's no evidence, none at all.' He was trying to persuade himself as much as the girl. Yet he couldn't forget the scene he had witnessed outside the Titanic Rooms, when Spendlove had flung his arms round Andrea, watched by Brett from his vantage point on the other side of the road. A small incident, but one that an unstable man might brood over until it became a source of rage. Homicidal rage, even.

'Remember, his two former partners have been killed.'

'Yes, but Rick Spendlove had nothing to do with their old firm, as far as I know, and that didn't save him.'

'It's dangerous to be a lawyer in Liverpool right now.' Her voice sounded distant.

Harry rubbed his sore ribs. 'Don't I know it?'

For a few seconds neither of them spoke. Then the doorbell screamed. He felt a surge of relief. It must be Daniel.

'Was that your door?'

'It's okay. I think I can guess who it is. Remember the mysterious Welshman?'

She gasped. 'He's come for you? Oh my God!'

'It's all right,' he said, 'there's nothing to worry about. Nothing at all, believe me. He's a bit odd, I know, he keeps harping on about vampires...'

He heard her moan and then the phone went dead. His visitor still had a finger on the bell. Swearing, he headed out into the hall. When he opened the door, he found that he had guessed right.

Standing outside was Daniel Roberts. He had a bulky lever arch file under his arm.

'I didn't mean to be late. You must have been wondering what's happened.'

Harry was conscious that he was still wearing his pyjamas. 'Don't worry, I overslept. Come in and tell me about it.'

Daniel followed him into the living-room and put the file down on the table in the middle of the room. 'The manuscript, as promised.'

'Thanks.'

Daniel sighed. 'A bloody Nissan ran into the back of me, miles from anywhere. I had to call out a repair truck. It took an age, but they managed to fix things so that I was able to limp over here. I'd have rung to put you in the picture, but I don't have a mobile and once I started, I thought I'd better keep driving.'

As an explanation, it was innocent enough, Harry thought. He had to believe it was true.

'Any damage done to you?'

'My shoulders are a bit sore, no more than that. I was lucky.' Daniel sighed. 'When you think of how easily these things happen. Remember, that's how our mother died. A split second disaster on the road.'

'Yeah.' Harry bowed his head. 'There's been another killing.'

'So I heard. I do have a primitive radio in the van, but the reception's usually hopeless. The dead man's a lawyer, isn't that right?' Daniel hesitated. 'Not someone you know?'

'Yes. An acquaintance, not a friend. He was a senior partner in a big firm. Fancied himself as a bit of a Casanova. I can't pretend we were bosom pals.'

'The reporter obviously believes there's a serial killer at work, doesn't he?'

'I didn't hear the news on the radio. Andrea Gibbs called. You remember, the girl you met at the Legal Group's office.'

'Oh yes.' Daniel rubbed his chin. 'I won't forget her in a hurry.'

'She's worried sick about Brett Young.' Harry gave a brief account of the conversation. 'She rang off as soon as I told her you'd arrived. Her nerves are in tatters.'

'That's one explanation,' Daniel said pensively.

'What are you getting at?'

'Oh, I don't know ... it was only a fleeting impression. Something and nothing, probably.'

Harry was about to press him further when the phone rang again. Andrea, calling back? He snatched up the receiver.

'Harry, mate ...' Ken Cafferty's tone was wheedling.

'What do you want?'

'No need to sound so suspicious,' Ken said, all injured dignity. 'Strange as it may seem, I want to pick your brains.'

'Go on.'

'You've heard the news, of course?'

'In the last few minutes. And the victim's Rick Spendlove?'

'Right. I'm at the scene now.' The crackling on the line muffled Ken's voice, but did not disguise his excitement. 'He was fished out of Benedict Dock, a stone's throw from the old Priory. A couple of kids turned up for a bit of late-night nookie and saw a car boot sticking up out of the water.'

'And the police are definitely connecting this death with the other two?'

Not even the poor reception could obscure Ken's chortling. 'It'd be nice to think that there were two separate crazed killers bent on culling the Liverpool legal profession. No, don't bother to quibble. At least you'd have less competition to worry about. Yes, of course they're bloody well linking the crimes.'

'And the vampire angle?'

'Not quite so sceptical now, eh? Well, the police have decided to go public. There's no way they can keep things quiet any longer, absolutely no way. Mind you, they're obviously rationing out the information, keeping as much stuff up their sleeves as they can get away with.'

'So Rick finished up with a stake through the heart?'

'Sort of.' Ken hesitated. 'That is, he was stabbed with a sharpened wooden stave. Funny thing is, the wound was superficial and they don't seem to think that's what killed him. Subject to the autopsy, of course.'

'I don't expect being decapitated did him much good.'

'Well, Boycott Duff are certainly looking for a new Head of Corporate Recovery,' Ken sniggered. Harry told himself that Ken wasn't really heartless, that the gallows humour helped him to cope with life's blackness – but he wasn't sure it was the whole truth. 'Bottom line is, though, he wasn't beheaded. Mitch Eggar says that his throat was slashed, but not fatally. They reckon the actual cause of death was probably drowning.'

Harry ground his teeth. 'So he may have been alive when he went into the water?'

'Seems like it. We'll have to wait for the pathologist's report for a definite answer. Oh, and one other thing...'

'Spare me the dramatic pauses, Ken.'

'Okay, my friend, no need to snap. Now, pin your ears back. Spendlove's killer had stripped him. Very ritualistic, by the sound of things. This is a front page story, no question. Look, I want a bit of inside track on Spendlove. Any chance you can come over here? I need to stick around for a while. There are people to talk to.'

'I'm not even dressed yet.'

'Christ, listen to you. Day of rest, eh? I've been out here since the early hours.'

'There's another thing. A friend of mine's here.'

Ken chuckled. 'Typical. No wonder you're not dressed yet. Bring her along if you like. I won't keep you long, then you can get back to taking care of the lucky lady. We can meet outside the

Priory, it won't take you long to nip through the tunnel. Don't bother to shave. Say twenty minutes?'

'Half an hour.'

Harry spoke with resignation, but part of him was burning with curiosity. After he'd put down the phone, he turned to Daniel. 'That was a crime reporter, someone I know. He's asked me to go to the scene, he wants background on the man who was murdered. It won't take long. When I mentioned you were here, he jumped to the conclusion you were a lady friend.'

'Can I come with you? If you don't mind, that is.'

Harry said slowly, 'No, that's okay. If you really want to.'

Daniel gave a bleak smile. 'Perhaps we share an inquisitive gene.'

A shower, a shave and a mouthful of toast later, Harry was driving through the Kingsway Tunnel. Daniel coughed and said, 'So is there a lady friend?'

Keeping his eyes on the curving road, Harry said carefully, 'There have been a few since Liz died. No-one permanent.'

'And at present?'

He wasn't ready to say anything about Juliet. Too dangerous. Besides, he still did not know his half-brother well enough. Couldn't even be sure how much he trusted him. 'I'm not in the mood to settle down with anyone.'

'Don't make the mistake I did, Harry. The single life's lonely. Lonely as hell.'

'You're not an old man. You might find someone.'

'The only woman I really get to talk to these days is Bronwen from the truckstop. Not exactly my type. Anyway, who would want to get involved with a tongue-tied middle-aged bachelor who writes unpublished four-hundred-page novels about an imaginary vampire hunter? You're younger, you're a partner in a law firm. You must have plenty of opportunities.'

'You may have the wrong idea about partners in solicitors' firms,' Harry said. 'Let's change the subject, eh? I don't suppose you know Birkenhead?'

'Not at all.'

'The old Priory dates back hundreds of years. The monks used to run the ferry. Now the place is a ruin. Typical bit of Mersey heritage, really. It's stuck between an industrial estate and a shipyard.'

They emerged from the mouth of the tunnel and Harry tossed a couple of coins into the basket at the toll booth. 'We're only a few hundred yards away,' he said.

'Seriously?' Daniel was looking round at the intersecting roads, the single-storey factory units, the yellow cranes on the skyline.

'I will admit it's not exactly Tintern Abbey. But a red rose grows out in Spanish Harlem, you know?'

Daniel laughed. 'Your taste in pop music is as out-of-date as mine in literature.'

'Here we are.'

As they rounded a corner, they could see flashing blue lights and a cordoned-off area. A knot of sightseers had gathered on the near side of the tape, peering in the direction of the docks. Looking past the police cars, Harry saw a vandalised length of fencing and a nettle-fringed track leading to cobbles on the nearside of the dock. Screens had been set up but they were not big enough to hide the bulk of lifting gear or the battered bonnet of a Porsche. Harry drove on past a couple of television vans and spotted Ken Cafferty waving from a throng of men and women gabbling excitedly into mobile phones. Ken was gesturing that he should park a little distance away by the sandstone wall which edged the grounds of the Priory.

As they climbed out of the MG, Ken was beaming, but he blinked when he saw the state of Harry's battered and bearded face.

265

'Bugger me. You had quite an argument with the car that knocked you down, didn't you? Who was driving, a disgruntled client? I'd sue, if I were you. Take legal advice, my friend, that's what you ought to do.'

Harry gestured towards Daniel, who was standing outside the padlocked gate to the Priory, gazing through towards the old Chapter House. 'This is Daniel Roberts, a relative of mine. He'd just called round when you rang.'

'Pleased to meet you. Not met any of Harry's flesh and blood before. Matter of fact, mate, going back to when Liz was done in, I had the impression you didn't have any family left.'

'Daniel lives in Snowdonia,' Harry said casually, as if that explained everything. 'He's a writer and vampires happen to be his speciality.'

'So you agree there's something in the vampire theory after all?'

'The man was immersed in water,' Daniel said softly. 'It's one of the vampire-hunter's favoured techniques.'

Ken scanned his face to check whether he was being sent up. 'You think that's why the car finished up in the dock?'

'Depend upon it. It's the same as the fire which killed the woman, Nerys Horlock. The murderer wanted to make sure his victim was dead.'

Harry asked, 'Have the police been able to reconstruct exactly what happened?'

'Things aren't clear yet. My guess is, the car was parked close to the dock when Spendlove was killed. Then the handbrake was released and – Bob's your uncle.'

'Then Spendlove must have had a rendezvous with the murderer?'

'I'd say it's the only explanation. Maybe Young contacted him. Perhaps he even pretended that he needed to seek Spendlove's professional advice. I make it a rule never to feel sorry for policemen, but I might just make an exception in Mitch Eggar's case. Never mind Symons, Horlock and Spendlove, it'll be Mitch's head for the chopper if he doesn't make an arrest very soon.'

'Hang on a minute. You seem very sure that Brett Young is guilty.'

'Listen, I know you love a mystery. Don't we all? But there can't be much doubt, can there? Young's definitely got a screw loose.'

'You're jumping to...'

Ken wagged a finger. 'Hear me out. Young lied about being a solicitor. He'd never passed the exams, but he inveigled his way into a job. Forged documents, concocted a c.v. that was more a work of fiction than one of my expense claims. Eventually he teamed up with Symons and Horlock. I don't say he had no skills at all. For all I know, he was probably a better advocate than half the people with proper paper qualifications. But he wasn't cut out for partnership. He didn't have much nous where business was concerned. It was the glamour of the law that attracted him.'

'Oh yeah, we all lead really glamorous lives. Even Rick Spendlove was doing his weekly shop the last time I saw him.'

'Well, I won't deny Brett was naïve. My theory is that Symons found out the truth and blackmailed him.'

'And Nerys Horlock?'

'I don't say she was a blackmailer, but if she did know Young's secret, he probably decided he couldn't allow her to live.'

'Rather over the top, don't you think?'

'Frankly, Harry, I'd say that driving a stake through someone's heart and then chopping their head off to make sure was astonishingly over the top. After that, pretty much anything else is a model of restraint.'

'All right, so what about Spendlove? Where does he fit in?'

'That's the one thing that bothers me. It's why I asked you over. There must be a motive, maybe you can figure it out. Did Spendlove ever have any business dealings with Young? Would they have crossed each other's paths in court?'

'No, they operated in different areas of the law. I can't imagine any reason why they'd want to meet, here or anywhere else. Spendlove was a business lawyer. Even Brett's wildest fantasies didn't stretch that far. Much the same as me. You don't find a Fancy Dan like Rick Spendlove down the magistrates'.'

'Wouldn't be seen dead there?' Ken sniggered. 'Unlike Benedict Dock, eh? All right. What about women, then? Spendlove was a naughty boy. I caught the tail end of that fiasco in the Maritime Bar, remember? Could there have been bad blood between them on that account?'

Harry shrugged and avoided Ken's eye, gazing past him towards the shell of St Mary's Church. He didn't want to say anything about Spendlove canoodling Andrea Gibbs in Old Hall Street. Ken could make out a convincing enough case for Brett's guilt without it. But it was impossible to forget the angry drumming of Brett's fingers on the steering wheel of the taxi that evening, as he tormented himself with what he had seen. Maybe Ken's instinct was right and Brett had taken a brutal revenge.

'It's all guesswork,' he said, trying to sound more casual than he felt. 'Speaking of which, where do you think your prime suspect might be hiding?'

Ken pursed his lips. 'Good question. Until Spendlove was killed, my bet was that he'd turn up dead. I thought he'd have topped himself after killing his two ex-partners and someone walking a dog somewhere would stumble over his body and a suicide note. If he's still around, then maybe he'll get in touch with his girlfriend. If he hasn't done so already.'

'You've talked to her?'

'Tried to. Strange girl. She wouldn't say much, but she was certainly doing a Tammy Wynette and standing by her man. Denied all knowledge of his whereabouts. I didn't take to her, but I was almost inclined to break the cynicism of a lifetime and believe she was telling the truth. In which case, God alone knows where

Young has got to. Perhaps not very far at all. He might be sleeping rough in Birkenhead Park.'

'And these vampiric elements,' Daniel asked suddenly, 'where do they fit in?'

Ken lowered his voice. 'Don't tell anyone I said this, but between the three of us, all that stuff's starting to look like a red herring. Certainly, this time around he's been pretty half-hearted about it all. Even though he did strip that poor bastard Spendlove stark naked.'

'What exactly happened?' Harry asked.

'The way I heard it, the stave only inflicted a glorified flesh wound and if a cut throat can ever be superficial, Spendlove's was. Assuming the water in the lungs did for him, it seems as if the vampire paraphernalia was all a bit of window dressing. Young's been trying to throw people off the scent.'

'Not a very successful ploy, if you're right.'

Ken shrugged. 'I never said the man was a genius. After all, even you passed the same exams he failed.'

Five minutes later, Harry and his half-brother were speeding under the river back towards Liverpool. They had left Ken making up a profile of Rick Spendlove, which from the early indications would bear as little resemblance to the reality as did tabloid obituaries of Diana, Princess of Wales to the real woman.

'Well, what do you think?' Harry inquired.

'I can't say I liked him.'

'Listen, Ken's not so bad. I meant, what do you make of the murder?'

'What he says makes sense, I suppose. But I gather you're still not convinced?'

'I see the logic of the case against Brett, certainly. Trouble is, logic has never been my strong point.'

269

'You agree with his girlfriend that he's innocent?'

'Look,' Harry said after a moment's pause. 'There's something I didn't tell Ken. The night Nerys Horlock was killed, Brett saw Spendlove putting his arms round Andrea. I'm sure there was nothing in it as far as she was concerned. The man's dick ruled his brain. But Brett wasn't exactly relaxed about it.'

'I see.' Daniel grunted. 'She's a curious girl, that one.'

Harry glanced at Daniel. Something had been puzzling him; he might as well mention it. 'I suppose I ought to tell you, she doesn't seem to be your number one fan. When I told her this morning that I could hear you ringing the bell, she threw a wobbler. I didn't get the chance to explain the connection between us before she banged the phone down. She probably still thinks you're stalking me.'

'Where does she live?' Daniel asked suddenly.

'I think Brett said she had a flat over a launderette in Fazakerley Street. Why do you ask?'

'Why don't we pay her a visit? I could put her mind at rest, let her see I'm nothing to be afraid of.'

'If you want.'

Harry shifted in his seat. He felt sure Daniel was keeping something back, but he couldn't imagine what it might be. There was so much about his half-brother that he needed to learn. Yet until they'd started talking about Andrea, he'd been beginning to relax in Daniel's company. It would be an absurd flight of fancy to imagine he had anything to do with the crimes, simply because he had an abiding interest in vampires. Wouldn't it?

Neither of them said anything else until they reached Fazakerley Street. The launderette was halfway down and Harry had to park on the kerb so as not to block the road completely. The door adjoining the launderette had a bell marked with Andrea's surname. When he rang, she opened the door on a security chain. She was wearing a T-shirt which revealed white arms as thin as a child's and impossibly tight jeans; both T-shirt and jeans were black. The vivid scarlet of her lipstick made a startling contrast with the pallor of her skin.

'Oh, it's you.' She caught sight of Daniel, standing by the car and gave a sharp intake of breath. 'What are you doing here?'

'We've just come back from Birkenhead,' Harry said in a briskly amiable tone. 'We had a look at the scene of the crime and we were wondering if we could talk. By the way, I ought to introduce you two properly. You know already this is Daniel Roberts. What you don't know is that he had a perfectly good reason for tracking me down. Would you believe, he's my long-lost half-brother?'

Daniel stepped forward, a grim smile on his face. 'It's quite true. Thank you again for the help you gave me in finding Harry. I'm sorry if I scared you. I don't realise sometimes what a gaunt and forbidding fellow I am. I suppose – I suppose I take my hobby too seriously.'

Harry became conscious of a current passing in the atmosphere between Daniel and Andrea. He found it impossible to analyse. It wasn't a matter of antipathy, or even fear. Rather, he sensed, something unspoken that they shared in common. He felt excluded, and at the same time, tantalised.

'Hobby?' she asked, fiddling nervously with the buckle of the belt to her jeans.

Daniel nodded. 'It's a sensitive subject round Merseyside at the moment, but I'm writing a book about a ruthless vampire hunter.'

Andrea stared hard at him and made a small noise. Then she sank to the ground in a faint.

Harry turned to Daniel open-mouthed. 'My God, you certainly have an effect on women.'

'She's not just any woman, Harry.'

Harry paused in the act of bending down to check that Andrea was all right. 'What do you mean?'

'Haven't you realised? She's a real vampire.'

Chapter Twenty-One

'When did you realise?' Andrea Gibbs asked twenty minutes later.

The three of them were together in her chilly room. Its small cobwebbed windows were set high in the walls and seemed designed to let no daylight through. As Andrea had recovered from her fainting fit, Daniel had murmured words of solicitude. When she'd struggled back to her feet, she had been about to slam the door in his face but he had managed to persuade her that he meant no harm. To Harry, listening in bewilderment, he had seemed like a tolerant father using a load of mumbo-jumbo to cajole a fey child into good behaviour. Yet in the end she had consented to invite them in. After trudging up here, he'd decided that anyone who spent much time in such a grubby hole could be forgiven for sinking into a pit of depression.

At Daniel's suggestion, she had directed him to where an old bottle of brandy was kept. Now she was lounging on a battered couch as she sipped from a glass with a chip in it. Harry was leaning against a sideboard that had been old-fashioned when John Lennon was a lad, rubbing his hands behind his back in a surreptitious effort to get warm. He could hear the rumble of the washing machines downstairs, the hum of traffic on the inner ring road in the distance. Daniel sat cross-legged on the threadbare rug at her feet, oblivious to the cold, not bothering to hide his fascination with her. He'd been describing his book, explaining his obsessive interest in *Dracula* and Van Helsing.

'There was something about you, that first time,' he said eagerly. He might have been describing a brief encounter with the love of his life. 'I had other things on my mind, I'd been desperate to find the one blood relative I had in the world. Even so, I could tell you were different. When Harry told me a little more about you, I began to wonder again. I've read so much about real vampires, but I've never met one before. This is amazing. Truly amazing.'

'You look baffled, Harry,' she said with a nervous laugh. 'If you didn't think I was certifiable before today, I suppose you're convinced by now.'

'I don't get it,' he admitted. 'You'll be telling me next that you're terrified of crosses.'

She shook her head. 'I don't believe in God, but that's not unusual. I don't have huge fangs, either. All that mock-Transylvanian crap I can do without. There isn't a coffin in my bedroom, you can check it out for yourself if you don't believe me. Bear in mind, vampires were around long before Bram Stoker. They've appeared in many cultures, going back into the mists of time.'

Daniel's eyes shone like those of a doorstep evangelist who meets a fellow believer. 'Lilith the Canaanite who sucked the blood of men in their sleep, the Empusae of ancient Greece who could transform themselves into beasts or salacious women at will. The Chinese, the native Americans, the Hindi, they all had stories which rang variations on the theme.'

'You know your subject,' she said softly.

Harry gritted his teeth. The two of them might have been talking a different language. He felt an obscure sense of disappointment that Daniel as well as the girl so plainly had a bee in his bonnet about all this stuff. He said roughly to Andrea. 'And you? How did you get into all this? Refuge from the harsh realities of law college, was it?'

She curled herself up into a tiny ball. She wasn't wearing shoes and he could see the outline of her ribs in the gap between her black top and her jeans. She could have passed for fifteen years old. 'I suppose I always thought of myself as different. Even as a child. My mother was a single parent and she died when I was fourteen. An aunt and uncle brought me up after that, out of a sense of duty, nothing else. I was pretty sickly and I used to get depressed a lot as well. I read a lot and I became intellectually interested in the law. I decided I might as well make it my career. But at the same time there was something missing from my life.'

'Yeah, a lot of lawyers think that,' Harry muttered.

Daniel glared at him. 'Go on, please, Andrea.'

'I used to be told I was moody, temperamental, attention-seeking. When I went through an anorexic phase just before I left home, my aunt's remedy was to tell me to pull myself together. She complained that I never considered anyone but myself. I found it impossible to make proper friendships. When I got interested in boys – and I did get *very* interested, my experiences were disastrous. They never stayed around for long, they used to say I was too much for them. They seemed to be wiped out after we'd shared a couple of nights of passion.'

She was speaking rapidly, as if desperate to explain herself and afraid that soon her chance would be lost. Daniel was listening to every word she uttered, an intent expression on his face. 'You needed to absorb their energy.'

'I only began to learn about myself when I went to university,' she said. 'I was on my own at last, away from my aunt and uncle, but things were still difficult. I called in at an occult shop one day. I'd always been interested, never done much about it. I picked up a magazine which had an article about real vampires. As soon as I read it, I recognised it was describing me, the way I felt. Everything. I had a vampire soul.'

Daniel turned to Harry. 'Real vampires are people who manipulate life force. It's called pranic energy. They absorb it from other living things. Humans in particular. Many of them never drink blood at all. But they are intense, moody, sensitive to light. They drain people they are close to. Especially lovers. It's not that they want to exploit others. They don't have a choice.'

'As the saying goes,' Andrea said, 'I am what I am.'

'Uh-huh.' Harry was experiencing an unexpected nostalgia for Juliet's enthusiasm for the Tarot and Feng Shui. This stuff was in a different league of loopiness, made no more palatable by the way Daniel was lapping it up.

'So many things suddenly made sense,' Andrea said. 'From the way I treated boyfriends to the fact that I felt more comfortable at night rather than during the day. I've always hated sunshine, people have said plenty of times how cold my skin is to the touch, even on a summer day. My aunt once called me a parasite, and though I didn't appreciate it at the time, actually she wasn't far wrong. As time has passed, I've tried to cultivate self-knowledge, learning to face the truth about myself.'

'Yet you didn't abandon the law,' Daniel said. 'Curious. There's no subject more rational.'

'You'd be surprised,' Harry murmured.

'You're right, Daniel,' Andrea said, ignoring the interruption. 'The idea of a game played by a set of coherent rules still appealed to me. At least it was something I could cling to whilst I tried to make sense of my own nature.'

'And how did Brett take all this?' Harry asked.

She faced him, her eyes wide. 'We skirted round the subject. For us, it was a kind of taboo.'

'So what do you imagine he reckons to all this – stuff about your vampire soul?' The words sounded even more brusque than he had intended.

'You don't understand,' she snapped. 'I've always dreaded people reacting in just that kind of way. It's a prejudice, don't you see, a form of discrimination? I've been afraid of being thought mad or some sort of pervert, that's why I've kept quiet over the years. Stayed in the closet, you might say. You've always struck me as a pretty tolerant guy, but I can see you've no time for what I'm saying. Brett was one of my bosses, remember. I could hardly confide in him.'

'You could have done it when you first started seeing each other.'

'I was afraid that telling him the whole truth would have ruined everything. I was sure he'd dump me and I couldn't bear that. We were good together. At last I'd found someone who gave me everything I needed. I gave him something in return, too. Trouble was, he sensed I was different, even if he wasn't quite sure how. Somehow we stayed together even after the firm fell apart and he had his breakdown, but at times he seemed terrified of me. I was desperate to confide in him, but I was afraid. It might have torn us apart. He wasn't strong enough to cope. I just hoped that slowly – in his own time – he might put two and two together. And I think he began to do just that. But I wanted more. I wanted him to come to terms with my nature, accept me for what I am.'

'Did he know that Carl Symons had sexually harassed you?'

She sat bolt upright. 'How did you hear about that?'

'You'd be surprised how word gets around. You complained to Nerys Horlock, didn't you? Woman to woman.'

'She made sure Symons laid off me,' Andrea said, fidgeting with a bracelet, keeping her eyes away from him. 'She knew I was a good lawyer, but she didn't like me. If she hadn't been a feminist, she'd probably have accused me of asking for it.'

'Did you feel bitter about her attitude?'

'What are you trying to say?' she snapped. 'I didn't kill her, if that's what you're getting at. She told me she'd had a quiet word with Symons and he didn't bother me again. There was no need to involve Brett, things would only have become even messier. I didn't murder Symons, either, by the way.'

Even while they had been talking, the room had darkened. Harry could see heavy clouds through the high windows; the forecast was for more rain. Andrea was like a slender shadow. He thought that if he tried to touch her, he might find nothing there.

'Tell me about Rick Spendlove, then. You seemed on very good terms with him, the night of the seminar. Brett saw the two of you smooching. So did I.'

She bent her head. 'Listen,' she said in a muffled voice. 'Things had been going badly between Brett and me. I was in a job going nowhere, he didn't have a penny to his name. He'd never told me that he'd lied about qualifying as a solicitor. I can't blame him for that, considering the secret I kept from him. I wish he'd trusted me, though. At least I would have understood better, understood why he sometimes talked about ending it all.'

'He threatened suicide?'

'Can you wonder? He even took an overdose once. Not a big one, and he knew I was due to turn up within the hour and I'd be able to save him. But it was a sign of his desperation. Symons had ruined him and Nerys Horlock had stood by and let it happen, so that she could get on with making a success of her career in a firm all of her own. Meanwhile our relationship was falling apart. He was at his wit's end. We both were.'

'And Spendlove?'

'I didn't know him well, but it was obvious he thought he was God's gift to the fair sex. He'd flirted with me. Then I went on a continuing education course put on by the Legal Group, to pick up enough training points to keep the Law Society happy. It took place in that new hotel on Lime Street. Rick bought me a couple of drinks in the bar and one thing led to another.'

'I see.'

'It meant nothing to either of us,' she said fiercely. 'I didn't mean to be unfaithful, but I was hungry for affection. Brett hadn't been – in the mood lately. I needed comfort. Rick Spendlove was there. That's all there was to it. He was a strong man – but I think he found me frightening. I drained him. He'd never have dared admit it, of course, he had too much ego.'

'That doesn't explain...'

'You're thinking about that incident in Old Hall Street? It was a big mistake. Stupid. My fault as much as his. I wish it had never happened. Spendlove had had a couple of drinks. They gave him courage and he started to pester me. I admit I didn't exactly push him away. He was good in bed, very good. Like I said, he was a strong man. But Brett had no need to be jealous, no need at all.'

'People aren't always logical about these things. He was afraid of losing you.'

'Just because we had a row that evening, the evening Nerys died, you shouldn't jump to conclusions.'

'Perhaps Brett didn't see it that way.'

She jabbed her forefinger at him. 'He didn't kill Spendlove, I'm sure of it! Or either of the others. You're as bad as the police, with your...'

'Hold on. I agree with you, for what it's worth.'

But she had already clambered to her feet. 'I'm sick of this! You come here, with your questions and your dirty insinuations. I've had enough of them. Would you go now?'

Harry glanced at Daniel, who gave an impatient nod. 'I only...'

Her hands were on her hips. 'Now, please.'

Daniel picked himself up from the floor and dusted his trousers. 'Goodbye, Andrea. Thanks for talking. It's been an experience, just talking to you.'

She turned to him. 'I made a mistake, didn't I? You're the one who understands me. Harry hasn't even tried.'

In a pub at Albert Dock, Harry said in a defensive tone, 'You don't really believe all that bullshit about real vampires, do you?'

They had lunched in near-silence. Harry's head kept throbbing. Perhaps it wasn't a surprise after all that had happened lately. He felt tired and frustrated and a little afraid. Three lawyers were dead; for all he knew, he might be next. Peter Blackwell had died as well and the terrifying – surely ridiculous? – possibility still lurked in the recesses of his mind that Juliet might have had something to do with that. Of course, it was ludicrous as well as disloyal. As much the stuff of nightmares as Daniel's barmy preoccupation with Count Dracula and his ilk. But however innocent Juliet might be, what future could the two of them have as a couple? It was only a question of time before Casper found out. Or, even more likely, before she tired of him.

The conversation with Andrea had left him confused and ill-tempered. He couldn't help blaming Daniel for encouraging her in her fantasy. All that crap about energy imbalance, inverted circadian rhythms and reversal of behaviour patterns belonged in the columns of a cheap magazine, not in the real world.

'She believes it,' Daniel said, putting down his tankard of bitter. 'That's what really matters. But to answer your question, yes, I suppose I do. I believe that some people do have vampire souls.'

'Oh, for Christ's sake. I thought I was gullible, but that takes the fucking biscuit!'

'Calm down,' Daniel said. 'Please, calm down. There's no need to lose your temper. I'm not saying they are fiends, not at all. Andrea Gibbs strikes me as deeply unhappy, afraid of what's happening in her life and with her boyfriend. I feel sorry for both of them.'

'Well, yeah. He's got enough on his plate without having the life drained out of him by an anorexic girlfriend whose head is stuffed with garbage.'

'You're being unfair. She's an intelligent woman, she's not insane.'

'You think not?' Harry asked sourly.

'No, I don't.' Daniel gazed at him. 'You told me you like mysteries. But you don't seem able to come to terms with any that you can't unravel.'

Stung, Harry said, 'Listen, Andrea Gibbs is a disturbed young woman who's filled her head with clap-trap and it hasn't solved one single problem in her life.'

Daniel sighed. 'That's one of the differences between us, isn't it? You keep looking for solutions. Answers to puzzles, everything neatly tied up in the final chapter. Me, I'm fascinated by the things that can't so easily be explained.'

Harry finished his drink. 'I'll get the bill.'

Daniel leaned across the table. 'What do you believe in, Harry?'

'Sorry?'

'You heard, I think. I asked what you believed in.'

Harry sucked in his cheeks. Every conversation with Daniel unsettled him. Partly because the man had made him question things he'd taken for granted all his life. Partly because he felt as if he were being measured, judged, as if his every word were being pored over, examined for inconsistencies. It was worse than being a witness at the Old Bailey. He wasn't ready to reveal his feelings to a near-stranger, whatever their ties in blood. Stubbornly, he demanded, 'What's that got to do with anything?'

'I made a mistake, didn't I, when we first talked? It was all about our mother, not about you and me. I want to know what makes you tick.'

'When I want psychoanalysing, I'll get in touch.'

'There's a bond between us, don't you feel it? We can help each other.'

You're just a bloke I hardly know who's crazy about vampires.

'Maybe.'

Daniel put his head in his hands. 'This isn't working, is it?'

He sounded like a lover at the end of an affair. Harry stood up. 'Sorry, Daniel. I've got things to do, you know? I'm back at work tomorrow. There's a lot of catching up to do.'

In a muffled tone, Daniel said, 'Can we talk again?'

Harry shrugged. 'I'll call you some time.'

Back in his flat, Harry picked up *The Journal of Quincy Harker*. By the time he put the manuscript down, he knew more about the Un-Dead than he could have wished to learn in a lifetime. The material was barmily melodramatic, the literary style at times clumsy and over-ornate. Unexpectedly, he felt an ache of disappointment. Perhaps he'd secretly hoped his half-brother was a literary *wunderkind* awaiting discovery. The truth was, the book was a potboiler, nothing more. And yet there was something in the whole farrago that made him keep turning the pages. The man could tell a story, that was for sure. If the book was rubbish, it was no more so than many of the paperbacks that crowded supermarket shelves. The only trouble was that Daniel wasn't simply writing a fantasy; he was trying to live one.

Harry sighed. In the quiet of Empire Dock, his conscience was troubling him as much as the sore ribs. He hadn't meant to be so blunt with his half-brother. Yet the nonsense about vampires, imagined and supposedly real, had been too much to take. Andrea didn't need humouring, she needed psychiatric help. Meanwhile, lawyers kept being murdered and the odds now must be that Brett Young was the culprit, had been the guilty one all along

On any logical view, Mitch Eggar and Ken Cafferty were right: Brett had motive, means and opportunity. Maybe this vampire stuff even related in some obscure Freudian way to the problems in his relationship with Andrea. Wherever he was hiding, surely the police would soon find him.

Harry winced as he thought that after their drinking session, Brett had gone out and set fire to Nerys's office with her body lying inside it. He had nothing, logically, to feel guilty about, but logic wasn't always his strong point. The killings were now the lead item on the national news, but he couldn't bring himself to watch the reports. He was sickened by the senselessness of the deaths – and tormented, too, by his inability to do anything to help bring the perpetrator to justice.

One thing he could do was get back to work, a desperate remedy designed to take his mind off the things that really mattered to him. He filled his briefcase with files and headed over to Fenwick Court. The office building was cold, dark and silent. Even though he'd worked there for so long, it seemed unfamiliar. Before he switched the light on in reception, the shadowy leaves of the yucca plant seemed to menace him, like knives in the hand of an assassin. His footsteps echoed as he walked down the corridor to his room. As he stepped inside and surveyed the files piled high on desk, chairs and floor, he sighed and told himself that he'd spent too long listening to malarkey about vampires. The real threat to his survival would come from the Law Society if he didn't catch up with the backlog of work.

He found his pager in the top drawer of his desk and shoved in a new battery. Normal service had to be resumed. It didn't take long to toss half the contents of his in-tray to the bin. Leaflets advertising unmissable seminars on tax avoidance, letters from recruitment consultants extolling job candidates keen to specialise in mezzanine finance – whatever that was – and gold-embossed invitations to subscribe to fine wine clubs created especially for solicitors with discerning palettes, all met the same swift fate. The correspondence that Carmel and his clerk Ronald Sou had left to await his attention proved heavier going. At least he could blame the fuzziness of his thinking on the after-effects of his accident. He dictated a dozen terse replies into the machine before taking a deep breath and started sifting through papers due to be produced in a High Court trial. In comparison, he thought gloomily, cleaning the Augean stables must have been a doddle.

At five past ten the pager began to bleep. Harry stared at it. How could he have forgotten how irritating that sound was? At least it offered a temporary reprieve from drafting a list of documents.

'Harry Devlin.'

'Back in the land of the living, then?' The catarrhal voice belonged to a veteran custody sergeant called Mortensen. 'Heard you'd had an accident.'

'I'm on my feet now.'

A throaty chuckle. 'More than can be said for some of your brethren, eh? You're not trying to eliminate all the competition, by any chance?'

'You know as well as I do, lawyers are like weeds. Uproot one and half a dozen more spring up in its place. Anyway, it's nice of you to ring for a chat, but...'

'Look,' Mortensen said, 'we've pulled in one of your clients. She's asking for you to represent her and so I said I'd give you a bell, see if you were around.'

'Who is it?'

'Sheryl Quigley.'

'What's the charge, Bob?' Harry asked as a matter of form. With Sheryl, there was only ever one charge.

'What do you think? She's like you. All she knows about is soliciting.' Mortensen gave a wheezy guffaw at his own wit. 'Matter of fact, she was in the back of a car with a priest. Teaching him that God moves in mysterious ways, I guess. They even had Radio 2 switched on. I've heard of elevator music, but that's ridiculous.'

'I don't suppose they were playing "Never On a Sunday"?'

Mortensen sniggered. 'Anyway, usual form. She'll be remanded to appear in the magistrates' tomorrow at ten. You want a word with her?'

'Put her on.'

Harry spoke briefly to his client and arranged to meet her in the cells at the main Bridewell before her court appearance the next morning. Sheryl was a realist. She agreed there was no point in protesting her innocence. The plan was to plead guilty and hope that the fine wasn't so heavy that she'd have to go straight back to the back streets of Toxteth to start earning the money to pay it off.

After he put the phone down, he gazed at the mound of documents. Perhaps he'd be more in the mood tomorrow. It was rather like Al Capone promising to jump on the wagon, but he'd had enough for one evening. He limped home, set the alarm and fell on to the bed. Within seconds he was asleep. If he dreamed of vampires, real or imagined, he didn't remember anything about it when the buzzer sounded the next morning.

He called in at the office on his way to the main Bridewell. Jim was already squinting at a set of title deeds in copperplate. 'Welcome back, Lazarus. What's on the agenda for today?'

'I was paged last night by Bob Mortensen. Sheryl Quigley has been arrested. She's been found in a priest's car, providing her own special brand of pastoral care. I'm seeing her at nine. Better be off, I'm late now.'

'Don't you want to hear about the new property work I've picked up?'

Harry could contain his enthusiasm. Tenancy agreements and building estates contracts couldn't hold a candle to court work. Whatever its shortcomings, at least it concerned human beings, human frailties. He waved a hand. 'Keep it as a pleasant surprise, eh? See you later.'

Sheryl proved, predictably, to be unabashed by her misdemeanour. She was a fat shameless girl with a gleeful sense of humour. Her spotty complexion attested to a lifelong love affair with doughnuts and chocolate eclairs. Harry had always had a soft spot for her. Where working girls were concerned, it made a change to act for one who was more likely to plough her earnings into confectionery than heroin. Her chins were apt to wobble as much as the massive breasts which Juliet would no doubt have described as her unique selling points. He had defended her half a dozen times over the years. She could turn her hand to most things, but her particular specialism lay in administering discipline. At one time she'd worked over in Manchester at a brothel catering for masochists. Maybe the priest was an old, guilt-ridden customer who'd wanted to soak up a bit more punishment.

'Usual fine?' she asked.

'You could go to prison,' he warned her, although they both knew it was unlikely.

'You won't let them do that, will you?' She laughed, shook her straggly dyed-blonde curls. 'Christ, I'm starving. When will they leave us alone, Harry?'

'Don't hold your breath.'

'It's my client I feel sorry for.'

'On the Lord's day, though.' Harry tutted.

'He's a man first, a Catholic second. I suppose they let him off with a caution?'

'First offence, why not?'

Sheryl gave him a wicked smile. 'You're sweet, Harry. You believe the best in people.'

It wasn't even true, he thought, as he wandered upstairs to the courtrooms. He was all too willing to imagine the worst. His suspicions of Daniel and Juliet, for example. Sheryl should have said what she meant and told him he was often naïve. That, perhaps, he couldn't deny. He ascertained that her case was to be heard in court number three. Most of the prostitutes were dealt with there; half of them were on first name terms with the clerk to the bench. It turned out that Suki Anwar was prosecuting here today. As usual, the court was a bear garden at this hour, full of lawyers, clients and witnesses, all of whom wanted to talk at the same time.

But today there was only one topic on everyone's lips. He heard Rick Spendlove's name a dozen times as lawyers joked nervously, asking each other who would be next. Eventually he spotted Suki in a corner, browsing through a wad of court documents, trying to familiarise herself with her caseload for the morning. He ploughed through the ruck of people so that he could have a word.

'Sheryl Quigley, you say? I've just been handed the papers,' she said briskly, keeping her eyes on the file. 'Guilty plea?'

'Uh-huh.'

'You're lucky, the chairman's soft on soliciting. She'll get off with a light fine.'

'And we all know how she'll find the money, don't we?'

She gave him a mirthless smile. 'At least justice will have been served.'

'Oh yes, I was forgetting that.'

'See you in there.'

'Wait,' he said as she moved away. 'Now that Rick Spend love has been...'

But she had moved quickly – deliberately? – out of earshot. Easy to imagine that she had no wish to discuss Spendlove or his death, but in that she seemed to be alone. Harry heard the name at least half a dozen times as he made his way through the ruck of people to take his place in the courtroom.

The case was soon over. Suki might not be in mourning for Rick Spendlove, but plainly she was in sombre mood today. Her usual style was to address the magistrates with eyes open wide, appealing to them to see the irresistible force of the prosecution case. Today, though, she kept her gaze fixed on her papers and spoke in little more than a mumble. It made no difference. Within five minutes the fine had been imposed and Harry was accompanying Sheryl down the stairs that led to Dale Street.

Her plump cheeks were pink, her eyes bright, her beam triumphant. In court, she'd seemed startled, unexpectedly overcome by the solemnity of her surroundings. But now he sensed that she would have been skipping ahead of him and taking the steps two at a time, had her buxom frame not been ill-equipped for it.

'Better result than you expected, then?'

'It's not that.' She burst into a fit of coughing, perhaps in an effort to contain her delight, and her mighty bosom swayed dangerously. 'It's just that...'

'Yes?'

As they reached the doorway that led on to the street, she turned to face him. 'Oh, Harry. I've seen some things in my time. But I must have seen everything now.'

'What are you talking about?'

'That woman, the prosecuting solicitor – it's Chantal!'

He gaped at her. 'I don't understand.'

'Oh, I don't suppose it's her real name.'

'You're talking about Suki Anwar? What do you mean?'

'She was at college in Manchester, of course, when I knew her. I remember her telling me that one day. It was like a holiday job to her. She'd run up a lot of debt.'

He gripped her wrist. 'You're joking, aren't you?'

'On my baby's life!' It was news to Harry that Sheryl was a mother, but he got the message. 'When I was at the Handcuff Hotel, Chantal was one of the girls who worked weekends. To make ends meet, she used to say. We had a good laugh about that, I can tell you.'

'You're sure about this? Suki Anwar was a prostitute?'

'Why so surprised?' Sheryl asked, all wide-eyed innocence. 'She's a prosecution brief now. It's not exactly a career change, is it? She's still dishing out the punishment.'

Chapter Twenty-Two

After he'd parted company with Sheryl, Harry wandered back to the office, pondering what her revelation might mean. He was sure she wasn't lying or mistaken. Sheryl might have her faults, but she was no fool. If she recognised Suki as a fellow prostitute, he wasn't going to argue. She'd even been generous in her appraisal of her former colleague's professional skills.

'She had what it takes, Harry, no question. Knew how to keep a client hungry for more. She could have gone all the way. Set up her own knocking shop, I mean. Chantal was no fool.'

No wonder Suki had kept her head down during the trial. An unforeseen encounter in the magistrates' court with a former colleague at the Handcuff Hotel must have featured high on her list of dread experiences. Unlucky to come across a working girl who'd plied her trade at the other end of the East Lancs Road, of course. She wouldn't have recognised Sheryl's real name when she'd read the file, wouldn't have spotted the need to feign sudden illness or make some other excuse to avoid having to come face to face with her.

He felt a rush of sympathy for Suki. He was well aware of the financial stresses suffered by people who wanted to qualify in the law these days. He'd talked to Carmel about it and what she told him made him angry. As far as he could see, politicians who talked a lot about equality had made it harder than ever for ordinary kids to compete with those who were better off. They looked after their own children, of course; the rest had to take their chances. If Suki had paid for her tuition fees by going on the game, he could understand it. But it was risky for any intending lawyer. What if someone found out?

As he turned into Fenwick Court, another question struck him. *Suppose Carl Symons had found out?*

Lost in thought, he walked into New Commodities House. A client was waiting in reception, reading the *Financial Times*. The sight was sufficiently unusual in the offices of Crusoe and Devlin for Harry to pull up short. People who came here tended to favour the sports pull-out of the *Daily Mirror*. The man was hidden behind the broadsheet, but it was easy to deduce from his polished brogues and immaculately pressed trousers that he wasn't a typical Crusoe and Devlin client. A sales executive from the fine wine club, perhaps? An envoy from the Office for the Supervision of Solicitors?

Suzanne was engrossed in study of her *vade-mecum*, *Feng Shui Can Heal Your Life*. Harry stifled a groan. Juliet had a lot to answer for. He could only hope that the author would recommend a change of job as an essential precursor to self-improvement. He coughed to attract her attention and mouthed: 'Who is he?'

For reply, she put down the book and mimed, 'We are not worthy.' Harry spun round in time to see the paper being lowered. It revealed the face of a man he had never met before, a face that was yet frighteningly familiar.

'Mr Crusoe?' Casper May asked.

'Er ... no. Sorry.' Harry was staring at him, hypnotised. It was like being trapped in a closet with a boa constrictor. 'I mean – my name's Devlin. I'm Harry Devlin. One of the partners here.'

Casper May got out of his chair. 'Oh yes,' he said coolly. 'I've heard about you.'

Harry felt his gorge rise. His legs were about to buckle under him. He clutched at the edge of Suzanne's desk to steady himself. He didn't know what to say.

'You're the litigation partner, aren't you? Good to meet you.'

Casper May stepped forward, his hand outstretched. Harry gripped it. He half-expected to be pulled to the ground and then pistol-whipped, but Casper's handshake was unexpectedly limp.

Somehow Harry found that rather shocking. He breathed out noisily.

'You okay?'

'Oh yes. Of course. Thank you.' He was jabbering wildly. 'It's just that – I didn't expect to be seeing you.'

'My property people have been handling the legal side so far, but I decided the time was right for me to meet you. I like to know the firms I'm dealing with.'

'Well, yes. Yes, naturally.'

'Congratulations on winning the tender, anyway. your partner put together a first class presentation, persuaded us he could handle all the work associated with transferring the homes into my company's name.'

'We've been well advised on our marketing strategy,' Harry said faintly. So the beauty parade Jim had mentioned was for the legal work associated with the old people's homes Casper was taking over.

'It shows. You're a small firm, but I don't have any prejudices about that. Who says size matters, eh?'

Casper laughed and Harry joined in. His cheeks felt warm; he was sure guilt was making him blush. He was remembering something Juliet had once confided in him.

The door to the corridor swung on its hinges and Jim bustled into reception. 'So you've met our new client? I tried to tell you that I was expecting Casper, but you were too busy rushing out to court.'

'If only I'd realised. I never expected to come face to face with – such an important client.'

'Don't get your hopes up.' Casper had a way of speaking that was pleasant yet icy. Harry could imagine him conducting a business negotiation in the same tone as giving an order to knee-cap a defaulting debtor. 'The fees you quoted in the tender, you won't be swanning off to the Bahamas on the profits. The work's price-sensitive. We want a quality service, naturally. But let's face it, the old folk in these homes are more bothered about incontinence pads than whether the leasehold agreements stack up. We need the legal stuff sorted out as cheaply as possible. That's why it's good to come here and see that – your overheads are kept rigorously under control.'

It was a euphemism, Harry realised, for saying that the yucca was visibly in need of intensive care and the coffee-stained copies of *Private Eye* on the reception table were six months old.

'Casper and I were planning to talk for an hour or so, then grab a bite of lunch,' Jim said. 'Care to join us?'

'Thanks,' Harry said, 'but I have to see someone else. Can I just have a word, Jim, before I leave you to it?'

He nodded to Casper May and led his partner back to his room. Once the door was safely closed behind them, he said urgently, 'You should have told me.'

'I tried, more than once. In the end, I thought I'd surprise you. The margins are tight, I shaved our quote to the bone, but it's good work and who knows where it will lead?'

Harry banged his fist on the desk. 'He's a fucking criminal!'

Jim stared at him. 'I don't believe this. What do you think your clients are? Boy scouts?'

'That's different. Casper May's a Premier League villain. We don't want to be beholden to a feller like that. He's bad news.'

'Listen, the money he's paying isn't bad news. We need it, Harry, or have you forgotten what the Loan Arranger told you?'

'Yeah, but there are limits.'

'We're drafting a set of leases, for God's sake, not selling a shipload of heavy armaments in breach of a UN embargo. I don't understand you. This is just the sort of break we've been looking for. What's the problem?'

'What about Juliet?'

Jim put his hands on his hips. 'I didn't consult her. Thought it better to keep her out of it, in the circumstances. When I was putting the tender together I kept in mind what she'd said about presenting to target clients, but that was all. Satisfied? Ethical dilemmas resolved?'

He fired the questions like arrows. His cheeks were red with anger. Harry ground his teeth. It was time to haul up the white flag. Otherwise the questions would get very awkward. 'All right, all right. I'm sorry. It was just a surprise, that's all.'

Jim placed a heavy hand on his shoulder. 'I thought you'd be pleased.'

'Sure. You've done well.'

'You're not convinced, are you?'

'No, you're right. We're not our clients' keepers. But let's just not get too close to him, okay?'

'No danger of that,' Jim said. He was relaxing now, honour satisfied. 'Apart from anything else, his aftershave makes me want to puke.'

As soon as Jim had departed to rejoin their new client, Harry dialled Juliet's number. 'I need to see you,' he said, keeping his voice low. 'Are you free?'

'What's the matter?'

'Tell you when we meet. I'll come over to your office, okay?'

'Yes, but I wish you'd explain...'

He was already on his way, tossing the receiver back on to its base and within five minutes, he was parking outside Juliet's office. Linda was in the outer room, tapping away on the keyboard as he arrived. When she looked up, he was shocked to see how haggard she looked. It was as if she'd aged ten years even since she'd visited him in hospital.

'Juliet's on the phone at the moment,' she said. 'She won't be long. She told me she was expecting you. You're on the mend, then?'

Harry nodded. 'And I realise it's a silly question, but how are you?'

'I'm still not quite sure Peter's death has quite sunk in yet. I keep hoping I'll wake up and find that he's still there, at the other end of the phone.'

'I'll always be grateful for the help he gave – that both of you gave – after Juliet found the body.'

Linda ducked her head. 'That was the start of things, wasn't it?' she said in a muffled voice. 'The death of Carl Symons. Do you think they'll ever catch the man who did it?'

'You mean Brett Young?'

'Yes.'

'Don't believe everything you read between the lines in the papers,' Harry said. 'I'm still not sure he's guilty.'

'But...'

Juliet's door opened and the familiar husky voice said, 'Harry. What's the problem?'

Harry glanced anxiously at Linda. 'It's Casper.'

'What's happened?'

'I was talking to him before I rang. Jim's only taken him on as a bloody client.'

Juliet's eyes opened wide. 'You'd better come in. Mind making us a coffee, Linda?'

She waved Harry on to the sofa in her inner sanctum and closed the door behind her. 'Linda's in a bad way. She insisted on coming in, but she's not up to it, that's obvious. After she's fixed the coffee, I'm going to send her back to Parkgate. And now you tell me your return to work hasn't gone to plan. What on earth's Jim up to?'

When Harry explained, she burst out laughing. 'It's priceless. Truly priceless. At least you're still in one piece.'

293

'I did wonder at one stage if he was measuring me up for a concrete overcoat.'

'Well, they are digging up Edge Lane at the moment,' she said, her eyes gleaming. 'You could still finish up buried in a trench if you don't play your cards right.'

He forced a grin but said, 'This isn't going to work, is it?'

'What do you mean? The mere fact you've met Casper, that Jim's handling a contract for him, it doesn't change anything. The Law Society hasn't issued a rule against sleeping with your clients' wives, has it?'

'I wouldn't be surprised,' Harry said. 'They've banned most of the other ways that your average solicitor gets pleasure. But that's not the point. Now I've met him...'

'What difference does it make? At least now you can put a face to the name.'

He looked at her. Teasing smile, strong jaw. A woman who knew what she wanted, a woman who liked to get her own way. His heart was pounding, but no longer out of lust. He'd never been cut out for an affair with her, he realised that now. He was boxing out of his weight. But for the time being, their relationship still amused her. She wouldn't let him be the one to end it. Rick Spendlove, he thought, must have felt like this, in the moments before he drowned. It was as if he were fighting for survival, as if his very life was at stake. But he could scarcely breathe any more.

He couldn't bring himself to go back to his desk yet. Instead he left his car in the park by the entrance to the Kingsway Tunnel and hurried back to the magistrates' court. He was about to go inside when he glanced down Dale Street and saw Suki Anwar a hundred yards away, heading in the direction of India Buildings, where she was based. Lengthening his strides, he weaved in between the shoppers and office workers and caught her up before she reached North John Street.

'We must stop meeting like this,' he said as he dropped into step beside her.

'And you ought to stop following me,' she snapped. 'Pestering me. Now if you don't mind, this briefcase is packed with files. I need to get back to work.'

'You recognised Sheryl, I presume?'

'Sheryl?' Her pace slackened, but she was doing her best to look blank.

'I don't suppose that was the name she used. Any more than you're called Chantal.'

A spasm of pain creased her face, giving him a glimpse of what she might look like when she was old and wrinkled. She paused on the kerb before crossing the road. Her shoulders had drooped. 'No,' she said, 'I'm not.'

At least, he thought, she knew him well enough now to understand that he would not give up, that it was easier in the long run to admit defeat. He gestured to a café on the other side of the road. 'Can we talk?'

'I told you, I'm rushed off my feet. Since Carl died...'

'Ten minutes. No more, I promise.'

'Why should I believe you?'

'So you've been entirely frank with me, have you?'

Her eyes were flickering to and fro, like an animal cornered by a hunter, trying to map an escape route, but afraid that there was no hiding place. 'Ten minutes?'

'Fifteen at most,' Harry said with a cheeky grin.

She didn't smile back. 'You can buy the coffee.'

'You're on.'

The café was called the Pool of Life. Carl Gustav Jung had coined the phrase for Liverpool in the early years of the century. According to rumour, he'd identified the concept of the collective unconscious after a night out in an Irish bar in Victoria Street. The Pool targeted the tourist trade and there were boards all over the place depicting pretty well everyone of note who'd had the faintest connection with the city. It wasn't yet lunch-time and the only other customers were a couple of old ladies in smart winter coats, probably on a day trip from Wirral, discussing their operations in penetrating high-pitched voices.

Harry chose a table at the back, next to a picture of Adolf Hitler. The Führer's other claim to fame was that he'd come to Liverpool to visit his auntie when he was nine years old; if only she'd had the foresight to push him under the wheels of a bus on Scotland Road. It took Harry ages to catch the waitress's eye and when she finally ambled over he had to fight the temptation to snap in guttural tones that his patience was exhausted. Once she'd finally taken his order, he turned to Suki and said, 'Tell me about it.'

'Why should I?'

He put his elbows on the table and cupped his chin in his hands. 'Because the cat's out of the bag. I know you worked at the Handcuff Hotel. Quite a secret for an ambitious young lawyer to keep. I'm not saying you'd kill to make sure the truth stayed buried, but remember how the caution goes. If you remain silent, it may harm your defence.'

'You bastard. This is none of your business.'

'Solicitors are being killed, Suki. The Law Society risks being made redundant. This isn't a time for finer feelings.'

'It's not your job to play detective.'

'No, but I'm not going to sit back and do nothing.'

She exhaled. 'You're not going to let this go, are you?'

'Can't. Sorry.'

'All right. What do you want to know?'

'Why you did it, for a start.'

She swept back the hair that kept falling into her eyes. 'Surely that's obvious. The money.'

'But there are plenty of ways of earning a few quid. Why prostitution?'

'I was desperate, okay? Halfway through my course I was up to my neck in debt. I'd fallen out with my parents, there was no way they'd give me a penny. I'd no idea of how to live on a budget, my tastes were pretty expensive and things got out of hand. Simple as that. I needed cash, and plenty of it, or I'd never make it as far as my finals.' She pushed the menu card aside and leaned across the table. Their fingertips were almost touching. He was conscious, more strongly than ever before, of her sexual appeal. He could understand why she'd gone down a storm in the Handcuff Hotel. 'The life my parents had as first-generation immigrants – it wasn't for me. Justice has always fascinated me. I wanted to help people, wanted to see justice done. And so I wanted to be a lawyer, wanted it more badly than anything else in the world. Can you understand that? I don't suppose you can.'

'Now you're doing me an injustice,' he said. 'Okay, then, how did you get mixed up with the Handcuff Hotel?'

'I shared a house with four other girls in Moss Side, near to City's football ground. One of them had a friend who'd spent a while on the streets, feeding a drug habit. I made a few enquiries, was put in touch with someone. And before I knew what was happening, I was being offered the chance to supplement my income, whipping men for fun and profit.' She gave him a bleak smile. 'They reminded me a bit of learned counsel, chuckling dutifully when the judge cracks a joke at their expense. But you know something? I became the queen of the torture chamber. The punters loved what I did, begged me for more. Me and the other girls, we reckoned they were football fans, Manchester City supporters. They had the same masochistic streak.'

The coffee arrived. Harry could hear one of the old ladies complaining about the quality of her hip replacement. Perhaps he ought to suggest that she took the hospital to court. He poured and then asked gently, 'Was Carl Symons one of your clients?'

Startled, she knocked her cup, spilling the drink over the melamine table top. Hoarsely, she said, 'What in God's name makes you say that?'

Harry picked up a napkin and mopped the coffee with neat, deliberate movements. Quietly, without looking at her, he said, 'I'm right, then?'

'You haven't answered my question!'

He glanced up into her scared eyes. 'You've answered mine, though.'

For a moment he thought she was trying to summon up the nerve to brazen it out, but her powers of invention deserted her. 'Yes,' she mumbled. 'That's where we met. People always thought he was a sadist, and so he was. But he liked to feel pain, as well as inflict it. He was the most odious man I've ever met. I'm glad he's dead, okay? No, more than that. I'm fucking ecstatic.'

He'd not heard her swear before and the brutal way she fired the last sentence made him shiver.

'Did you kill him?'

'If I had,' she said, 'do you seriously think that I'd admit it to you?'

'Why not?' He licked his lips. 'Come on. It's good to talk. Besides, I'm not the police and you're in confession mode.'

She took a sip from her cup. He sensed she was fighting to regain her composure. 'I asked you, how did you know Symons patronised the Handcuff Hotel?'

'I've never understood why you let him get away with rape. You don't lack guts. He must have had quite a hold over you, I decided, he must have been able to threaten to destroy your career if you even breathed a word.'

'I owe you an apology,' she said. 'I've underestimated you. When Symons was killed, I thought you were just a nosey-parker

I could pump for information to make sure no-one would suspect the truth about my past. And here I am, telling you my darkest secrets.'

'I've never denied being a nosey-parker.' Harry sighed. 'I suppose you and he both thought you were safe. Symons remembered the old adage about not fouling up in your own backyard. He wasn't foolish enough to patronise the Liverpool brothels, so when he wanted a good thrashing he drove down the motorway. You'd pushed it all to the back of your mind, presumably. You'd qualified, you'd found a good job. I don't suppose you ever dreamed that one day you'd come face to face with a former client.'

'I remember his big fat arse,' Suki said viciously. 'Even that wasn't as ugly as his head. Or as bald.'

'What happened when you met in the office?'

She shook her head. 'Both of us were stunned, I guess. He recovered his composure first, as you might expect. At first, he was fine. Talked about the need for discretion. He wanted to test me, I see that now, find out how much he could get away with. It sounds stupid, but it was almost like a bond. Each of us could have wrecked the other's career. It's pathetic, but I was so grateful that he was determined to keep things quiet.'

'I see.' Harry thought he could picture Symons toying with her, planning how to shift the relationship of exploiter and exploited from the seedy confines of a Mancunian brothel to the bland environment of a government office.

'Work kept us together. I reported to him. He was helpful, even made jokes about turning the tables and showing *me* the ropes. I guessed that people would start thinking that we were having a relationship. When I mentioned it, he was relaxed. "Let them," he said. "Better that than they have an inkling of what we used to get up to, don't you agree?" What I didn't realise was that he was using it as a cover, so as to help him explain things away if and when he took things further than I wanted. Because, you see, I'd put the

Handcuff Hotel a long way behind me, but Carl Symons' sex drive was still as strong as ever.'

'He made you do things?'

He could see tears forming in the corners of her eyes. 'It was partly my fault. I was a fool. I wanted to get on. To begin with, he was happy to offer a *quid pro quo*. My first appraisal was marvellous. The countersigning officer asked with a twinkle in his eye if I'd written it myself. Of course I had. But afterwards, I was Carl's prisoner, you see. He started to demand things – that weren't on offer. He threatened to out me if I said no. When I retaliated, said I'd ruin his career, he pointed out that if he was destroyed, he'd take me with him. He was ambitious, but he had a reckless streak too. He'd risked everything just by visiting the Handcuff Hotel. I couldn't be sure that he wouldn't ruin my career as well as his. He was a gambler, I realised. He might have been bluffing. But I couldn't take the risk.'

'And then,' Harry said softly, 'he raped you.'

She inclined her head. The tears were trickling down her cheek. Her voice was almost inaudible. 'I won't go into details, okay? Not for you or anyone else. All I'll say is that even Symons realised afterwards, he'd gone too far. He'd robbed me of every last shred of dignity. I'd reached the point where I'd almost stopped caring whether I lived or died, let alone what happened to my brilliant career in the CPS.'

'So he backed off?'

'Yes, he might have been a risk-taker, but he was a coward beneath it all. He knew he'd gone too far. I presented at least as much of a danger to him as he did to me. Especially when I started seeing Nerys.'

'You met her in the courts?'

'Yes, I'd decided I was off men for good by that stage. She offered a shoulder to cry on. Then something more. She was lonely. She was a workaholic, she'd spent years on the law, the whole law and nothing but the law. Once she said to me, "I've spent all this time, fighting to get to the top. And when I did, there was nothing there." We became very close.'

'How much did you tell her about Carl?'

'I was highly selective. I didn't give her all the gory details of the rape, let alone mention the Handcuff Hotel. I didn't think she'd sympathise. I was afraid she'd see it as something of a betrayal of feminism. Maybe she wouldn't, maybe she'd have understood. Too late now to find out.'

'So when you pulled the plug on the tribunal claim, she was angry because she didn't understand?'

'Exactly. I was furious with her, too. She had no right to put a claim in behind my back, when I'd already told her I wanted to let it drop. We had a blazing row, and that was that. The two of us split up.'

'What about Rick Spendlove?'

She dried her face with a napkin and gazed across the table at him. 'Building up quite a case for the prosecution, aren't you?'

'You're the expert in that field.'

'What about him?'

'He embarrassed you at the Maritime Bar when he mentioned the tattoo on your bum.'

She gave him a cool look. Already she was beginning to recover her composure. 'If you think that's a credible motive for murder, you're not as smart as I thought.'

'I never claimed to be smart. I only said I don't give up.'

'Whatever. Tell the police if you think the tattoo matters. Personally, I wouldn't want to distract the forces of law and order if I were you. They have their man in the frame. For what it's worth, I didn't kill any of the victims, let alone all three. I wasn't physically strong enough, apart from anything else. Since we last spoke, I've talked to a few people and found out more about how Symons and Nerys died. To cut off their heads' – she gave an involuntary shudder – 'that would have required brute force. Or a lot of skill.'

'Maybe. But you're young and fit. It wouldn't have been physically impossible, especially if you'd knocked them out first. And you could easily have killed Spendlove. Unless you've managed to come up with an alibi for the night when he was killed.'

'Afraid not. Terrible lack of foresight.' She narrowed her eyes. 'This is a game to you, isn't it? You don't seriously believe I'm a murderer.'

'No, it's not a game.'

'Come on,' she urged. 'It's obvious, isn't it? Brett's gone over the edge. He's the one the police are looking for. Symons must have found out that he wasn't qualified. It explains a lot.'

'Nerys knew as well, didn't she?'

'She never mentioned it to me,' Suki said. 'But I think Symons had told her. Looking back, on the odd occasions when she mentioned Brett, there was a sub-text. I never paid much attention at the time, but now I think that she'd discovered he should never have been in a solicitors' partnership in the first place. So she had no sympathy when things began to get rough for him.'

'And Spendlove?'

'Your guess is as good as mine. Maybe he was rogering Brett's bit of stuff.'

'So you think Brett's a triple killer?'

'Put it this way, he's going to need a bloody good lawyer himself after the police have caught up with him. And they aren't so easy to find around here. He only has himself to blame for thinning the ranks. Perhaps he'll give you a ring.'

She treated him to a dazzling smile. Harry was struck by the way her confidence had returned during the course of the conversation. She was even sitting up straighter in her chair. She reminded him of a suspect in a police interview room who suddenly realises that the detectives don't have enough evidence to make a charge stick.

Or perhaps she had simply persuaded herself that he would keep the secret of her past to himself.

He tried to catch the waitress's eye. 'Sorry. I didn't mean this to take so long. Thanks for your time.'

'You're welcome.' She picked up her briefcase. 'But now I really must dash. See you around.'

He watched her go, hips swinging jauntily beneath her sober black skirt, and wondered if she was right. For Suki, Brett was a convenient scapegoat. If only he could find the man. And find him alive.

One of the old ladies was saying that she'd always been a martyr to arthritis and that hip replacements weren't all they were cracked up to be. The waitress had abandoned the task of ringing up the price of the coffees on the till in favour of a chat with a brawny youth who had emerged from the kitchen. Harry wasn't bothered; he was in no hurry to get back to the office and resume his onslaught on the backlog of desk work. He turned in his seat and scanned the café. There was an information board on the pillar behind him. A picture on it caught his eye. It depicted a pipe-smoking Victorian patriarch, complete with top hat and walking stick. The caption was *The Mole of Mason Street – King of Merseyside's Underworld*. The phrase caught his attention and, craning his neck, he read the rest of the paragraph and the acknowledgment of its source.

As the words sank in, an idea began to form in his mind. He clambered hastily to his feet, knocking his chair over in the process. The old ladies glanced at him and tutted audibly. Another black mark for the younger generation – if he still qualified for membership of the younger generation. He pulled his wallet from his pocket and tossed Casper May's business card on to their table.

'In case you ever need looking after,' he murmured, giving them a wolfish smile as he hurried to the counter.

The waitress paused in her conversation to say she wouldn't be a minute.

'I haven't got a minute,' he said, tossing a fiver at her and hurrying for the door. If his guess was right, it just might be that every second counted.

Chapter Twenty-Three

Half an hour later, he was reversing his MG into a small unmarked car park on a slope off Smithdown Lane. He yanked a book out of the glove compartment and crammed it into his jacket pocket. It was a paperback he'd bought from the shop in the Bluecoat Art Gallery after leaving the Pool of Life. One chapter was entitled 'Joseph Williamson – The Mole of Edge Hill.'

Harry had skimmed through the pages every time he hit a traffic light on the way here. He'd heard of Williamson; his name cropped up in newspapers or on regional television once in a while. Yet beyond the fact that Williamson had built a network of tunnels under nineteenth-century Liverpool, he knew little about the man. The King – aka the Mole – of Edge Hill was the sort of person who fascinated tourists; locals took their city's past for granted.

Williamson's story was strange but simple. A tobacco merchant celebrated for his eccentricity, he'd been smart enough in his younger days to marry the boss's daughter. He'd made a fat fortune and after giving up work at fifty he'd bought a tract of barren land in Edge Hill on which he proceeded to build an estate. His retirement coincided with the aftermath of the Napoleonic wars and the city's first wave of mass unemployment and poverty. Troubled by the signs of deprivation all around, he recruited an army of men from the neighbourhood and offered them wages in return for hard work. Because he had few material needs, he set them to build huge brick arches behind the houses in Mason Street, where he lived. When that was done, he had them dig below ground. As time passed they constructed a maze of tunnels and caverns, stretching for miles beneath the city streets.

It was, Harry reflected as he stuffed the book into his jacket pocket, the ultimate job creation scheme. Williamson had spent a fortune paying people to do work that lacked any purpose.

Nowadays, he would probably have been in charge of the Millennium Dome. Yet it was impossible not to admire him. His heart had been in the right place. He'd given people the chance to regain their self-respect.

It was beginning to drizzle as Harry turned into Smithdown Lane and paused to check his bearings. In the books were maps and pictures of the area. The sandstone wall which ran alongside the pavement had been crudely repaired over the years with brick and concrete. According to the text, the wall had marked the boundary of Williamson's land. He found himself outside a forbidding pair of metal gates, through which he could see a derelict courtyard. This must be the old Lord Mayor's Stable Yard. His destination was on the other side of the gates. Just two little snags. First, the site was plastered with signs saying *Smithdown Security – Eternal Vigilance*; their logo was uncompromising, a mailed gauntlet inside a ring of barbed wire. Second, on the opposite side of the road towered a six-storey police station. A burly man in shirt sleeves was watching him curiously from a first floor window. Harry gave him an anxious nod and began to retrace his steps.

He passed an old bricked-up house and climbed a mound next to the car park. Now he was above the stable yard and could see the tops of the old buildings. Slates had been stripped from some of the roofs and he could see huge nettles and bushes growing in between the cobbles on the ground. A tall fence topped with razor wire bordered the site for twenty yards, then give way to another sandstone wall. This time the old blocks hadn't been mended. Time and vandals had made gaps which might afford hand-holds if he were desperate to explore the courtyard. And he was desperate.

He looked over his shoulder. A tattooed youth in frayed jeans was wandering around the car park, casually testing the vehicle doors. Harry took his wallet out and called out to him. 'A tenner if you give me a leg up over the wall.'

The lad stared at him. He evidently found it difficult to reconcile the near-respectability of Harry's sober if aged suit with a reckless determination to indulge in an apparently pointless act of trespass in broad daylight.

'There's no harm,' Harry urged. 'I'm a surveyor for the people who are going to develop this site and I've left my padlock key back in the office.'

'Yeah, and Everton just signed the Pope as first team coach.'

'Come on, mate. I can't do it on my own. It's good money for ten seconds' work.'

'Piss off. How do I know you're a fucking surveyor? Besides, have you seen the traffic? That's a main road over there. I'd have to be out of my mind.'

'Twenty quid.'

'All right. But get a move on.'

The money changed hands and the lad bent down. With his help, Harry managed to haul himself up the wall. There was a loose coping stone on the top and for a moment he thought he was about to fall, but he managed to cling on. As the lower half of his body dangled over the wall, he glanced in the direction of the main road and spotted a motorist in a passing car staring at him. Brakes screeched as the car almost collided with a van overtaking in the opposite direction. The lad had vanished. Harry could hear the echoes of footsteps pounding across the gravelled car park and into the distance. He jumped down to the ground. The impact knocked the breath out of his body. He felt a sharp pain in his damaged leg and his ribs began to ache. But at least he'd made it.

Gasping with the effort, he limped across the cobbles. The ground was overgrown with weeds and old tyres and bits of iron lay all around. Old stable buildings fringed the yard. Their windows had been blocked with sheets of corrugated iron, some of which were peeling away from their fixings. He glanced through one of the gaps, but the stables were empty except for litter and other rubbish.

He checked in his book and made for the corner of the yard. Trees formed a natural tunnel; at the end there was a large arch, lined with brickwork. An entrance to the labyrinth. He peered into the darkness and saw that the passageway was filled with rubble. Better give that one a miss.

To the right was a small opening. Again he looked inside. The roof of the opening was lined with bricks. Stalactites were hanging from it. A musty smell hung in the air. He consulted his book, only to be told that the passage led to an underground well and no further.

'Brett!'

He could hear his voice bouncing back off the walls of the chamber. No reply. Perhaps it had been stupid to imagine that Brett might be lurking in such a hell-hole. He moved towards the right-hand corner of the yard. He could see a gap there. As he drew nearer, it became clear that there was another opening in the brickwork. The second entrance to the tunnel. He bent down and called Brett's name again. No answer. He felt foolish and glanced over his shoulder. If anyone had noticed his illicit entry into the stableyard, they had yet to give chase. Encouraged, he stepped into the darkness.

He'd bought a pocket torch on his way from the Bluecoat to the car. He switched it on, and although the beam was weaker than he had hoped, it lit up the cave. The floor was uneven and strewn with stones and bits of rubble. The far end seemed to be walled up. Careful not to miss his footing, he advanced with care and found that he wasn't confronted by a dead end after all. There were two gashes in the rock. Bending down, he entered the right-hand passageway, but soon found that the roof sloped down and that further progress was impossible. Retracing his steps, he took the left-hand entrance.

He hadn't expected it to be so cold. He found himself wishing he'd come better prepared. A thermal vest wouldn't have gone amiss. Yet he'd persuaded himself that he dare not delay. It wasn't the first time in his life he'd surrendered to impulse and then had cause to regret it. As he moved forward, the tunnel began to shrink around him. He was breathing unevenly, suffering the first pangs of claustrophobia as he was forced to bend double. His feet slipped on the algae-slick ground and when he put a hand out to steady himself he cut his wrist on a jag of rock. Soon, he thought, he would be crawling on his hands and knees. Suitable for praying that there wouldn't be a roof-fall.

Suddenly the tunnel opened out into a vast cavern. Relief washed over him, then he put his hands on either side of his mouth and bellowed, 'Brett! Are you there?'

As the question echoed around him, he closed his eyes and concentrated, breathing in the stale underground air. What was the movement that he could hear – surely something more than the nervous scurrying of a disturbed rat?

'It's Harry Devlin!'

His name reverberated in the cavern. An egotist's dream. Carl Symons would have loved it. Again he thought that he could hear an answering noise in the distance. He had to believe that he'd guessed right, that he'd found Brett Young.

'I'm alone!' he shouted. As soon as the words left his lips, it occurred to him that they were unwise. If Brett were the murdering kind, he might need little encouragement to add to his tally of victims. It would have been more sensible to imply that a squad of armed detectives were bringing up the rear. Too late now.

He moved forward. The cavern floor was silted and wet. Peering though the gloom, he could see a number of dank holes leading from the cavern. Brett might be hiding in any of them.

'Let's talk!'

At last he heard a sound he believed he could identify. Boots clambering over rock. The noise was coming from the tunnel to his left. He crept towards it. Somewhere in the darkness, boulders clattered.

'Shit!'

Brett's voice, hoarse and tired, but unmistakably Brett's voice. Harry clenched his fists. He'd guessed right. No, *deduced* right.

'Come on,' he hissed, shining his torch into the tunnel. 'There's nothing to be afraid of.'

He couldn't see Brett, but was sure that he was drawing nearer. He could hear scraping sounds, as if the other man was carving a path through mounds of debris. Finally, his torch picked out a shape emerging from the gloom.

Brett looked like an extra from *The Night of the Living Dead*. His jacket, jersey and jeans were tattered and torn. His face and hands were dirty and bruised. Blood was seeping from a cut on his cheek. His eyes were blank, expressionless.

'What do you want here?'

'I need to talk to you.'

Brett's voice rose. 'Why couldn't you leave me alone?'

'Like you left me alone when you hit me in the car park at Empire Dock?'

Brett bowed his head. 'It was an accident.'

Harry leaned back against the sandstone wall and folded his arms. In a casual, chat-over-a-garden-fence tone, he said, 'Sure, but you didn't stop to find out how bad an accident, did you?'

A pause. Brett took a couple of stiff paces towards him. Now he was so close that Harry could feel sour breath on his cheek. 'I didn't mean to kill you.'

'I realise that. The accident was my fault, not yours. I was trying to get away from someone and I stumbled in front of your taxi. I suppose you panicked.'

'That's right.' Brett stretched out his arms, as if in supplication. It was as if, having spent days in the darkness, he was learning how to talk again to a fellow human being. 'I'm sorry I scarpered. I should have called for help.'

'Doesn't matter. Someone else did that.'

'Looks like you've made a pretty good recovery. Not sure about the beard, though.'

'At first I felt as though I'd been steamrollered, but I'm fine now.'

'I'm glad. You see, I'd wanted to talk to you that Sunday. I couldn't think of anyone else.'

'What about – Andrea?'

'Not Andrea,' Brett said harshly. 'I knew you'd listen – but then you ran under my wheels. I simply lost it. I drove off and left the Sierra near Paddy's Wigwam.' There was an awkward pause. 'How did you find me?'

Harry gestured at their surroundings. 'You're interested in Merseyside's underworld, aren't you?'

'Well, yes, but...'

'I saw a book in your flat with that title, the night Nerys was murdered. *Merseyside's Underworld.* At the time, I assumed it was all about true crime, stories about protection rackets and drug wars, that sort of thing. Then I came across the phrase again this morning. You know the Pool of Life café in Dale Street? I saw the words on a display board featuring Joseph Williamson. The text was an extract from the book. A couple of things suddenly clicked into place.'

'Such as?'

'I remembered you had another book, about pot-holing. Suppose you were keen on tunnels, knew the network of caves under Mason Street? You'd decided to disappear off the face of the earth. Where better to hang out than in a ready-made hiding place a few minutes' walk from your home?'

Brett blinked. 'Clever of you.'

'It was a neat trick, a bit like that story by Edgar Allan Poe. You're right under the nose of the police, yet this is the last place they'd look for you.'

'The security people are more of a worry. They're pretty efficient, they patrol the site regularly. The guards come with their Alsatians, at any time, day or night. I have to make sure I keep well out of their way. So I've only been above ground a couple of times since I arrived here.' Brett frowned. 'But you didn't come here just because you read a tourist sign in a cafeteria.'

'No, I decided to check my idea out. I found *Merseyside's Underworld* in the Bluecoat shop. The author's introduction expresses thanks for assistance from colleagues in the Subterranean Merseyside Society. Your name's included.'

'I joined years ago. Not that I've been to any meetings since the firm folded. Too much else on my mind, you know.'

'He even mentions that you're a particular *aficionado* of Williamson and his mining activities. It all added up so I raced over here. Of course, I've never been inside the tunnels before, but I thought it must be worth taking a look.'

'I'm sure you weren't disappointed,' Brett said. He was looking a little less like a zombie, showing animation at last. This was his domain, he was talking about his special subject. 'Spectacular, isn't it? Look at the way the sandstone has been cut and shaped in this chamber. Doesn't it remind you of the pyramids of Ancient Egypt?'

The comparison was a bit fanciful, but Harry couldn't help nodding. 'There's a whole lost world down here.'

'You've not even seen the Banqueting Hall yet.' Brett was starting to gabble with excitement. 'That's the most famous cavern, but it's not the biggest. In one place, the caves are as deep as the police station outside is tall. The audacity of it simply takes your breath away. The tunnels go on for miles, you know. Nobody knows how far.'

'You've stayed here ever since you knocked me over?'

'That's right. I – I panicked. I dumped the car, but then I didn't know what to do, where to turn.'

'You could have talked to Andrea. She's been worried sick about you.'

'How could I trust her?' Brett hissed.

Harry said carefully, 'Did this vampire nonsense...?'

Brett shuddered. 'So you know about that, as well? Let's not talk about Andrea, eh? She and I are finished.'

'Don't be so sure.'

'Finished, I said.' Brett's voice had begun to rise again. 'We're incompatible, understand?'

'She cares about you.'

'And I'm crazy about her, but it's no good. It can never work. We're wrong for each other. In the end I decided this was the safest place to be. I know my way around. There are a couple of entrances that no-one else knows about. You can't find everything in the guide books. I was sure I could stay here – well, more or less indefinitely. I could come and go as I pleased, as long as I made sure that no-one who mattered saw me if I ever needed to leave to get fresh provisions. Follow me and I'll show you where I've been sleeping.'

He led Harry through an opening the shape of a keyhole and into a narrow, curving tunnel. 'You'll have to wriggle on your belly, there's no alternative. Come on. Just till we get round the bend. It's not far.'

'All right,' Harry grunted, 'I needed to buy a new suit anyway.'

'You ought to have come properly equipped if you were planning to look for me down here,' Brett said severely.

'I'm a bit short of pot-holing gear,' Harry muttered as he tried not to crack his head against the roof of the tunnel.

Brett manoeuvred himself round the bend with the ease of long practice. Scrambling after him, Harry saw that the passage opened out into another chamber. The air was fresher than he would have expected; there must be ventilation shafts nearby. It wasn't too cold, either, considering the time of year and that they were beneath the ground. In the corner was a heap of belongings: warm clothes, a pillow, a mattress, a handful of books.

'Home sweet home,' he muttered as he wiped the dirt off his jacket and trousers.

'I needed time to myself. After Nerys died, the police started closing in. It was only a question of time before they discovered that I'd never qualified as a solicitor. Then they would find out that Carl Symons knew the truth.'

'How did he find out?'

'One of my tasks was to deal with all the paperwork for the Law Society. Carl and Nerys were happy with that – one less job for them to worry about. It was the only way I could keep pulling the wool over everyone's eyes. The trouble started when I took a holiday and Carl started to sniff through my private filing cabinet. He soon realised that something didn't stack up.'

'That's when he started blackmailing you?'

'He didn't put it like that, of course. To listen to him, you'd have thought he was doing me a favour. The way he put it, I'd jeopardised his career and livelihood. He'd teamed up with me in the utmost good faith. It was up to me to make reparation. And you know the funny thing? I could see his argument.'

'He was a lawyer. He could argue any cause.'

'Yes, we're good at that, aren't we? If nothing else. So I had to pay the price.'

'Even though it was crippling.'

'Oh yes. Pulling out of our partnership cost Carl nothing. It ruined me, in every way. You see, I had nothing to lose by coming down here. I could think things over, try and get myself sorted out.'

'And have you?'

Brett shrugged. 'It's not so easy.'

'Perhaps you should have stuck with local history instead of getting involved with the law.'

'Oh, I became fascinated by Williamson after I moved to Liverpool, but I was always keen on the law as well. You don't need to have letters after your name to be seduced by the idea of courtroom drama. When I was growing up in Maryport, I set my heart on becoming a solicitor. But I couldn't cope with Law College. I kept flunking the exams. It didn't seem fair. I had the knowledge, the commitment. There were worse lawyers than me who sailed through.'

Harry wondered uncomfortably if he was one of them. 'Yeah, I suppose that's dead right.'

Brett leaned forward, jabbing Harry's chest with a finger to emphasise his point. 'You meet them all the time in private practice. People whose advice to clients is positively dangerous. I'll tell you something, Harry. Whatever lies I may have told, no-one ever suggested that I wasn't a good lawyer.'

Harry took in a lungful of air. Brett had a point: a cynic would say that telling lies was part of a solicitor's job. 'So you decided to pretend you were qualified. Didn't people check up on you?'

'I went to London for a while. There was nothing to keep me in the north. Besides, no-one knew me down there. Firms were crying out for staff. They weren't too fussy about checking the paper trail. I interviewed well, spun a few yarns, forged a couple of documents. It was like playing a game. You'd be surprised how easy it is. Easy to succumb to temptation, to get in deeper and deeper.'

'Uh-huh.' It took all sorts, Harry thought. From time to time, he too fantasised about what it might be like to lead a Walter Mitty existence. But he'd always envisaged it as a way of escaping from legal practice, not as a means of signing up for it.

'Before I knew what was happening, the wishful thinking had come true. I was offered a job. I suppose I should have stopped there, but the line between my little game and the real world was getting pretty blurred. For me, I suppose it always has been. I had the opportunity to become Brett Young, solicitor of the Supreme Court of Judicature. Chance of a lifetime. So I took it.'

'Yet you came to Liverpool. Bit of a contradiction there, surely?'

'Don't knock it. The place isn't so bad and I wanted wider experience, simple as that. I saw a job offered in the *Gazette* and applied. By now, I had a track record. I'd shown what I could do. It didn't bother me too much that I didn't have the right qualifications. Why should it? I'd earned that job, earned it on merit. I didn't think I was deceiving anyone. Not really.'

Harry was familiar with that kind of logic. His criminal clients used it all the time. And so, sometimes, did he. He said gently, 'Did you resent the fact that Carl and Nerys were qualified and you were not?'

'Why should I?' Brett raised his eyebrows. 'Still looking for a motive for me to kill them?'

'The police will want to know. You may as well be prepared for their questions. They won't mess about. Not with Rick Spendlove dead as well.'

'You wouldn't be trying to trap me, would you?' Brett demanded. He hadn't twitched with shock at mention that Spendlove was dead, but there was a wildness in his voice which made Harry edge away from him.

'How would I do that?'

'You think I know Spendlove's dead because I killed him, but it's not true. I've not spent all my time down here, you know. I've been out a couple of times, once at night, once first thing this morning before the security guard did his round. I went to the mini-mart on Congress Street and bought the *Daily Post*. Look for yourself, it's over there. And it's full of Spend love's murder.'

'Well, then,' Harry said softly. 'What do you make of it?'

Brett glared at him. 'You still believe I killed them, don't you?'

Harry had his back to the cavern wall. Maybe attack was the best form of defence. Launching into cross-examination mode, he leaned forward, starting to wag his finger like a latter-day Rumpole. 'Didn't you see them as vampires? Carl and Nerys because you thought they'd conspired to wreck your career. Your whole life. Spendlove because he took a shine to Andrea and you were afraid he'd steal her from you.'

Brett shuddered. He seemed to want to shrink away, to curl up and try to fade away into the darkness. 'No! It's not true!'

'A stake was driven through Carl's heart.' Harry spat out the words. He wouldn't go easy on Brett. It was too late to relent. 'Same thing with Nerys. Their heads were cut off. With Rick Spendlove, it was similar, though maybe the killer was disturbed before he could finish the job. Nerys's office was burned. Rick's car was dumped in the dock. Fire and water, you see? Tell me – how much have your troubles with Andrea played a part in this? The whole thing has been about destroying vampires, hasn't it?'

Brett's breathing had become laboured. 'You're fucking well out of your mind.'

'I'd say whoever killed those three lawyers was the crazy one, wouldn't you? You have to be pretty disturbed to decapitate a corpse, don't you agree? Besides, there's more. There's the business of the tunnels.'

Brett stared at him. 'What about the tunnels?'

'When I glanced at the book that told me about Joe Williamson, I had a quick look at some of the other chapters. One thing I never realised is how many tunnels there are in Merseyside.'

'Oh yes,' Brett muttered. 'They're all over the place. People simply don't understand.'

'Smugglers' tunnels on the Wirral, for instance. Dawpool's mentioned in the index. The place where Carl Symons lived, you remember. Contraband used to be taken from the ships that docked in the anchorage. That's why a customs officer had to be based there.'

'So fucking what?'

'Nerys's office is only a few hundred yards from here,' Harry persisted. 'Handy for the Williamson tunnels. And Rick Spendlove was drowned within a stone's throw of Birkenhead Priory. The Priory's mentioned in *Merseyside's Underworld*, too. Something about a legend that a couple of monks were buried alive in a tunnel which led to the river. They were trying to hide the Priory plate from Henry VIII's heavy mob.'

'What in God's name are you getting at?'

Harry gazed at Brett's white face, trying to ignore the doubt that nagged him like a bad tooth. Driving over here, an idea had begun to form inside his head. He hadn't had time to work out the details of his latest theory, but the big picture looked persuasive. Once he'd seen Brett's name in the author's acknowledgments, he'd decided he must be on the right track. The tunnels must be significant. Perhaps the killer had lain in wait beneath the ground, or used the tunnels to store the tools of murder: stake, axe, petrol to start the fire. Everything pointed to Brett's guilt. He was the tunnel expert, he was hiding down here, for God's sake.

'You used the tunnels before you killed them.' He was making it up as he went along. 'You kept the weapons there, you...'

'Hold on a minute,' Brett said fiercely. He clutched at Harry's sleeve. 'Suppose you're right. Suppose it just for a moment. Wasn't it stupid of you to come down here on your own? I could kill you easily and your body would never be found. You hear stories going back a century, of people who came to explore the tunnels and were never seen again. There are so many places I could leave a corpse to rot.'

'You won't do that,' Harry said. His hands were clammy and his heart was pounding, but he was determined not to let his fear show. 'It's not part of your plan. I'm no vampire. You don't need to murder me. What would be the point? You can't stay here for ever. Sooner or later, you'll have to go back above ground. Look, why don't you come back with me? We can talk to the police, see what we can sort out.'

Brett's eyes widened. 'Are you serious?'

'You need to face up to things,' Harry insisted. 'It's the only way.'

'No, I was talking about the tunnels. I mean, have you *studied* the book?'

'Of course not. I haven't had time.'

'Give it to me.' Brett reached out and snatched the book, a gesture so sharp and swift that Harry almost lost his footing. He flicked through the pages and then thrust it back into Harry's hands. 'There. Something you missed when you skimmed through. Read it.'

Harry glanced at the text. '*Attractive though the legends about passageways running from the Priory are, there is sadly no truth in them. The opening which can be found in the crypt leads nowhere. Indeed, no evidence is available to suggest that there ever existed even a short underground tunnel to the Mersey, far less the supposed network extending as far as New Brighton in one direction and Ince in another.*'

'I don't believe everything I see in black and white,' he said mutinously. 'You said yourself that the stuff about Williamson and these tunnels is incomplete. Maybe you're aware of stuff that no-one else knows.'

Brett shrugged. 'If there are tunnels at the Priory, I've yet to come across them. As for Dawpool, there is supposed to be at least one tunnel, but I've never got round to exploring that area, just the old colliery workings further down the river at Neston.'

'So you say.'

'Why should I lie? If I'm as deranged as you seem to believe, you're dead meat anyway.'

'You can't just brush aside what I've said.'

'Why not? It's a load of bollocks. I've never killed anyone.'

'All right.' Harry's heart wasn't beating quite so fast now. It was absurd, but he had the feeling that he was being pushed back on to the defensive. As he had driven over here, his reasoning had seemed watertight. Down here in the labyrinth, it was starting to resemble a wild stab in the dark. 'Even if you didn't make use of the tunnels for the murders...'

'Get real, Harry. You're talking nonsense. Most of the tunnels you're talking about don't exist.'

'You had the motive...'

'Christ, I've never denied that I was glad when Carl Symons got his come-uppance.' Brett puffed out his cheeks. 'But I wouldn't say I hated Nerys, even when she sided with Carl. Not so that I would kill her.'

'And Rick Spendlove?'

Brett glared. 'He was a bastard. In his way, he was as bad as Symons. I won't pretend to any remorse about his death. He treated women like shit. Led them on until he had his wicked way, then dumped them. Nerys acted for one of them, a woman called Tuesday Jones.'

Harry blinked. 'Tuesday Jones?'

'Yes, sort of name that sticks in your mind, isn't it? She was Spendlove's secretary and they started an affair. She thought he was going to marry her, but when he realised she was serious, he kicked her into touch. That's the kind of man he was. I tell you, he was no loss, Harry. No loss at all.'

Harry rubbed his chin. 'Why don't we talk to the police?'

'You must be joking. I'm the obvious suspect. You've said as much yourself. They'd lock me up.'

'You can't stay down here for ever.'

Brett shrugged. Eventually he said, 'We'll see what happens.'

'I ought to be going.' Harry spoke in a measured, deliberate way but his mind was working frantically.

Brett waved in the direction of the way out. 'No-one's stopping you.'

'Aren't you afraid I'll blow the gaff?'

Brett chewed at his lower lip. 'Not really,' he said at length. 'You're no fool. And it won't help if you confuse the issue. After all, you know I'm innocent, don't you?'

Harry let out a breath. 'Yes. I suppose I do.'

Chapter Twenty-Four

Five minutes later he was back in the Lord Mayor's Stable Yard, blinking hard as he adjusted to the light in the outside world. His hands and face were filthy and his suit jacket and trousers were torn. Next to him, the average scarecrow would resemble Beau Brummel. He could smell the fumes of the traffic and the drizzle had turned into a downpour, yet coming out into the open from the caverns was like emerging from the snow-covered mountains into the valley of eternal sunshine in *Lost Horizon*.

His final questions had nonplussed Brett Young. 'What are you suggesting?' Brett had asked, after telling him what he wanted to know. 'Surely you don't think she...'

'I'm not suggesting anything yet,' Harry said. 'I learned my lesson when you shot down my idea about the tunnels. This time I'm going to check my facts. Something they used to teach at law college, remember? I shouldn't have been so hasty.'

'I'm not ready to talk to the police,' Brett said, his cheeks reddening. 'You understand that? I won't let them put me through the third degree.'

'You can't stay here for ever.'

'I'm not giving myself up.'

'Maybe I could go with you to the police station. Once they've heard what I have to say, I don't think they'll arrest you.'

'You've been wrong before.'

'That's true.' Harry forced a grin. 'I'm relying on the law of averages.'

Above ground again, he began to splash across the cobbles back to the wall he had climbed. To get out, he'd need something to stand on. He looked around the courtyard and his eyes fell on an old rusting water butt. He mauled it through the puddles and the undergrowth and was just turning it upside down to form a platform when he heard keys rattling in the padlock of the main gate. A dog began to bark. Harry clambered up on to the butt, but his foot went through it and he had to reach out and cling on to the wall to save himself. The bottom of the upturned butt was rotten and he'd cut his ankle. He swore. A bout of tetanus was all he needed.

'Hey!'

Eternal vigilance, he remembered, was the slogan of the security firm which looked after the Stable Yard. He swore again and pulled himself up the wall. He could hear the dog bounding across the cobbles. It sounded as if it hadn't eaten for days. The guard had broken into a run. Harry could hear him panting with the effort.

'Come back here!'

His arms aching, Harry gave a final heave and hauled himself over the wall. A quick glance over his shoulder took in an Alsatian with bared teeth and a uniformed Schwarzenegger hot on his heels. He dropped over on to the other side. The grass was slippery because of the rain and he lost his footing, but he pulled himself back to his feet and hobbled to his car as fast as his injured legs would allow. Thank God the lad with the tattoos hadn't nicked the MG. As he unlocked the door, Harry could still hear the dog's howl of fury. He was sweating, yet somehow euphoric. At least he'd avoided becoming a late lunch for man's best friend.

He drove home and had a hasty wash and change before returning to his office. From the severity of Suzanne's expression, he assumed he'd wafted in with a current of bad Chi. She was firing questions before he could draw breath. 'Where have you been? What have you been up to? Your cheeks are bruised and you've a cut on your hand. It's nothing to do with all these murders, is it? You've not been attacked?'

'It's a man's life in the Liverpool magistrates,' he said. 'Get me the CPS, will you? I need to speak to Suki Anwar. Put her through to my room. And pass me the first aid box.'

Suki's voice came on to the line as he was unwrapping a bandage for his damaged ankle. She listened to his request in silence. When he'd finished explaining what he was after, he demanded, 'Are you still there?'

'Yes, but what's this all about?'

'I'll explain later.'

'I'm not sure I can track down the papers. Even if I could, I'd be taking a hell of a risk. If anyone found out...'

'Listen, Suki, it won't be the first time you've ever broken a rule. See what you can do. Please? I'll meet you in the Dock Brief at six, is that okay? Bring the file with you.'

He put the phone down feeling tired yet strangely exhilarated. His whole body was aching; his leg was stinging. He rolled up his trouser leg and inspected the damage: a nasty gash, but hardly life-threatening. It wouldn't stop him, he thought, as he put on the bandage. Soon, he was sure, he would know the truth about the vampire killings.

His next call was to Windaybanks. He asked for Irma Jackson. They had spoken once or twice in the past when he'd been on the other side of a case from Nerys Horlock; she sounded like a sergeant major on parade even when taking a call-back message. When he said he needed to see her urgently, he could almost hear her brows knitting together.

'You're not up to your old tricks? You have a reputation for poking your nose in when a murder's been committed.'

'And now three people have been killed. One of them Nerys.'

A pause at the other end of the line. 'It's terrible. People here can't talk about anything else.'

'Can you blame them? Look, I've had an idea which may have a bearing on her death. I'd like to ask you a couple of questions about one of her clients.'

'What on earth do you think...?'

Jim's face appeared round the door. 'I'll explain later,' Harry muttered. 'Can you see me after work? We could have a drink, if you like.'

'I'm teetotal,' she barked.

'Fine, I'll buy you a lemonade. Will you come?'

A pause. 'It all sounds very peculiar to me. I mean, what about client confidentiality?'

'Remember what happened to Nerys,' he said grimly.

She hesitated, then said, 'I'll give you five minutes. No more. I have a bus to catch at ten to six. I'll meet you outside your office, just after half past. If you're not there, I won't be hanging around.'

'I'll be there. Thanks, Irma.'

Jim groaned as Harry replaced the receiver. 'Your first day back, and already it's as if you'd never been away.'

'Thanks.'

'It's not a compliment. You look like you've been dragged through a hedge backwards. What the hell's been going on? Carmel was getting a search party together to look for you. We thought you must have keeled over in the magistrates' court.'

'I'm often tempted. But as it happens, things cropped up. I had to change my plans. You know how it is.'

'Not really. I thought it was only God who moves in mysterious ways. Are you going to let me in on your little secret, whatever it is?'

'Soon, I promise.'

'On second thoughts,' Jim grunted, 'perhaps I'd rather not know. Ignorance is bliss where your activities concerned.'

'Something I have in common with Casper May.'

Jim flushed. 'Look, I don't like May any more than you do. I know he has a dodgy reputation.'

'I don't know,' Harry said with a shrug. 'Give him six months and he'll be advising his pals in high places on how to implement an ethical business policy.'

'All right, you've made your point. But he's offering us legitimate work and decent money. And we could do with some of that.'

'Sure. I'm not complaining. You did well to win the contract. Besides, why shouldn't we act for him if we're happy to hire his wife?'

'Yes, old son, I've been thinking about that.' Jim cleared his throat. He shifted from foot to foot, not meeting Harry's eye. 'Maybe it's time for us to call it a day with Juliet. Her fees are very reasonable. She's even given us a hefty discount. Very good of her. But I think we've probably done as much as we can with her help. We need to stand on our own two feet.'

An icy finger ran down Harry's spine. *Jim knows about Juliet and me. Or, at least, he suspects that something's going on between us. And he wants me to drop her before Casper finds out.*

'Well,' Harry said carefully, 'you probably have a point. You're going to let her know?'

'Thought I'd drop her a line in the next couple of days. If you agree, that is.'

'Fine. Fine. No problem. No problem at all.'

'That's settled, then.' Jim hesitated. 'She's quite a lady. It was worth consulting her. But we must be the smallest firm she acts for, by a mile. We're not really in her league.'

The phone rang. 'Juliet May,' Suzanne announced.

Harry covered the speaker with his palm. 'Juliet's on the line. Do you want to have a word?'

'No, no,' his partner said. 'Uh, better do it in writing, don't you think? More businesslike. I'll leave you to it, shall I?'

As the door closed behind him, Harry muttered into the phone, 'Can we get together tonight?'

'Well, well,' she said, 'you're not usually so direct.'

'Can we?'

'As it happens, darling, we can. Casper's out at a dinner with a group of councillors. He won't be back until after midnight.'

Perfect. He clenched his fist in suppressed exultation. Trying to sound calm, he said, 'Can we meet at your place?'

'What's come over you?' she murmured. 'You sound different. Forceful. Not that I'm complaining, mind. You've never wanted to pay me a visit before.'

That was because he'd never been able to handle the thought of sleeping with another man's wife in the matrimonial bed. But this was different.

'We need to talk,' he said.

'I won't cook.' She giggled. 'To tell you the truth, I'll have other things on my mind besides conversation.'

'Me too,' he said. 'Me too.'

'She was all fur coat and no knickers,' Irma Jackson grunted. 'I never had much time for her. Not from the moment when she first rang up to make an appointment with Nerys. She said she was personal assistant to the head of Corporate Recovery at Boycott Duff. It didn't cut much ice with me, I can tell you. I've always called myself a secretary and been proud of it. I had to laugh to myself when it turned out that she'd only been promoted from the typing pool a couple of months before. Once she started sleeping with him, needless to say.'

'She and Rick Spendlove were definitely having an affair?'

Irma sipped at her mineral water. They were perched on bar stools in a poky winebar in Water Street. Rain was drumming against the roof, almost drowning the Sinatra compilation playing in the background: Harry could barely make out ol' Blue Eyes crooning about strangers in the night, exchanging glances.

'Oh believe you me, she was as bold as brass about it. She was pleased with herself, thought she'd found herself a rich man to marry second time around. But it wasn't exactly an achievement, going to bed with that creep. If I'd been daft enough to take a job with him, he'd probably have propositioned *me*, he was that randy.'

One of the things Harry liked about Irma was that she was devoid of self-delusion. With her cropped brown hair, shapeless body and muscular legs she was never likely to set pulses racing and she knew it. It didn't help that she had the clothes sense of a bag lady. Her Age Concern overcoat had a couple of buttons missing and when he'd met her ten minutes earlier, he'd noticed a hole in one of her mittens. She didn't bother with make-up, presumably reasoning that it was wasteful to throw good money after bad. But Nerys Horlock had been shrewd enough to realise that Irma's mind was as sharp as her tongue. He guessed that her judgment of Nerys's client, however harsh, was seldom wide of the mark.

'Yes, she'd fallen for his sales patter hook, line and sinker. She wasn't bad-looking in a common sort of way, you know. Frizzy hair dyed blonde, though her roots needed doing. And a big bosom, of course. She made the most of her assets, believe you me. There were times when she came to the office and even in the depths of winter she was wearing a skimpy top and no tights.'

'I don't suppose that impressed Nerys.'

'It most certainly didn't. The thing was, dressing like a tart was second nature to someone like that. She wasn't interested in what other women thought. She knew what men like. They don't see beyond that sort of thing.'

She glared at him, as if well aware that he was as susceptible to mindless lust as the rest of his sex. As Sinatra launched into a cautionary tale about the tender trap, Harry said hastily, 'So she actually thought that Spendlove was going to do the decent thing?'

Irma sniggered. 'She wasn't as smart as she thought, was she? She liked to make out that she was street-wise, but he was too fly for her. I gather she'd been brought up in Toxteth, though you'd never guess to hear her talk. She liked to come over all middle class. Anyone who didn't know would have imagined she'd been to some snooty ladies' college on the Wirral. She wasn't going back to Toxteth, that was for sure. Her first marriage had obviously been a big disappointment. She wanted to live the life of Riley second time around.'

'You said that Spendlove recommended her to consult Nerys?'

'She'd told him that she wanted to dump her husband. He'd never matched up to her expectations. He wasn't earning good money any longer, he was throwing everything away for the sake of a stupid obsession. Boycott Duff don't handle divorce work, it doesn't fit with their image. So Spendlove suggested she consult the toughest matrimonial lawyer in town. Someone who could get blood out of a stone. I suppose he was keen to make sure that Tuesday would never be dependent on him.'

'And Nerys drove a hard bargain in the negotiations?'

'Ruthless.' Irma rolled the word off her tongue with relish. Nerys had been a heroine to her, Harry realised. Who knows, maybe she'd even been a little bit in love with the boss. 'He didn't like solicitors, he wouldn't take advice until it was far too late. A big mistake. Nerys wrapped the judge round her little finger. Her ladyship came out of it with the house and a bit of cash as well, far more than she deserved if you ask me. Her husband was bitter and no wonder. But he only had himself to blame. If he'd checked early on in the proceedings, he would have found out that Nerys wasn't someone you messed with. When he refused to settle out of court, she made up her mind to take him to the cleaners. It was a matter of professional pride for Nerys. Even if she didn't care for her client, she never gave less than her best.'

'What happened to the affair?'

'Just what you'd expect. One evening she came back to the office unexpectedly. Left her handbag behind or some such excuse. If you asked me she wanted to see if she would catch Spendlove out. Well, she did. He was misbehaving with a trainee solicitor. Had the girl over the photocopying machine, would you believe?

Her legs were wrapped round his neck, the way I heard it. And a Cambridge graduate too! Thank goodness I left school at sixteen, if that's what a posh education does for you.'

'So she broke it off with Spendlove?'

'Rushed out in tears and never went back to work. She told Nerys she could never face him again. So he wriggled out of any kind of commitment, as per usual, which I suppose was exactly what he was angling for. But she soon got over it. A fortnight later she met some footballer in a nightclub and moved in with him the next week. When he was transferred to Italy, she followed him and his fat pay packet over there. Oh yes, she was that sort. The kind who always fall on their feet in the end.'

'And her husband?'

'Utter pain in the backside,' Irma snorted. 'Even complained to the Law Society about the way Nerys had handled the case. It didn't do him any good, needless to say. You can make a fuss about your own solicitor messing things up. It's a bit rich to moan because your ex-wife's lawyer has given you a hard time.'

Harry finished his drink. He was on mineral water too. He hadn't wanted to risk booze; something told him it was going to be a long night and that he'd need all his wits about him before it was over. 'Thanks, Irma. I appreciate your help.'

She thrust out her lower lip. 'Go on, then. What's this all about? Tell me why you're asking all these questions. And be quick about it, my bus goes in a couple of minutes.'

'I told you, it's all to do with Nerys's death.'

'Come on. You're not seriously telling me the divorce had something to do with Nerys being murdered?' The sceptical look in her piggy eyes turned slowly to horror. 'Are you? Are you?'

'I couldn't bring the file,' Suki Anwar said as he handed her a Bacardi and coke fifteen minutes later. 'Too risky. I've enough black marks against my name as it is. God, you're wet through.'

He was dripping all over the scuffed table that separated them. On the way here from the wine bar, his umbrella had collapsed and he'd hurled it into a litter basket in disgust. But for the moment he was oblivious to the damp and the cold. 'Did you get a chance to take a look at the paperwork?'

'Yes, but I still don't understand...'

For all the hubbub in the Dock Brief's saloon bar, he lowered his voice as he leaned across the table. 'Carl was the prosecutor in the case, am I right?'

'Tell me why you want to know.'

Suki wasn't as patient as Irma. As he explained his latest theory, her eyes widened. At one point she clutched at her throat and he wondered if she were about to vomit.

'You're serious about this?' she demanded when he paused for breath.

'I'm hardly likely to make it up, am I?'

'I – I don't know what to say.'

'Just tell me if I'm on the right track. Was it Carl's case?'

When she nodded, he let out a breath and slumped back in his chair. At last he'd fathomed it. He'd been wrong, terribly wrong, when he'd changed his mind and decided that Brett Young must be the killer. This time, though, he was sure there was no mistake. And, as had happened in the past, he felt no sense of triumph, no urge to order champagne in a fit of self-congratulation. To solve a puzzle was to do much more than merely to play a game. Learning the truth laid bare the lives of others, exposed their secrets and lies, provided a reminder – as if he needed one – that no matter how deeply passions burned, killing someone was beyond excuse. He'd known several people who were murderers. Some had been clients whom he had done his best to defend. He wouldn't have described many of them in tabloid terms, as evil through and through. Yet their crime, even when committed in a moment of aberration, set them apart for ever. Murder, he kept finding, could be explained but never justified.

'Carl had a habit of calling a conference with victims of crime to explain his decision not to prosecute in a case of that kind,' Suki said. 'He was always careful to play it strictly by the book. His file was immaculate. You couldn't argue with his judgment or suggest that he'd been hasty or not cared enough to do the right thing. Lack of evidence strong enough to enable a jury to convict, that was the point. It's never easy to prove guilt beyond reasonable doubt. The police hated him, you know. They'd bring him a case and he'd knock it back, saying that they had to do more work. Even if they'd sweated blood to pin the crime on the suspect.'

'I remember you telling me that he liked to pick winners,' Harry said. 'It made his figures look good. When Carl Symons prosecuted, you could bet the accused had no hiding place.'

Suki nodded. 'Funny kind of ruthlessness, wasn't it? The sort that lets the guilty go free, rather than be tarnished with failure to have them sent down. It isn't only the do-gooders who are soft on crime.'

'Thanks for your help.'

'Wait a moment. I copied this for you.' She delved into her handbag, pulled out a photocopied sheet and, with a quick glance round to make sure no-one was looking, shoved it into his pocket.

'What is it?'

'A note of Carl's meeting when he explained his decision. Destroy it after you've read it, okay? You'll see he admits he didn't make himself popular. But then, he never cared about that.'

'No.' Harry sneezed. 'He never did.'

'Are you all right? I'd get changed out of those wet clothes, if I were you.'

'I'll be fine,' he said as he got to his feet. The hard work of the evening was still to be done. 'You didn't have to slip me the note. Thanks anyway.'

'It's okay. And – about the things we were talking about the other day, you will keep quiet, won't you?'

'Trust me.'

'I think I do.' She laughed. 'Even though you're a solicitor.'

'I hope things run a bit more smoothly for you from now on.'

'Did I mention that my section leader has given me the chance to act up until Carl is replaced? He even dropped a hint that I'll be in line for a permanent promotion next year if I keep him happy.'

'Congratulations.'

'Yes.' Her dark brown eyes had begun to shine. Perhaps it was the buzz from the alcohol after a long hard day in court. 'It's true what they say, isn't it? Every cloud has a silver lining.'

Last spring, the Mays had moved house. Casper had decided that someone who rubbed shoulders so regularly with the great and the good ought to live in suitably prestigious premises, so he'd acquired one of the most spectacular homes on the peninsula, a black and white manor house overlooking the Dee at Parkgate.

Harry drove slowly along The Parade. He remembered visits here in the summers of his childhood, when his parents had always treated him to a Parkgate ice cream whilst they devoured the local shrimps. The three of them had walked along the front and he'd gazed across the silted-up river and the salt marsh, struggling to picture the resort when the Dublin packet and the Welsh ferry had sailed from here, in the days when Parkgate had been one of England's major ports. Lady Hamilton had lived here as a girl, Handel had visited en route for the first performance of *The Messiah*. Milton's Lycidas had been shipwrecked nearby. Talk about Paradise Lost.

On a cold, dark and wet November evening, as the rain slanted down on to the promenade, it was hard to believe the place had a notable history. There were no pedestrians in sight and hardly any cars; the windows of the houses and flats were curtained against the night. He caught sight of the bell tower of a private school at the end of the promenade, a landmark that told him he had almost reached his destination. He pulled up outside wrought iron gates whose centrepiece was Casper's initials and announced himself into the entryphone.

'You found it easily enough, then,' Juliet's disembodied voice said.

'Parkgate's pleasant enough, but there aren't too many million-pound mansions perched above the promenade.'

'We're going to have an unforgettable night,' she said dreamily.

You never spoke a truer word. He watched as the gates swung open and headed up the long curving drive. As his car passed through the trees and eased to a halt in front of the gabled porch, he felt a little like Philip Marlowe, arriving at the Sternwood place. But his suit wasn't powder-blue and he'd never claim to be well dressed.

She was waiting for him, opened the front door before he'd stopped leaning on the bell. She was looking at her best: silk top, leather skirt, black stockings. Her hair shone; he longed to touch it. She was about to greet him with a kiss, but when she saw his expression, she hesitated.

'Is something wrong?'

'Yes,' he said. It was a good way of putting it. 'Something's wrong.'

Chapter Twenty-Five

Fifteen minutes later, the two of them left the house in silence. As they stepped outside, the security lights switched on automatically. Strange to think of the Mays guarding against burglars, for which petty thief in his right mind would dare to rob Casper? The harsh glare showed up the streaks that tears had left on Juliet's face. What he had told her had left her distraught. He hated himself for causing her pain. But what else could he do? The truth had to be told at last.

Pulling his jacket up over his head, he raced across the gravel courtyard. When she had caught him up, he rapped on the door of the annexe. He could tell that the building had once been a stable block. In the estate agents' phrase, it had been sympathetically converted into living quarters. Suitable for a family retainer. Apt, really. Nowadays a place like this might be called a granny annexe, but at present it was a refuge for Juliet's personal assistant.

Linda Blackwell opened the door. She wasn't wearing her glasses and she blinked several times, as if trying to make sense of their blurred features. When she recognised Harry, with Juliet behind him, she took a step back. Her features had frozen in a mixture of bewilderment and fear.

'Harry ... what is it?'

'I know the truth, Linda.'

She swallowed. 'I don't understand.'

'I know all about Peter. And what he did.'

'What? You're not making any sense.'

'He was a murderer, Linda.'

Juliet pushed him to one side. 'Tell him it isn't true, Linda. Tell him it isn't true.'

But Linda Blackwell had begun to weep. The tears flowed as if a dam had burst. Her knees buckled and she gave out a wail, a terrible and elemental sound. She was like an animal, a creature of the wild, a mother about to witness the betrayal of her young.

Compared to the average granny flat, Harry thought, the converted stable block would have provided suitable accommodation for the Queen Mother. Juliet evidently had more sophisticated taste when it came to interior design than she did in her men. The beamed living-room was stuffed with more antiques than the Lady Lever Gallery, yet the effect was somehow homely. In the background, a clock chimed every quarter hour. the armchairs were deep and comfortable. He guessed that Linda Blackwell was yearning to be swallowed up in the upholstery as he explained the reasoning that had brought him here.

'When we were talking, Peter said something about Tuesday. It didn't sink in at first that it was his ex-wife's name. It was only when I learned that Rick Spendlove had once had a fling with a secretary called Tuesday Jones that I made a connection.'

'She was one of those who liked to keep her maiden name,' Linda said. 'It's the modern thing, I know. Feminism. Personally, I was glad to take my husband's name. That's what marriage is all about, isn't it? Sharing everything.'

'And you were very happily married,' Harry said softly.

'Yes. We always were. You know what they say – "'til death do us part."'

'But Peter wasn't so lucky, was he? Tuesday began an affair with Spendlove after your husband died. The accident knocked both you and Peter sideways, didn't it?'

She bowed her head. In a muffled tone, she said, 'It came out of the blue. Ron was still a young man. Young at heart, that's for sure. He went out that morning full of the joys of spring.'

Harry breathed out. He wasn't used to hearing about happy marriages. To a lawyer whose wife had left him and who handled his fair share of divorce work, the idea that a couple could live together in harmony often seemed like an absurd flight of fancy. He told himself not to be jealous, that Linda was only talking like this out of desperation. She'd lost her husband and her son.

'And he never returned, did he?'

'Those wicked boys,' she said, her voice hollow. 'If only they'd realised the harm they'd done. If only they'd been made to realise.'

'It was a group of kids, wasn't it, throwing stones from a bridge over the M62? They hit the car and your husband crashed. The police had an idea who the culprits were, but couldn't prove anything. Besides, most of them were under ten. The age of criminal responsibility.'

'But the ringleaders weren't,' Linda said. 'An example could have been made of them.'

'You and Peter both demanded a prosecution, I gather?'

'It wasn't a question of vengeance,' Linda said earnestly. 'Not so far as I was concerned. It was just – the right thing to do.'

'The CPS reckoned there wasn't sufficient evidence.'

'Peter said it was a cover-up. They'd been so slow making a decision. We were patient for a long while, we understood the police needed to carry out proper investigations, but we thought it was only a question of time before someone was charged. We spoke to the detective who was leading the inquiry. He was sympathetic, he warned us it would be difficult, but he wanted to bring them to court. The police always know the guilty ones, you know, even if they can't prove it.'

'I'm not sure that's always true,' Harry said gently.

Linda sniffed. 'It was Carl Symons' case and he pulled the rug out from under us. Peter was incensed. He wrote letters to the newspapers, he got in touch with his MP. None of it made a blind bit of difference. Nobody took much notice. People made sympathetic noises, but they said nothing could be done.'

'Symons met him to explain his decision, didn't he?'

'Yes, he tried to make out that he was being sympathetic to the bereaved. Really, it was a back-covering exercise. Peter saw through that straight away.'

'I've seen Symons' notes of the discussion. It's obvious there wasn't a meeting of minds. The irresistible force had met the immovable object. Didn't you want to attend, see if you could do anything to persuade the authorities to change their mind?'

For the first time in their acquaintance, Linda was looking her age. The lines around her eyes and mouth seemed to have multiplied. 'I couldn't face it. By that time, I'd had enough of the whole sorry business. I told Peter that we were powerless, that there was nothing we could do, but he simply wouldn't give up. He wanted to see justice done for his father. He was a good son. The best anyone could have.'

'Did you realise that your neighbour was the lawyer dealing with the case?'

'Not at first. This all happened before Symons moved in next door. It was only when Symons sent that snotty letter to Peter about blocking his garage access that Peter told me who he was.'

'He blamed Symons personally, didn't he? Symons had let the youngsters he thought responsible for his father's death get off scot free. He let the death of your husband eat away at him, it became an obsession.'

'Loyalty, that's all it was, Harry. Perhaps you wouldn't understand.'

Harry bit his tongue. He reckoned he did know a bit about loyalty, but now wasn't the time for an argument about it. 'I suppose that's how he developed his grudge against lawyers. This feeling that they'd conspired against the two of you. Cheated you both out of revenge for your husband's death.'

'Oh, I tried to persuade him that it was time to move on, that we couldn't spend the rest of our lives in mourning. But it wasn't easy.'

'Maybe because you weren't entirely convinced of that yourself?'
She spread her arms. 'Possibly.'

'And the more he dwelt on your husband's death, the further he
and Tuesday grew apart?'

'They were never suited. I had to let him go when he wanted to
marry her, but I knew it would never work out. A pretty face and
a nice chest are never enough. They didn't have much in common.
He was intelligent, she had as much brain as a second-hand rag
doll.' Her voice was shaking. 'Where Peter was sensitive, Tuesday
simply wanted a good time. A marriage needs more than physical
attraction to make it work. A mother always knows whether a
woman is right for her son, Harry. Your mother will have been the
same with you, I'm sure.'

'I've learned something about families lately. Logic doesn't play
much of a part where blood ties are concerned.' He sighed. 'So
Tuesday took up with her boss, Rick Spendlove?'

'I doubt if he was the first man she'd slept with since marrying
Peter. What changed was that she stopped caring about whether
he found out about her affairs or not. Eventually, of course, he
discovered what was going on. Even then, he was willing to forgive
her. But she would have none of it. She thought Spendlove was
going to marry her when the divorce came through. Her fancy man
didn't touch matrimonial law himself, no-one in his firm did. Not
lucrative enough compared to corporate stuff, I suppose. So he
recommended her to consult the Horlock woman.'

'And Nerys screwed Peter in court.'

'She ruined what was left of his life.' For the first time in the
conversation, Linda's voice broke with emotion. 'I never met the
woman, but what she did was unforgivable. She treated it like a
crusade, as if it were her personal mission to bring my son to his
knees.'

'Nerys was always a formidable opponent,' Harry said. 'She
never varied her style.'

'Perhaps, but what mattered to me was the way she set out to cripple him. You saw the hovel he was living in. He was drinking far too much. I wasn't blind, I could see it. So I begged him to come and live with me, but he wouldn't agree, even though I stayed with him regularly, just wanting to be near him. But he said he needed his own place, it was a question of dignity.'

'Nerys was only doing her job.'

'If that's true,' Linda said with sudden brutality, 'her job was a bag of shit.'

For a little while, nobody spoke. Eventually Juliet said, 'Did you have any idea what was going through Peter's mind?'

'That he was planning to kill them? No, of course I didn't. If I had, don't you think I would have stopped him? I thought no more of the three of them – Symons, Horlock and Spendlove – than he did. But I didn't want him to wreck his health, make things even worse than they already were, just because of those stupid lawyers.'

'He saw them as vampires, though,' Harry said relentlessly. 'Did he talk about that?'

'Oh, we talked all the time. We'd always been close. I couldn't have wished for a more devoted boy. He came to think that every solicitor was as bad as the ones who had tormented him. I did my best. I'd tell him there were a few rotten apples in every barrel. They used to say that about bent policemen, didn't they, until they found out the barrel was full of them? Anyway, it was no use.'

Harry nodded. 'I could feel his hostility the moment I mentioned I was a solicitor.'

'Can you wonder?'

'Oh, I see why he resented us, persuaded himself we'd shattered everything he cared for. The way he saw it, a solicitor had protected the people who'd killed his father, prevented them from getting their just deserts. Another solicitor had slept with Tuesday and ruined the marriage. A third helped Tuesday to cripple Peter financially. Hardly surprising that he felt the whole profession was conspiring against him.'

'He had nothing left to live for,' she said, 'it was desperation that drove him to murder. Not that I realised it at the time. He'd talked about making them pay, but I thought that was sheer bravado. What can one man do against the legal establishment? I blame myself. Perhaps I should have done more.'

'He was a sick man,' Juliet said. 'It wasn't your fault. You did your best for him.'

'So did you,' Linda said. 'You made sure he had the best help money could buy. I thought he'd turned the corner. You gave me hope, I'll never be able to repay you for that. When he came out of the hospital, he seemed to be getting back on an even keel. I knew it was going to be a long haul, but I didn't have a crystal ball, not even your Tarot cards. I couldn't guess what was about to happen.'

'Which was why,' Harry said, 'you were happy to let Juliet borrow your house on the night of the storm. It was a way of showing your gratitude. Besides, you could stay with Peter as you had so many times before. Did you want to keep an eye on him?'

'We talked on the phone every day and I liked to get over there whenever I could. So it was no hardship to do Juliet a favour when she needed somewhere off the beaten track. Of course I should have rung Peter to let him know I was coming, but sometimes I went over on the spur of the moment anyway. He was always there, he said he loved to see me. I actually thought it would be a pleasant surprise for him.'

'Instead of which, he was nowhere to be found when you arrived?'

'I assumed he couldn't have gone far, especially on such a shocking night. I had a key, so I let myself in and waited for him to turn up. And waited. And waited.'

'When did he finally show up?'

'Ten minutes before you rang. By that time, I was worried sick. All sorts of things were going through my mind. I even wondered about ringing round the hospitals. And then he walked through the door. At first I felt an almighty surge of relief, but then I saw his face. He looked as if he was in the middle of a waking nightmare. Which in a way, I suppose, he was.'

'Did he tell you what he'd done?'

'No!' The veins were standing out on her temples. Harry felt sure she was telling the truth. Her eyes weren't focused on him; it was as though she were talking to herself, trying in vain to make sense of it all. 'The fact is, he could barely utter a word. It was as if he'd changed, seen something – terrible.'

'And then,' he said slowly, 'I rang you up and your worst fears were realised.'

Linda shook her head. 'It wasn't as simple as that. I couldn't bring myself to believe that he would actually kill someone, even though I'd already worked out that something ghastly had happened. Which was why I snatched up the receiver the moment I heard the phone ring.'

'I remember,' he said. 'You sounded as if you'd been poleaxed. And yet – you came out to the cottage straight away and I never dreamed what was going through your mind.'

'I've never known a night like it. I felt as though I was sleepwalking. Part of my house had been smashed, my boss was asking me to lie to the police – and none of it mattered. I hated myself even for wondering if Peter might be responsible. I was afraid I was jumping to conclusions, but I knew that if I could do that, so could the police. If he was falsely accused, he might finish up convicted of a crime he hadn't committed. It's happened many a time before. The law doesn't protect the innocent. I decided that all I could do was to play the part you were suggesting, try to make sure that no-one suspected my son.'

'You certainly managed that,' Harry said. 'You were bound to be in a state of shock, given the damage that the fallen tree had done. We were just grateful for your help. It never crossed my mind that either you or he had something to hide. And I realise something now. The police will have checked the calls from the mobile as a matter of routine. They'll have seen that the phone was answered at Peter's flat before I dialled 999. It's almost as if I gave him an alibi.' He shook his head. 'One thing might have stuck in my mind. Peter had planned to become a surgeon. I guess he made use of his knowledge of anatomy when it came to killing Symons and decapitating him. That was the difference between the first two murders and the third. The heads were efficiently severed, the stave went right through the hearts.'

Linda gulped in air. 'After Peter died, I found a diary in his flat. Of course I shredded it once I'd read it all. Like I destroyed all the other evidence.'

'The police never suspected a thing, did they?'

She shook her head. 'You could say he'd committed the perfect crimes.'

'And the diary?' Juliet asked.

'It broke my heart to read it. He described how he'd been biding his time for months, waiting for an opportunity to kill that man. The weather forecast was so bad, he was convinced the man would be at home that evening and there was little or no danger that anyone would see him making his way to the Harbour Master's Cottage. He parked on the top road that leads to West Kirby. There's a short cut through the trees that not many people use. It isn't a path, barely a track. The weapons were taken from Ron's old shed in the garden. An axe, a mallet and a wooden stake which Peter had sharpened in readiness. He clambered over the wall in the darkness, unlocked the shed and picked up the bag he'd put them in.'

'And then,' Harry said, 'he committed his murder. Forced his way in, knocked Symons out with a blow from the axe handle, so he was defenceless.'

Linda trembled. There were tears in her eyes. 'When you put it like that...'

'Sounds pretty brutal? Well, that's the way it was. A cruel sadistic killing.'

'No-one mourned Symons,' she blurted out. 'He was a hateful man. So far as I can make out, everyone is glad he's gone.'

Harry grimaced. He cast his mind back to Suki Anwar, revelling in the demise of the man who had tormented her, relishing the prospect of taking over his job. 'Even so...'

'Ron wasn't like that,' she said. 'People admired him. Peter and I worshipped him. He was irreplaceable.'

'And you think he'd have been happy about being avenged through murder? The murder of a man who hadn't done him any harm but do his job, a man who'd committed no crime.' As he uttered the words, he remembered that Carl Symons had been a blackmailing rapist. But did that make any difference?

'Peter felt he had to do it. The diary explained everything. It helped me to understand the pain he'd been going through.'

'Didn't you talk to him after the police had finished with you? I know you hadn't read the diary, but you had your suspicions. Why not challenge him?'

'How could I?' she demanded. 'How do you say to your son that you think he's committed murder? I told myself I was mistaken, I was being a neurotic mother. It would have been terrible for him to be falsely accused, especially after he'd been through so much. I couldn't bring myself to add to his suffering. I wanted to look after him, keep him safe.'

'So you're saying that you had no idea that he intended to kill Nerys Horlock?' Harry asked coldly.

'No!' she shouted. 'No, I did not! Do you think I'd have let him out of my sight, let alone gone back into work if I'd guessed what was going to happen? I'm not a mind reader. His diary said he felt he'd had no choice. He'd become fixated on this idea that lawyers were like vampires. They earned their living out of the misery of others. That was why he'd set fire to Horlock's office once he'd murdered her. It's a way of making sure that a vampire is dead. I think he wrote it for me to read, as well as some kind of therapy. But he couldn't bring himself to confess to me, face to face.'

'And the night Nerys died, what were you doing while he was killing her?'

She reddened. 'Sleeping. I don't sleep well, the doctors had given me tablets. He persuaded me to turn in early, said I wasn't looking too well and the rest would do me good. He waited till I was out of it and then he set off for Liverpool. It was all in his diary. Perhaps he thought one day I'd find it, perhaps he wanted to explain.'

'And when you heard the news that Nerys Horlock was dead? You knew she'd acted for Tuesday. Didn't you put two and two together?'

'I was beside myself, if you want the truth. But I had no proof. He told me he'd been up late that night. Reading. Perhaps I didn't believe him, but I had to protect him. *Had to.* Oh, neither of you would understand. You're both childless, you can't imagine how it feels when your own kid is threatened.'

Harry sensed Juliet stiffening beside him. He'd come too far to give up now. Recklessly, he demanded, 'So did you kill him, Linda? Did you push him down the stairs?'

She stared at him. 'You shit! I would never do that! Not to my son, my only child.'

'Not even when he was a killer, a deranged double murderer who stabbed and beheaded his victims, did his best to incinerate the second?'

'How dare you!' She had risen to her feet, was standing over him, her small fist balled-up. 'I would have stood by him, no matter what he was accused of, no matter what he'd done. That's what mothers are for. He was troubled, yes, deeply troubled, but who wouldn't be, after everything that he'd been through? His death was an accident, I tell you, a terrible accident.'

'So tell us how it happened.'

'He'd been drinking heavily. I think he must have realised I was afraid for him. There was this guilty secret that hung in the air between us, but neither he nor I could bring ourselves to talk about it. I had to leave his flat to pick up something for us to eat. By this time, I was living from hour to hour. When I got back, I found him sprawled across the floor at the foot of the stairs. I think he'd meant to go to the loo and opened the wrong door in his confusion. He fell down the staircase and broke his neck. I'd lost the only two men I'd ever loved. They were taken from me. How *dare* you say I killed my boy, you utter bastard!'

All of a sudden she crumpled back into her chair and curled up into a foetal shape. She was weeping uncontrollably. Juliet went over and put an arm round her, held her tight. 'I'm sorry, Linda, I'm so sorry.'

There was no stopping the great gasping sobs. Juliet whispered softly to her friend whilst Harry slumped back in his chair, his eyes closed. He would need to ring Mitch Eggar, tell him that at last the mystery was solved. Before he did, though, there was one last question to put, so that the picture was complete. He waited miserably, wishing that the truth would sometimes cause less pain.

When Linda had finally been calmed, she sat huddled up next to Juliet, who paused in murmuring words of comfort to address Harry. 'I think enough's been said, don't you?'

He could read the look on her face. *Stop here, stop right here. You mustn't torture her for a moment longer.* He wasn't unkind, he could scarcely imagine the agony Linda Blackwell was enduring, but he had to satisfy his curiosity, couldn't bear simply to walk away and leave it all to Eggar and his team. And yet he guessed that if he pushed any further, he was finished with Juliet. She could forgive many things, she could go back time after time to the thug who beat her, but she would not tolerate him making her friend confess the worst.

Even so, he had no choice. Just as Linda must have felt she had no option but to choose the course she had. He cleared his throat and said, 'I've been asking myself why you murdered Rick Spendlove? Was it because you felt you owed it to your husband and your son?'

'Harry!' Juliet cried. 'For God's sake!'

He brushed her protest aside with a sharp wave of the hand. 'Peter's diary made clear what he'd had in mind, didn't it? Spendlove was to be his third victim, the revenge wouldn't be complete without the destruction of the third vampire. You decided you had to finish the work he'd begun.'

Linda turned her ravaged face to him. There was no sign of outrage, even as Juliet swore with fury at him. Probably it was a flight of fancy, but he told himself that he saw in her pale blue eyes a mute plea for understanding. Might she even be grateful that the truth was known, that the time for denial had passed?

'That's how it was, Linda,' he said, 'I'm sure of it. As far as you were concerned, Spendlove had to die. Partly because that way, you thought no-one would link the first two killings with your son – or the third with you. Partly because you felt you owed it to Peter to carry out his plan. And you were lucky. Brett Young had done a runner. When you visited me in hospital you were keen to persuade me he was guilty. I should have guessed what you were up to. Of course, he was the ideal scapegoat.'

She bowed her head. He could see the mousy roots of her hair. Juliet's face was wiped of expression, but he guessed that inside, she was beginning to despise him for the relentlessness of the case

347

he was building for the prosecution. He was awash with a strange feeling of guilt, as if he were the one who was doing wrong, yet he could not help himself. His throat was parched, but he had to keep talking.

'So you set out to seduce Spendlove, anyone could have worked out that was the way to catch him off guard. I suppose you learned a good deal about him from what Peter wrote?' Linda flinched and Harry took it that his guess had been on the mark. 'You're an attractive woman, he was sex-mad, it wasn't too difficult. Did you pretend to be a potential client or did you simply let him pick you up at a club?'

She found her voice at last, although she spoke so faintly that it was hard to make out the words. 'Peter knew where Spendlove lived. I followed him to a bar. I couldn't believe how easy it was. It was like a waking dream.'

'So the two of you arranged a tryst at the waterfront in Birkenhead. His idea was to make love to you in the back of his car, but when he was naked and defenceless you had him at your mercy.'

He glanced at Juliet. Her face was still a mask. The clock chimed the hour. He waited until it had fallen silent.

'And you didn't let him escape, Linda. You'd taken Peter's weapons, I suppose you'd found them hidden in the flat. The axe, the hammer and the wooden stave. You didn't have the strength or expertise for a precise copycat killing. It didn't matter. You knocked him out and dumped the car and his body in the river. He wasn't dead when he hit the water, but so what? You'd carried out the plan.'

In his mind he could hear Spendlove's voice, extolling the virtues of older women. *They don't yell and they don't tell.*

'That's right,' she said and suddenly she flung out her arms in a gesture of triumph. 'I'd avenged the men I loved. They could rest in peace. Rest in peace for ever, once the last of the bloodsuckers were dead.'

The Letter

I read between the lines of your letter

and have been in an agony.

I am watching as you sleep. I feel your soft breath on my cheek. It would be so easy to end it by pulling a pillow over your face. I have come so close to destroying you, and in more ways than one.

But I cannot do it. Must not do it. It would not be an end, but rather the beginning of the worst nightmare of all. And I have had my fill of nightmares. Already I hate myself too much. Hate what I am or have become. I have sucked the life out of you for far too long.

I loved my mother and when she died, I felt the bitterness of betrayal. The passage of time dulls pain, but I can never quite forget. Then I see what I am doing to you, how I am draining the life from you, and I feel ashamed.

I need to do what my mother failed to do and say goodbye. The guilt is burning my soul. If one of us must die, let it be me.

I ask one thing, and one thing only. When you read these words, think of what I have done not as self-indulgence, nor even as desperate and cowardly. Think of it instead as an act of love.

Chapter Twenty-Six

A week after Linda's arrest, he rang Juliet. They hadn't spoken since that night at Parkgate. He'd half expected that he would never speak to her again. A few times he'd picked up the phone, once he'd even started to dial her number, but then he'd thought better of it. Perhaps they didn't have much left to say to each other. But he couldn't let her go without a word.

'I visited Linda today,' Juliet said. Her voice was unsteady. 'She barely recognised me.'

'Where is she?'

'A high security unit. They seem to think she won't be fit to plead. Turns out there's a family history of psychiatric illness. Her father died in what they used to call an "institution". I didn't have any idea. She never told me about it, she always seemed so calm and composed. Oh God, it's so...'

He coughed. 'Look, I meant to call you sooner, but...'

'It's all right. I didn't expect to hear from you again. Not after that terrible night.' He thought he could hear a stifled sob. 'I suppose you're thinking what I'm thinking? That it's run its course, our – thing together.'

The honest answer was yes, but he'd been a lawyer too long. Like most lawyers, he was cautious to the point of cowardice. 'Well – don't you?'

'Perhaps we should cool things down for a while,' she said after a pause. 'Jesus, I said some stupid things that night, Harry.'

She had, too, after Linda finally broke down. Bitter, wounding things. But you couldn't judge someone by what they said when they were in the depths of despair. They weren't uttering secret truths, just lashing out blindly as a way of easing the pain.

'Forget about it. The two of you were very close. You were bound to be distraught when you heard the truth.'

After a pause, she said, 'You know something? Even though she kept things from me, she was the best woman friend I've ever had. I've always got on a lot better with men than my own sex.'

'I didn't set out to destroy her,' Harry said. 'Or hurt you. Does that matter?'

'Of course it matters.'

'I needed to be sure, you see. I'd already made one mistake. Earlier that day I'd accused Brett Young.'

'I hear he's back in circulation.'

'Sort of.'

'There was a paragraph in the paper saying that the police had interviewed him about his deception. I see you're representing him, they printed a quote from you.'

'Brett's still got a heap of problems, even though he isn't a killer. I got that badly wrong.'

'But you were right about Peter and Linda.'

'Shall I tell you something? I wish I'd fouled up again and they were innocent.'

'It's not your fault, this mess. None of it.'

He kept quiet. She hadn't been so understanding out in Parkgate.

'It's an obsession with you, isn't it?' she said eventually. 'The need to discover the truth – whatever the cost. But sometimes the price is too high to be worth paying.'

'Maybe I need counselling,' he said, trying to make a joke of it. 'Have you come across anyone who specialises in Compulsive Detection Syndrome?'

If he'd hoped she would laugh, he was disappointed. 'I ought to tell you,' she said, 'Casper's been appointed to the north-west task force on eldercare.'

A fragment of an old song swam into his mind. *Hope I die before I grow old.* 'I'll tell Jim. We ought to pass on our congratulations. It isn't every day one of our clients gains preferment. The closest most of them come to government patronage is picking up their giro cheques from the social.'

'What it means is, he'll expect me to accompany him to various functions. He's talking about moving in different circles.' She giggled, making an effort to sound a bit more like the old Juliet. 'I'm not sure whether that means lobbyists with loads of hair gel or incontinent geriatrics. Either way, my pulse isn't exactly racing. But you know how it is.'

'Yeah.'

'Well, I suppose I'd better be going. Boycott Duff have given me a brief. The senior partner's a bit miffed about the media coverage of Spendlove's death.'

'I thought no publicity was bad publicity?'

'They prefer their partners to die of strokes through overwork. It's difficult to put a positive spin on things when your head of Corporate Recovery is stripped and drowned by a middle-aged widow bent on revenge.'

'Think of it as a challenge.'

'I gather they want to reposition themselves in the marketplace. They're talking about increasing their commitment to *pro bono* legal advice for the underclass. Sharks in Samaritans' clothing is the only slogan I've come up with so far. A tad more work needed yet, I'm afraid.'

'Good luck,' he said softly.

'I'll see you around, Harry.'

'Sure,' he said. His stomach was churning. He didn't know whether he would ever see her again, or whether he wanted to.

After he'd put the receiver down, he sat staring at the phone for a long time. He was thinking about families. The way Linda had covered for her son, then killed the man that Peter had planned to murder himself.

And then there was Daniel. Someone else he hadn't phoned. Suzanne had taken a couple of messages, but he hadn't returned the calls. He hadn't been sure what to say. The simple truth was that the two of them didn't have a great deal in common. So much divided them. Townie and country boy, English and Welsh, would-be writer and courtroom hack. God alone knew why, after so many years, his half-brother had sought him out. Harry felt as if a crushing burden had been roped around his neck. He couldn't give Daniel a place in their mother's life. Flesh and blood they might be, but the past was gone. They hadn't shared a childhood, they hadn't shared the pain at her sudden death. Now it was too late. Wasn't it?

On his wall was a year planner. He'd taped it up there, as a nod to administrative efficiency. He looked at the coloured stickers his secretary had fixed on to it. Blue meant a day in court, red marked the last day for issuing a writ before the time limit expired, yellow signified her holidays. The year was nearly up and what had he to show for it?

Suzanne buzzed him. 'It's the listing office at the Employment Appeal Tribunal. They want to talk dates for the hearing of that unfair dismissal appeal.'

He took a deep breath. 'I'll ring them back. I've got another call to make first.'

She grunted. 'Suit yourself.'

He'd scribbled the number on his blotter, not sure if he'd ever want to dial it. Hurriedly, as if he feared being seen in the act of committing a petty crime, he punched in the numbers.

Half a dozen rings, no more. If he doesn't answer, then it's not meant to be. I won't try again.

'Hello?'

'Daniel,' he said quickly, the words tumbling out, 'it's Harry here. I'm glad I caught you. I've been thinking ... I mean, I wondered if we might get together again some time. I read your manuscript, by the way.'

'Yes?' The voice was eager. 'It needs a lot of work, of course.'

'I'm glad you let me see it. But there is one thing.'

'Yes? Tell me.'

'When we see each other next time, not a word about vampires. Okay?'

The noise roused Brett Young from sleep. As consciousness returned, he realised that someone was trying to open the window of his room. It was a tall old window which overlooked the small yard at the back of the building where he lived. Since moving here, he'd never bothered to let in the air. The wooden frame made a sound like an animal in pain as it was lifted. He peered through the early morning gloom.

Andrea was naked. He could see the outline of her ribs as she stood by the open window. She'd always been thin, but it seemed to him that she'd been wasting away for a long time now. Yet there was no mistaking the tenderness of her gaze as their eyes met.

He levered himself up into a sitting position. He felt exhausted and his neck felt sore. He could dimly recall her biting him as they made love earlier in the afternoon. He guessed he must be bruised; she never knew when to stop. It had been a wild and passionate coupling, almost enough to make him believe that they could put the past to one side and start again.

'What are you doing?' he mumbled.

'I'm sorry,' she said.

'Sorry about what?' He was blinking the sleep out of his eyes. 'I don't understand.'

She pointed to the bedside table. He turned his head and saw a lined exercise book, open at the first page. It was filled with her handwriting. She had an extravagant style, full of loops and underlinings.

'I've left it for you.'

'What is it?'

355

'An explanation. You see, Brett, I do love you. More than life itself.'

His skin was cold. 'Andrea, why are you talking like this?'

'You thought I'd killed them, didn't you? Symons, Horlock and Spendlove.'

'I never...'

'I don't blame you,' she said softly. 'I blame myself. I may not be a predator, but I've been a parasite for long enough. I've drained the life out of you. It's tantamount to murder.'

'No! I love you!'

'But you've said it yourself, many a time. We've been destroying each other. It can't go on any longer. You do see that, don't you?'

She turned around and stepped through the window on to the tiny ledge outside, slim fingers clinging on to the sides of the window frame. Her long hair billowed in the breeze. Her whole body was trembling.

'For Christ's sake!' he cried. 'What are you trying to do? Come back inside!'

Her voice was wafted into the room by the breeze. 'Read my letter.'

He leaned over to the exercise book, scanned the first few words.

How long have you been afraid of me? Last night I noticed you glance in my direction when you thought I wasn't looking – and I saw the dread deep in your eyes.

His throat was parched. She was right. He'd been frightened. Still was. Tears blurred his vision. The words on the pages seemed to merge with each other. Yet odd phrases sprang out at him.

No more deceit: the choice is simple. One of us has to die ... Yesterday I cut my wrist ... So much better to die young, wouldn't you agree?

He could feel her eyes upon him as he stared at the message. As if she were feasting upon him.

I need to do what my mother failed to do and say goodbye. The guilt is burning my soul. If one of us must die, let it be me.

He made a choking sound, trying to force out her name.

'And – Andrea...'

'At least I tried to explain,' she said. 'So – goodbye, darling.'

The words floated in like a cloud of dust. Even as he watched, she released her grip on the window frame and launched herself forward and down. As she disappeared from view, he let out a roar of pain that drowned her scream.

'Oh God!' he cried. To emptiness.

Then he rushed over to the window, felt the smack of the wind against his cheeks. She had thrown herself on to the wicked spikes on top of the wall that enclosed the yard. The blood was oozing on to the ground. One of the spikes had impaled her. Brett knew at once that it had ripped through her heart.

Excerpt from *All the Lonely People*

Chapter One

Your mind's playing tricks, Harry Devlin said to himself.

As he reached for the front door key, he could hear a woman laughing inside his flat. Yet when the police had called him out on duty four hours earlier, he had left the place in darkness, empty and locked. For a moment he paused, as if frozen by the February chill. Had she come home again at last?

The laughter stopped. In the silence that followed he glanced up and down the third floor corridor, sure he must have been mistaken. But a long evening in Liverpool's Bridewell, trying to persuade grizzled detectives that two and two did not make four and that his latest client was innocent, had drained his imagination. It was midnight and he was too cold and weary for make-believe.

She laughed again and this time he knew he was not dreaming. He would have recognised that sound of careless pleasure after an eternity, let alone a lapse of two years. A wave of delight swept over him, succeeded after a moment by puzzlement. He realised that the door was ajar and, taking breath in a deep draught, strode through to the living room.

"So what kept you?"

She spoke as though resuming a conversation and the lazy tone was as familiar as if he had last heard it yesterday. Curled up in his armchair, she was watching television: Woody Allen's *Love and Death*.

He drank in the sight of her. The black hair - in the past never less than shoulder-length - was now cut fashionably short. Nothing else about her had changed: not the lavish use of mascara, nor the mischief lurking in her dark green eyes. All she wore was a pair of Levis and a tee shirt of his that she must have found in the bedroom. She had tossed her jersey and boots on to the floor. On the table by her side stood a tumbler and a half-empty bottle of Johnnie Walker. She scarcely glanced at him as she murmured her greeting; she was captivated by Diane Keaton, turning Woody down.

"Liz." The croakiness of his voice was embarrassing.

In response she favoured him with the gently mocking smile that he remembered so well from their time together. She said, "Your reactions may be slow, darling, but there's nothing wrong with your memory."

"How did you get in here?"

"The duty porter. I told him I was an old friend. The truth, if not the whole truth, you'll agree. I explained it was your birthday and that I wanted to give you a surprise. He seemed to think you'd be pleased to see me. Showed me up himself." She pulled a face of comic disapproval. "You ought to complain about the lousy security. I might have been your worst enemy."

With a rueful grin, he said, "Aren't you?"

"Careful, that's almost grounds for divorce."

The heating in the room was oppressive. She had switched it up to furnace level. Already he felt a moistening of sweat on his brow. Shrugging off his raincoat and jacket, he dropped into an armchair, scarcely able to take his eyes off her.

"Nice place you have here."

A wave of her slim hand encompassed the lounge. It was furnished in the same home-assembly teak they had bought during their engagement. In one corner, a top-heavy cheese plant leaned precariously towards the curtained windows. The walls were lined with book-crammed shelves: *Catch-22, Uncle Silas* and *Presumed Innocent* sandwiched a clutch of old movie magazines and an ink-stained guide to the Police and Criminal Evidence Act. Sheaves of paper spilled from every available surface, covering half the carpet.

Legal aid claim forms awaited completion amid scrawled notes about his cases and a jumble of junk mail.

"Splitting up must have suited you," Liz said breezily. "No one to nag about tidiness."

Crazy, he thought. He'd rehearsed this moment a thousand times, when she came begging for a second chance. The right words should come easily. So why did he feel a schoolboy's tongue-tied inadequacy?

He contemplated an elegant tracery of cobwebs, hanging from the ceiling above her head. "Life's certainly different these days."

"I'll bet. So where have you been, you old stop-out? I was here before nine. Good job you don't lock the drinks cupboard."

"The police lifted a client of mine. A petty burglar, trying to finance his taste for smack. I've been down in the interview room all evening."

"Harry, why do you bother?"

"Guilty or innocent, he's entitled to justice. Same as you or me."

Liz groaned as if hearing a joke for the hundred[th] time. He knew that she knew that for most of his criminal clients, conviction was an occupational hazard. And once more tonight, after the drawn-out sequence of questions and lies, bluffs and denials, the ritual had ended with the man's signature scratched on the statement that would send him to jail, enabling everyone else to go home, their jobs done. Chances were that tomorrow or the next day he'd have a change of heart and solicitor and some cowboy from Ruby Fingall's firm would try to get his name in the papers, building a case on police brutality.

"I know what you're going to say." He mimicked her old refrain: "'How can you defend those people?' But it's my job, remember?" Fishing in his pocket for a pack of Player's, he said, "So why have you turned up after so long?"

"I thought you might want someone to celebrate with. Thirty-two today, or is it Thursday morning already? Only a couple of birthday cards up, I notice," She hiccupped. "Sorry I haven't brought a present. You'll have to make do with the charm of my company. Many happy returns, anyway." She raised the tumbler and added as an afterthought, "Am I right in thinking you've put on weight?"

In the background, Woody Allen was soliloquising. Harry strode over to the television set and switched it off with a force that almost snapped the knob.

"You bastard. I was enjoying that."

"You didn't tell me what brings you here."

She shifted in the chair, stretching her slim figure like a self-confident cat. "Aren't you glad I'm here? Surely you've missed me, just a little?"

He sighed. "You were my wife, for God's sake."

"Still am, Harry."

"Yes."

He watched her finish the drink. Curious, he said, "Have you run out on Coghlan?"

"Sort of." She bit her lip. "But - I'm frightened, Harry."

The smile had vanished and her eyes, large and luminous, held his. Liz hadn't forgotten how to hypnotise him. To break the spell, he got to his feet and walked to the window, pulling the curtains apart. The flat was on the river side of the Empire Dock building, a converted warehouse which had once stored tobacco and cotton, with walls built to withstand fire, tempest and flood. In the distance, he could hear teenage delinquents shouting unintelligibly. Joyriders, hooligans or petty thieves perhaps. Tomorrow's clients, anyway. A police car siren wailed and nearer by, the site security guard's Alsatian began to bark. Meanwhile, the Mersey below snaked away into the shadows. A string of lights gleamed along the water's edge, trailing beyond Empire Dock as far as Harry could see. On the opposite side of the river, he could make out the angular outlines of the shoreside cranes, looming like creatures on an alien landscape. It was a Liverpool night, like any other.

He swiveled to face her. "I don't believe you've ever been frightened in your life."

The long-lashed lids were lowered now. "Harry, it's the truth."

"Convince me."

She studied her crimson fingernails. "Mick and I have drifted apart. He's back in his old ways, hanging around with his cronies up at the gym. Keeps making mysterious phone calls and throwing a fortune away on the horses. Sometimes I don't see him for days on end. I'm on my own so much, I even started working again. With Matt Barley at the Freak Shop."

"So I heard."

"You did?" She sighed. "Poor Matt, he's always been kind."

"You work part-time, he told me."

"Yes." An evasive look flitted across her face. "It fits in well with - other things. And it's a break. I'm not made to be the little lady, sitting at home whilst my feller spends every spare minute with a bunch of Second Division crooks." She resumed her scrutiny of her hands. "I've finally decided to ditch him, Harry."

His stomach muscles tightened. He hardly dared hope that she was back to stay. Forget that idea, he warned himself: a re-make is never as good as the original movie. But he could not forget it. Not wanting to say anything, he gazed at a bit of the carpet which was free of his papers. It was patterned in grey; he had chosen the colour that would best hide the dust.

Liz began to speak rapidly, the words running into each other. "I know you think I'm reaping my desserts. I can't blame you, there's no excuse for the way I behaved. I'm not asking for sympathy. But these past two years haven't been easy. I reckon I loved Mick once, but now I hate him and he hates me. He's mean and he's selfish and his temper is vile."

Harry waited.

Head bowed, she said, "And I've met somebody else. I need him badly. Don't wince - I'm serious. I've made all my mistakes. This is for real."

He closed his eyes, said nothing. There was nothing to say.

She talked on, though he hardly listened: "I thought Mick had no idea. I was afraid of how he might react. We've been so careful to keep it secret. But Mick's been too quiet lately, it isn't natural. Withdrawn, scarcely bothering to rant or rave if I burn his meal . . . as if he's planning what to do with me. He's even had me followed. I'm scared, Harry, I swear it. I believe - I believe he wants to kill me."

Liz always had a flair for melodrama, he thought. Like a heroine from one of those soap operas that used to glue her attention to the TV screen. Why did she never go on the stage? No actress could match her talent for fantasy. Long ago in their married life he'd learned that she would never be content; she had a child's thirst for new excitements.

Eventually, she said, "Well?"

"What are you asking for, Liz?"

She stifled an exclamation of impatience. "Your advice, of course. That's your job, isn't it? Giving the lawyer's impartial view. Solving problems. I don't know why you never made more money." She flushed. "Sorry. Me and my big mouth. But I do need your help. I trust you, Harry, always did. Tell me what to do."

He made a don't-care gesture with his shoulders. "If you're worried about Coghlan, move in with your new fancy man. He'll protect you."

"That's difficult." She licked the tip of her forefinger; an old, unconscious mannerism. "Trouble is, he's married."

Typical, Harry reflected. Aloud, he said, "And his wife?"

"His wife is - well, let's just say she's neurotic. He needs to pick his moment to break the news that he's walking out."

That struck a chord. He recalled the slow torture of those last few days before she finally left him one winter's evening. The skirting round of conversational no-go areas. Meaning less small talk at the dinner table. Silence in bed. And the awareness of a marriage rotting like so much dead grass.

"I get the picture."

She averted her face. "Mick's away at present. Down in London, or so he says. All the same, I can't go back to that house tonight, can't take the risk that he might turn up. Harry, he's violent! Dangerous. I daren't imagine what he intends to do. It's best to hide until everything's worked out. So - it occurred to me - I mean, would you mind if I stayed here for a day or two?"

Only Liz would have the nerve to ask, he thought. Her gift for making an outrageous request seem logical would be envied by any lawyer who ever made a speculative application for bail. The darkness of her hair, the height of her cheekbones, were the only clues to her Polish ancestry: in her instinct for the main chance, she was Liverpudlian through and through.

Wryly, he said. "Are you sure you'll be safe here?"

She treated him to her best knee-melting smile. "As safe as anywhere in the world. And I won't give you any hassle. I'll be out of your hair soon, I promise."

He stubbed out his cigarette and immediately lit another. She frowned and asked, "When did you start smoking again?"

"Day after you last saw me." He blew a smoke ring and waited for her to make a know-all comment about lung cancer or the nicotine stains on his hands. But for once in her life she had the sense to keep quiet and eventually he said, "Okay, you can stay."

"Thanks. That's wonderful." Almost to his surprise, he sensed that her gratitude was genuine.

"Where are your things?"

"I travel light, remember? I have a bag with me. Tomorrow I'll pick up the other odds and ends, if I'm sure Mick's still out of town." She smiled. "Let's talk more in the morning. I've so much to tell you, you wouldn't believe it. But there's plenty of time. Tell you the truth, right now, I feel as if it's my birthday, not yours, and there are a hundred candles on the cake."

Yawning, she stood up. Even her simplest movement was invested with that feline grace. He couldn't help saying, "You look no different from the woman I married."

"Flattery will get you anywhere." Their eyes met for a moment, before Liz moved away and said, "Well, maybe not everywhere. I went on a tour whilst you were out. You only have one bedroom."

The bed was their old kingsize. "It's all I need."

An I'm-not-to-be-tempted look flitted across her face. Her tone was gentle but firm. "The last few weeks have been hell for me, Harry. Truly. I must have a good night's rest. So what are the options?"

He weighed up her expression for a moment and then said, "The sofa folds down."

"Would that do for you? I mean - you know how it is?"

When he didn't reply, she leaned forward and kissed him lightly on the cheek before disappearing into the bathroom. Already she was at ease with the geography of the flat, gliding around as if it were home. He heard the shower running and said to himself: That's your wife in there, this is your chance to make it happen again. But he knew that he, too, was in danger of succumbing to fantasy and all he did was pour himself a whisky and settle back in his chair.

Soon she re-emerged, a towel wrapped round her hair. She had stripped off the jeans; her bare legs were as smooth as ever. "I'd forgotten what a mess you make of the toothpaste," she said. "You need a woman to take charge."

"My trouble is, I attract the wrong type."

She laughed. "I deserved that."

"You deserve much worse." He couldn't help grinning. For all her faults, Liz had always been able to make fun of herself, as well as of those around her.

"I like this flat," she said gently, "but it's lonely. You don't have anyone special?"

Only you, he wanted to say.

"No."

"That's ridiculous. You're not a bad-looking feller in a poor light."

Reaching for an ashtray, Harry said dryly, "My next door neighbour thinks all I need is a little female company. She keeps inviting me round for coffee and I'm running out of excuses."

Liz beamed encouragement. "Get together with her. It'll do you good. The bachelor life is fine, but if you don't relax, you'll never make it to thirty-three." Her left arm reached out and stroked the heavy stubble on his chin. For a short while, neither of them spoke, but at last she said, "Goodnight, Harry." Her tone was soft, almost tender, and the words hung in the airless emptiness of the room as the bedroom door shut behind her.

Harry remained motionless, staring through the picture window into the darkness outside. Despite the heat of the room, a chill of fear had suddenly touched him for when he had looked down at her slender wrist, he had seen the angry red stitch marks which criss-crossed it - marks that he recognised as the stigmata of a failed suicide.

The Making of *First Cut is the Deepest*

By the time I came to write *First Cut Is the Deepest*, the seventh book in the Harry Devlin series, I felt I'd come to know the character of Harry, and his world, pretty well. The success of the earlier books in the series had also given me a great deal of confidence as a writer, and I had more than enough energy and enthusiasm to set myself fresh challenges.

Writing a series has many benefits, but it also carries risks – above all, that you start producing the same-old, same-old. There are attractions in sticking to the tried-and-tested, and it is certainly easier, and less likely to trouble one's publishers, who tend to assume that loyal readers don't want their expectations to be confounded in any way. After all, people keep reading a series because they like what it has to offer. But I cling to the belief that they also like an author to vary their diet from time to time, as long as the qualities that attracted them to his or her writing in the first place are not diluted.

One "given" in a crime series is that, whatever trials and tribulations the hero or heroine may face, he or she will live to fight another day. Of course there are exceptions – Conan Doyle tried to kill off Sherlock Holmes, Nicolas Freeling disposed of Van der Valk, and so on – but it's an extraordinarily bold step to take; I once heard P.D. James say in an interview hat she thought it was very foolish, and many writers would agree.

This means that series authors face a challenge: how to keep readers on the edge of their chairs, when they are well aware it's overwhelmingly likely that the protagonist will survive - in contrast to the fate of protagonists in stand-alones written by, say, Cornell Woolrich or Barbara Vine. I decided to face up to that challenge in this book by putting Harry in jeopardy in not one but three different ways.

First, he's embroiled in an affair with Juliet May that threatens his well-being because she is married to a dangerous and ruthless man. Second, while engaged in a tryst with Juliet, he encounters a decapitated corpse, and finds himself plunging head-first into an elaborate murder mystery. And third, he is being stalked by the enigmatic Daniel Roberts. I won't say any more about the Roberts sub-plot, except to say that the idea behind it didn't occur to me until I started plannng this particular book. The idea appealed because it gave an extra dimension to Harry's life. That's one of the joys of a series – rather like a soap opera, characters' lives and backstories develop in all kinds of ways that were never part of the original concept.

Not long before starting to plot the story, I read Dracula, and found that Bram Stoker's original novel far surpassed in merit the various film versions that I'd seen. The first part of the book in particular strikes me as a superb example of exciting popular fiction that has stood the test of time. The fact that Jonathan Harker is a lawyer, and that the Count is versed in English law caught my fancy, and I thought up a potential link with an idea for a mystery plot about a series of murders of Liverpool lawyers. As a Liverpool lawyer myself, the notion appealed to my (no doubt warped) sense of humour, but I hasten to add that there wasn't an element of wish fulfilment in disposing of professional rivals – honest! In fact, as I mentioned in the acknowledgments in this and other Devlin books, fellow lawyers in the city have always been astonishingly generous in supporting my literary efforts – not least in contributing the occasional joke or snippet of legal lore. I did think, though, that readers might be entertained by a story which linked lawyers and blood-suckers. As Harry reflects, the mountains of Transylvania are a long way from Toxteth, but when my researches drew my attention to "living vampires", I realised I'd discovered another ingredient to put into the mix.

The settings of the key scenes needed, I felt, to be as vivid as possible, and I wanted many of them to differ from those used previously in the series. Again, this is part of varying the diet. So the story opens on a wild night on the edge of Wirral, above and below the river that divides England from Wales. I lived in Wirral for seven and a half years before moving back to my native Cheshire, and the peninsula's many contrasts fascinate me. Later in the story, Harry's travels take him to such diverse spots as Birkenhead Priory – ancient remains reeking of history, cheek-by-jowl with a dockyard and modern urban life – and the rather charming former port of Parkgate.

I was also keen to set a scene underground in the centre of Liverpool, and I consulted a group of fellow writers – '"The Liverpool Scribblers", who dined convivially at a different city restaurant each month. The group included several crime writers (Margaret Murphy, who has kindly written an introduction to the new e-book publication of *I Remember You*, was one of them) as well as horror writer Ramsey Campbell and the late Jim Hitchmough, a TV sitcom writer. I asked if anyone knew of a fascinating subterranean location in the city that hadn't been used in fiction before, and John Owen, who wrote crime short stories and radio plays, suggested Williamson's Tunnels. Nowadays, the Tunnels are well known, and a road sign directs tourists to the entrance, but it wasn't so at the time I started writing this book and I wasn't familiar with them. However, the more I discovered about the Tunnels, the more intrigued I became, and I was lucky enough to manage a visit in person before writing the scene in question. I also found the website of the Friends of the Tunnels a mine of useful information, and an excellent example of how the internet can assist a writer's researches, as long as it doesn't become a complete substitute for personal experience.

The plot and structure of the book were complex, and the story was the darkest I had written, something which reviews, for instance in *The Times*, highlighted. I set out to enrich the texture of the story, and add some light relief, by including a miscellany of jokes and references to books and films. The opening line, for instance, comes from the opening line of *Pulp Fiction*. Few people will confuse my work with that of Quentin Tarantino, but it amused me to tip my hat to the legendary director while kicking off a story which, for all its embellishments, is at heart a detective mystery that seeks to respect the classic values of the genre while holding up a mirror to a group of people and their society at the end of the twentieth century.

I thought – and still believe – that the book is a taut, fast read, but so much is crammed into it that, unavoidably, it became the longest novel I'd written up to that time. When my Italian publishers, Mondadori, made an offer for it, they laid down a condition that, to fit in with their requirements, the book should be cut down in length. I agreed, but left it to people at Mondadori to do what was necessary, as I was reluctant to take a hatchet to the text. How successful the editing was in artistic terms, I still don't know, as I can't read Italian. Better to remain in blissful ignorance, perhaps. Mind you, the Italian editions all sold very well, which did make me appreciate the skills of the translator.

When I came to the end of the book, and it was accepted by Hodder, my UK publishers, they proposed a deal for me to write another couple of books in the Devlin series. I'd thoroughly enjoyed writing *First Cut is the Deepest*, and I was excited to have found an American publisher at last for the Devlin books (though oddly, they started with the fifth book in the series, and the books were subsequently taken up by another publisher). But I wanted to stretch my talents as far as I could, and I had an idea for a non-series book which excited me enormously (this later became *Take My Breath Away*). Because I was working full-time as a partner in a law firm as well as writing novels and legal books, it didn't make sense to commit to writing three brand new novels at that stage, and I opted to take the risk of putting the Devlin series on hold for at least a couple of years.

As things turned out, my writing career changed course unexpectedly after that. My editor left Hodder, and *Take My Breath Away*, a book whose complexity meant it took a couple of years to write and went through countless revisions, eventually appeared under the imprint of Allison & Busby. By that time, I'd also completed the last novel by the late Bill Knox, *The Lazarus Widow*, for yet another publisher, and started work on a historical novel featuring the life and misadventures of Dr Crippen – *Dancing for the Hangman* – which did not see the light of day for another five years. My new editor at Allison & Busby, David Shelley, proposed that, rather than resuming the Devlin series, I should write a new series set in rural Britain; this led to the first of the Lake District Mysteries, and the success that *The Coffin Trail* and later books in the series enjoyed meant there was little time for writing about Harry. However, when Liverpool's year as European Capital of Culture was approaching, I decided to seize the opportunity to bring Harry's career up to date, and to tackle the changes in both his life and in his native city since the events of *First Cut is the Deepest*. The result was *Waterloo Sunset*, a book which proved to be a joy to write. It appeared in 2008, ten years after this book's first appearance, and Harry's return gave me, as well, I hope, as plenty of his fans, a great deal of pleasure.

Will Harry return again? It's a question I'm often asked. And the answer is: I hope so. He's someone I like a lot, and I would love to find out what happens to him next.

Martin Edwards: an Appreciation

by Michael Jecks

Both as a crime writer and as a keen exponent of the genre, Martin Edwards has long been sought out by his peers, and is now becoming recognised as a contemporary crime author at the top of his form.

Born in Knutsford, Cheshire, Martin went to school in Northwich before taking a first class honours degree in law at Balliol College, Oxford. From there he went on to join a law firm and is now a highly respected lawyer specializing in employment law. He is the author of Tottel's *Equal Opportunities Handbook*, 4th edition, 2007.

Early in his career, he began writing professional articles and completed his first book at 27, covering the purchase of business computers. His non-fiction work continues with over 1000 articles in newspapers and magazines, and seven books dedicated to the law (two of which were co-authored).

His life of crime began a little later with the Harry Devlin series, set in Liverpool. The first of his series, *All The Lonely People* (1991), was shortlisted for the CWA John Creasey Memorial Dagger for the first work of crime fiction by a new writer. With the advent of his second novel, Martin Edwards was becoming recognised as a writer of imagination and flair. This and subsequent books also referenced song titles from his youth.

The Harry Devlin books demonstrate a great sympathy for Liverpool, past and present, with gritty, realistic stories. 'Liverpool is a city with a tremendous resilience of spirit and character,' he says in *Scene of the Crime,* (2002). Although his protagonist is a self-effacing Scousers with a dry wit, Edwards is not a writer for the faint-hearted. 'His gifts are of the more classical variety - there are points in his novels when I think I'm reading Graham Greene,' wrote Ed Gorman, while *Crime Time* magazine said 'The novels successfully combine the style of the traditional English detective story with a darker noir sensibility.'

More recently Martin Edwards has moved into the Lake District with mystery stories featuring an historian, Daniel Kind, and DCI Hannah Scarlett. The first of these, *The Coffin Trail*, was short listed for the Theakston's Old Peculier Crime Novel of the year 2006.

In this book Martin Edwards made good use of his legal knowledge. DCI Hannah Scarlett is in charge of a cold case review unit, attempting to solve old crimes, and when Daniel Kind moves into a new house, seeking a fresh start in the idyllic setting of the Lake District, he and she are drawn together by the murder of a young woman. The killer, who died before he could be convicted, used to live in Kind's new cottage.

Not only does Edwards manage to demonstrate a detailed knowledge of the law (which he is careful never to force upon the reader), with the Lake District mysteries he has managed to bring the locations to vivid life. He has a skill for acute description which is rare - especially amongst those who are more commonly used to writing about city life.

More recently Edwards has published *Take My Breath Away*, a stand-alone psychological suspense novel, which offers a satiric portrait of an upmarket London law firm eerily reminiscent of Tony Blair's New Labour government.

Utilising his legal experience, he has written articles about actual crimes. *Catching Killers* was an illustrated book describing how police officers work on a homicide case all the way from the crime scene itself to presenting evidence in court.

When the writer Bill Knox died, Edwards was asked by his publisher to help complete his final manuscript, on which Knox had been working until days before his death. Bill Knox's method of writing was to hone each separate section of his books before moving on to the next, so Martin was left with the main thrust of the story, together with some jotted notes and newspaper clippings. From these he managed to complete *The Lazarus Widow* in an unusal departure for him.

More conventionally, Martin Edwards is a prolific writer of short stories. He has published the anthology *Where Do You Find Your Ideas?* which offers a mix of Harry Devlin tales mingled with historical and psychological short stories. His *Test Drive* was short listed for the CWA Short Story Dagger.

Edwards edits the regular CWA anthologies of short stories. These works have included *Green for Danger*, and *I.D. Crimes of Identity*, which included his own unusual and notable story *InDex*. In 2003 he also edited the CWA's *Mysterious Pleasures* anthology, which was a collection of the Golden Dagger winners' short stories to celebrate the CWA's Golden Jubilee.

A founder member of the performance and writing group, Murder Squad, Martin Edwards has found the time to edit their two anthologies.

When not writing and editing, Edwards is an enthusiastic reader and collector of crime fiction. He reviews for magazines, books and websites, and his essays have appeared in many collections.

He is the chairman of the CWA's nominations sub-committee for the Cartier Diamond Dagger Award, the world's most prestigious award for crime writing.

Martin Edwards is one of those rare creatures, a crime-writer's crime-writer. His plotting is as subtle as any, his writing deft and fluid, his characterisation precise, and his descriptions of the locations give the reader the impression that they could almost walk along the land blindfolded. He brings them all to life.

(An earlier version of this article appeared in *British Crime Writing: An Encyclopaedia,* edited by Barry Forshaw)

Meet Martin Edwards

Martin Edwards is an award-winning crime writer whose fifth and most recent Lake District Mystery, featuring DCI Hannah Scarlett and Daniel Kind, is *The Hanging Wood*, published in 2011. Earlier books in the series are *The Coffin Trail* (short-listed for the Theakston's prize for best British crime novel of 2006), *The Cipher Garden*, *The Arsenic Labyrinth* (short-listed for the Lakeland Book of the Year award in 2008) and *The Serpent Pool*.

Martin has written eight novels about lawyer Harry Devlin, the first of which, *All the Lonely People*, was short-listed for the CWA John Creasey Memorial Dagger for the best first crime novel of the year. In addition he has published a stand-alone novel of psychological suspense, *Take My Breath Away*, and a much acclaimed novel featuring Dr Crippen, *Dancing for the Hangman*. The latest Devlin novel, *Waterloo Sunset*, appeared in 2008.

Martin completed Bill Knox's last book, *The Lazarus Widow*, and has published a collection of short stories, *Where Do You Find Your Ideas? and other stories*; 'Test Drive' was short-listed for the CWA Short Story Dagger in 2006, while 'The Bookbinder's Apprentice' won the same Dagger in 2008.

A well-known commentator on crime fiction, he has edited 20 anthologies and published eight non-fiction books, including a study of homicide investigation, *Urge to Kill* .In 2008 he was elected to membership of the prestigious Detection Club. He was subsequently appointed Archivist to the Detection Club, and is also Archivist to the Crime Writers' Association. He received the Red Herring Award for services to the CWA in 2011.

In his spare time Martin is a partner in a national law firm, Weightmans LLP. His website is www.martinedwardsbooks.com and his blog www.doyouwriteunderyourownname.blogspot.com

Also Available from Martin Edwards

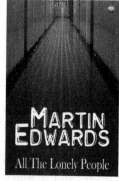 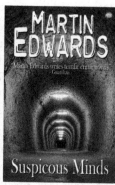 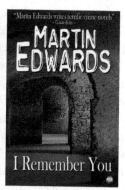

All the Lonely People   *Suspicious Minds*   *I Remember You*

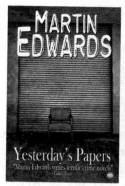 

Yesterday's Papers   *The Devil in Disguise*

Lightning Source UK Ltd.
Milton Keynes UK
UKOW06f0647050917
308613UK00010B/234/P